I0614254

KINDRED HEARTS

ROWAN SPEEDWELL

Dreamspinner Press

Published by
Dreamspinner Press
4760 Preston Road
Suite 244-149
Frisco, TX 75034
http://www.dreamspinnerpress.com/

This is a work of fiction. Names, characters, places, and incidents either are the product of the author's imagination or are used fictitiously, and any resemblance to actual persons, living or dead, business establishments, events, or locales is entirely coincidental.

Kindred Hearts
Copyright © 2011 by Rowan Speedwell

Cover Art by Reese Dante http://www.reesedante.com

All rights reserved. No part of this book may be reproduced or transmitted in any form or by any means, electronic or mechanical, including photocopying, recording, or by any information storage and retrieval system without the written permission of the Publisher, except where permitted by law. To request permission and all other inquiries, contact Dreamspinner Press, 4760 Preston Road, Suite 244-149, Frisco, TX 75034
http://www.dreamspinnerpress.com/

ISBN: 978-1-61581-898-3

Printed in the United States of America
First Edition
May 2011

eBook edition available
eBook ISBN: 978-1-61581-899-0

For my beloved brothers and the sisters they gave me, and for the next generation in whom our hopes reside. And for Bunnie, who keeps us all in line.

Because I'm lucky to have kindred hearts, and it *is* all about family.

Ah! Sure some stronger impulse vibrates here,
Which whispers friendship will be doubly dear
To one, who thus for kindred hearts must roam,
And seek abroad, the love denied at home.

—George Gordon, Lord Byron

ROLOGUE

1790

THE hand resting on his shoulder felt heavy as a stone. His thin legs, still wobbly from the weeks he'd been ill, trembled from the strain of holding up his head, his body, that heavy hand.

In front of him, the ground was still raw and black and grassless; a fading bouquet of flowers rested at the foot of the headstone, the markings on it also raw. "Alice, Lady Ware," it read, and some dates. Below that was another name, "Emily Northwood, 1790." Mama. And Baby Emmy.

"You weren't well enough for the funeral," Papa said above him, his voice growly and as physical as the hand on his shoulder.

The words washed over him, meaningless. The only thing he saw was the headstone and the fading flowers. Mama was dead. The last time he'd seen her, she was bending over him, wiping his forehead and telling him to go to sleep, to rest, that she would be there when he woke up. But she wasn't. And crying for her didn't help, didn't bring her the way it always had.

Instead, it had brought Papa, who'd stood at the foot of the bed, frowning at him. Papa always frowned; it had frightened Tris into silence, as it usually did. He was afraid of Papa, but never more so than when he'd come into his room instead of Mama. He didn't remember Papa ever coming into his room. "Where's Mama?" Tristan had asked bravely, his voice sounding strange, thin and thready. His throat hurt.

Papa had looked even angrier, but his voice was quiet as he spoke. It scared Tris even more. "She's gone."

"Bring her back," Tris said. He was trying not to cry, but tears were leaking. "Bring her home, please."

"I can't. She's dead. She and the baby died from the fever. It's just us now."

Then his father did something horrible. He smiled. Tris had never seen Papa smile. It terrified him, and he screamed and screamed. Nurse came in and tried to calm him down, and sometime during his screaming, Papa went away and didn't come back until this morning, when Tris was finally well enough to get dressed and go outside.

He looked over the raw headstone toward the vicarage. A large van was parked outside, and Mrs. Vicar was standing directing the men moving furniture into it. "Why are they taking Vicar's furniture?" he asked his father.

"Mrs. Redding is going back to her people," Papa said.

"Why? Who will take care of Vicar and Rob and Will and Cressy?" Rob and Will were his best friends. Cressy was only four, and a tagalong, but she was all right for a baby and a girl.

"Vicar Redding and the children died of the fever also," Papa said. "They were buried near their home parish, not here, though."

Tris looked up at Papa in consternation. "But—who will teach me? Who will I play with now?"

"You're going to Westminster in a few months, as soon as you are fully well again. That's school. I'm sure your mama talked to you about school. You'll make new friends there." Papa was quiet a moment, then said, "Pretty soon the grass will grow here, and it will be a lovely place for you to come and visit your mama and Emmy."

"Why would I visit them?" Tris asked. "They're *dead*." He ducked away from Papa's hand and ran down the hill to the carriage. When he got there he was too out of breath to climb in, so he stood beside it, crying, until Papa came and lifted him up into the gig and took the reins. They drove back to the house in silence.

Nurse met them in the hall and led Tristan upstairs, where she put him back into his nightshirt and tucked him back into bed. "You're still not ready to be outside," she said gently, "but soon you'll be all healthy and can go out and play again."

Tristan said nothing, but rolled over and pretended to sleep. He was still pretending when Papa came into the nursery. He stood for a long time at the foot of the bed, and Tris thought he knew that Tris was only pretending, but he didn't move or say anything, and so neither did Papa. Finally Papa went away and Tris really did go to sleep.

OH, ALICE, James thought, looking down at the tiny, wasted little figure huddled in the bed. *What am I to do with him? I don't know the first thing about children.* He sighed, then left the room and went down to his library. In the big family Bible, he wrote the dates of Alice's and Emily's deaths, beneath the entry dated less than a year ago for Emily's birth. Alice had been so delighted with Emily, already teasing him about her future beaus and the awkward Seasons she'd have, flirting and parading her conquests before her doting papa. That future was gone now, erased as completely as snow in spring. His own future was equally gone, with no Alice to share it with.

Theirs had been a love match: he, a second son, happy in his studies at Trinity, vying for one of the hotly contested lecturer positions in mathematics, had had no intention of marrying but had rather planned for a bachelor academic career. Alice, the only child of a wealthy importer, had been introduced to him by a friend of his elder brother, and he had, to his own great shock, fallen desperately in love with her. His courtship had been cut off by her father, who was uninterested in acquiring a mere second son, no matter how ancient the family name. Alice, for her part, had steadfastly refused to marry any of the other suitors her father had dangled in front of her, stating calmly that if she could not marry James Northwood, she would marry no one. For a year, they'd spoken only through letters, hers written and smuggled from the house by a faithful maid; his scribbled in the dark of his scholar's carrel.

Then Albert had died of a winter fever and suddenly James *was* the heir. Alice's papa's reservations vanished, James was torn from his beloved scholarship, and before he knew it, he was married.

He smiled despite himself and ran his finger lightly over the notation of his marriage ten years earlier, and the birth of his beautiful son Tristan two years later. He'd missed Cambridge, but he wouldn't have wished it any other way. Only now....

Above the fireplace hung the portrait he'd had painted right after Emily's birth: Alice, her silvery eyes bright beneath the fringe of dark curls, Emily in her christening gown cradled in her arms, and Tristan, standing at Alice's knee, looking up at her. The painter, an up-and-comer named Thomas Lawrence, had caught the expression in Tristan's face exactly: a soft, adoring look that perfectly echoed James's own feelings about her.

God, how would he live without Alice? He knew nothing about children; all his expertise was in finance. The children had always been in Alice's purview. He supposed he should consult with Nurse about what to do with Tristan; he had a vague idea that children needed supervision and management, and supposed it should just be approached as any of his other business interests, with common sense and logic. But not today. It was the first time he had visited the graves since the funeral, and he was too exhausted.

Tomorrow, or perhaps the day after. He sat at his desk and made a note of it in his memorandum book, then looked at all the other things he had to do, and sighed. Perhaps the day after....

Book One

London, 1810

CHAPTER 1

"SIR? Sir?"

Tristan Northwood opened one eye gingerly, feeling the rasp of eyelid across sandy eyeball. An impossibly bright light burned his retina; he quickly shut the eye but not before the flash of light revealed a face he thought he might recognize. Illumination came, though thankfully not the literal kind. "Reston," he grated, his eyes still screwed shut. "What time is it?"

"Ten thirty, sir," the valet's voice said. It seemed to have an unnaturally loud, booming quality. Then the words sank in through the fog.

"Ten thirty? In the *morning*?"

"Yes, sir."

"Reston, you're *sacked*."

"Yes, sir. Would Mr. Northwood prefer the green waistcoat for today or the blue?"

"Mr. Northwood would prefer that Reston, along with all waistcoats of whatever hue, go straight to the devil."

"Yes, sir. Prior to my leaving, however, may I remind Mr. Northwood that he has an appointment with Baron Ware at eleven thirty this morning?"

"Bloody hell."

"Yes, sir."

Another attempt at vision was made, this one more successful. Reston was in the process of drawing the drapes against the vicious morning sunlight. When the room was sufficiently dimmed, he picked up the tray he'd set on the table by the window and brought it to the bedside. "Your coffee, sir."

Tristan sat up, grabbed at his head just as it was about to fall off, and said hoarsely, "You're not only rehired, Reston, but I'm raising your wages." He took the cup gratefully.

"Yes, sir. The blue or the green?"

"The blue. No. Where's that orangish one I bought last week?"

There was silence in the room, then Reston's sere tones. "I'm sure I couldn't say, sir."

"Why not? You're my damned valet."

"Yes, sir. However, that was the waistcoat you wore last Thursday evening. You were not wearing it Friday morning when you returned home." Nor the cravat, shirt, or boots, though the boots were later found where Mr. Northwood had apparently dropped them, in the mews some thirty yards from the stall where he himself had been discovered, dead drunk and wearing only trousers and a greatcoat. Reston privately thought it was only the pickling properties of the immense volume of alcohol that his master had imbibed that had kept him from freezing to death in the chill April air.

"Damn. I liked that waistcoat."

"Yes, sir."

Tristan drank his coffee moodily, then said, "Which is more likely to irritate my father?"

"The blue, sir. The—er—iridescent quality of the fabric is quite—eye-catching."

"Blue it is. I suppose there's no time for a bath?"

"Not if one wishes to be on time."

"One doesn't, but one wants to get this month's lecture over with, so I suppose I shouldn't dillydally. Damn. I wonder where I left the waistcoat? I don't suppose I can advertise for it, after all—'left in some lady's bedchamber, one orangish-red waistcoat'."

"Nor the shirt or cravat," Reston said mildly.

"All that? I must have been on the verge of being discovered," Tristan said. "Oh, well, that was last week and no one's called me out yet, so I suppose I evaded capture that time as well."

"Yes, sir."

"It's not like anyone could identify whose waistcoat it was, anyway—it was the first time I'd worn it, and... Lady Abernathy?"

"No, sir. Sir is accustomed to visiting Lady Abernathy on Wednesdays."

"Drat. Oh, well. It's not like I can't afford to lose one waistcoat. I know—I'll purchase another of the same hue, then if anyone *does* suspect, he'll be flummoxed by the fact that I apparently still have it. Take care of it, will you, Reston?"

"Yes, sir."

"What would I do without you?"

"I'm sure I couldn't say, sir."

Tristan threw off the coverlet to find himself still nearly fully dressed. "Ballocks," he said irritably and peeled off grimy trousers and drawers and shirt, then strode over to the washstand and soaped up a flannel with the cold water. Reston picked up the discarded clothing and said, "I'll bring these out and return in a moment to help you shave and dress, sir."

"Mm," Tristan replied, staring at himself in the washstand mirror. He looked like hell, unshaven, eyes bloodshot, skin gray. He looked forty instead of his true twenty-eight. Twenty-eight, and still as tightly under the thumb of his father as he had been at eight. Worse—at eight he'd still had his mother to advocate for him. A year later she'd died and his newborn sister with her, leaving Tristan and his father to deal with their grief in their own separate ways. His father had chosen to control every waking moment of Tristan's life, and Tristan had chosen to defy him just as thoroughly.

He was tired of it. Tired of waking every morning hung over or still drunk, with little or no memory of the night before; tired of rogering endless women with their soft, clinging hands and soft, clinging bodies and pervasive, nauseating perfumes; tired of hours spent in one club or another with the same obnoxious friends. Tired of the rebellion that never seemed to end, never seemed to do more than annoy his father. Not that the old man hadn't tried everything to rein his heir in, including cutting his allowance. Tristan had merely cut his expenses to compensate, leaning on his friends and drinking cheaper gin instead of brandy, until his father got tired of hearing about it from his own friends and given in. He wasn't a gamester, at any rate, and had never been a glutton; those activities bored him and did nothing to make him stop thinking. Sex and drink, those were the tickets to oblivion. But they never lasted long enough, and he was tired of waking up afterward. Tired of waking up, period. It was pointless, at any rate—even oblivious, he knew that he was a completely worthless individual, his sole value being that he was the heir to his father's extensive properties. His father had made sure he knew that. "Ballocks," he said again, and done washing, he pulled on fresh drawers and trousers just as Reston came back in, hot water and shaving gear in hand.

HIS father was waiting in the library of his town house in Clarges Street when Tristan arrived on the stroke of eleven thirty. The butler showed him in, his face expressionless as usual, though Tris knew he was as much a disappointment to Fulton as he had ever been to his father. It was his role in life, and he was nothing if not consistent. After a moment of his standing in the doorway, his father looked up and said irritably, "Come in, then, don't dillydally. Awful waistcoat—what made you spend your blunt on that atrocity?"

"The sure knowledge that it would annoy you," Tristan said casually.

"You look like hell."

"Thank you, sir. May I return the compliment?"

"Don't try to be clever, boy. You missed the boat on that one years ago. Your way of life is going to be the death of you."

"Life is the death of all of us, sir," Tristan said, and dropped into the chair in front of the desk, lounging back carelessly. His father's eyes narrowed at him, but he did not address the issue.

Instead, the baron drew a piece of paper from the stack on his desk. "I've been hearing things about you far too much lately, Tristan. Your drinking has become an embarrassment to the family name."

"Everyone drinks," Tristan said with a shrug, "and everyone drinks to excess. Far be it for me to fail to follow the example of those wiser than I— which I understand from you is everyone."

"And this business of your womanizing...."

Tristan said lazily, "I have yet to be accused to my face of anything of the sort."

"God, I hope so!" The baron glared at him. "But there are rumors, and they are growing. You will end up looking down the barrel of a pistol at this rate."

Tristan shrugged again. "Dueling is illegal, or hadn't you heard?"

"That doesn't mean it doesn't still go on!"

"I'll take my chances."

"You will not!" Baron Ware stood and glared down at his son. "You have sown the last of your wild oats, my boy. I'll not stand by and watch you piss away what's left of your life without leaving anything behind. I've arranged a marriage between you and—"

"Marriage? Me? My God, what poor woman has you so annoyed with her that you'd burden her with myself?"

"Lady Charlotte Mountjoy. The Earl of Chilson's daughter. She's twenty-four, and she's agreeable."

"I would think so," Tristan said, "seeing as if she's twenty-four and unwed and apparently invisible, since I have never met the chit, she must be not only on the shelf but unattractive to an apparently amazing degree. Or is she one of those who prefers the company of her own sex and thereby a womanizing sot who'll leave her alone is precisely the kind of marriage she wants?"

"You may be a womanizing sot, but you'll not leave her alone, if you mean leaving your marriage unconsummated. Your legacy—and the freedom you so cherish—is dependent upon getting an heir off this woman, assuming you haven't caught some filthy pox that has destroyed your ability to do so. Or at least making a fair attempt to get an heir. And to answer your question—or rather assumption—Lady Charlotte is not at all unattractive. She does, however, prefer the country, so has spent little time in town."

"Well, that's good, then," Tristan said. "Since I don't want her in town anyway."

"You'll have her in town until you've got an heir on her—preferably two. After that point the two of you can both go to hell, or wherever you choose." His father flung the document across the desk at him. "Sign it and show up Monday at St. George's at ten a.m.—sober and not hung over."

"Don't I get to at least meet my blushing bride before the wedding day?"

"And have her cry off? Hardly."

Tristan reviewed the document. He'd expected the usual sort of thing, settlements and whatnot, but this was specifically aimed at him. He was to produce a minimum of two children, at least one of them a boy, after which his father proposed to settle two of his properties and their income upon him personally and one on his prospective bride, for the maintenance of her and her children, with a trust that would increase for each additional child. He would live with his bride until the two children were born and during that time he would continue his usual allowance with the addition of a lease on a townhouse. His wife would receive the same allowance. Between them it was assumed they would be able to maintain a reasonable standard of living.

There was an option for him to refuse—with the result that his allowance would cease, the lease on his rooms at Albany would be canceled, and the only concession to his living arrangements would be the offer of a purchase of a cornetcy in the cavalry. Tristan stared at this last in disbelief. "You'd cut me off?"

"No, but I would insist on your going into the army," his father said coldly. "I have failed to make a man of you; if you choose not to let a wife make the attempt, perhaps the army will succeed instead. Lady Charlotte's twin brother Charles has made a successful career as a cavalry officer; I don't doubt that you'd do equally well. If you put your mind to it."

"No doubt," Tristan said, equally coldly. "You'd prefer me to be someone else's responsibility? Or is it that you'd rather see me dead than your heir? I'm sure that distant cousin would be more amenable to your plans."

"I am *trying* to save your damn life, boy! You have pissed away every opportunity I have given you. You have one last chance to turn your life around."

"One last chance to let you control me," Tristan said bitterly. "One last chance to show the world that the great Baron Ware can manage his heir just as well as he manages all his wealth and properties and investments and businesses. Well, do you know what, Father? Make your damn arrangements. I'll be at St. George's, and I'll give you your bloody heirs, and may you be damned with them." He snatched up a quill, shoved it unceremoniously in the inkwell, and scrawled his name at the bottom of the paper. "I'll fuck your Lady Charlotte until she bursts with children, and then shove her back into the damned country where she belongs and then your 'rumors' will seem like nothing in comparison to the mud I'll drag your precious name through."

His father's lips were a thin seam, but he took the sheet wordlessly and placed it in the pile on his desk. Tristan stood, dropped the inky quill on the carpet at his feet, and walked out.

COLLECTING his coat, hat, and gloves from an expressionless Fulton, Tristan stormed out of the building. At the end of the street, instead of turning right toward home, he walked down Curzon Street, crossed Park Lane, and entered the park, abandoning the more traveled paths for a sheltered spot he knew altogether too well. A bench sat on a slight rise beyond the Serpentine, with a view of the water though almost hidden from the strollers nearby. He flung himself onto the bench and covered his eyes with his hands.

Marriage. Not the kind of marriage he'd always sort of dreamed he'd have, with a woman he truly cared about—even if he'd never yet met her—but the kind of marriage he'd made such a career out of flouting. Marriage to a stranger, a woman with whom he shared no interests, no common acquaintance that he knew of, a woman he'd never even *seen* before. He'd never met the Honorable Charles Mountjoy, but knew what was meant by a "successful cavalry officer"—one who sat on his fat arse while sending his men out to die. Not the kind of man he would find interesting. He knew her brother, the Honorable Daniel Mountjoy, slightly; they belonged to some of the same clubs, but where Tristan and his friends frequented Angelo's and Jackson's, Mountjoy's set preferred the gaming hells Tristan found boring. He wondered dully if Mountjoy's sister was a gambling sort; if so, he'd soon put a stop to it.

He shook his head wearily. What made him think he would have any more control over his wife's behavior than he did anything else in his life? Everything he did seemed to be a reaction rather than an action: drink too much because his father disapproved of it, take meaningless risks because he was his father's sole heir, bed women he couldn't marry for much the same reason. God knew that at this point he didn't sleep with women because he got any great enjoyment out of it. Work to get the woman satisfied, then a few minutes of his own pleasure, a moment of blissful oblivion, and then it was over. Barely worth it anymore.

The sound of footsteps, and an automatic reaction; he leaned back, his arms across the back of the bench, his legs crossed and one Hessian swinging idly, the very picture of an idle buck enjoying the April morning. A pair of girls came giggling up the path; they hesitated on noticing him, but when he touched the brim of his curly beaver, they curtseyed hastily, giggled again, and hurried off down the way.

They made him feel old. Did his betrothed giggle? He hoped not—she was twenty-four, after all, and a woman that firmly on the shelf had no right to giggle like a schoolroom miss.

His betrothed. God. Maybe the cavalry was the right choice. But then he thought about having to bow to the demands of one of the officers he knew: arrogant, privileged, more concerned with their own comfort than that of their men, quick to lash out at imagined insult, quicker to punish imagined rebellion. Of the parade of battered veterans begging on every street corner, of the lists of casualties printed in every edition of the Times, the retired officers in his clubs missing an arm, a leg, an eye. He was a coward, he knew it, but the idea of coming back half a man frightened him worse than not coming back at all—perhaps crippled, forever helpless at the hands of a man who hated him…. He felt ill. No, marriage, even to a woman who despised him, would be better than that. And she would despise him, there was no doubt in his mind about that.

He climbed to his feet, shaking his head to clear it. No matter. He had an appointment for lunch with his friend Gibson and after that, a lesson with Henry Angelo. He would keep his appointment with his wedding with the same consistency as those, as unappealing as it was—he made it a point of honor to never miss an appointment, no matter how drunk he might be. He might be a womanizing sot, but he was by God an *honorable* womanizing sot. He snorted a laugh at the joke, and was laughing still as he headed down the path toward the street.

CHAPTER 2

"MR. TRISTAN NORTHWOOD."

Tristan's hostess hurried forward at the sound of his name, reaching out a hand to grasp his. "Mr. Northwood! So happy to see you. You must tell us *all* about it! Such a wicked boy to keep such a thing a secret!"

"I take it the notice was in the Times today," Tristan said.

Lady Raegood nodded. "I was not even aware that your family was acquainted with the Mountjoys, and here you are betrothed to Lady Charlotte! Such a sweet girl. I was at school with her, you know."

"I didn't," Tris admitted, then said with a smile, "but she must have been years ahead of you."

"Oh, go on," Lady Raegood simpered. "Oh, we were separated by some years, but I shan't say in which direction! Of course, she was always more mature than her age—such a difficulty, being the only girl in *such* a family."

Tristan raised an eyebrow.

"Oh, not that they're not perfectly acceptable," his hostess amended quickly. "But all *men*, you know. So difficult for a young girl. Her twin brother is delightful, of course."

"I understand that he is in the cavalry?"

"Yes, one of the dragoon regiments. He's in Spain or Portugal or one of those other heathen places." She sighed dramatically. "We were all quite in *love* with him when he came to visit Lottie. That uniform! Those eyes! Those *shoulders*!"

"He sounds quite a paragon," Tristan said dryly.

She laughed. "Oh, quite. But we were just silly schoolgirls at the time." She flirted her eyes up at him.

Inwardly he sighed, but only said, "I trust I may have the honor of a dance with you later in the evening?"

"Of course, Mr. Northwood." Her voice dropped to a husky whisper. "You may have as many as you like."

He smiled down at her gallantly, suppressing the urge to run back out into the rainy night. He was to meet Gibson and Berkeley here; an hour or two to socialize, then they'd be off to a certain pub for some more pleasant entertainment. "We'd best keep to two," he said, "else there will be talk. As long as one of them is a waltz?"

"Of course," Lady Raegood said instantly. She glanced over her shoulder. The middle-aged Lord Raegood was with a group of his cronies, guffawing over some joke. In an undertone, she said, "Perhaps later we could meet in a more... private setting?"

"Alas," Tristan said smoothly, "I've another appointment this evening. Another time?"

She looked disappointed, but rallied. "By all means," she cooed. "I drive in the Park most afternoons; perhaps if you were walking there I could take you up for a turn or two?"

"It would be my pleasure," Tristan said. He took her card and wrote his name next to two dances, noting that the other waltz was taken by Geoffrey de Salis, another of the more disreputable rakes of the ton. So little Betsy Raegood was hedging her bets? Good for her. And with Geoffrey in the running, he himself didn't need to take on another inamorata—at least not just yet. Betsy Raegood *was* a prime piece; he'd thought her devoted to her older husband, but apparently appearances were *very* deceptive. He felt a little depressed at another example of the faithlessness of the aristocracy, of which he was such a prime example, but smiled encouragingly down at her before taking his leave and going to find Gibs.

He hadn't quite escaped the ballroom when he came face to face with Barbara Abernathy. "Rumor has it that you're getting married." She flared her fan and peered at him coquettishly over the top.

"Yes, it's true. An arrangement between our parents. Cash for her, posterity for my father." He took her arm and led her a little aside, into an alcove where they could be seen clearly, but not overheard.

"Then I trust you will respect the bonds of matrimony as well as you ever have?" she said, giggling.

He glanced down at her. "Of course," he said dryly. "I don't see where my life needs to change in any substantive measure." He considered, then went on. "No doubt, however, I will not be able to visit next Wednesday as usual—I would imagine my bride expects some sort of honeymoon or something of the sort. The following Wednesday will, I'm sure, be a different story."

"It's so obliging of William to keep to such a regular schedule," Barbara observed. "I do wish I could see you more often, but his Wednesday card games are the one time I can be absolutely sure he will remain occupied. Besides, you keep to a rather busy schedule yourself, do you not? I understand Mrs. Foote's husband was quite irate with her over a coquelicot waistcoat found in her bedchamber Thursday week."

"Oh, good God," Tristan sighed. "Deborah Foote. I had quite forgot her. I met her at the Templemoors'."

"I *thought* that was your waistcoat. You have impeccable taste in everything except waistcoats." She fingered the gold-and-cream-striped example he wore today. "This one is not *too* horrible, but some of them…!"

"I wear them to irritate Baron Ware," Tristan said. "I don't often see him, but I know a number of his friends regularly report back to him about me."

"Ah," Barbara said. "Is *that* how you ended up in this pickle?"

He shrugged. "Hardly a pickle. For a minor inconvenience, I win more or less free of his interference—at least for a while. And I suppose it is inevitable—I am quite nearly thirty, after all. Time to start the nursery and all that."

She snorted delicately. "It's different for a man, age."

"My delectable darling, 'age cannot wither you nor custom stale your infinite variety'."

"That sounds like a quote," she said suspiciously. "Shakespeare, I think?"

"You think correctly," he said. "Antony, referring to Cleopatra. Though I trust my upcoming marriage will not encourage you to engage the services of an asp?"

"My darling Tristan," Barbara said in the same tone, "I haven't the faintest idea what an asp is."

He chuckled, bowed correctly, and took his leave.

CHARLOTTE MOUNTJOY sat serenely in the chair in front of her father's desk, regarding calmly the mess of papers, quills, half-empty drinking glasses, stray playing cards, and snuffboxes. It was Papa's mess; she didn't think she'd ever seen it any other way. It was comfortable in its own way, a representation of the way the household worked. He let her run the rest of the house the way she wanted; he was free to mess up his bookroom as much as he wanted. Unspoken, but no less an agreement.

On the other hand, Papa himself looked uncomfortable, which was unusual. Papa rarely let things make him uncomfortable; if they did, he either ran roughshod over them or ignored them, whichever was appropriate. She was perfectly happy being ignored. As long as there was plenty of food and drink, he was as perfectly happy as she.

This discomfort threatened to disturb that happiness. She had an inkling of what it was about, and hoped she was wrong.

For the last three years, ever since her last Season on the Marriage Mart, he'd occasionally made comments about her unmarried state. She mostly hadn't paid attention, since he quite depended on her for his comfort, and as he was quite as selfish as she, she doubted that he would make any attempt at any activity that would result in him losing her as housekeeper. He'd been happy enough to oblige her and turn away her several prospective suitors during her three Seasons. She was only a girl, after all, and the substantial gift from her mother had left her quite well enough off that she need not marry for money as so many of her contemporaries did. There seemed no reason to be rid of her.

But over the course of the last several weeks, subterranean grumbling overheard between him and his heir, her older brother Daniel, signaled a shift in the Earth's surface. Money troubles. Her plans for a settled, retired spinsterhood were about to be disrupted.

Two weeks ago Papa had uprooted the family from their country home and dragged the household to their drafty townhome in London. The first week Charlotte had been obliged to supervise the cleaning of the place top to bottom, as well as the hiring of several new servants, since Papa had of course both neglected to advise the London staff that they would be arriving and neglected to inform her ahead of time so that she could do so. So it was a full seven-day of housecleaning, shopping, organizing, ordering, and reordering. Thank God for Ellen Bayes, her cousin and companion, whose natural domesticity got and kept things running smoothly. All Charlotte had to do was make decisions.

Charlotte herself was undomestic—her sole household skill was hiring excellent servants. She was quite good at reading people. But in order to find honest, organized, hard-working servants, one had to have a selection to hire from, and the various agencies seemed to be taking delight in sending her absolutely unacceptable candidates. It took her nearly the whole fortnight to fill three staff positions, the last only this morning.

And now she had to deal with whatever Papa's febrile brain had come up with.

She folded her hands and waited placidly.

He stared at her, his bloodshot eyes vague. After a moment, he said, "Er. Humph."

"Yes, Papa," she said agreeably.

"Harrumph. Well. Lottie. Past time you were thinking of getting married."

Oh, drat, she thought. She'd been right. With a faint sigh, she said, "If you think so, Papa."

"Right. I do think so. Gel your age ought to be thinking about settin' up your own household, not managing your Papa's."

"Yes, Papa."

He frowned at her, then pointed his unlit cheroot at her. "Thinkin' about it, are you?"

"Only since you mentioned it, Papa."

"I've arranged a thing for you. Ware's whelp. Good age. Ripe for settlin'. Told Ware you were willin', 'cause you are, aren't you?"

"Ware's whelp"? She thought a moment. Oh, Baron Ware. His son was Something Northwood. Something fanciful—Lochinvar? Lancelot? No—Tristan, that was it. One of her many correspondents had just written her about him, something about a drunken theater party and him ending up on stage after the romantic lead had stormed off in a huff. He'd taken up the role instead and finished to laughter and great applause.

Hmm. Not a restful sort. But presumably he wouldn't require a great deal of attention. Besides, she'd learned how to manage his type—hadn't she lived with them for the last twenty-four years? She glanced up at her papa's face, with its pattern of broken blood vessels and the bags from too much drink and too little sleep, and sighed faintly. "As you wish, Papa."

"Good settlements. Took care of you. You'll have your mama's gift, of course; tied that up so even your husband can't get his hands on the principal. For the rest—well, that's business, and of no interest to you."

Ah. The reason behind this. "Baron Ware is anxious to get his heir wed, I take it?" she asked in her mildest voice.

"Well, he's twenty-eight, you know. And a bit of a hey-go-mad fellow. Best to get his grandson off him and settled up before the son breaks his neck on the hunting field or one of his wild undertakings."

"Is Daniel quite rolled up, then?" she asked, still in that mild tone.

It didn't fool Papa. He gave her a sharp look at odds with his bleary physiognomy and said, "Aye. Far more than I can manage."

"That explains it." Ware, apparently, had agreed to settle Daniel's debts in return for Daniel's sister.

"Northwood's got a bad reputation, but I've never heard that he ever mistreated a woman," Papa said firmly. "He's only a bit wild, not unkind. And a handsome lad, from what I've seen of him. Ware seems to think that he just needs marriage to settle him down. Has to wed sometime. No reason it shouldn't be you."

"None at all," Lottie said agreeably. *Well*, she thought, *so much for the retired-spinster plans*. On the other hand, one might expect that once she had produced the required heir, she might be permitted to retire to the country, anyway, and leave her husband to go to hell in his own way. That would be acceptable. Besides, Papa seemed quite resolved.

She glanced again at the disarray of the desk, echoed in the general disarray of the bookroom. Perhaps it might be entertaining to be mistress of her own establishment, after all. And she did trust Papa to look out for her welfare, as much as he could be expected to, so the terms of the marriage should not be too onerous. "Well, Papa, if Mr. Northwood is agreeable, so am I," she said, rising from the chair.

"Is Monday next too soon for you? I know you ladies will want to shop for trousseaux, that sort of thing?"

She considered it a moment. "I have no objection to Monday," she said thoughtfully. "Ellen and I can certainly shop in the meantime. I've several ball gowns I've yet to wear which should be suitable for the wedding itself. I presume we will have a wedding breakfast here?"

Papa waved his hand dismissively. "Ware's taking care of all that. We just have to be there. St. George's, of course."

"Of course," Charlotte said mildly.

"I say, Lottie, you're taking this well. Didn't expect a fuss from you, but you did have that damnfool notion of setting up your own household once upon a time. Wouldn't have done, you know."

"I suppose not, Papa," Charlotte said.

"This will be quite well. Much better for you."

"If you say so, Papa." She hesitated. "Will we be entertaining Baron Ware and Mr. Northwood prior to the wedding?"

"I don't see the need," her father said absently. "Ware's a dead bore. His son's more lively, but I don't see the point of invitin' one without the other. Ware's the one in charge in this matter—his son's got nothing to say to the point. Now, run along. Tell Ellen."

"I shall." She dropped a polite curtsey, then left the room in search of her companion.

"SO YOU'RE marrying Daniel Mountjoy's sister? Better keep a tight hand on the checkbook, boyo."

Tristan finished checking the harness on the pair hooked up to his curricle and glanced up at Gibson. "Say what?"

"Daniel Mountjoy. Man's a leech. Worst judge of horseflesh I've ever seen and don't ever stake him to a hand of cards. Bet that's why Chilson's so eager to marry her off—get her off his books before his heir pisses away her dowry. Don't imagine there's much of that to begin with, eh?"

"Haven't a clue," Tristan said disinterestedly. "Ware dealt with all that. All I've got to do is show up on Monday. Never even met the chit." He tightened a buckle, then looked across the innyard to where Hapwell was talking to his tiger. Another few minutes, then; it looked like Hapwell was deep in instructions. Stupid to take a tiger on a race, even one like this one, over well-maintained roads at five in the morning, when the only traffic would be the odd farmer bringing vegetables to the Covent Garden market. Dangerous for the tiger, and that much more weight on the carriage. Of course, Hapwell's carriage was barely more than wheels and a seat; he probably needed the tiger for ballast. His own was more substantial, but so lightly balanced he was perfectly confident that he'd beat Hapwell handily over the five-mile round trip course they'd laid out in the bet at White's last night. Or was it this morning?

"Hardly a chit, must be damn near twenty-five by now. Solidly on the shelf."

"Have you met her?" Tristan ran his hand along the back of the nearer horse, feeling the tension in its muscle. The horse soothed at his steady, confident touch—steady, despite the fact that he'd been drinking pretty well continuously since supper the night before. He knew how much liquor he could handle before a race—and, well, a little pickling relaxed him, made his hands lighter on the ribbons.

"What, you're marryin' a pig in a poke?" said Berkeley groggily from where he leaned against the curricle, finally catching up with the conversation.

"Guess I am." Tristan stretched, then shoved Berkeley, so that the tankard of ale he'd just lifted to his lips splashed over his cravat. "Never met her, anyway."

"I did." Berkeley dragged a hand across his mouth to wipe away the ale that had managed to get to his lips from his cup. "Came out at the same time as m'sister. Not a bad-looking girl—had a few interested parties but nothing came of it. Don't know whether they never came up to snuff or she turned 'em all down, or her pa did. Only spent a couple Seasons in Town. Don't know what the problem was."

"I don't care," Tristan said. "All women look alike in the dark, eh? Throw her nightgown over her head and I won't care what she looks like underneath. Nobody says I have to pay any other attention to her."

"I say," Berkeley frowned. "Not very gentlemanly. Girl is a lady, after all."

"Yes," Tristan said, "but nobody said I was a gentleman." His lip curled in a sneer. "My father least of all."

"Your father," Berkeley said, then he belched. "Your father... is an ass. You're not as bad as all that." He looked at Gibson. "Is he as bad as all that, Gibs?"

"No. He tries, but he's a lousy rake. Only beds married women, won't debauch an innocent or an honest wife. Doesn't gamble to excess...."

"Gambling is boring," Tristan said absently. One couldn't count races like this one, at any rate. He hadn't done it for the money, though he was sure the betting was going heavy, from the crowd of gentleman gathered in the shabby yard. It was for the fun of it—and to prove to Hapwell that skill at driving was more important than the carriage beneath one.

"And always lends me money when I ask for it. Drinks too much, but don't we all? No, Woodsy is an abject failure as hellspawn." Gibs shook his head sadly. "Berks, you're more of a hellspawn than poor old Tris here."

"I am?"

"Yes. For no other reason that you refused to spot me a pony last week."

Berkeley sniffed. "I draw the line at subsidizing your gambling excesses."

"You, sir, are not drunk enough if you can still pronounce subdisi... dubsidize... that word," Gibson said, in the clear, careful tones of the very inebriated. "We are drinking to Northwood's wedding. Drink up."

"You, sir, are going to end up facedown in the gutter one of these days, and you'll be robbed and stripped naked. Then what will you do?" Berkeley said, belching again.

"Stand up and stagger home naked," Tristan said absently. "Just as I would."

"Your wife'll like that," Berks said.

"I assume you mean me, since Gibs hasn't a wife. As to that, I daresay she'll have many things not to like about me," Tristan said. A barmaid came out of the inn with a brimming pitcher; he intercepted her and held out his own mug. "Fill 'er up, luv; I'm off to Hammersmith in a moment," he said, giving her a noisy buss on the cheek. "Will you long for me when I'm wed, sweetheart?"

"From wot I 'ear of you, luv, *that* won't change your life none," she retorted pertly.

He laughed and gave her a gentle pinch on her round arse before letting her go. She flirted her skirts at him as she walked away. "I should marry that one," he said, and he took a drink.

"I say," Berks said, horrified, "you *can't!*"

"Of course not," Tristan replied. "I'm already betrothed." He stood up, raising his mug high. "To my blushing bride!"

A roar of approval rumbled through the yard, and he tossed back the ale, pleased with himself. "There. As proper a toast as you'll ever see."

"I hope it don't," Gibs said.

"Don't what?"

"Change your life none."

"I don't see where it should. She's just a woman."

"Well," Gibs sighed, "right now, it's just a woman. But later there will be children; I mean, didn't your pa say that was the whole point?"

Tristan shrugged. "I don't know anything about children. That's her area of exper, experzeet. Ex-per-tease." He grinned in triumph. "Expertise. At least, I assume so—she's a woman, after all. It's what they're good for."

"Not all they're good for," Berks said.

Tristan laughed and held up his tankard in silent salute, then handed it to Berks. "Hold that for me," he said. "I'll need it when I come back. Assuming I haven't broken my neck on the way."

"You won't," Gibson said. "Charmed life."

Tristan gave him a brief, bitter smile, then vaulted into the seat of his curricle and gave Gibson the nod to let go of the horse's head. Hapwell followed suit, his tiger jumping up behind, and they trotted out of the innyard to where a string lay across the Hammersmith road. "Ready, then?" Hapwell called, and Tris called back, "Readier than you, Hap!" with a laugh.

Someone dropped a Belcher handkerchief and they were off.

It was a beautiful morning for a drive, the road dry, the sky lightening and bright with the promise of sun later. Tris took an easy lead, his heavier carriage holding the rutted road better than Hap's, which had a tendency to slide. He grinned, enjoying the rush of excitement he'd always felt when racing: the chill breeze in his face, the rumble of the hooves and the wheels and the road, the thrill of those moments when the carriage shot up a rut and hung for a moment in midair before striking the road again…. It was like the hunt, when one felt the horse's muscles bunch beneath one and suddenly one was flying. Moments like these he could forget his past, his future, time, and life, and his father's disapproval. Moments like these he was no one, nothing, a leaf in the wind, the wind itself, an echo of his own voice. He laughed aloud, and his horses, used to the sound, picked up the pace until he no longer heard Hapwell's wheels behind him.

He made the turn just past Hammersmith, and passed Hapwell on the way back to Kensington, overtaking a wagonload of turnips and slowing his pair to a cooling trot as he wended through the arch to the still-dark innyard. There were cheers and groans of disappointment, and he waved his whip in salute as he drew up, tossed a coin to the ostler's boy, and jumped down from the seat. The boy took the pair off to walk them, and Tristan went back to join his friends.

"I trust you both made a profit?" Tristan asked, drawing off his gloves and wiping his forehead with his handkerchief.

Berkeley grinned and handed him his tankard. "As usual," he said. "Where's Hapwell?"

Tristan shrugged. "I imagine about halfway back from Hammersmith. He hadn't yet arrived there when I saw him last. Sun's up; that will slow his eastward trip, I imagine."

The sun came up over the innyard walls and one of the menservants came out to douse the flambeaux. "I'm for home and bed," Gibs said. "Coming, Woods?"

"You go ahead. I have to wait for my cattle to cool, then take the curricle home. Maybe by then I'll be sober enough to manage London traffic."

"Send them home with a postboy," Gibson suggested. "I'll take you up. I imagine you're ready to knit the raveled sleeve of care?"

"God, you and your quotes," Berks complained.

"Shut up, or I won't give you a lift," Gibson threatened good-naturedly.

The barmaid came out with the pitcher again and refilled their tankards. Tristan watched her walk away, his eyes narrowed.

"It isn't right," Tristan said suddenly.

"It isn't?"

"What id'nt?" Berkeley inquired.

"I'm getting married on Monday, and here 't is Wednesday and I've never even met the woman!" Tris looked around the innyard as if he'd find the woman in question lurking somewhere there.

"Is it Wednesday?" Gibson asked no one in particular.

"I think so. At any rate, it isn't right that the poor girl should be expected to marry someone she's never met!"

"I like you, Woodsy," Gibson said. "Allus thinkin' of other people."

"Besides," Tristan said reasonably, "if she dislikes me intensely p'raps she'll cry off. I wonder if I have to go into the cavalry if she's the one that cries off?" He shrugged. "Ah, well. Don't matter. Might as well be in the cavalry. At least it has horses, right?"

"Could be worse," Berkeley mumbled. "Could be infantry."

"Oldest damn cornet in history," Tristan complained, and drained his tankard. "Her twin's four years younger than me and is a bloody captain already. Bloody twin."

"Whose twin?"

"My finance. Finnish. Betrot'd," Tristan said, sketched a bow, and went after his curricle.

He tipped the ostler and swung up into the seat without too much trouble; a little voice awoke and said that perhaps it wasn't the best idea to go calling on his betrothed while he was, if not completely pickled, then certainly well-to-live. He ignored it, as he had ignored it most of his adult life, but he did stop at home to change his curricle for the Brat, and for a quick wash and fresh cravat, so he was inadvertently a bit more sober when he trod up the steps to bang on the front door of the Earl of Chilson's townhouse.

*C*HAPTER 3

A SUPERCILIOUS butler, no doubt valedictorian of the Supercilious School of Butlering, answered the door and regarded him askance. "Sir?"

"Tristan Northwood. Here to see Lady Charlotte."

"I will enquire if her ladyship is at home," the butler intoned, but took his card and permitted Tristan into the hall. Tristan glanced around curiously; he thought he might have attended a ball or two here, but then again, it was decorated much the same as any other townhouse, fashionably, with too much Chinese influence and too little taste. He shrugged carelessly. *He* didn't have to live here, and when it came time to decorate his own townhouse—he wondered vaguely where it would be, since his father had promised him the house after he married, and that was only a few days hence. He should probably contact his father's man of business—what was his name? Finchley? Fitzleigh?—to find out where he was supposed to take his bride since he couldn't very well take her home to his rooms after the wedding, and.... His thoughts ran down as the butler came down the stairs to say, "If Mr. Northwood would follow me?"

"WAS that the door?" Ellen asked curiously.

Charlotte glanced up at her companion from the letter she was reading. They had only just finished breakfast and retired to the drawing room. "Door?" she asked vaguely.

"Yes, I'm quite sure I heard knocking. Who do you suppose it could be?"

Charlotte thought. "Well," she said, "it wouldn't be Papa; he wouldn't knock. Neither would Daniel, unless he'd lost his key. Neither Papa nor

Daniel was particularly quiet this morning when they got home, so I doubt that either has gone out again. So I would have to say that I do not suppose it could be anyone. What time is it?"

"Just past eight."

"Odd time to make calls," Charlotte said, and went back to her letter. "Liesl says that she has some visitors from Naples. Apparently Mr. Murat is rethinking his alliance with the Austrians, and causing trouble with some of the Germans there. He is not making friends."

"I wouldn't think so. What is he, Bonaparte's brother-in-law? That family has no sensibility." Ellen got up and went to the window, glancing down at the street. "Just a horse, so a gentleman. I suppose he must be looking for Daniel. Not one who knows him, at any rate; if he was a friend he would know Daniel is never awake before noon. So a stranger."

"My goodness," Lottie said with a little laugh. "You are so logical! Calculating all that!"

"Aren't you curious?"

"No," Lottie said. "I do not think I am a curious sort. I imagine Jeppson will be in shortly to tell us who called. I have noticed that he does do that frequently."

"I should hope so," Ellen said, and sat back down again, giving her charge a rueful smile. "You are so practical, Lottie."

Lottie just smiled serenely.

To both their surprise, Jeppson appeared sooner rather than later. "Mr. Northwood to see you, ma'am," he said to Charlotte. "Are you At Home to him this morning?"

"Mr. Northwood?" Charlotte blinked in surprise. "Mr. *Tristan* Northwood?"

"Yes, Lady Charlotte." The butler presented a silver salver with a card on it. Ellen got up and took the card.

"Tristan Northwood. Well, well, well." She glanced at Charlotte. "Shall you meet him, then?"

"I suppose I ought."

"I should advise Lady Charlotte that it appears that Mr. Northwood has been drinking."

"Oh, dear," Ellen said, and looked indecisive. "Already?"

Lottie laughed. "Oh, it's probably 'still'. Good heavens, someone's always drinking around here. Send him up. I find that I am a curious sort after all."

"Charlotte, are you sure?" Ellen asked anxiously as Jeppson left the room. "It's not a proper hour for calls, and if he has been drinking...."

"My papa would not betroth me to anyone who is not a gentleman," Charlotte said, as she set her embroidery aside. "Do ring for tea, Ellen, dear."

"Yes, of course," Ellen said, flustered, and did so. A moment later they heard footsteps on the stairs, and Jeppson entered, followed by a tall young man.

"Mr. Northwood," Jeppson said.

"Thank you, Jeppson." Charlotte rose and crossed the room, her hand outstretched. "How do you do, Mr. Northwood?"

"Fine, thank you." He glanced from her to her companion. Charlotte took the hint.

"Ellen, may I present Mr. Northwood? This, sir, is Mrs. Ellen Bayes, my companion."

"My pleasure." Mr. Northwood bowed.

Charlotte led the way back to the pair of chairs before the fireplace she and Ellen had occupied moments ago. "Will you take a seat, sir?"

"Thank you." He waited for her to sit, then followed suit.

Charlotte regarded him thoughtfully. Handsomer than she'd expected; though there was a tired, dissipated look about the gray eyes, he did not yet possess the broken blood vessels in the nose and cheek that were the hallmark of the perpetual drunk. His dark hair was tousled, but only fashionably; his cravat was neat and clean, and his coat tidy. His face seemed to have the conformation of one who smiled often; there were small wrinkles at the corners of his eyes. He was well-built as well, broad-shouldered, long of limb and lean of hip. All in all a very pretty sight... except for those eyes.

He smiled at her. "Have I earned your approval, madam?"

"That remains to be seen," she said. "Your appearance is quite satisfactory. I am much surprised."

As was Tristan. He'd come expecting at the very least an antidote; instead, he found a very pleasant-looking woman. Not pretty, no: her snub nose and round face were not those of an Incomparable, but neither was she ugly. Just—ordinary. But pleasant enough. And a trim enough figure beneath her simple gown. Fair hair—curled, but he could not quite tell if that was natural or the product of curling-irons—in a plain style appropriate for a morning at home. And she looked... peaceful. Undemanding. Something inside of him unwound at that thought, and he smiled again. Perhaps this would not be quite as horrible as he'd suspected.

"I am pleased that my appearance is satisfactory. I hope I may reassure you on any other points you may question."

"Indeed." She glanced up as the footman came in with the tea tray and set it down on the table between them. "I do of course have a number of questions for you. I hope you won't find them too personal."

"Lottie...," Mrs. Bayes said, pleating the plain gray stuff of her gown anxiously.

Charlotte smiled at her friend. "Oh, Ellen, dearest, don't be concerned. Mr. Northwood is my betrothed. He and I can have no secrets, can we, Mr. Northwood?"

Tristan stared at her a moment, nonplused, then shook his head. "I suppose not." *Like hell*, he thought, *am I telling you all* my *secrets!*

His fiancée said to her companion, "You see? It would be quite proper for you to leave us in private for a short while, Ellen, dear. It would *not* be proper for you to hear a discussion between two affianced people." Her smile was an amazing thing, Tristan thought in weird fascination, a sort of placidly immovable expression, as if she had no doubt that her will would be obeyed. Suddenly he wondered if he were up for it after all....

"Lottie?"

"Shoo. Come back in fifteen minutes." Lottie studied him a moment, then went on. "That should be sufficient for the discussion I intend to have."

"Fine," Ellen said, "but it is against my better judgment." She rearranged her shawl and sailed out of the room, nose in the air.

"It's a sad duenna so easily routed," Tristan observed.

Charlotte wrinkled her nose. "Is that a foreign word, 'duenna'? Because it sounds like a foreign word. It sounds like something my brother Charlie might write. He's in the Peninsula, you know."

"I do now," Tristan said.

"What does it mean?"

"'Chaperone', I believe."

"Oh, Ellen isn't my chaperone. She's just my companion, to keep me company, you know. Not that I really need company; I'm perfectly happy by myself. But Papa prefers that I have someone with me when I want to go riding, or walking, or shopping, and so I hired Ellen. She's actually...." She frowned, wrinkling her nose again. "A second cousin or something. Her husband died and she was quite bored, so she was happy to come here."

"She may continue to live with you when we are married," Tristan offered magnanimously.

"That would be nice," Charlotte replied. "She can keep me company when you are out. I suppose you have a very busy life. Men seem to."

Yes, of course, Tristan thought. There were many demands on his time, drinking, swiving, attending mills, attending the opera—for the sole purpose of picking up the stray opera dancer, of course....

"Do you attend the opera?"

He blinked. "Yes, of course," he said automatically.

She wrinkled her nose again. She was rather amusing, he thought dazedly. Like a puppy. "I went once. I fell asleep."

"Well, it is...."

"My brother Daniel says most men attend to look at the pretty ladies on the stage." She chuckled, a low, warm sound. "He then had to explain to me that the stage in opera is not the same as the stage one rides on to travel around. Isn't that silly? Of course, I was quite young at the time, not yet out."

"He said that to you when you were still in the schoolroom?"

"Oh, I was out of the schoolroom. But not 'out' yet, you know. When a girl is presented and all that."

"Yes. Yes, I understand."

"I thought you might," she said complacently. "You look like a clever person."

He opened his mouth, then closed it again, bereft of any comment suitable for mixed company.

"I am not at all clever," she said. "But I have no difficulty asking people to explain things. Some people do, you know. But I don't. For instance, I would like to ask you a question."

"Fire away," Tristan said.

"Would you like milk? Oh, that isn't the question. That's just an inquiry."

"No, nothing, thank you."

"Well, tea, of course, so not quite nothing." She poured him a cup of tea and handed it to him.

He had just taken a sip when she asked, "Are you diseased?"

With an effort, he kept from either spitting it out or choking on it; when he'd managed to swallow, he asked, "I beg your pardon?"

Her demeanor was as calm as if she'd just asked him the time. "Diseased. I overheard my brother Daniel discussing you with my papa, and he said I would be lucky if you weren't diseased. He said that you made a habit of... well, I can't say the word, it's most improper, but it *means* that you lie with ladies and that that frequently breeds disease." A faint frown appeared on her forehead. "I don't understand quite how that would happen, but I thought I'd better ask."

He gave a bark of laughter. "No," he said in amusement, "I'm not diseased. I take precautions to avoid, er, engendering offspring, and it seems to have a salutary effect on the spread of... illnesses."

She cocked her head, like a little wren. "What *sort* of precautions?"

"This is a most improper conversation," Tristan said, fighting back the little imp of depravity that was encouraging him to elaborate.

"But we are betrothed. I do most sincerely wish to confirm that you are not ill before I marry you. Please explain how you prevent this."

"Are you *serious*?"

She blinked. "Yes, why?"

"Well-bred ladies do *not* discuss such things with gentlemen they have just met."

"Perhaps if they did," she said meditatively, "there would be less spread of illness."

He opened his mouth, then shut it again. And sipped his tea. Finally, he said, "I always use a French letter."

She frowned. "A French letter? You mean one of those like the *c* with the little squiggle beneath, or the *o* with the hat?"

He laughed out loud. "Lady Charlotte, you are a delight. No, it is a sheath that fits over the—" He started to say, "Membrum virilis," which was how his tutor had described it when he'd given Tristan "the talk," but realized quickly that she would have no idea what he was referring to. So he took a breath and went on, "The male member. My dear Lady Charlotte, you must *swear* that you will never repeat a word of this conversation, or your papa will have me horsewhipped!"

Her eyes met his, thoughtful and innocent. "Of course not. It is a private conversation. How does this prevent engendering?"

"By keeping a man's seed from the woman. Did your mama or your governess ever tell you *anything* about how babies are born?"

"Of course not. They said my husband would explain it to me. And you are my husband, or you will be on Monday, and that is quite the same thing. I thought since you were here you might take the time, because I'm sure on Monday we will be *quite* busy with the wedding, and the wedding breakfast, and all."

"Right." He took a deep breath. "Babies are engendered by the man placing his male member inside the woman in a special place between her legs and releasing seed. There. That's it, in a nutshell."

She pursed her lips, thinking. "But if you don't want to engender babies, why do it?"

"Because it is an exceedingly pleasant experience. However, there is always the danger of babies. And disease, if your partner is not completely clean."

Again the wrinkling of the nose. "I should not want a partner who was not clean."

"Neither would I, but it is not something that one notices in one's excitement," Tristan said dryly.

"Do you lie with a great many ladies?"

"Lady Charlotte…."

"That is very personal, is it not? I apologize."

"No need. I can understand that it would be a concern of yours. Pray believe me when I tell you I will do nothing that will cause you any harm."

"Except lying with me and making me have babies," she said. "I have often heard that women die in childbirth. It makes me wonder why they bother."

"For the propagation of the species," Tristan said, confused. Didn't all women want babies? Well, all ladies, anyway—a good number of the women he consorted with would be horrified to find themselves increasing, but not because of fear of death in childbirth. He blinked. "Don't you want babies?"

"Oh, I suppose one or two would be acceptable," Charlotte said. "As long as one can afford nurses and whatnot. Do the ladies you lie with not want babies?"

My God, this girl was a mind reader. He shook his head. "No—at least not mine."

"Pity. I would imagine you would have pretty babies. I trust any babies I have of yours will be pretty." She took a sip of tea. "I will, of course, be placing my life in your hands, but I suppose it is necessary for you to have an heir. Papa explained that to me when he told me I would be marrying you."

"'Told you'? He didn't ask you?"

Her eyes went wide. "Whatever for? I do not have an opinion on the matter."

"You don't? You aren't being forced into this or anything?"

"No, of course not. I knew I would be married eventually. Papa and Daniel both found you agreeable—except for the issue of disease, of course, and I am most satisfied with your answer. So how should I object?" She cocked her head again, birdlike. "I am quite satisfied, Mr. Northwood. You are a gentleman, you have answered my questions honestly, I believe, and you are not unattractive, so our children should be pleasant to look upon. And Papa tells me you are comfortable financially, and heir to a great deal more, as well as to an honorable title. No, I am quite content. I would prefer to correspond with my brother Charlie about this; I am used to taking his advice, for he is a very wise man. He is a cavalry officer, you know."

"I have heard," Tristan said between his teeth.

"However, there is certainly not enough time for that! No matter. For my part, I assure you I will not object to your continuing in your habits as before; I certainly do not expect you to dance attendance upon me. I expect that once I have produced an heir—and perhaps a second child, just to keep him company—I will be permitted to return to the country. I have no great love for Town."

Tristan stared at her blankly. He hadn't quite expected to come here and make love to the girl, but he had at least expected to have to charm her a bit. She was so completely disinterested in their marriage that it shocked him, despite his familiarity with loveless society unions—and the bored wives that resulted. He'd expected that his own would end up that way as well, but somehow he felt that Charlotte would not even consider expending the energy to have an affair. Peculiar creature.

Still, he was getting what he wanted: a wife who would not interfere with his activities and would provide him with the heir his father demanded.

"Yes, of course," he said with a feeling of relief. "I myself prefer Town living, but I do have a very nice hunting box in Leicestershire, not far from my family home—which of course we will inherit in due time. It's called Lilac Cottage. The hunting box, not my family home—that's Wareham." He was vaguely aware that he was rattling. "And even had I not, the settlements include a property that will be yours outright upon the birth of your second child. So you will be able to be mistress of your own establishment, and not required to tolerate the company of the baron unless you wish it."

"I probably shall not," she said. "I've met him, of course, but I don't see the need to maintain any great acquaintance with him. Thank you. A small manor will be quite acceptable. And until then, a townhouse here, and your Lilac Cottage."

"Well, then. If you have no more questions?"

"Just one." Charlotte put her tea cup and saucer back on the table and folded her hands. "You said that the engenderment process requires a man to place his member inside a special place in a woman. I believe I am acquainted with the area you mean, from suffering the monthlies as all women do. However, do not men possess the same orifice?"

"No. Our equipment is entirely external." Really, this conversation was the strangest Tristan had ever experienced.

"Hmm. Then when two men lie together, how do they manage?"

A vision roared through Tristan's head at her words: an accidental drunken stumbling into the wrong inn room late at night, the sight of broad shoulders, lean flanks, the arch of a back golden with sweat and firelight; a pair of equally muscular legs wrapped around that strong back and a man's voice urging the other on with incomprehensible cries. The sight had never left Tristan since that drunken night three years before. Sometimes, just as he was ready to spend, the memory came again, blocking out the face of the woman beneath him. "I *beg* your pardon?!" Tristan's face burned with unaccustomed embarrassment, and he wasn't sure if it was at her words or at the memories they dragged up.

"Well, they do, sometimes, you know."

"And how the dev— How would you know that?"

She cocked her head and regarded him thoughtfully. "I do not think I should say," she said finally. "It was a private conversation—much like this one."

"Well, you should not have had that conversation, and if I ever find out who it was I shall horsewhip him myself!" Tristan said furiously. "That sort of union is an abomination, not only illegal but immoral. Men who lie with men are deservedly hanged. It is appalling that anyone should have sullied the ears of a gently bred lady such as yourself!"

"Oh. It is very bad, then?"

"A terrible sin!"

She nodded, not flustered in the least. "Interesting." Then she smiled at him. "It's very kind of you to be concerned about my well-being," she said in the same sweet voice. "I'm very happy that you should be anxious about it. It bodes well for our acquaintance."

He sat a moment, speechless. Then the door opened and the companion peeped in. Lottie glanced up and smiled at her with the precise same smile she'd given him: sweet and warm, but ultimately dispassionate. "Come in, Ellen. We're quite done here." She stood and he followed suit, taking the hand she held out to him. "Mr. Northwood, thank you for stopping and for setting my mind at ease. I am quite looking forward to Monday morning. Ellen, dear, would you see Mr. Northwood out?"

"Certainly," Mrs. Bayes said, and opened the door wider for him. He went out and down the stairs beside her, still reeling from the strange conversation he'd just had.

As he took his hat and coat from the butler, Mrs. Bayes said, "She's not stupid, you know. Or slow. People think that about her, but it isn't true. She's actually very bright in her own way. So you needn't worry about your heir being daft or anything. She's just… different."

"So I see," Tristan said dryly. "Well, thank you, Mrs. Bayes. Oh, and I would like to invite you to continue as my wife's companion after our marriage. I… am often away, and it will be good for her to have your friendship."

"Yes, I understand." The eyes that met his had none of Charlotte's vagueness, and none of her naïveté. "Good day, Mr. Northwood."

"Good day, Mrs. Bayes."

CHAPTER 4

THE stone of the balustrade under Tristan's bare feet was cold, but at least not icy. His toes curled around the edge as he balanced, hands tucked under his arms to keep his fingers warm. Behind him, the light and warmth and laughter of the party spilled out onto the balcony, forming almost a solid presence at his back.

"By Gad, it's cold out here!" Gibson complained. "How can you stand it, Tris?"

"It's a bloody dare," someone else said. "Someone dared him, so he's got to stand it, don't you, Northwood?"

"No one," Tristan said, "shall call me a coward without proof—and shall get none from me."

"Nobody called you a coward, old boy," Gibson said.

"They said I wouldn't do it," Tristan said. "I must prove them wrong." He hiccoughed gently, careful not to lose his balance.

"You're completely mad," Gibson said.

"No, he's completely naked," Berkeley said. "Needs his hat. Everyone needs a hat. Where is it?"

Someone passed Tristan his hat. Balancing carefully, he set the hat on his head and looked out at the still-dark sky. The sky in the east was definitely lightening—*turning into a fine spring day*, he thought absently. *A perfect day for a wedding.* Right now, though, it was a little cold, and he was naked, and he really wished the sun would hurry up and rise so he could do the crowing-like-a-rooster bit and get down and get a tot of something warm and alcoholic in him. He was sobering up too quickly, although the very fact that he was on a balcony four stories above a cobblestoned London street and the wind was picking up and his balance was not of the best because of all the very warm and alcoholic beverages he'd been drinking all night—well, all of that was rather exciting. Despite the shock of cold that had shriveled it moments ago, his cock started to wake and he laughed wildly. *On the edge of forever*, he thought through the laughter; one step and he'd be suet on the cobblestones below, freed of obligations, freed of expectations, freed of the necessity of marriage, freed of his father, freed of *decisions*.... He laughed again, and the sun edged up over the buildings on the horizon, and his laugh turned into a triumphant *ark-aroooo!* as he flapped his elbows, arched his back and crowed.

And overbalanced forward, hanging for a split second over the cobblestones far below, and a warm wash of peace, of acceptance, flowed through him—until hands on his elbows yanked him backward, and he did indeed fall, but into a half-dozen pairs of arms that bore him back into the brightly lit salon. Someone threw a coat over him, and his bearers dropped him on a sofa, and a girl he'd met earlier but didn't remember the name of knelt at his side and gave him a smacking kiss. "Lor' luv ye, ducks! I can't say if ye're brave or foolish, but ye're no coward!"

"Oh, I am," he assured her. "I am the greatest of cowards, but I'll hear it from no man—nor woman, either."

She giggled, and her hand drifted south beneath the coat to curl around his rising cock. "Well, what have we 'ere, ducks?"

"Madam," he said somberly, "if you do not know, I must not as a gentleman educate you." Then he hiccoughed again.

The girl pushed the coat up onto his chest and climbed on the couch, straddling him, the warmth of her body finishing the work his exhilaration had begun; but the exhilaration was gone, faded into his usual emptiness, and he sat up, pushing her gently away. "Not now, love," he said. "Gibs!"

Gibson pushed through the chattering crowd. "What the hell was that about, Northwood? Bloody thought you were goin' t' end up takin' a dive. Don't do that to me again, boyo."

Tristan shrugged. "No great matter if I had. Where's my hat?" It had fallen off when he'd tumbled back off the balustrade.

Berkeley dumped a pile of clothing into his lap, the hat perched on top. Under the cover of the coat, Tristan squirmed into his drawers and trousers, then pulled his shirt over his head. Berkeley observed him in puzzlement. "You've been standing on a balcony with your pizzle in the wind for a quarter hour, but you can't put your breeches on in public?"

"Shut up," Tristan said, and he pulled his own greatcoat on. "Whose coat is this?"

"Mine," someone said.

Tristan tossed it in the general direction of the voice. "I must away," he said dramatically, and swept a bow, then set his hat on his head. "I have a wedding to attend. In"—he took his watch from his coat pocket and glanced at it—"four and a half hours. Just enough time to sober up. Ladies.... Gentlemen...." He bowed again and sailed from the room—in his own mind. In reality, he staggered a bit, tripped over the doorsill, and only avoided falling because Gibson and Berkeley were following him and caught him before he measured himself out on the shabby carpeting of the hallway.

HE WAS stone sober several hours later as he stood in the echoing nave of St. George's, watching his bride walk down the aisle toward him. Her hand was on her father's arm, but her figure, in lavender silk appropriate for the spring day, was upright and confident. He was relieved that she was so calm about the whole thing; it would have been impossible if he'd been expected to take on a fragile, weeping flower. One of her bridesmaids was already that, sniffling into a fine lawn handkerchief.

Beside him, Gibson shifted uncomfortably. "Buck up," Tristan said in an undertone, "it'll soon be over and then you can have a drink."

"I'm supposed to be the one reassuring you," Gibson hissed back. "Aren't you *nervous*?"

Tristan considered it. "No," he said finally. "She's only a woman. I know how to deal with women."

"That's true enough...."

"Shh!" That was Berks, behind Gibson. Charlotte and her father were arriving at the altar.

Tristan shook the Earl's hand politely, then turned to his bride. She smiled up at him with that serene, unflappable expression. "Hullo," she said.

"Hullo," Tristan said back.

AND they were married.

THE manager bowed them into the drawing room of their suite. "Grillon's finest," he said, "just as the baron required. I trust you will enjoy your stay. Will you take dinner in your suite tonight?" His eyes twinkled at them.

Tristan glanced at Charlotte, who looked enquiringly back at him. "My dear?" he asked.

"May we eat in the dining room?" she asked. "I've yet to dine here, although I understand the food is quite good."

"As you wish. I've tickets for the theater this evening, so would you prefer to eat before or after?"

"After, I think. The wedding breakfast did go on quite long. Perhaps tea?"

The manager bowed. "I will have tea sent up, and reserve a table for you for after the theater."

"Thank you," Tristan said, and dismissed him.

Charlotte wandered around the room, picking up bibelots and setting them back down again. "It was quite nice of your papa to choose such a nice suite. It must be expensive."

"It's the most expensive suite in the hotel," Tristan said. "Nothing must be spared to show the world what a patient and generous man Baron Ware is."

She turned and looked at him. "You don't care for him at all, do you?" she said thoughtfully. "You barely spoke at the breakfast."

"No," Tristan said with a tight smile. "I don't care for him at all."

"Hmm," she said, but she didn't pursue it, just giving him a vague smile. "We're going to the theater, not the opera?"

"No. You said you didn't care for opera. I don't recall if you told me what type of theater you did like, so I chose something light."

"Oh, that's fine. I've never seen real theater. It will be interesting."

"Did you have a pleasant time at the wedding breakfast?" Good lord, was he really asking such a banal question?

"Oh, quite pleasant. All my friends were there, which was quite nice. Your friends seem amiable."

"Yes. Quite." Oh, God. Now he was starting to sound like her.

"I wish my brother Charlie had been able to make it. I shall write him this evening, of course. Do you wish to read the letter before I send it?"

"Of course not! Does your father read your correspondence?"

"Oh, good heavens, no. He couldn't care less about that."

"Well, I see no reason to either."

"Very well. I was not sure if you would prefer it. I would like to begin as we intend to go on, you know."

"I have no interest in anything you may write your brother."

She cocked her head in that birdlike fashion and said, "I shan't write anything detrimental. I'm curious as to what Charles will make of you when you meet. I think he will quite like you. I don't say that you will like him— that is understood. Everyone likes Charlie. He doesn't necessarily like everyone. But I think he will like you."

Tristan pinched the bridge of his nose. "I'm sure I will be quite fond of your brother," he lied through his still-clenched teeth.

He tucked his hands into his pockets. "I meant to tell you—it was kind of your companion to take on the project of organizing the household. I haven't seen the townhouse yet." Tristan was getting desperate. What else could he possibly talk to her about? Was this to be the rest of his life, this stilted small talk? "Sherry?" he asked, sighting in relief the pier table holding the decanters of spirits.

"No, thank you. I don't take stimulants."

"Well," he said, in an attempt to be jocular, "that makes us almost complete opposites, then, does it not?"

"My papa and my brothers drink, of course. It's not that I disapprove, although in my opinion far too many people drink spirits far too much. I just don't care for the taste. But, please, do not let me stay your hand. Thank you for inviting me to the theater, by the way. I am quite excited to go. Because Papa's funds did not often stretch to frivolous entertainments, and I am so rarely in town, I have not had the opportunity. Will we be going to Drury Lane?"

"No, I'm afraid not. It burnt down several years ago. They are in the process of rebuilding, I understand, but are not yet finished. It took them less time to rebuild the Covent Garden Theatre; they finished that last year. That is where we are going tonight."

"Two theaters burnt down?" Her lip worried her teeth. "Are they so dangerous?"

"Not at all. Mere coincidence." He really had no idea but didn't want her to back out. He'd planned this evening carefully so that they would have to spend a minimum amount of time in each other's sole company. "No more dangerous than any other building."

A knock on the door signaled the arrival of the tea tray; after the maid had departed and Charlotte had poured out, she said, "There is something I wish to speak to you about, Mr. Northwood."

"I would prefer you call me Tristan," Tristan said, "and I shall call you Charlotte, if that is acceptable."

"As you wish," she said, with a faint smile. "At any rate, I simply wanted to make it clear that I do not expect you to dance attendance on me. I understand that men have different interests and habits, and that they rarely overlap with those of ladies." Her smile deepened. "I am *quite* sure that you would find my own activities deadly dull. So I was wondering if you could tell me what you normally do, and I will arrange my own schedule so that it does not interfere with yours."

Tristan stared at her blankly a moment, then said, "Am I interfering in your schedule today, Lady Charlotte?"

"Oh, good heavens, no! I certainly did not mean to infer that! On the contrary—I know that it must be dull for you this afternoon to be closeted alone with a woman you barely are acquainted with, and simply wish to understand what you *do* find interesting."

"Oh. Well." There was that strange second sight she seemed to possess, at least as far as he was concerned. Or was it that he was so totally predictable? "I usually rise late as I am frequently out until dawn," he said, quite honestly, "and spend most of the afternoon at Angelo's or Jackson's, or riding, or at my club. I attend social events in the evenings. Nothing too unusual."

"I tend to rise early," Charlotte mused, "and don't attend many social events, although I suppose that may change, now that I am married and fixed in town for the time being. Do you regularly lunch at home?"

"Usually," Tristan said wryly, "though I generally call it 'breakfast'."

She laughed. "Well, then, perhaps we should be sure that what is served will suit us both. Perhaps occasionally, too, we could share an afternoon ride? I enjoy that and try to manage it a few times a week. What is Angelo's?"

"A fencing master," Tristan said. "And Jackson's is next door, and teaches boxing."

She wrinkled her nose. "Like fisticuffs?"

"Like fisticuffs, but there is science involved. It is something most men find interesting, if only to observe, so there are usually many spectators at such events. I prefer to participate myself, but not in public, of course." Except that one time in the Green Park....

"Never?" Was she smiling?

"Well... once. On a dare."

"Did you win?"

Despite himself, he laughed. "Yes, as a matter of fact. Bloodied my opponent's nose."

"What was the dare?"

"Well, it was more of a challenge, over something stupid. I can't remember now—I imagine I was pretty well-to-live at the time. But someone challenged me to a boxing match in the park, I refused because one *doesn't*, of course, not in public—and then he dared me to do it." He sighed theatrically. "I simply cannot refuse a dare."

"Why not?"

He blinked. "Well... I don't know. Perhaps it's because the inference is that if you refuse, you're a coward. You have to accept because otherwise you'd be painted as a coward for all time."

"I wouldn't think so," Charlotte said thoughtfully, "but if you feel that way, of course you must be right."

He laughed again, but this time there was a bitter note in the laughter. "That would be a first," he said, then changed the subject. "So, tomorrow—do you wish to visit our new home after breakfast? We can confer with Mrs. Bayes and determine what changes you wish before we move in. Then in the afternoon, I thought—if it's not too childish an entertainment—we could visit Astley's...."

She squealed in delight. "Astley's! I have forever wanted to go there, but Papa would never take me. And Gunter's for ices afterwards?"

He took her hand and kissed it. "Of course, my dear. Whatever you like."

"I think," Charlotte said, grinning up at him, "that I will like marriage to you quite well!"

TRISTAN stood at the suite's windows, looking out over a sleeping Albemarle Street. Behind him, in the dark, Charlotte slept the sleep of the not-quite-so-innocent-any-longer. *No*, he thought, *still innocent, just not a virgin.* His fingers tightened on the drapes he held clutched in his fist. He'd done his best, he'd thought, implementing all the patient little tricks and teases to coax a woman to climax; the stroking, kissing, licking that they all seemed to love so much, that made their bodies respond and welcome him. It was part of what fueled the rumor that he was such a good lover—that he took his time and made sure his partner always spent first before he did, at least once and hopefully more than that. And Charlotte was not unattractive; it had been no hardship for him to make love to her slowly and thoroughly....

Until she'd lifted her head and said thoughtfully, "Is all that really necessary? You needn't fuss, you know."

He'd been flabbergasted. "Fuss?" he'd echoed indignantly. "Fuss?"

"Really," she'd replied calmly. "The kissing, and, and such. It's pleasant, but I would really rather just get it over with, if you don't mind."

Get it over with. *Get it over with*? It was a miracle he'd been able to complete the act with that echoing in his ears. The strange thing was that even as his balls grew tight and the sparkling feeling shot through his spine, he thought she'd climaxed herself, her face tightening and her eyes screwed shut and her voice gasping little cries. But when he'd spent himself thoroughly in her and eased himself from her warm little channel to lie beside her, all she'd said, in a complacent little voice, was, "Well. Thank goodness *that's* over with," and rolled over to go to sleep.

He'd lain most of the night staring at the ceiling and wondering what the hell had just happened. He'd heard enough whining from the women he'd bedded about their husbands just rogering them and then rolling over to fall asleep, when they'd wanted foreplay and cuddling afterward—which *he* had always made sure to provide. It was a strange little irony that here he was, in the same boat as all those women…. Well. Not exactly the same boat, and no doubt there were men out there who would be delighted to be married to a woman who made no demands on him. He should just stop feeling… what? Sorry for himself? Insulted? After all, *he*'d been satisfied. Or at least, he'd spent. Not quite the same thing, but close enough.

He dropped his forehead against the cool glass. Well.

When he'd turned seventeen and was just about to go up to Cambridge, his father had called him into his study. Heart pounding, wondering what he'd done wrong *this* time, Tristan had obeyed, standing hipshot and insouciant, faking the picture of careless youth, the pose he'd always taken in view of his father, at least since he'd figured out that nothing he could do would ever please him. The baron had given him a long, severe look, then said abruptly, "What has your tutor told you about women?"

Tristan had blinked, then replied carefully, "What *about* them?"

"About…." The baron waved his hand. "About relations with them."

Tristan shrugged. "He explained the process."

"You're seventeen."

"Amazing recall you have," Tristan drawled.

The baron ignored him. "Have you ever had relations with a woman?"

Tristan considered the question. He hadn't, actually; not unless one counted snatching a kiss from a barmaid in the company of his friends. Did he want his father to know that? No—that wasn't what he was asking. He was asking about the Real Thing. "Not yet," he said, still in that lazy, drawling voice (which he'd discovered a year or so ago drove his father insane). "I'm sure I'll be rectifying that in the near future, however."

To his surprise, the baron didn't answer right away, merely studying his heir through narrowed eyes. Finally, he said, "You're a good-looking boy; I imagine you're right. Do you know what a French letter is?"

Tristan blinked again. "Yes, sir," he said in surprise.

"Use them. It's unkind to a woman not to, and although you have many faults, I have not heard that unkindness is one of them."

Unlike you, Tristan had thought, but merely inclined his head in acknowledgement of his father's comment.

"One other thing." Baron Ware had turned and walked to the window of his study, glancing outside. Over his shoulder, he'd said, "It is also only kind that you see to the pleasure of your partner before your own. A gentleman never spends first. Do you understand me?"

"Yes, sir," Tristan said. After a moment, he added, "My tutor said that ladies do not climax as men do."

"Ladies may not. But women do. And in the end, they are all women." Baron Ware turned back to Tristan. "Not as men do, precisely, but they do take pleasure in the act. Or they *can*, if a man is patient and considerate. It is a selfish and ignorant man who sees to his own pleasure without taking care of his partner. While you have thus far proven yourself both selfish and ignorant, I trust that your behavior toward women in whatever walk of life will not reflect those flaws in your character. And should you think that in doing so will be another slap in the face to me—understand that I will probably never know about how you treat women. *They*, however, will know. And whatever your feelings for me, they do not deserve unkindness from you."

"Sir." Tristan clicked his heels and gave a curt bow of his head.

"You leave for university next week," Ware said, returning to his desk and reseating himself. "Franklin will be in contact with you regarding your allowance and living arrangements. I expect a regular report of your progress in your classes. You've shown an aptitude for numbers, therefore I've enrolled you in a program of mathematics. Franklin has the details. I give you good day."

"Sir," Tristan had said again.

He was almost to the door when his father spoke again. "Tristan."

"Sir?"

"There will be plenty of opportunities for you to experience the intimate act. Do not be in a hurry." Ware gave his son a humorless smile. "Hurry is never a good thing at such a time."

"No, sir," Tristan drawled, giving him the same insincere smile back. "So I understand."

HE'D never hurried. It was the one piece of advice from his father he'd ever followed. He supposed the baron was right—women did not deserve unkindness, and it wouldn't matter to the baron if he was unkind, so it was no hardship to take his time with his women. And it did make the whole process more enjoyable; not so much the actual activity, which he frequently could have done without, but witnessing someone take such intense pleasure at his hands. It was the one thing he *knew* he did well.

And now his wife—his *wife*—had shattered that illusion.

His eyes stung, and he rubbed them impatiently, only realizing when his hand came away wet that he was crying. *Crying.* Over something so stupid. He was an idiot. So Charlotte didn't care for lovemaking. He had the rest of his life to teach her. And in the meantime, he still had the rest of the world—the female half, anyway—who *enjoyed* him. His lips thinned. If Charlotte didn't want him—and he didn't care, anyway, if she did or didn't; the only advantage to sleeping with her was that he *finally* got to feel what it was like to be naked inside a woman—there were other people who *did*. He'd never promised her fidelity.

But God, he so wanted to. He wanted a wife who was a *lover*, a wife who would save him from those other women, those other beds. A wife who would care for *him*, not for his position or expectations.

Still—he had time. And maybe, just maybe, Charlotte would come to care for him the way he needed to be cared for, and he could do the same for her. He snorted softly. Once, he'd felt that way about his father—that if he was just patient enough, just obedient enough, just *good* enough, the baron would come to love him. But he hadn't. And when Tristan was thirteen, he'd given up waiting. Four years he'd given the baron. He owed his marriage at least that. And surely, surely by then they would love each other. Surely, surely four years was enough to build a real life together? Surely, this time, he would be good enough?

Hope in his heart, he turned and went back to bed.

Book Two

LONDON, 1814-1815

CHAPTER 5

November, 1814

TRISTAN,

I am given to understand that you are looking to sell your string of hunters. I can only assume that this is an indication that you are rolled up. I find it difficult to understand how you have managed this, given your and Charlotte's quite-generous allowances, but I suppose you have engendered gambling debts or something of that nature. I cannot see where a sporting-mad man like you would otherwise be willing to dispose of a set of animals so painstakingly acquired. To say that I am disappointed will of course be unnecessary, as unnecessary as taking this step.

You may give the list of your debts to Franklin; he will present it to my solicitors in London, who will resolve the debts. The only recompense I expect is that you will remove your family from Town and return to Wareham or to Lilac Cottage for the holidays, remaining there until at least the beginning of the Season. Perhaps if you cannot control your gambling impulses in Town you will be able to restrain yourself in the Country.

I would appreciate it if you would keep me apprised of such situations before they arise again.

Ware.

Tristan folded the letter, his fingers idly pressing on the broken wax seal as if he could reseal it, and in doing so, pretend he hadn't read the contents. He should be used to this by now, he thought bitterly. Ware might spend most of his time in the country, but his spies were everywhere. Not solitary spies, but whole battalions.... And of course he would put the worst possible interpretation on his son's actions.

He glanced up as Franklin came into the library. He liked the old man; it wasn't his fault that he took his orders as much from Ware as he did from Tristan. He'd retired three years ago, leaving the complexities of Ware's business interests to younger men, but had found retirement irksome, and when Ware had suggested he take on a much less demanding position as Tristan's man of business, he'd been quick to agree. Tristan had had no interest in finances at that point, so he'd acquiesced reluctantly. Despite his connection with the baron, however, Franklin had proved to be an honestly helpful resource for Tris and Charlotte's young establishment. Tris was fairly sure that Franklin respected Tristan's privacy as much as possible, and the only things that reached Ware's ears were things that were public knowledge, like the sale of his hunters. Well, not public knowledge, per se, but certainly public rumors. He tapped the edge of the folded letter against his lip.

"Good afternoon, sir," Franklin said cheerfully.

Wordlessly, Tristan handed him the letter. The older man settled in the chair before Tristan's desk and drew out his spectacles before examining the piece of paper. His lips pursed, but he only shook his head.

Tristan took the letter back and folded it again, tucking it into the drawer of the desk where he kept his father's missives. "I trust that you will not be distressed if I fail to present the list of my debts for Ware's solicitors?"

"Gambling debts," Franklin said, and he shook his head again.

Franklin's tone of voice so precisely echoed the tenor of his own thoughts that Tristan chuckled. "Well, then. Shall we begin with our real work?"

TRISTAN reviewed the document under his hand before signing it. "I'm only transferring funds from one account to another," he said in annoyance. "Why must it require so much paperwork?"

"To keep otherwise unoccupied men of business occupied," his man of business quipped. "That's the last of it, until the sale of your hunters."

"When will that be?"

"The notice will be in the papers next week. Should there be no interest at that point, we'll have to bring them up from Leicestershire to sell at Tattersall's, but I don't expect that it will be necessary."

"I should hope not," Tris said. "They're exceedingly fine animals. I've had plenty of offers in the past. But I haven't hunted in two years, and all they're doing is eating their fool heads off. Plus there's the waste of maintaining a staff to tend them. Eventually I'll put the house on the market, too, unless Mrs. Northwood prefers I keep it, but in the meantime I see no reason to maintain the stables as well." He thought a moment, then added, "Put in the articles of sale for the string that the buyers are to hire the three younger grooms as well. Riley and Martin are old enough to retire—write something up including a decent pension for them. They can stay on at the hunting box until they find a cottage or something to retire to, or until I decide to sell the place."

"Pension to come from the trust?"

Tristan thought. "Yes—they won't be much of a drain on it. Fifty or sixty pounds a year each, I think."

"Most generous."

Franklin's employer snorted. "Mrs. Northwood spends more on hats."

"One last item of business." Franklin noticed Northwood's glance at the mantel clock but went on. "The owners of this house are inquiring if you would be interested in purchasing it when the lease expires."

"No," Tristan said flatly. "When does the lease expire?"

"The first of June. Do you wish me to tell them that you prefer to continue leasing, then?"

"No," Tristan repeated. "Mrs. Northwood's confinement is expected in April. At that point the baron will be signing over a property in Lincolnshire that is presently empty. I intend to move my family there as soon as my wife is able to travel. We will not require a London residence. If I need to come to Town, it's cheaper to stay at my club."

Franklin regarded his employer thoughtfully. He'd known Tristan Northwood since the rebellious boy had first been sent to Westminster, when Franklin himself had been Baron Ware's estate manager. Tristan's marriage four years ago had been intended to settle him down, but Franklin had seen little evidence of it until the birth of his heir some eighteen months ago. Then over the following year and a half, Tristan's personality had undergone a complete change, no longer the devil-may-care rogue known for hard drinking and wild living.

From what Franklin could see, he was still drinking as heavily as any other man of the ton, but on a schedule as clockwork as any businessman could wish. He was stone-cold sober when he met with Franklin three times a week at nine a.m.; from ten to eleven thirty he was closeted in the nursery with young Jamie; then from eleven thirty to twelve thirty he lunched with his wife, with whom he was on cordial if not warm terms. Then he left the house, for his club, or Jackson's Saloon, or to ride in the park, returning in the early evening in time for supper or to escort his wife to a scheduled social event.

On their return, however, after his wife had retired for the evening, Mr. Northwood would settle in his library. At two a.m., per his precise orders, two sturdy footmen would "assist" him to bed, leaving his long-suffering valet to attempt to get him disrobed and comfortably in bed. Then he would rise again at seven or eight to start the whole cycle over again.

Franklin and Reston, the valet, were longtime friends, and what Franklin did not witness with his own eyes he heard from Reston. What he heard did not reassure him or the valet. "It's like he's not all there, Franklin," Reston said. "He's here, but there's nothing inside him. He's walking through his life, not living it."

Tristan Northwood was no different from many another gentleman of means in London. The difficulty for both of his two old retainers was that for most of his life, Tristan Northwood *had* been different. Wild, true, but never cruel in his jokes; he had dozens of friends, too many lovers; he was a wit, a bon vivant, a charming rogue. A smiler.

Franklin thought regretfully, *He never laughs anymore.* A perfunctory smile where there had once been a broad grin; a businesslike attitude where there had once been cheerful carelessness. It was as if his interest in the financial security of his family had taken the joy out of his life. And yet Franklin was willing to swear that Tristan adored his little boy. What was it about being a father that had changed him so, taken the life out of him? Franklin sometimes got the impression that there was a caged animal looking out of Tristan's cloud-colored eyes, one desperate to escape. But from what?

A thought struck him and he studied his employer surreptitiously as he put his papers away. No—he didn't look ill: a little thinner than a year ago, but by less than a stone if Franklin were any judge. His eyes were tired, true, but averaging five hours of sleep a night, plus too much brandy, would do that to a person. "Will that be all, then, sir?"

"If you've no further business." Tristan gave him a brief smile that didn't reach his eyes. "I have another appointment, as usual."

HIS appointment was waiting anxiously when he came into the nursery, and all the stress of business and the ache of his morning hangover vanished at the sight of that beloved face. "Papa!" Jamie cried, and shook the wooden frame of his cot. "Papa-papa-papa!"

Tristan crossed the room in a rush and lifted him into his arms with a loud smacking kiss that set the toddler chortling. Tristan glanced at the nursery maid, who bobbed a curtsey.

"If you please, sir, he's been fed and his nappy's been changed and he's just woke up from a nap," she said in her usual rush. "I'll be right next door should he need me."

"He won't," Tristan said to the little boy in his arms, "will he, my little man?"

The baby gurgled at him happily. Then he squirmed to be let down and when he was, toddled over to pick up a stuffed dog with well-chewed ears. He brought the toy back to Tristan. "Papa," he said decisively, holding it up to him.

"Thank you," Tristan said seriously, then grinned and scooped the little boy up, tossing him into the air. The baby squealed delightedly, and Tristan pretended to drop him, setting him off into giggles, before settling them both on the floor to play with his blocks. While he did, he studied Jamie, amazed all over again at the little miracle that was his son. Wide, dark eyes like Charlotte's; dark, curling hair like his own; and a personality and a temperament that was all Jamie—quick to laugh, rarely fussy, and even at eighteen months quick to learn new things. He showed Tristan one now, stacking his blocks by size so that he could build a pyramidal structure as tall as he was himself. Tristan picked up the stuffed animal and went to put it on top of the smallest block. "No, no, Papa!" Jamie said. "B'ocks! No puppy!"

"You are a very smart boy," Tristan said soberly to him.

"Papa give," he ordered, and Tristan gave him the puppy. Jamie cuddled it, crooning to it tunelessly. Charlotte often sang him to sleep; sometimes on his way out for an evening, Tristan would stop by the nursery to see her sitting in the rocking chair beside the cot, rocking Jamie and singing some lullaby. She loved Jamie every bit as much as Tristan did, he thought. She was an excellent mother. She was a good wife, too, even if he was a poor example of a husband. The smile faded from his face.

Jamie noticed. "Papa sad?"

"No, love. I'm fine." Tristan smiled at him.

He worried that Jamie would miss him when he was gone, and the older Jamie got, the more likely that was. He needed to do this quickly, but he was hampered by Charlotte's pregnancy. Once the baby was born and he'd got them settled in the country.... He supposed he could lessen the blow to Jamie by becoming more like the other fathers of his acquaintance, only having contact with their children on rare occasions, but he was too selfish for that.

He enjoyed Jamie. He just hadn't thought ahead when he'd got into the habit of spending time with his son, hadn't expected that Jamie would come to enjoy his time with his father as well.

He remembered the day when it had been brought to his attention just how foolish he'd been. It had been about four months ago; he'd gone to the nursery just as he always did, and found Jamie standing up in his cot, holding onto the wooden slats. And Jamie's face had lighted up at the sight of him. It staggered Tris. Jamie was *happy* to see him. Happy to see *him*. It shook Tristan to his core.

And then he'd gone down to lunch, and Charlotte had casually mentioned that she was increasing again, and he'd realized that that would be another little being who would come to look forward to seeing him, to care for him, to expect to be cared for. He'd managed to find the right words to say to Charlotte, half-hearing her complacent statement that he no longer needed to come to her at night, and he'd thought, *Never again*. He hadn't been able to bring himself to lie with any other woman, either. He'd shut himself off from that part of his life for good—it was too *dangerous*. The idea of bringing *another* life into the world that might look to him....

He couldn't bring himself to stop visiting Jamie. But he'd started in train his plans for the future—arranging things so that Charlotte and his children would be settled, so that when the time came, he could take himself out of their lives. Set them free of him, for good.

Smiling at Jamie, he reached out and tickled his plump little belly. Jamie chortled, and with a laugh, knocked over his tower of blocks.

"Oh, *no!*" Tristan exclaimed in mock horror. "What do we do *now?*"

"Again!" Jamie yelled, and Tristan laughed.

CHARLOTTE was reading a letter when he came down to luncheon; one hand held her fork immobile in midair, the chunk of chicken dripping sauce onto the plate while the other held the letter up. It was a not-uncommon sight—Charlotte had dozens of correspondents across the whole of Britain and not a few elsewhere in the Empire—but she usually managed to eat and read at the same time. This letter held her rapt.

He'd served himself the chicken and settled into his chair to eat before she put the letter down and turned to him. "News?" he asked mildly.

"Charlie's coming home," she said happily. "He's coming back in the next month or so. He doesn't say why; just that he's well and looking forward to being home again. It's been years, hasn't it?"

"I can't venture to say," Tristan observed dryly, as he poured himself a glass of wine. "I was not acquainted with Major Mountjoy the last time he was in England."

"Although Charles had been on Lord Wellington's staff, he didn't come back to England when his lordship did for the Honors last summer. He transferred to Lord Castlereagh's staff just about then. I think he was last here in 1808," Ellen said prosaically. "You two weren't yet married. And as I recall, he was only here on a flying visit. He came down to Chilson on his way with his regiment to the Peninsula."

"Oh, yes, that was about Grandfather's legacy," Charlotte nodded. "I remember now. He doesn't trust Daniel to handle his funds for him."

"I should think not," Tristan said austerely. "Still, it will be nice for you to see him again."

"I wonder if he's just coming for a visit, or if he's selling out?"

Ellen said, "With the war over, surely he's selling out? You don't think he's being posted to America?"

Tristan said, "I wouldn't think so. The Ghent negotiations will be resolved soon enough, and we'll be done there; Gambier and Goulburn seem to expect that we'll be able to reach some accommodation by the end of the year. If the major is smart, he'll sell out as soon as he can while his commission is still valuable."

"I don't understand any of that," Lottie complained. "It's all above my head."

Tristan shook his head. "Lottie," he said, "don't play stupid. It's beneath you."

"But it's entertaining," Lottie said complacently. "And it's good practice for when I'm bored with someone at social events. They get this glazed look in their eyes, and I know it's only a matter of a few minutes before they go away and I can look for someone *interesting* to talk to."

"It's no use," Ellen said to Tristan. "I've been trying to get 'round her for years. She's as stubborn as a rock."

"I noticed. Jamie seems to take after her."

"Oh, as if you're not as obstinate as a mule," Charlotte retorted.

"Children," Ellen sighed. Tristan and Charlotte exchanged a conspiratorial grin.

CHAPTER 6

December, 1814

"I THOUGHT we'd got rid of you days ago," a voice said from the doorway.

Major Charles Mountjoy glanced up from the bureau, a stack of cravats in his hand, and grinned. "You've got rid of my trunk—that was sent out on Tuesday. But His Grace demanded I stay on through last night's soiree at the Margrave's. How was Venice?"

"Cold. Wet," Captain Randall said, dropping into the small room's one chair. "And it smells. But the ladies are *quite* nice. Almost made it worthwhile."

"And your mission successful?"

"More or less." Randall made a face. "We have promises."

Charles echoed his expression. "Promises. Wonderful." His tone of voice made it anything but. "Have you seen His Grace yet?"

"Are you joking, Monty? Went straight there in all my dirt. He seemed pleased, though, so I suppose I'm just being cynical."

"Perhaps. Who did you deal with?"

"Gian de Luca."

"Oh, de Luca." Charles shrugged. "He'll come through."

"You know him?"

"Met him a few times in Portugal. He was with the Venetian contingent there, trying to deal with their investments in Lisbon in case Boney made it across the border. One of the more sensible men I've had to deal with. Came through in a couple of tight spots when we needed a bit of assistance; he's got a good relationship with the Duke." Charles put the cravats into his traveling case and went back to the bureau, this time to pour them each a sherry from the decanter on top. Handing the glass to Randall, he said, "And speaking of Portugal—how's Keighley working out?"

"Brilliantly," Randall said, and toasted Charles. "Thanks to the genius that is Charlie Mountjoy. I would have hated to lose him; he's one of the best sergeants I've ever worked with. I can't believe how he's turned around since you spoke to him."

"Sometimes," Charles said, dropping onto the narrow bed and regarding the sherry through the glass, "all a person needs is someone he can talk to. Poor Keighley was stuck in the rough spot so many sergeants seem to end up—all the men above him are nobs, all the ones below report to him, or resent him for raising himself up above the common muck. And his fellow rankers? Too many are irretrievable drunks or bullies. I hate waste." He took a sip of the sherry. "Losing Keighley to the drink would be a waste. From your reports he wasn't like that as a corporal, so I knew there had to be a way to reach him. It was simple enough."

"Simple for you, perhaps," Randall said. "I don't understand—you're not a martinet, but you're not *easy*, either, and your brigade was one of the tightest, best-run of them all."

"I had good men," Charles said.

"Hah! I knew half your men when Coverdale was your battalion's major, and they were *not* good men. Talk about bullies and drunks...."

"The key word is 'half'," Charles said. "The ones I could work with, I kept, and transferred the ones that were irretrievable. For the rest, it was simply a matter of gaining and keeping their respect, and unlike most of the officers in this man's army, I knew that wasn't by handing out floggings like they were Christmas sweeties." He shook his head. "You can't always choose the people you work with, but you can choose to learn how to deal with them. They're all different."

"The Duke says you're the best judge of character he's ever known. And he should know—he's damn good at it himself."

Charles shrugged. "Perhaps. Perhaps I'm just lucky. Or maybe just observant."

"So then why are you selling out? I'd think he'd be demanding you stay, now that he's here."

"The kind of character judgment you need in the ranks is different from the kind of character judgment you need when dealing with politicians. It's not my style. I did what I could for Lord Castlereagh, but Wellington's got a better grasp of the politics involved here than I ever could learn." Charles took a sip of sherry. "Plus, there are enough German-language interpreters around that he doesn't need my services here. We've put paid to Bonaparte; there's nothing for me on the Continent, and I'm not eager to go running off to America. They're mad over there."

"Says the man who insists there are no madmen."

"I didn't say there weren't any madmen. I just said that there are men called mad who might still be brought to reason, if one could only reach them. And not by the methods used in the average madhouse."

"You still think of him, don't you?"

Charles nodded. "Winstead should never have been in that place—should never have died, not like that. If Warren had only *listened* to me...."

"You were a mere captain then, Warren a colonel—and one not likely to listen to anyone. I can't say I was broken up when I'd heard he'd bought it at Ciudad Rodrigo."

"I'm just glad he wasn't involved with Badajoz," Charles said dryly. "He would have made it even worse than it was. I don't know how; I just know he'd have managed it."

"Absent friends," Randall said, raising his glass. "Oops—it's empty. The toast to Warren must be canceled."

Charles snorted. "Just as Warren was canceled. There is justice in the world, somewhere. Warren's dead, and Keighley, at least, is alive."

"For which I'm grateful."

"Well, if you're *smart*, you'll make sure he's made a lieutenant before too much time passes."

"A lieutenant? Keighley?"

"He wouldn't be the first to rise through the ranks, Randy. I know he hasn't the funds to buy a promotion, but find a way. He needs the challenge. More than that, he needs the status. Make him a lieutenant, and he'll walk through hell for you." Charles drained his glass. "Me, I've got a walk through hell to deal with tomorrow. Or at least a ride through bloody Germany. In December!"

Randall took a sip of sherry. "So, you're leaving just as I return?"

"Almost. Tomorrow morning, after one last meeting with His Grace. I only stayed after Castlereagh left because he knew I'd been one of the Duke's aides-de-camp in the Peninsula and he'd asked me to help get the Duke up to snuff with what's been going on here."

"Well, if we've one last night, let's go find some supper and a lass or two to entertain…. Whoops! Speaking of lasses!" Randall dug in the pocket of his greatcoat and pulled out an envelope. "The Duke told me to take this on to you; it came in today's packet."

Charles took the envelope and looked at it, then smiled. "It's from Lottie. I wrote her a month ago that I'd be returning home. D'ye mind waiting a bit?"

"Not at all." Randall leaned back in his chair.

Charles broke the seal and opened the letter. It smelled of lily of the valley, Lottie's favorite scent, and was written in Lottie's execrable English instead of German, their preferred language for correspondence. That was deliberate, to annoy the English censors who read all correspondence back and forth out of Austria and required all personal letters to be written in English—and another reason he would be happy to be going home. With the crossing of the lines to conserve paper, reading her letters was a project.

Dearest, most wonderful Charlie!

I was Extatic to hear from you that you would be Returning Home from the Wars at Last!! I have Missed you terably. I cannot wait for you to meet Jamie. He is quite the Little Man now, and is walking and talking, though not very Well. But he is very Smart. He must get it from Tristan, for as you Know, I am Not at All Clever.

I am Espeshully glad that you are returning Home, for I am Much Troubled in my mind. Tristan has assured me that we are not at all Rolled Up, but he has put his Hunters up for Sale, wich I do not understand at all, Altho he says it is because they are Wasteful. I do not understand this because Father and Daniel do not consider Hunters wasteful. Perhaps they have different Speesies of Horses? Tristan has changed much in the last few Months and is much more Sereous than he ever was before. He treats me as well as always. I cannot Complain of him. He is always Gentle and most Kind to me, espeshully now that I am Increasing again. I am so Happy about that, for Tristan has Promised that after this child is born, he will settle us in the Country again, which is of all things what I most Desire. He says he has lost Interest in Town. I am Distressed for him, for he has always Loved Society, but he does not Partisipate in many ton Activities as he did once. I hope that you will be Friends with him and Engage him in more Activities, for he is a Social Creachure, which I am not!!

I know you are Aware of his past Deeds, and hope you do not Judge him too Harshly. He has always been Discreet, but I do Believe that he has been Faithful to me for some Time now. I do not Understand all about the

Ways of Men, but I think it espeshully Kind that he does not Importune me for Favors any longer, under the Circumstances. I have never Enjoyed such things, and he has Assured me that I need not Concern myself with That any longer. He is such a Good, Loving Husband. I am more Blessed than I can say. Partickulerly since my Best Loved Brother is on his way Home to us!!

>*Your delighted,*

>*Charlotte*

Charles reread the letter, a sinking feeling in his gut. Northwood? Tired of London? He recalled a quote—was it Ben Jonson or Samuel Johnson who said "When one is tired of London, one is tired of Life"? Maybe it was Samuel Pepys. He always got them all confused.

"Bad news?"

He glanced up at Randall. "No. No. Lottie's excited about my return, of course." He folded the letter and put it back into the envelope.

"But?"

"'But?'"

"Your voice is not as certain as your words, my friend. I may not be as good a judge of character as you, nor as clever in managing men, but I know you."

Charles sighed. "She's worried about her husband. He seems to be under some kind of strain; he's put his hunters up for sale, although he told her that it wasn't because they were done up. And he's tired of London."

"That should make her happy—isn't she always complaining how much she hates it there?"

"It does, but… Northwood's a bit of a skylark. He's far more social than Lottie, and has a wide circle of friends. Even when he's in the country his place is an endless house party, much to Lottie's annoyance. I can't imagine him being happy in Leicestershire very long. Particularly not without a string of hunters."

"Well, then, he'll go back to London and leave her there, where's she's happy. You've said that they don't live in each other's pockets."

"No, but they've become quite good friends over the years. She's fond of him."

"What do you think about him?"

Charles shrugged. "I can only judge him from his treatment of Lottie. And if he treated her unkindly, she would have mentioned it. She tells me everything."

"What do you mean—have you never met the man?"

"I haven't been back in England since '08," Charles said. "They were married in 1810, or thereabouts."

"Hm," Randall said, and subsided into thoughtful silence.

Charles opened his traveling case again and took out a bundle of envelopes, his letters from Lottie over the last few years, and slid the new one under the ribbon tie. "Well, I'll find out soon enough," he said over his shoulder to Randall.

STILL, it didn't stop him from taking the letter out and rereading it later, by the flickering light of his candle. Lottie was a placid, sensible girl; it took a lot to get her fluttered, and her skylarking husband didn't normally do it, wild as he could be. She'd known about her husband's amours and wild living long before she'd ever even met him, through her capacious correspondence with, as Charles could nearly figure it, every woman and some of the men of the ton.

If Lottie was worried, Charles was worried. And not just for Lottie's sake.

He sighed, and folded the letter again, holding it against his nightshirt-clad chest. He'd heard stories about Tristan Northwood long before the news had come that his twin had married the man; at the time, he'd just written him off as another one of the restless, drinking, gambling, whoring young sots of his generation, a company of men that Charles himself had never shared. Of course, going into the military at the age of sixteen meant that he'd never had the time, freedom, or money to indulge. Northwood had plenty of money—that was, of course, why Charlotte had married him—and too much time, with his father still hale and hearty and apparently disinclined to turn any of his own responsibilities over to him.

As for freedom… he knew of Baron Ware; knew of the immense wealth the man managed. To Charles it seemed as though that much wealth was more of a burden than a blessing. It *loomed*, like a thundercloud, all that responsibility—for land, for people, for things. How could anyone feel free with that sort of thing hanging over his head?

With a sigh, he put the letter away and folded his arms beneath his head, staring up at the peeling ceiling. Tristan was becoming serious, Lottie had said, and it worried her. Charles knew about things like that. A skylark turning into a wren…. It meant more than just a man maturing. There was something *wrong*.

Charles knew people. He could look at a man, talk to him for a moment, and understand just exactly what drove him. More than that, he could listen to others' opinions of him and know how to handle him. It was part of what made him valuable to His Grace; part of what made him such an exemplary officer; part of what got him his position as an ADC to Wellington at the young age of twenty-five. He knew people. He *understood*.

Keighley wasn't the first troubled officer he'd worked with; it seemed that people with problems gravitated toward him. Randy himself had been a lost soul when they'd first met, but his grief was simply homesickness and the recent loss of his sister. With Charles's help, he'd settled into the life of a young officer quickly enough. Keighley, with his resentment and anger and bitterness, was more of a challenge, and it had taken a good many long conversations over ale in the closest pub before he'd opened up enough for Charles to help. But he was worth it—smart, dependable, quick-witted, and courageous.

He'd got the same impression of Tristan Northwood.

Charles pulled another letter from the stack. This one was dated some nineteen months previous.

Dear Charles,

Well!! You are an Uncle!! And believe it or Not, your Silly sister is now a Mother!

My beautiful boy was born yesterday and Already I Cannot remember what it was to Be without him. The Deliv'ry was not Bad; the Acosher (I do not Know how to spell this, and it is a Man, so I cannot Call him a Midwife, tho that is what he Is) said it was a very Easy birth. I do not Remember much of it; I know it was Painful, but now it Seems hardly Important.

Poor Tristan was Frantick, however. He came in during the Thick of Things and was Appaul'd (no Doubt at my Looks, as I was Not at my Best!). Afterwerds, he Insisted that I should Not go through it again, Despite the Contrackshuel Obligashuns we have. I Assur'd him I was quite All Right, but I think he has been Trawmettised. Poor Tristan. He could not be more Upset if ours were a Love Match.

This is not to Say that we are not Fond of each other. We have become Quite good Friends in the last few years. Hearing of his Anticks from his friends—for he does not boast to me—is so Entertaining!! Only Tuesday last someone dared him to swim the Serpentine and he DID. I scolded him Quite Severely because he could have Cawhgt a Chill, but he did Not. He does not Gamble, for which I am Greatful, but he Cannot turn down a Dare. Some of the Challenges are quite Silly and some are Dangerous, which Worrys me, as I Think he does not Tell me of the truly Dangerous ones. But he has such Energy and High Spirits that I cannot bring Myself to Sqwash him down.

We have Named the baby James Tristan Charles Eustace Northwood. Tristan did not want to name him James for that is his Father's name, and as you Know, Tristan does not Get Along with his father. He said he should be named for Papa, but I will Not Permit anyone to Name a child Eustace!!! When I told Tris what Papa's name is, he Agreed. We have instead tucked the Eustace down near the End of his names in Hopes that no one will Notice, and will call him Jamie. He is Quite Beautiful, and Tris doats on him Already.

The Baron, for that is how Tris Refers to his Papa, has come up to Town for the Christening. He has a House here, but spends Most of his time in the Country, coming up only for the Season or when he has a Vote in the Lords he is Intersted in. While his Estate and Tristan's Hunting box are quite close, we do Not visit much when We are in the Country. But he was Most Delighted with his Grandson (as who could Not be?) and says we Must bring him to Wareham this Summer. Tris only Snorts when this is Mentioned.

Charles put the letter back into the stack and folded his arms behind his head. Over the years he had received any number of letters from his sister, and more from his cousin Ellen, about the young man who had bought—or been bought—into his family. He had been prepared for his sister's sake to like the man as long as she was content with him, but between them, his sister and his cousin had described a person who was not only likeable, but strangely lovable. Ellen's letters had been interesting, to say the least; she was a more careful correspondent than Lottie, and originally she had been doubtful as to Northwood's character. But as time went on, the tenor of her thoughts changed. He recalled a line from one of her letters: *"Mr. Northwood never permits his burdens to overcome him; he is, from first to last, a gentleman to all those who deserve gentlemanly behavior, no matter how he behaves in the company of those who do not."* It took him a while to realize what Ellen meant, and even now he wondered what sort of "burdens" his brother-in-law carried that he kept from his wife, but that his more perceptive cousin-in-law recognized. He had asked Ellen in his next letter what she had meant by his "burdens," but apparently his letter had gone astray and her next reflected no inkling of the subject. He wondered, too, if Ellen referred to not only the various soiled doves and adulterous wives Tristan Northwood was notorious for cultivating, or if she included his despised father in "*the company of those who do not.*"

What burdens?

CHAPTER 7

THE butler was waiting when Tristan came in from his club on a blustery day early in January. "Mrs. Northwood's brother has arrived," he said, "and is with her in the drawing room. She has asked that you join them when you return."

"Bother," Tristan said. What did Daniel want now? He'd been up to town twice in the last six-month, both times making a point of stopping by to see his sister, but the only time he ever saw Tristan was when he wanted to borrow money. Tristan handed his hat and cane to the butler, smoothed down his hair, and figuratively girded his loins for the pitch and the inevitable argument. It wasn't that he minded loaning Daniel the odd fiver. It was when he came looking for serious money to invest in one of his crazy schemes that the battles began; Daniel because he rarely took "no" for an answer, Tristan because he had no intention of pissing away funds better spent on planning for his family's future.

He heard Charlotte's low, musical laugh and waited for Daniel's distinctive guffaw. What he got instead was a deeper version of Lottie's, a smooth baritone rumble. Frowning in puzzlement, he pushed open the door to the drawing room and froze.

The man seated across from Lottie was one he'd never met before, but somehow no stranger. Hair the same texture but a brighter shade than Lottie's, streaked from sunlight; eyes the same brown but under strong brows; the blunt, insipid features of Tristan's wife translated into a tan, more masculine, livelier form. He wore a dark blue cavalry uniform, but with a black silk neckerchief instead of the usual stock. Rising as Tristan entered, he held out a large hand. "Mr. Northwood?" he said in a voice that matched the laugh, smooth and strong and rich and sending chills through Tristan's suddenly tense body. "Charles Mountjoy, Lottie's brother. Pleased to make your acquaintance at last." He smiled in a friendly manner.

That smile shattered Tris, like a blow on a bell too quickly cooled in casting. Dazedly, he took the man's hand, and it closed, warm and steady, around his. "Major Mountjoy," he managed, then realized he was still holding the man's hand and released it quickly. Well-honed social skills kicked in just in time. "Welcome. Lottie mentioned you were returning home. Are you back for good, or just on assignment?"

"For good, I'm afraid," he said with a chuckle. "I'm not cut out for the diplomatic life, so I've been sent home in disgrace."

"Nonsense," Lottie said. "You're being silly."

"Actually, yes, I am—no disgrace involved. The Duke has plenty of advisors far better suited than I to diplomacy. It was an honor to be taken on as one of his ADCs in the Peninsula, but that was primarily due to my German translation skills. His Grace speaks very little German, and most of the King's German Regiment very little English. I was transferred to Lord Castlereagh's staff when the Duke was made ambassador to France, for the same reason, and went with Castlereagh to Vienna, but now he's come home and Wellington's in Vienna in his place. There are plenty of bilingual staff in Vienna these days, so I've decided twelve years is enough of playing at soldiers, and am temporarily posted to the Horse Guards while my regiment is overseas. Until I sell my commission."

"And I will hear nothing of your putting up elsewhere while you do," Lottie said, apparently carrying on the conversation Tristan had interrupted. "We've plenty of space here, and it would be silly for you to waste your blunt on rooms when we're so close to your headquarters. Besides, I'm sure you won't have any funds until the sale comes through."

"I've plenty in my pocket," the major said with that smoky laugh. "Despite the expense of Vienna's sartorial demands. Plus, unless Daniel's managed to get his hands on my allowance, I should have some funds in Barclay's."

"You do. Daniel is so very annoyed that he can't get at it," Lottie said complacently. "He's perpetually asking Tristan for money."

The major's brows drew together sharply. "He does? You don't comply, do you, Northwood?"

Tristan shook his head. What had the major asked? Oh. Right. Daniel. "Rarely, and then only a few guineas. Daniel's judgment on fiscal matters is pathetic." He smiled briefly and met the major's warm, dark eyes; they held Tristan's a moment, then glittered faintly as the well-shaped lips curled upward in response to Tristan's expression. That bell-like chord rang again. Tristan turned his head away, breaking the connection, and shook his head in confusion. When the hell had he started noticing the shape of a man's mouth or the warmth of a man's eyes?

When he'd walked into the drawing room.

"Are you all right, dear?" Lottie asked placidly.

"Yes, of course," Tristan said. "A bit of headache, that is all."

"Perhaps you should have a lie-down before dinner," she said. "Charles, you'll be joining us, won't you?"

A vision flashed into Tristan's head then, of lying on his bed, that tall, powerful figure beside him, stripped of that blue uniform, that tanned skin and bright hair golden in firelight. He shook his head again, swallowed hard, and said thickly, "Excuse me. I must…," and he turned and almost ran from the room.

HE WAS relieved to find his room empty, Reston off doing something other than tending his wardrobe. Using the much-despised boot jack to remove his Hessians, he tossed his coat over a chair and crawled fully dressed onto the bed, curling up on his side as though defending against a kicking. It had been years since he'd had a sudden physical reaction like this, a fully extended cockstand already throbbing with aching need. And for a man? He felt feverish, hot and clammy and sick with desire, and confused as hell. Nothing had ever hit him like this before. No—wait. Once. Once, drunk and stumbling into the wrong inn room. Firelight golden on strong flesh, muscled legs and men's low voices…. God. He'd never forgotten that. He'd pushed it aside, hidden it in his deepest memory, but it had never gone away, popping up at inopportune moments, when he was lost in sexual excitement. Was that a clue? Was that his body telling him something he had never wanted to admit to himself?

He ached to unbutton his trousers and take himself in hand, but to do that was to cave in, to admit—what? That he was damned. That he desired another man—not only another man, but his bloody brother-in-law. Adultery was one thing; he knew he was damned for that, but even that was forgivable. This—sodomitical tendency—was not. Could not be. It wasn't him. He'd never….

But he had. He knew he had. Not only in the firelit inn, but other times. Watching a mill, caught up in the excitement, the press of warm male bodies, the scent of sweat and blood and gin.

At Angelo's, watching supple forms dance in their deadly minuet.

At Jackson's, half-naked in the company of other half-naked men, relishing the contact of blows on muscled flesh.

His blood had heated, his body hardened. He'd tossed it off as purely physical excitement. It had meant nothing. But it had. He'd lied to himself, but it had meant something. Something that needed to be slaked in a woman's willing body.

Slaked, but never satisfied.

Shaken, he found himself weeping, as if he'd lost his soul.

Sleep came after tears, but a sleep shattered by dreams: of that scene in the inn room, but with the golden head turning to face him where he stood in the doorway; Major Mountjoy's face looking at him, smiling that warm smile, inviting him to join them, or worse, smiling, but not inviting him, laughing as he stood there watching, forever shut out of that warm embrace, that heated, firelit fucking....

When he awoke, it was to Reston laying out his clothes for dinner. He rose, nodded at Reston's greeting, then washed up. His head still ached, but he was determined not to show his despair and went down to dinner composed, if not content.

"OH, DEAR," Charlotte said placidly. "I hope he is not unwell."

Charles stared at the door. So *that* was Tristan Northwood.

He was thinner than Charles had expected; he had had an image of the typical bluff and hearty squire of the drinks-too-much, eats-too-much variety, but Tristan was tall and lean and there were hollows beneath those cool pewter eyes. God, what eyes—like stormclouds lit from beneath by a setting sun. The rest of him was equally striking: the dark wing of eyebrow, the long, chiseled nose, the curved, sensuous lips—the mouth of a hedonist, of a small, spoiled boy, and yet, when he smiled, there was something sweet and innocent in his face that hit Charles like a brick. "I trust," he said, then he paused, cleared his throat, and went on, "I trust I said nothing to distress him?"

"Oh, probably not. Tristan sometimes gets these headaches—I don't think he sleeps particularly well, at least according to his valet. He insists there's nothing wrong, and refuses to see a physician. Perhaps you might have more influence on him. He doesn't like me to worry."

"He does care for you, then." Strange—he'd got the impression that he had disturbed Tristan fully as much as Tristan had affected him. But if Tristan loved Lottie…?

"Oh, we are quite good friends," Lottie said.

"I *meant*," he said patiently, "that he loves you."

Lottie considered this a moment. "I think he does, but not in a *romantic* sort of way," she said meditatively. "He is a very romantic sort of person, but I don't think he feels romantic about *people*. I think he just expects people to disappoint and so doesn't have very high expectations of them."

"Do you disappoint him?" Charles asked curiously.

"I don't think so." Lottie thought a moment. "I think, probably, because I never promised him anything. He doesn't expect anything of me, nor I of him, and so we can be quite comfortable." She patted her rounded abdomen contentedly. "As comfortable as I get these days."

"Don't you want anything more from your marriage, Lottie?" he asked, taking her hand in his.

She smiled up at him. "Of course not. I am *not* a romantic sort of person, Charlie, not like you and Tristan. I don't care for the marriage act, and don't really need much of anything. Tristan suits me quite well." She shook her head. "I sometimes think that *he* needs more than just fondness, but there isn't much I can do about that. When we were first married… well, that's all done now, anyway."

"What's all done?"

"You know that he was unfaithful to me," Lottie said. "I think he was still… I don't know. *Looking*. As if he thought maybe he could find someone who could love him in a romantic sort of way. But he never did. It is a shame. He does so want to be loved."

Charles swallowed. Lottie patted his hand, which still clutched her other one, and slipped into the German the two of them spoke when discussing sensitive or private things, a holdover from their childhood with a German nanny. "I don't know if he would be… *open* to your kind of love, Charlie. I asked him about that sort of thing—oh, years ago now. He was quite… appalled at the idea. And yet… I don't really think he *enjoys* the marriage act."

Releasing her hand, Charles covered his eyes. "You didn't tell him about me, did you, Lottie?"

"No, of course not." She rested her head against his shoulder. "I would never do that. You told me a long time ago that one must *never* under any circumstances reveal details of a private conversation, and I hope I will always obey that rule."

"You understand that if you were to slip, my life would be endangered," Charles said carefully.

"Yes—and that is why you must be very, very careful with Tristan, Charlie. I don't *think* he'd do anything against you, but one can never tell, can one?"

"No," Charles said ruefully in English, "one can't."

TRISTAN drank his way through dinner, barely touching his meal. Charles watched him covertly while talking to Lottie; his brother-in-law was quiet, not sullen, but seemingly lost in his own thoughts. He answered pleasantly and readily enough when addressed directly, but the only time his eyes met Charles's was when Lottie mentioned that she'd had the room next door to his prepared for Charles's habitation. Then he glanced up, startled, to meet Charles's steady gaze, and flushed. "That's fine, Lottie," he said, turning hurriedly to his wife.

"Is it? I hoped so," Lottie said serenely, "but I wasn't sure. You may, of course, lock the adjoining door if you feel the need." She turned to Charles. "This house is rather small; there are only four bedchambers on the second floor, and a sitting room across the back of the house that Tristan and I share. All of the bedchambers connect; Ellen is of course next door to me, and Tristan and you will be across the hall. Your and Ellen's rooms are a little smaller than ours, but not much, are they, Tristan?"

"No, not by much," Tristan said, and took another drink of his wine. It was his sixth or seventh glass—Charles had lost count—but he did not seem affected. Charles supposed that with the amount of drinking that went on in society these days, especially among the gentlemen, that putting away entire bottles of wine was no great matter.

"Excellent vintage," Charles said to Tristan. "Do you keep your own cellar?"

"A small one," Tristan said. "I've a few bottles of decent enough stuff laid away, but for entertaining we usually order through Berry's."

"We dine simply enough at home, as you see," Charlotte said, "so a bottle or two is plenty for us."

"Of course," Charles said, giving her a smile. "And you don't like wine anyway, do you, *Liebling*? Or have your tastes changed since your marriage?"

"Not much," she admitted, "but I don't mind this red, or the white stuff we have with a fish course. I still don't like port."

"Neither do I," Tristan said, almost belligerently, "and I don't like lingering over it after dinner, as has become fashionable. I think it's rude to the ladies."

"And I tell him that it merely gives us the opportunity to dissect the characters of the gentlemen among ourselves," Lottie said, chuckling.

"Ouch," Charles said in amusement. "Well, then, since it is not the custom of this household, you and Ellen will have to wait until later to dissect our characters, eh, Northwood?"

Tristan frowned faintly, then raised his glass to Charles. "As you say, Major."

"I trust," Ellen said mildly, "that you shall give us no reason to, Charlie."

"I hope not. But being men, we are of course of coarser clay than the ladies."

Tristan turned to Lottie. "Shall I give your regrets to Mrs. Osborne, Lottie? I assume you will prefer to stay home this evening to visit with your brother?" Tristan glanced at Charles again briefly. "Or did you both plan to go tonight?"

"Oh, I'd rather stay home, but if Charlie wants to go out, then…."

"Not tonight, please. I would like to settle in and make sure my batman knows his way around. I took the liberty of introducing Reid to your Reston, Northwood. I trust he won't distract your valet too much from his duties."

"That's quite all right," Tristan said.

The table conversation turned naturally to the latest word from the Peace Conference in Vienna, and moved into the drawing room when Charlotte directed. Tristan visited for a short while before disappearing upstairs to change for the evening.

"I hope you aren't hurt that Tristan decided to go out tonight," Lottie said. "But we did have an invitation, and while people are *quite* used to me not coming, he has friends there that will miss him."

"Not at all," Charles assured her. "We are virtual strangers, after all, and he's just been notified I'll be living next door to him. It would be outside of enough to expect me to live in his pocket as well."

"He did say something to Lottie about sponsoring you at Boodle's, and White's," Ellen said in her quiet way.

"That is quite generous of him, seeing as the only knowledge of my character he can have is filtered through my devoted baby sister."

"'Baby sister'!" Charlotte poked at him with her fan. "I'm barely five minutes younger than you are."

"But it was a very long five minutes, according to Papa's reports. No, don't poke me again—my ribs won't take it."

"Hah," Lottie said. "Big strong soldier, you."

"Mr. Northwood was very quiet at dinner," he said, changing the subject. "Is that normal, or is it because of me?"

"He was a *little* quieter than usual," Ellen told him, "but he seemed to be distracted about something. I trust all is well with him, Lottie?"

"I assume so," Charlotte replied. "He has not said anything to me to the contrary. He did have one of his headaches this afternoon, so perhaps that is it."

"Ah," Ellen said, "perhaps that was the reason."

"I think I will check with Reid and make sure he's managed to get everything put away," Charles said. "If you ladies will excuse me a moment?"

"You will come back downstairs?" Charlotte asked with a faint frown.

"My dear Lottie," he replied, "I doubt that I shall find any reason to remain upstairs." He bowed to them both, then went up to his room.

The connecting door was unlocked; he turned the knob and opened the door. It opened inward, into his own room.

Tristan looked up from the pier glass where he was adjusting his neckcloth. "Found your quarters all right, then?" he said politely.

"Yes, thank you. I'm sorry—I didn't realize you hadn't left yet. I hope I'm not disturbing you."

There was a moment of hesitation, then Tristan said coolly, "No, not at all."

"I do want to thank you for letting me stay here, and hope that it's not too much of an imposition. I expect once I've sold my commission, I'll have enough funds to manage a set of rooms at least. Lottie said that prior to your marriage you lived at Albany—do you recommend it?"

"It was fine. It is a bit expensive, though."

"Ah. Then perhaps I shall set my sights a bit lower."

"You are welcome to stay here," Tristan said stiffly. "It would delight Charlotte if you did."

"But not her husband?" Charles's voice was soft.

Tristan shook his head. "It would be fine with me," he corrected. "It's not as if we don't have the room. But I must warn you—we'll be giving up the lease on this house this spring, probably before the forthcoming Season is over. Once Charlotte is delivered, we'll be retiring to the country. Charlotte prefers it."

"And Charlotte's husband? Does he prefer the country as well?"

"Charlotte's husband has no preference one way or the other," Tristan said flatly.

"I'm sorry to hear it," Charles said. "I would hope that you would be as enthusiastic as my sister at the prospect. She is quite delighted."

"I'm glad," Tristan said. He hesitated, then said, almost unwillingly, "Do you wish to accompany me to the Osbornes'? Charlotte's condition limits her social activities, and this will be quite a small party—no dancing, just music and cards, which is why she had originally agreed to go. I shall only be there an hour or two, and then expect to meet friends. You are welcome to join me, if you like."

"Some other evening, perhaps," Charles said with a smile. "I really would like to settle in tonight after doing so much traveling. I feel like I've barely made it to port."

"You came direct from Vienna?"

"Yes, and traveling from there across the Alps in midwinter was an experience I'd not like to repeat," Charles replied.

"From what Lottie says, nothing seems to bother you," Tristan said. Was there a note of annoyance in his tone?

"Not much does," Charles admitted. "Stupidity, arrogance, and waste, but not much else."

Tristan was quiet a long moment, then said curtly, "Well, if I'm to spend any time at the Osbornes' before my next appointment, I'd best be leaving. Good evening to you, Major, and if I didn't say it before, welcome."

A most grudging welcome, Charles thought, and wondered what in his previous words had triggered the abrupt withdrawal from conversation.

THE Osbornes' was insipid, but Gibs was late and Tristan stuck there until he arrived, since they hadn't previously decided on where they would be meeting Berkeley. He drank a little, conversed a little, but the rooms were hot and he was—anxious, he decided the feeling was. Anxious was as good as any word to describe it.

It was all Lottie's damn brother's fault. Who was he to come into Tristan's life and turn it awry like this? And why *should* Tristan's life be turned awry? There was something—*peculiar* about him. Not just the way he made Tris feel, but the way he'd said that: "Stupidity, arrogance, and waste…." It was as if he'd summed up Tris in three small words carelessly tossed off. Charles, the war hero, Charlotte's beloved brother, the admired staff officer. Of course he would despise Tristan if he knew him. Tristan was all of what he least admired.

Tris found his way out of the main rooms and into what was apparently a sitting room, but one with French doors out onto a balcony. He opened the doors and went outside into the frigid January air. *No*, he thought, leaning his elbows on the balustrade and resting his forehead on his palms. There was nothing peculiar about Charles. What was wrong, was wrong with him.

The realization he'd come to this afternoon terrified him. He thought he'd known who he was, what he liked and disliked, what his admittedly limited future held, knew what his standards were and his (again limited) morals were. But what he was thinking, what he was *feeling*, was so far outside those parameters that he wasn't sure who had got in and taken over his head. Certainly not Tristan Northwood the notorious womanizer, the Corinthian, the man's man. That man would never look twice at another man, not in *that* way. That wasn't right. Wasn't *decent*.

Oh, God.

He was going to hell. He'd always expected it after his years of adultery, but always in the back of his mind he'd hoped for leniency on God's part. After all, everyone did it. But this—lusting after *men*—this God couldn't forgive. He was doomed.

And he didn't care. *Oh, God*, he thought again, what was he to *do*?

"There you are," a voice said behind him. "Good Lord, Tris, aren't you freezing?"

He turned, social mask in place, and grinned at Gibson. "Too beastly hot in there," he said lightly. "Where the devil have you been?"

"Stuck at my sister's," Gibs said. "Sorry about that. I've done the pretty to our hosts, so I'm ready to leave."

"Good," Tristan said, elbowing him lightly as he went past. "I need a drink."

"I heard you've a visitor," Gibson said as they moved through the crowd.

Tristan stopped and blinked at him. "How did you find that out?"

"Osborne said you'd mentioned it. Lottie's brother?"

"Yes." Tristan started moving again, smiling, bowing, nodding at acquaintances as they made their laborious way through the crowded rooms to the door. Taking their coats from the footman, they moved out into the night.

In the dark, knowing Gibson couldn't see his face, it was easier to talk. "Yes, Major Mountjoy is selling out and has deigned to grace us with his presence," Tristan said lightly.

"Oh, one of those pompous types?" Gibson said.

Tristan sighed. "No, actually, he's quite pleasant. Personable. I suppose I'll put him up for membership in my clubs; he's selling out, so I suppose he'll have to meet people sooner or later. I'll introduce him around. I think you'll like him."

"If you do, I probably will," Gibson drawled.

"He's all right," Tristan said dismissively and changed the subject.

IT WAS still quite dark when Charles woke suddenly, disoriented for a moment in the strange bed. Then he remembered where he was, but wasn't quite sure what had woke him. Then he heard it again: the soft scrape of footsteps, the creak of a stair, a muttered word. He rose quietly, drew on his dressing gown, and opened the door a crack.

Reston, Tristan's valet, was coming up the stairs, candle in hand. Behind him, two of the household's footmen supported the master of the house as he stumbled up the stairs.

Charles opened the door wider. "May I help?" he asked softly.

Reston looked up and shook his head wearily. "No, thank you, sir," he said equally softly. "Mr. Northwood is very tired and just needs to retire." He opened the door to Tristan's bedroom and stepped in. The footmen half-carried Tristan in behind him.

Charles waited until the footmen had again left the room before he closed his own door and opened the adjoining one. Reston was efficiently stripping Tristan, and pulled the voluminous nightshirt over the thin body with practiced movements. Charles watched silently. Finally Reston looked up and said wearily, "There is nothing wrong, Major."

"He does this every night?" Charles surmised.

The valet said only, "I am not unaccustomed to the process, Major. Mr. Northwood will sleep the rest of the night. Thank you for your concern." He bowed politely, then reached past Charles for the knob, and pulled the door shut in Charles's face.

Charles studied the grain of the wood in the panel before him a moment, then went back to bed.

DESPITE his interrupted sleep, when Charles woke at dawn, he felt quite rested and decided to go for a ride before breakfast. He walked over to the Horse Guards' stables, where his cattle had temporary lodgings, and roused his groom to saddle Paragon, then rode the gelding to Hyde Park for a quick shake-down run along one of the few paths that had been swept clear of snow. It was on his way back to the gate about a half an hour later that he met Tristan, on a rangy bay that pranced about energetically, its breath puffing white clouds in the cold.

"Good morning," Tristan said politely. His eyes were bloodshot, but otherwise he showed no sign of the intoxication that had required two men's assistance earlier that morning, and his gloved hand on the restive bay was steady and strong. "You're out early."

"Yes," Charles said. "I was about to head back, but if you're up for some company...."

"By all means, if you don't mind the cold," Tristan said, and Charles turned his mount to ride beside his host. "That's a mannerly gentleman," Tristan nodded at Paragon.

"He is," Charles replied, patting the gelding's neck affectionately. "His name's Paragon, and he is. Steady and strong and sweet-mouthed. I bought him in Portugal, about five years ago."

Tristan's bay reached his head out—Charles didn't know whether he meant to nip Paragon or just investigate him, but the gelding calmly stepped aside without breaking stride. Tristan chuckled. "He's a smart lad too," he said, slapping the bay's neck gently. "Behave, Brat," he said to the horse.

"That's his name? Brat?" Charles raised an eyebrow.

"It's appropriate," Tristan said. "He's not a bad lad, but he's mischievous. He wouldn't have bitten your mount, but he might have pretended he was going to up to the last second. I think he likes to test. But he's a nice, smooth ride."

Charles's eyes flicked up, meeting Tristan's. To his amusement and interest, Tristan's cheeks blushed briefly scarlet, then the other man looked away, over toward the other side of the park. "Oh, lord," he said with an exaggerated sigh, "here comes Bab Abernathy, without a groom as usual. I don't think she's seen us yet. It's early enough—race you to the Serpentine?"

"You're on," Charles said.

"Ready, steady… go!" And Tristan was off, Charles at his heels.

THEY'D drawn up at the edge of the frozen water and were walking to cool the horses (Tristan had won by a whisker) when Charles said, "Who's Bab Abernathy and why were we avoiding her?"

"Oh, you'll meet her soon enough," Tristan said. "She's Lady Barbara Abernathy. She was… a bit of an inamorata of mine a few years ago. Sometimes she'll catch me here in the mornings and try to… well, you know. I lost interest in that connection, and she doesn't quite want to believe me." He glanced at Charles. "She is quite lovely," he said honestly. "I could introduce you, if you wish."

"I'm sure I'll meet her sooner or later," Charles said lazily. "No need to interrupt a perfectly good morning ride. Do you normally ride at this hour?"

"Most days," Tristan said, turning Brat's head back toward the gate nearest the house. "When it's clear like this. Brat doesn't mind the cold."

"Is this usual weather for late December?" Charles inquired. "It seems cold for so early."

Tristan shrugged. "Perhaps a bit more snow than usual," he said, "but they've kept the roads clear enough. Does the cold bother you, after your years in the Peninsula?"

"People have this strange idea that Spain is a hot country," Charles mused. "When in fact, it's an *extreme* country. Madrid and the northern part of the region get *much* colder in winter. And of course that's where we were, mostly. On the other hand, when it's hot…." He laughed. "*Madre de Dios!*"

"I suppose you speak Spanish fluently," Tristan said. Was that a wistful note in his voice? Charles cocked his head and studied his companion.

"Well enough to be understood," he conceded, "but I speak German much better. As does Lottie, of course."

Tristan blinked. "Lottie speaks German?"

"You didn't know? Our mother was German, and she brought her own nanny with her when she married. Between the two of them, we all grew quite fluent in it. Daniel lost his facility with the language when he went off to school, but Lottie and I always spoke it to each other, and when I went off to Eton we wrote to each other. And of course spoke it on holiday." He chuckled. "I don't know how she's managed to keep hers up, but I've used it quite a bit dealing with the Prussians and Austrians the Army has had contact with. They speak two quite different dialects, but I can manage in both."

"I can read Latin and Greek, a little, but don't have any modern languages," Tristan said, then he shook his head. "I'm not a scholar—never have been. Too busy, and never bright enough." His voice was careless. "Well—cold enough yet? I'm ready for breakfast."

"Lead on," Charles invited, and he followed Brat from the park.

TRISTAN might have been ready for breakfast, but to Charles's surprise, ate only a few pieces of toast and a spoonful of eggs. He did drink a large mug of ale, followed by several cups of coffee. Charles thought about the glimpse he'd had of Tristan last night, before Reston had enveloped him in the nightshirt. The man was too thin for his height, despite the broad shoulders. "Is that all you're eating?" he asked curiously.

"I never eat much breakfast," Tristan said, again in that careless voice.

"Does Charlotte eat at this time too?"

"No, she has a tray in her room, usually. I suppose with you here, that may change," Tristan said. He poured himself another cup of coffee. "We usually lunch together."

Charles helped himself to more ham. "This is delicious. I thought your cook did a fine dinner last evening, but she's outdone herself with breakfast."

"Mm," Tristan said. He opened the newspaper and began reading.

Snubbed, Charles grinned faintly and set to work on the ham.

A few minutes later, Tristan glanced up from the paper and said, "Are you interested in joining any of the clubs? I've memberships at Boodle's and White's. Well, and Brooks's, but Prinny and his brothers frequent that place, so I'm rarely there."

"You dislike the Regent?" Charles raised an eyebrow. "I had understood that he had a certain charm about him. Was I misinformed?"

"Not at all," Tristan said. "He is quite pleasant-natured, usually. I don't care for his hangers-on, however. I don't think they're a good influence. At any rate, my question is whether or not you're a member of any of the clubs, and if not, if you'd care for my sponsorship? I believe your Duke is a member of Boodle's."

"He is, and I'm not. I've spent very little time in London as an adult; think of me as a foreigner with an excellent accent and you'll be spot on."

"A babe in the woods, eh?"

Charles laughed. "Quite. So I must trust you not to lead me astray." He let his eyes hold Tristan's a moment too long and was rewarded with that charming blush again. So. Interesting. His sophisticated brother-in-law wasn't immune to a bit of flirting—and despite Lottie's warnings, Charles thought he was, after all, attracted to Charles.

Interesting.

"Boodle's and White's, eh?" he said, stabbing another piece of ham and adding a dollop of potatoes. "I think both would be within my means. I don't gamble much, though."

"Nor do I," Tristan said. "I find it tedious, unless it's for entertainment with friends. I'm not above a pleasant game of whist or piquet, but vingt-et-un is simply a matter of luck, not skill."

"No, I agree," Charles said. "I too prefer games of skill over games of chance. I suppose for me it comes of years in the military—there is so much that is beyond our control that we learn to appreciate achievement, rather than just advancement. At least some of us do."

"Lottie says your own advancement was awarded, not purchased. That's quite an accomplishment for someone as young as yourself."

"Someone seemed to think I'm a good leader," Charles said absently. "But that's done. I'm technically on extended leave until the sale of my commission goes through, but I'll still be reporting daily to the Horse Guards headquarters until then. It's a small price to pay to get them to house my cattle until I can arrange their sale."

"How many horses do you have?"

"Three, including Paragon. Speaking of which, thank you for letting me have stable-room for him this morning; I'll take him back to the Guards after breakfast when I report in. Then I am at your service after lunch."

"Fine," Tristan said. "I'll take you around, introduce you to some people." He glanced at the clock. "If you will excuse me—this is the time I usually spend with my son. Have you met him yet?"

"Charlotte introduced us last evening," Charles said. "He's delightful."

A slow, soft smile spread over Tristan's face, and he met Charles's eyes with ones that glowed with love. "He is, isn't he?"

Charles stared at him blankly, his heart flipping over. *My God*, he thought dazedly, *what I wouldn't give to have that look be for me.* The pewter of Tristan's eyes had warmed to something softer; the smile, so different from the brittle grins he'd flashed before, went straight through Charles like the musket ball he'd taken in the side years ago, the oddly painless shock of impact before the pain began. But this time there wasn't any pain. This time there was a rush of heat and dizziness, as if he'd been holding his breath and only now taken in air. And in the wake of the shock a slow, bittersweet understanding.

He'd thought he'd found Tristan attractive before. Seeing him now, smiling with love, Charles realized that it was more than just attraction, more than just the appeal of a handsome, arrogant, moody young man.

That face—that love—belonged to a man who could steal Charles's heart. Not even Gregory, whom he'd loved, had ever struck a blow like this one. With just a smile, he undid all Charles's carefully constructed defenses, stripped him bare, and left him helpless.

"Yes," he managed, and he wasn't sure if he was answering Tristan's rhetorical question, or submitting to Fate.

CHAPTER 8

"WELL, then, all settled in? Rumor had it that you were back."

Charles closed his book and grinned up at Dr. MacQuarrie, one-time physician to Arthur Wellesley and his cadre. "Mac!" he said in delight as he shook the man's hand vigorously. "I didn't know you were posted back here!"

"Well, not much for me to do in Lisbon once you fellows had gone off," the physician said as he dropped into a chair across from Charles. "His Lordship—excuse me, I suppose it's 'His Grace' now—never really needed a personal physician any road; I'd swear the man was made of iron. Besides, Hume suits his temperament better than I ever did. So once my leg healed, he had me sent back here. Not that I minded—I'm getting a bit too old to follow the drum."

"How is your leg?" MacQuarrie had broken it during an earthquake in Lisbon several years prior.

"Gives me fits on cold damp days, which is why I'm living in this godforsaken city instead of a civilized place like Edinburgh." He snorted. "Not that London's much better, weather-wise. I'm inclined to retire to someplace like Sicily for my old age. Someplace hot and dry. Maybe Egypt."

Charles laughed. "Well, don't retire too soon. I'd been meaning to write to you, anyway; it's even better that you're here. You're a member of this club?"

"Since before you were born, you young upstart. Who sponsored you?"

"Tristan Northwood."

MacQuarrie raised an eyebrow. "And how do you know that lively lad?"

"He's my brother-in-law—married my twin a few years ago. Do you know him?"

"Had the privilege of patching him up a year or more ago after one of his lunatic escapades. Someone had challenged him to round up all the swans on the Serpentine. A blow from one of those wings can break a man's arm; in his case he was lucky enough to get off with a badly sprained shoulder. He did it, though. I don't know how—swans are mean-spirited creatures for all they're so beautiful. Penned them all in an enclosure he and his friends had set up, until a pair of watchmen threatened to arrest them all." MacQuarrie snorted. "So they turned them loose on the beadles, but one went after Tris. He was the only one hurt in the aftermath, luckily."

"Sounds like Tris," Charles said. "From what I've heard, his little games usually don't hurt anyone but himself."

"If he were a little more careful about the dares he takes, he wouldn't get hurt as often as he does," Mac said. "He's been lucky so far that he hasn't done much damage to himself—carriage races and suchlike are bloody dangerous. He's a regular at Jackson's and Angelo's, so he's got good reflexes—I think that's what's saved him so far. Though I haven't heard much of him lately—your sister seems to be a good influence on him."

"Oh, I doubt if anyone could have much of an influence on him," Charles said. "Except his little boy."

"That would do it," Mac nodded. "So what did you want to talk to me about? I'm here, and not likely to go anywhere else."

"You trained in Edinburgh, didn't you?"

"And where else would a good Scotsman train? The best education in the world, particularly in medicine, my lad. Why? Are you thinking of taking up the caduceus yourself?"

"I am, but I'd rather not have to travel all the way to Edinburgh for it. Can you recommend somewhere a bit closer to home? I'm trying to sell my commission, but since I've been promoted to Major, it's got a bit harder. I don't want to sell it too cheaply, but since the peace broke out, takers are getting particular."

"Hold out for the most you can," MacQuarrie advised, "or sell cheaply to someone you respect."

"That was my intention," Charles said. "And none of those who've expressed interest are ones I'd like to see taking over my old troops. Even if most of them are now in America under Forrester."

MacQuarrie beckoned to a waiter, who went away and came back with a glass of whiskey. "Another for you, lad?" he asked, glancing at Charles's half-drunk wine.

"No, thank you," Charles said to the man, who nodded and vanished in the way of all good servants.

Mac said, "To be licensed as a physician with the Royal College, you'll need a few years of classes—the official number is five, but there are ways around it, of course. If you're interested in surgery, that's more of an apprenticeship—less prestigious, but more practical, and you'll be practicing in no time. On the other hand, the poor don't mind if you don't have an a FRCP after your name. There are a couple of physicians I know in the process of training at one or another of the hospitals here; they're desperate for help. I can give you a few letters of introduction, if you like. Or, if you'd be interested, I can work with you myself—I'm affiliated with St. Joseph's London Hospital in Spitalfields—not the best quarter of town, but you won't find a more diverse body of patients. Excellent teaching hospital; and if you decide to go for the degree, it's affiliated with London University. Surgery and medicine, though of course you'll have to choose. If you pick medicine, I've built up a tidy practice outside the military since I've been back, and I'd like to have someone worth leaving it to when I retire."

"I'm interested, and grateful that you are as well." Charles sipped his wine, then went on, "Some of what I've seen during my military career makes me think that there's more honor in mending a man than in damaging him."

"I've always felt that way." MacQuarrie studied him from under bristly brows. "I've watched your career with great interest since you advocated for that young man—Winstead? Was that his name?"

"Yes," Charles said. "Gregory Winstead."

"I never thought he was mad," Mac said, "but Warren had had it in for him from the beginning. Never understood it—the boy was fine, a good soldier, until Warren took command of his outfit. I didn't know much about the situation."

"Warren took a dislike to Greg," Charles said, "and baited him mercilessly. Greg was a good lad—never said boo to a goose. But Warren wouldn't be placated, wouldn't be swayed by reason, and seemed to take delight in how much he could poke at and torment the boy. If anything drove Greg mad, it was Warren." He swallowed the last of his wine. "Sorry. It still infuriates me, and they're both dead."

"I've often wondered…." Mac trailed off, staring into his glass.

"Wondered?" Charles prompted.

"Well… see here—you went to public school, did you not?"

"Eton. Yes."

"And you knew boys who were a… particular kind of bully…."

"Oh, yes," Charles said softly, coldly. "I knew them. Cowards."

"Certain things that were said of Warren made me think he enjoyed disciplining his men a little too much. That he *got* a little too much out of the activity, if you know what I mean. And certain… gentler types were meat and drink to that kind of man." He met Charles's eyes finally. "As a physician, you're required to keep the confidence of your patients, no matter how much you personally may be offended by their actions or their beliefs. I've always felt it was rather like being a papist priest in the confessional. But I suppose it doesn't matter now; the boy is dead, and from what I understand has no family to be damaged by the facts."

"You mean the fact that Gregory was a sodomite," Charles said calmly. "I knew. He confided in me, even before the business with Warren started. And you're right—I believe that Warren targeted him because of it. Even though Warren didn't know—couldn't have *known*—he suspected it, and that was enough for someone like Warren. And yes, I believe that Warren had leanings that way, and became a bully to compensate for it."

MacQuarrie leaned back in his chair and studied Charles. "That's very interesting," he said thoughtfully. "And Warren pushed the boy just a little too hard, so that all it took was a simple sentence to drive him over the edge?"

"The proverbial straw that broke the camel's back," Charles said.

"What did he say?"

"I don't know. I was too far away to hear. I just saw Greg sitting quietly polishing some harness, and Warren came up and said something. And Greg just went berserk. Tried to strangle Warren with the harness. They took him away screaming, and put him in the local madhouse. And he died there." Charles rubbed his forehead wearily. "What a waste. He was an excellent soldier, and a good man. If he had been in my company I would have been able to intercede long before it got to that point, but he was in Captain Hanson's, and Hanson was never one to tolerate interference." He rubbed his head again. "I should have interfered, and damn the consequences."

"No, you shouldn't have," Mac said levelly. "It wouldn't have made a difference in the end, and your career would have been over. And I'm aware of a number of other men that you *did* help, including that one you made your batman, who would have ended up cashiered or worse if you hadn't been there."

"It doesn't feel that way," Charles said bleakly.

MacQuarrie nodded. "I know. You're caught up in the 'what if's. But you can't do that if you plan on making a medical career for yourself. You do your best. You do what you think is right. And you don't second-guess yourself. That way lies chaos." He tilted his head. "There are some physicians who are beginning to specialize in mental and emotional disorders. Are you considering moving in that direction?"

"I hadn't thought about it," Charles admitted. "I was focused on getting the training as a generalist first. I don't know enough about it."

"Well, I can help you with the generalist part. I'll send over a list of books to get you started; it would help if you read Latin or Greek…."

"It's been a few years, but I did have *some* education—Eton, you know. Even if I didn't go to university."

"Good. You'll need to brush up on it, at the very least, to take your examinations in a few years. Most of the classic texts are available in translation. There are also some good German texts which I think we can get that way as well."

"Ah, there, I have you. I read German better than I speak it, and I'm fluent, thanks to a German nanny. That was why I spent so much time running after Wellington and Castlereagh."

"Oh, yes, I'd forgot. That was why you were in Vienna with Castlereagh. Good. Get the books, and in a week or so I'll get in touch with you and arrange to have you accompany me on rounds at the hospital. See if it's something you'd be interested in, talk to the other students, and so on. We'll deal with your formal education when we get to that point. What's your direction?"

"I'm actually living with the Northwoods, temporarily." Charles dug in his pocket for a card and penciled the address on the back. Handing it to MacQuarrie, he smiled in relief. "I'm much obliged to you, Mac—I've felt at a loose end lately, after running around after Wellesley for the last year. This gives me a sense of purpose."

"Everyone needs a sense of purpose, lad," MacQuarrie said soberly. "A man can't live like a skylark, flitting on the breeze. He needs a reason, or he's wasted. And we know you hate waste."

Charles nodded and rose, shaking the man's hand. "Now," he said, taking up his book again, "I've got to get home—we're dining out tonight and I need to change. I'll talk to you in a week or so?"

"My hand on it," Mac said, and they shook again. "Good day to you, Dr. Mountjoy."

"Not yet," Charles said, grinning, "not yet."

TRISTAN was waiting at the foot of the stairs when Charles came down, tugging awkwardly at his new tailcoat. The front was shorter than the military tunics he was used to, exposing the lower edge of his waistcoat, and the back was longer, the tails brushing the backs of his thighs. But if he was going to be a civilian, he needed to start thinking like one—or at least dressing like one. He glanced up to see Tristan staring at him, his face blank. "Does it look that bad?"

His brother-in-law blinked. "No, no, of course not. It's just—I'd become accustomed to you in your uniform. It seems odd to see you in civilian dress. It looks… quite nice. Weston?"

"At your recommendation," Charles said. "I could have fed my entire brigade for a week for what it cost me, but Lottie informed me that I would be expected to look my best for this evening." He cocked his head as he stepped onto the tile of the entry hall. "What makes this evening so special?"

"We're dining with the Morpeths. Lady Morpeth is a dear friend of Lottie's. Viscount Morpeth is the Earl of Carlisle's heir and a prominent politician, but for all that a tolerable fellow. He's a member of Boodle's."

"Did I meet him there? I don't recall anyone by that name."

"No, he wasn't there then."

"Wait a moment—Carlisle's heir? Then his wife would be Georgie Howard?" At Tristan's nod, Charles grinned. "Of course. Lottie wrote me about her frequently. Usually when she's just been brought to bed of another hopeful Howard."

"That doesn't surprise me," Tristan laughed. "They have nine. *Their* Charles is just about six months younger than Jamie. Their mothers are already planning on them becoming the best of friends."

"Good luck to that," Charles said. "I admit my experience with children is limited, but all the attempts like that I've seen have engendered mutual antipathy in the victims."

"No doubt," Tristan said. "Fortunately, I was never forced into that position."

"No cousins your age your parents expected you to automatically be fond of?" Charles remembered a few disasters like that.

"No—I am happily bereft of relatives. Should Jamie and I predecease the baron, the title will pass on to a distant relative I have never met." Tristan glanced up the stairs. "Ah, Charlotte. You look lovely."

"I look *fat*," Charlotte corrected, smiling, "but since it's the Morpeths we're dining with, that shan't signify."

"Georgie *enceinte* again?" Tristan asked.

"Not that I know of. Good heavens, Tris—little Charles is not even a year old yet!"

"Well, considering they have had nine children in nine years, I wouldn't think that would be unusual."

"There's more than two years between Blanche and Charles," Lottie said complacently.

"Which only means that there is less than that between several others," Tristan pointed out.

"Good God," Charles said faintly.

Lottie chuckled. "They're a fond couple."

"So I imagine." Charles shuddered. He glanced at Tristan, who was frowning. "What is it?"

"Do you dislike children?" he asked.

Charles shook his head. "Not at all. I just think it's brutal to put your wife—whom one assumes one has *some* affection for—through the trauma of childbirth so often. Not to mention the discomfort of pregnancy."

"Which one doesn't," Lottie said sternly, "in polite company."

"Sorry, *Liebchen*," her brother said penitently. "I forget."

"We'll civilize you yet," she retorted.

"I don't know," Tristan said abruptly. "I rather like him uncivilized." Then he seemed to realize what he'd said, and went crimson.

Charles jerked his head around to stare at him. Their eyes met a moment, Tristan's wide and shocked at his own words. "I didn't mean that the way it sounded," he said awkwardly.

"How did you mean it, then?" Charles asked in a low voice.

"Just that—that—that it's refreshing to hear someone speak honestly and straightforwardly for a change. I didn't mean to intimate that you're, you're... uncivilized. Or barbaric, or anything. You're not. You're just not...."

Charles regarded his averted face, then said, "I didn't take offense."

Tristan whipped his head up, met his eyes again, then turned away. "Thank you. Well. Shall we go? Lottie, here's your wrap. Charles, would you see if the carriage is outside? I sent the footman for it a while ago. Oh, here he is. Charles, your coat." He handed Charles his top coat and took his own from the footman, busying himself to cover his acute embarrassment.

Charles shrugged into his coat and put on his hat and scarf while Tristan fussed over Lottie, then escorted her outside, leaving Charles to follow. He shook his head. This was going to be a long evening.

It was, although the Morpeths were most pleasant company, as were the rest of the guests. They engaged in Tristan's despised after-dinner port, but Tris gave no sign of his disapproval, acting the gracious guest. He showed unsuspected talent as a raconteur, taking his turn in the story-telling with anecdotes that set the table laughing, though more at his own expense than anyone else's—a particular favorite was one about him slipping on a patch of ice and nearly taking down an old lady with him, and his frantic efforts to avoid it. Tristan laughed as hard as any of the others in the retelling. It was the first time Charles had had the opportunity to see Tristan in, to coin a phrase, his native habitat; his behavior was as polished and sophisticated as his interactions with Charles had been awkward and uncomfortable. It was almost as if he'd taken on the persona of another person, a Tristan Northwood who was debonair and self-confident and charming.

And he *was* charming; all the ladies brightened when they came into the drawing room after their prescribed half hour with the port, and their attention was focused on Tristan. He obliged them by paying distinct attention to every single lady there, from the youngest debutante to the oldest dowager. He admired needlework, fetched cups of tea, turned pages at the spinet, drew out the shyest so that she bloomed under his regard. Charles more than once glanced at Lottie to see her watching her husband and smiling approvingly. "He does have a way with the ladies," she murmured to him once when he'd stopped by to take her cup for a refill.

"I see that," he replied in the same low tone.

She gave him a steady, assessing look, then waved him away as she turned back to Lady Morpeth.

It was foolish, Charles knew, to feel so much for someone who might never return his regard, but he was so sure in his gut that Tristan was not indifferent to him. That must have been why it hurt so much to watch him gently courting each lady, after having to watch him charm his male counterparts. Each person he spoke with had his full attention, even if that person was a bore or an ass; he was patient and just-appropriately-friendly with each. No wonder he was so sought-after socially....

"You're scowling," Lottie said when he brought her tea cup back to her.

"Am I? I didn't sleep well last night," he said.

"Did they wake you when they brought Tristan up?"

"You know about that?"

"Of course. It's part of his routine," she said dryly. "Lurk in the library drinking until two in the morning, then have the footmen and Reston haul him up to bed. You'll get used to it."

"That's appalling," he said in an undertone.

"If you can stop him, you would have my gratitude," she replied. "I like Tristan, and his drinking is not healthy."

"He doesn't listen to you?"

She snorted. Lady Morpeth leaned over and said, "Is it a joke?"

"Hardly, Georgie," Lottie said. "We were talking about Tris."

All three of them looked over at where Tristan was seated beside Lady Morpeth's mama-in-law. The countess was laughing, and as they watched, she smacked Tristan's arm sharply with her fan. "Lady Carlisle is entertained," Georgie said. "Thank God. She's impossible to deal with when she's annoyed. And at least no one will accuse Tristan of flirting with her the way Rutland does when he talks to Elizabeth."

"Does that anger Rutland?" Lottie asked in concern. "Because Tristan flirts with everyone."

"Oh, once it might have," Georgie waved her hand dismissively. "But Tristan has become much more circumspect since he married you, Lottie."

"Did Tristan and *Elizabeth*...?" Lottie asked curiously.

"Lottie!" Charles said sharply.

Georgie laughed. "Oh, good heavens, *I* don't know. I doubt it, though. Elizabeth's not the type."

"But Tristan is," Lottie said thoughtfully. She glanced at Charles. "And it's no good scolding me, Charlie. I knew very well what Tristan was when I married him."

"But he's not like that anymore," Charles pointed out. "You said so yourself."

"It doesn't change the past, Charlie."

"But one should give him the benefit of the doubt," her brother said, frowning. "He deserves to make a fresh start if he can."

"Tristan has a stalwart defender in your brother, Lottie!" Georgie said. "That's so nice. So often men just want to drag each other down."

"It seems to me that that is a fault of both genders," Lottie shot back.

"True enough," Georgie admitted. "And Tristan is such a sweet boy, despite the awful things he's done, that one can't help but quite forgive him, can one, Lottie?"

"Of course not," Lottie said. "I am quite fond of Tristan, and count myself quite lucky to be the one who snapped him up."

"You ladies are entirely too disrespectful of my poor Tristan," Charles said sternly.

His sister gave him a calculating look; Georgie only laughed.

TRISTAN stood, bowing, to let the Countess of Carlisle's companion take her seat, said something politely meaningless, and wandered off in search of a drink. A voice at his elbow said, "Rumor has it that you've become quite the Darby to Lady Charlotte's Joan."

He turned. "Lady Barbara," he said, with a curt half-bow.

"It was Bab and Tris between us not so long ago," she purred.

He studied her discreetly. She had lost none of the beauty she'd always had, but he was unmoved. He'd broken with her not quite a year after his marriage, replacing her with a series of shorter-lived affairs with women less demanding, but the ennui he'd attributed to his growing boredom with Bab Abernathy hadn't dissipated; the other women bored him too. "You're looking well," he said distantly.

She cocked her head and studied him. "I've heard nothing of your taking on a new mistress," she said coolly, "and several people have said that you've sworn an oath of fidelity to your insipid bride. Nonsense, I told them, Tristan Northwood has never had any truck with something as banal and bourgeois as fidelity. Certainly not to a woman as dull and uninteresting as his wife. Too bad her brother got all the looks in the family—he's quite handsome."

Automatically Tristan glanced up, looking for Charles, and found him, laughing at something Lady Morpeth or Lottie had just said. What Lady Barbara had just said wasn't quite true: Lottie was neither insipid nor dull, and she was attractive in an ordinary sort of way. It was just contrasted to her twin that she came off the loser; his strong features and graceful build were more than just a masculine version of Lottie's. Lady Barbara was right in one respect: he was—quite—handsome.

"My God," Bab said faintly. "You *are* besotted."

He turned back to her, paling. *Oh, God, did she just see him lusting after Charles?*

"I can't believe you're actually *in love* with that pale passive princess," she went on in disdain. "But that look on your face tells me a different tale. Really, Tris!"

He made her another half-bow, said, "Thank you for your felicitations, Lady Barbara. If you will excuse me?" and strode across the drawing room to his wife—and her brother. Taking Lottie's hand, he tucked it into his arm and smiled down at her.

Lottie said dryly, "Lady Bab becoming importune again?"

"You know it," he said in the same tone.

She laughed brightly and patted his sleeve, as if he'd just said something flattering. "Witch."

"I wish I hadn't had to invite her," Georgie said, "but her mama is a friend of my mother's, and we've been forced to associate since we were children."

"Odd," Lottie said, "to think of Bab as a child. I always sort of thought of her as being, oh, I don't know, hatched or something."

"Conjured," Georgie said, giggling.

"Transformed from a poodle, like Mephistopheles in *Faust*," Charles said.

"From a *poodle*?" Georgie said. "What is *Faust*, Major?"

"A book by the German writer Goethe. I don't think it's been translated yet," Lottie said. "Charles sent it to me last year; it's been quite the rage in Europe. Mephistopheles is a devil or demon or something that makes a bet that he can steal a man's soul. It's quite frightening."

"The devil's a poodle? One of those German hunting dogs?" Tristan laughed.

"I thought it was supposed to be cats that have the relationship with Satan," Georgie observed.

"Cats are quite angelic in comparison to Lady Bab," Lottie pointed out.

"Goethe? Isn't he the one who wrote that terribly sad book about the young man who shoots himself?" Georgie asked.

Tristan's blood ran cold. He glanced over at Charles, who was, thankfully, looking at Lady Morpeth. "Yes," Charles said. *"The Sorrows of Young Werther.* It's about considerably more than just a foolish young man's suicide, though. It started a revolution in German culture. Lottie's named for the heroine."

"Really?"

Lottie smiled at Lady Morpeth. "My mama always said so, but the fact is my grandmama's name was Charlotte, too, so it's only partly true. Besides, I can hardly imagine anyone perishing for love of me."

Tristan raised her hand to his lips to hide his trembling. After a moment he released her and said, "Don't sell yourself short, love."

"My dear Tristan," Charlotte said in amusement, "some of us need love to breathe, and you are one such. Others, like me, see the whole concept as something to write stories or operas about and little more. I should think being the subject of a passion such as that to be sorely uncomfortable. And I certainly could not reciprocate. Charlie, on the other hand...." She gave her brother a mischievous look. "He has all the passion I lack, don't you, dearest?"

Tristan saw Georgie giving Charles an interested look. "Oh, have you a grand passion, Major?"

"Of course, if my sister says so. Alas, the object of my affection is wed, so I must not share the name." Over Georgie's head, Charles's eyes met Tristan's and held them a long moment before turning back to his sister. Tristan's breath went short.

"Oh, no, you must tell, mustn't he?" Georgie turned to Lottie. "We promise to keep it a secret."

Laughing, Charles shook his head. "Oh, no, my lady. I am content to worship from afar, and to give a name will only ruin the innate chivalry of my passion."

"How *romantic*," Georgie breathed. "Is it a lady of the ton? Or someone you know from abroad?"

"Someone I've only met recently."

Georgie turned to Tristan. "Mr. Northwood, you *must* know who it is. You know everyone."

"I'm afraid I don't know who he means," Tristan said shortly. "Sorry. Besides, what does it matter if the lady is already wed? They can have no future."

"That," Lottie said complacently, "sounds like something I would say."

A SHORT while later, he managed to corral Charles in an anteroom as they were fetching the ladies' wraps. "I need to speak to you," he said sharply.

Charles glanced at him. "I would think that would be easy enough to do," he said, "inasmuch as I live in your house."

"This can't wait until later," Tristan snapped. "What the devil were you playing at in there?"

"I beg your pardon?"

"That comment about the subject of your passion being wed. Was that a slap at my infidelity? I'll have you know I'm faithful to my wife; have been for months now. It's not fair that you should judge me by my past behavior...."

"What? Slow down, Tris!" Charles raised his hands placatingly. "I had no such intention. I was merely being honest. I *am* in love, and the subject of my affection *is* married."

Tristan scoffed, "You've hardly been in society enough since you've been back to form any such attachment."

"'Whoever loved, if not at first sight'?" Charles quoted softly.

"That's drivel," Tristan said scornfully. "Well, if you insist that it wasn't an insult, I'll have to accept it. Society would look askance at me if I call out my brother-in-law."

"'Call out'? You aren't serious?"

Tristan drew himself up and looked down his nose at him. It wasn't easy; while they were close in height, Charles had an inch or two on him. "Are you calling me a coward?"

"Good God, no! Tris, I don't know where you got this bee in your bonnet about my insulting you. I meant nothing of the sort. And there are no circumstances under which I would meet you in a duel." Charles put his hand on Tristan's sleeve. "Tris, please trust me in this. I meant nothing by my statements, and neither Lottie nor Lady Morpeth took them any way other than surface comments. No one questions your fidelity or your courage."

The heat from Charles's hand burned through Tristan's coat. "No," Tristan said, suddenly tired. "No."

"Cry friends again?"

He glanced up, but Charles's brown eyes were simply their usual merry, warm selves. There was no significant intent in their expression, no condemnation, no judgment, nothing but friendliness. He managed a faint smile. "Of course. Do you have Lottie's coat? I think this is her shawl."

CHAPTER 9

CHARLES had been in residence for a week or so before his books arrived from Dr. MacQuarrie. He met the package with delight, already bored with both Tristan's frenetic social life and Charlotte's placid one. He enjoyed the afternoons he spent with Tristan at Jackson's or Angelo's or riding in the Park on clear days, but the evenings of endless parties and dinners to which he, a new, eligible single male, was invited were beginning to pall. Thus it was a relief to have an excuse to turn down another evening party in favor of his new studies.

He was deep in the description of the symptoms of malarial fever when he heard the door to the library open. Tristan came in and headed right for the brandy on the sideboard, pouring himself a glass and tossing it off before refilling his glass and turning toward the desk. He froze, obviously not expecting Charles to be there. "Oh. Up late, aren't you?"

"Am I?" Charles glanced at the ormolu clock on the mantel. "I suppose I am. I got quite absorbed and didn't realize the time. Shall I yield the library to you, Tris?"

"No, no," Tristan said, "I'm in no hurry. Brandy?"

"Thank you."

Tristan blinked. "Really?"

"Yes. Why? Did you think I was a teetotaler? You've seen me drink."

"Wine, with dinner. Ale, at Jackson's. I've never seen you drink brandy before. Certainly not late at night."

Charles shrugged. "I don't feel the need to drink before bed, other than a cup of tea, or chocolate. I sleep well enough."

"God, I wish I did," Tris said, half to himself. He poured Charles a glass of brandy, then brought it over to where he sat. Propping himself up on the corner of the desk, he set the glass down at Charles's right hand. "What keeps you so interested so late?" he asked, angling his head to look down at the text open in front of Charles.

"It's about malarial fever," Charles replied. "Cinchona bark seems to be the best remedy for it, but even though we've known about it for centuries, the disease itself is still mysterious."

"You're interested in *diseases*?" Tristan asked disbelievingly.

Charles laughed. "Not per se," he admitted. "I'm studying to become a physician. One of the ones that attended us in the Peninsula is living in London now and has offered to take me under his wing. I'll need to return to school, but it will be worth it."

"A *physician*? But why?"

"I have to do something," Charles said reasonably. "I'm a younger son, my half-pay won't last once I've sold out, and you know yourself my family fortune is minimal. It doesn't stretch to supporting indigent relatives."

"You could always marry an heiress," Tristan pointed out.

Charles laughed and shook his head. "No, thank you," he said merrily. "I can't imagine selling myself that way. I have no intention of marrying."

"But a *physician*?"

"You say that as if it's a surgeon or something lower-class like that," Charles said. "Physicians are one of the few careers a gentleman can enter, along with barristers—and I'm not cut out to argue the law. But I've had enough experience with medicine to know that it's something I could find interesting—and I've enough desire to know that I can follow through with it. Besides, I'd be bored to insanity if I had to live a life of leisure."

"A life like mine, you mean?" Tristan asked bitterly.

"Yes," Charles said gently.

"Well, better you than me," his host said, once again in that careless voice. "I haven't the brains for such a thing."

"Oh, I think you're wrong there. Here." He pulled another book from the stack. "Look at this and tell me what you think." It was a simple anatomical text, and he opened it to a plate of a human skeleton. "You've got an analytical mind—don't you see how all the bones fit together? Like a puzzle. Isn't it fascinating?"

Tristan set his glass down on the desk and leaned over to study the plate. "Good Lord," he said in amazement. "I never saw anything like this at university. We have all those bones inside us?"

"Something like 208. The actual numbers vary. Newborns have more—almost half again as many."

"You're joking!" Tristan blinked. "What happens to them all?"

"They fuse into other bones as the child grows." Charles sat back in his chair, watching Tristan's face in the lamplight. Tristan's expression was solemn, intent as he studied the plate; he reached out with a finger and drew it down the illustrated spine, tracing the rib cage and the pelvis. Charles felt as if it were his own body Tris traced, felt the ghost finger along his spine, curving over his abdomen to trace the lower edge of ribs, the taut muscles, then down along his hip, sliding inward…. He caught his breath silently.

Tris looked up, his eyes bright. "Is there more of this?"

Wordlessly, Charles flipped the pages to a plate illuminating the muscular system. Tristan sucked in a breath. "This… this is amazing! How do they know how these are all shaped, and where they go?" He pointed to a spot on the plate. "The muscles attach to the bones?"

"Yes, or cartilage. All muscles attach at both ends—except one. Only one attaches at one end."

"Which one?" Tristan asked curiously.

Charles met his eyes. "The tongue," he said softly. "The most dangerous—and the strongest—of all the muscles."

"I see," Tristan said. He'd looked back down at the page, but his neck above his cravat had darkened. He didn't move for a moment, then turned the page and looked at the next plate. "What is this? Is this in German?"

"Yes. There is a strong scientific bent to the German mind, I think—some of the best medical texts come out of Prussia and Austria. I brought that one back from Vienna, along with a few others. But I believe it's also been printed here, in English translation. I could look for a copy, if you're interested in studying it?"

Tristan laid his hand over the plate, which was of a detailed drawing of the shoulder structure. "You would do that?"

"Of course," Charles said in confusion. "Why wouldn't I?"

His host met his eyes, a wry smile twisting the graceful line of his lip. "People don't, in general."

"Don't what?"

"Give me things. At least not things that are, well, things I want, if you know what I mean." Tristan closed the book. "Yes. I'd like to see more of this. It's interesting."

"Believe it or not, you have some very interesting books in this library," Charles said. "There's a very nice copy of Culpeper's *English Physitian*, if you're interested in herb-lore, and what looks like a first edition of Fuller's *Pharmacopoeia Extemporanea*. That one must be an hundred years old and is in prime condition."

"I bought the library lock, stock and barrel from George Roberts' widow when she was selling all their lumber," Tristan said, then he cocked his head and studied Charles in mild amazement. "You're really enthusiastic about all this, aren't you?"

"I've always been interested in helping people," Charles said, adding wistfully, "it's such a *change* from killing them."

Tristan slid off the desk and drew the guest chair up to lean on it opposite Charles. "You didn't like being in the military? Why did you stay so long, then?"

"Oh, I didn't dislike it, precisely," Charles said. "Particularly after Wellesley tapped me for a staff position after Badajoz. God, what a nightmare battle *that* was. It wasn't any easier—God knows that he works his ADCs to death!—but at least I didn't have to *watch* my men die." He rubbed a hand over his forehead. "As an officer you're in the best position to protect your troops, but there was only so far you could do that, and ultimately, it was you who gave the order for them to fight. And dying in battle is a horrible way to go. It's rarely quick, and more often slow, bloody, and painful. The screaming… God save you should never experience that."

"Were you ever wounded?" Tristan asked.

"Yes, a couple of times. Kept me out of action for a few weeks, but nothing of consequence." Charles sipped at his brandy. "But in between the battles, there were so many shared experiences—and even bivouacking in the cold, or ghastly forced marches in the rain, were easier to take when you knew everyone else was going through the same thing. Sometimes it was just… funny. There comes a point in misery where you just go beyond a certain point, and it doesn't matter anymore." He smiled to himself in remembrance. "And when you're all making common cause, that makes it worthwhile." He looked up at Tristan. "Didn't you have close friends at school that you could always rely on to buck you up when you were miserable?"

"Yes. Gibs and Berks—Roger Gibson and Jasper Berkeley. We met at Westminster, a bunch of scrubby schoolboys. Watched each other's backs and got each other into mischief, through public school and all the way through Cambridge."

"Did you take your degree?" Charles asked curiously.

Tristan flushed. "I didn't do well," he said. "I was only twelfth."

"Twelfth what?"

"Twelfth Wrangler."

"*Twelfth Wrangler*?" Charles gasped. "Good God, Tris! That's first-class honors!!"

"It's *twelfth*," Tristan said. "And besides, the Tripos is just a test of memorization. You learn the rules, it's easy."

"For you, perhaps. Good God, Tris, if I were Twelfth Wrangler, I'd have it engraved on my calling cards."

"It's *twelfth*," Tristan muttered.

Charles reached out and ruffled Tristan's hair. "It's brilliant," he said softly. "I'm proud of you."

Startled, Tristan raised his head and gazed at Charles. Charles blushed and drew back his hand. "Sorry," he said quickly. "I didn't mean to be so familiar…. It's just that from Lottie's letters, I feel like I know you so well—I do apologize."

Tristan smiled faintly, his cheeks blooming. "No, that's all right," he said quickly. "I don't mind. It's…. No one's ever given me that, either, you know."

"Given you what?"

"Said that. Said they were proud of me." Tristan shook his head and sat up, leaning back carelessly in his chair. "Well, why should they, at any rate? Another brandy?"

"No, thank you." Charles studied him a moment, then said, "That Culpeper's on the table over there if you want to take a look at it."

Tristan glanced over his shoulder. "Might as well," he said, still in that careless tone; but he got up and went to the table, picking up the book respectfully and settling back in the chair to read. Charles watched him a moment, smiling to himself, then went back to his own book.

Over the course of the next few hours, Charles watched subtly as Tristan went back and forth to the shelves, looking at the well-organized titles and picking out new books to read. Once in a while he'd draw Charles's attention to a passage and they'd discuss it based on Charles's experiences and current medical practices. "Was George Roberts a medical man?" Charles asked finally, as Tristan showed him another old gem he'd discovered.

"Not that I'm aware of," Tris said. "I think his widow said he'd bought the library off someone else years ago. We of the ton do that a lot, you know. Better to *look* educated than to actually *be* educated."

"I can't imagine that," Charles said thoughtfully. "I can't imagine not building a library of your own if you've the money and space. I've only a few books—rather hard to haul a library with you all over God's green Earth. I sent them home as I traveled, and my father has them down at Chilson."

"You're welcome to...." Tristan's smile faded. "I was going to say you're welcome to have them here, but I forgot that we'll only be in this house another couple of months, and by then you'll have found your own lodgings. You won't want to rusticate with us while you're studying, so there'd be no point joining your library with ours. But until we do move, you are welcome to use whatever texts you find here."

"Thank you," Charles said soberly. "And I do promise to find you those English translations I mentioned."

"Thank you," Tris began, but he was interrupted by a knock on the door, followed by Reston poking his head in. He looked surprised.

"Mr. Northwood? It's two of the clock...."

Tristan blinked, then his eyes shot to the clock on the mantel. "Oh, God," he said faintly. "It's bedtime—and I'm still sober!"

"Is that a problem?" Charles frowned.

Tris gave him a quick, humorless smile. "I don't sleep well," he said dryly. "And I hate laudanum—it gives me horrible headaches. Brandy usually does the trick—but it will take me hours to reach a sleepy state."

"Brandy is as bad as laudanum as a sleep aid," Charles said. He rose from the desk. "However, I have some herbal powder that's effective with less aftereffects. Reston, if you'll bring tea to Mr. Northwood's room, I'll fetch the Scutellaria."

"That sounds dreadful," Tris said wryly.

"It sounds worse in the vernacular," Charles shot back. "It's called 'skullcap'. I know, that's just a hat—but to me it always reminds me of the fairy tale of the Red Cap—the evil ogre that dyes its hat with the blood of its victims. My mother was quite fond of the darker German fairytales. The Scutellaria is much more benign. It's from North America—a native plant, so you won't find it in Culpeper's."

"I suppose that means I must trust you," Tristan said, giving him a skeptical look.

"You must." Charles grinned. "I promise it's safe."

Tristan shrugged. "As long as it works, I don't care if it's safe."

Charles's amusement faded, and he said grimly, "Well, I care. I've no desire to injure you, Tris. In any way."

TRISTAN felt his face heat—not an unusual feeling when Charles said anything that could even *remotely* be taken wrong. He was beginning to think that Charles deliberately said things he knew Tris would misinterpret, as if he suspected Tris's feelings for him and was taunting him. But he didn't think Charles was that unkind. God, he was confused. He rubbed his hands over his face. "I didn't realize it was this late," he said. "I must be tireder than I thought."

Charles curled his fingers around Tristan's elbow. "Come, then," he said, his voice gentle, "we'll get you your tea and Reston can put you to bed. I'm sorry to keep you up so late—I hope you've enjoyed the evening."

Tris lowered his hands and met Charles's concerned eyes. "Yes," he said, and to his surprise it was true—not just because he was with Charles, but because he'd honestly become interested in what he had been reading and discussing with him.

"Good," Charles said, releasing him as they reached the door. "Because I'm hoping that you don't mind my using the library for my study on occasion. And repeating this evening's experience when you're not elsewhere committed. I've enjoyed it."

Oh, God, Tristan thought as Charles gave him that affectionate smile. *I am so lost.* He followed Reston up the stairs, painfully aware of Charles's solid presence behind him.

Charles went into his room and came out a moment later with a small packet of herbs, which he gave to Reston. "Here. Steep this in Mr. Northwood's tea for ten minutes. It's as bitter as any tea," he said to Tris, "so you might want to add some honey to it."

"Thank you, Major," Reston said, and to Tristan, "I shall be right back with the tea, sir," and went back down the stairs.

Charles and Tristan gazed at each other a long moment, then Charles said, "I'd best get to bed. It's later than normal for me." Was it Tristan's imagination, or did he sound reluctant?

"Yes," Tris said curtly. "Good night," and he turned and went into his own room. A moment later he heard Charles's door close quietly. He shed his clothing quickly, pulling on the nightshirt Reston had set out, and climbed into the big bed, curling up on his side with a pillow tucked in his arms, just as he had that day when he'd first met Charles, and come running upstairs to hide in his room. Then, he'd only lain miserable, fiercely aroused and not daring to do anything about it, because doing something about it meant that it was *real*, that he was aroused by a *man*. Now he knew it was much worse—that he thought he was in love with Charles. It couldn't get any more real than this.

How much longer could he go on? It was barely the middle of January and Charlotte wasn't due for nearly three more months. He needed to survive until he could safely bring her down to the country—what would that be? Four months? Five? Five months of living next door to a smart, funny, beautiful man, a man Tristan couldn't *have*? Five more months of dreaming of Charles, of waking to wet sheets and terror that he'd cried out Charles's name in the throes of his dreaming? Five more months of living what was rapidly becoming a nightmare of his own devising?

Or he could find some way to put this behind him. To forget that he was in love with Charles, that he didn't feel that warmth every time Charles spoke his name or addressed a comment to him. That he didn't long for Charles's approval far more than he had ever wanted his father's, with no more probability of ever earning it. How could he, when Charles was always so kind, so thoughtful, so considerate, things he'd never experienced in his adult life from another man. Was that all it was? Was it merely that Charles was kind to him, that he never seemed to *expect* anything from him? Was it only that Tristan was so hungry, so desperate for Charles's friendship that he had convinced himself that it was love?

But these feelings had started before he really knew Charles—when he'd first met him, before he'd experienced Charles's kindness. The desire wasn't for friendship. That was physical, purely and simply. He *wanted* Charles—wanted those strong arms, that lovely mouth, those horseman's thighs—wanted him naked, in bed, with him. Wanted him to *love* him.

There was a scratching on the door and Reston came in, the tea tray in his hands. "Oh, sir," he said in distress, "you should have waited—I would have helped with your clothes."

"I'm sorry, Reston," Tris said wearily, "but I was too tired to wait. Sorry about the boot jack."

"It's nothing, sir. Your Hessians will be quickly mended, I assure you." Reston set the tray on the table and poured the tea. "Shall I add the honey as the major suggested? It *is* quite bitter."

"Yes, please." Tristan took the cup and tasted it, making a face at the bitterness. "Thank you, Reston."

"You're welcome, sir." Reston busied himself picking up Tristan's clothing and setting everything to rights, then turned back to Tris. "Will there be anything else tonight, sir?"

"No, Reston. Go to bed."

"Yes, sir." At the door, Reston paused and turned back. "Sir?"

"Yes?"

"It's not my place to say, but if you'll be so indulgent, I would like to express my admiration for Major Mountjoy. He is a very considerate gentleman."

"Yes," Tristan said sadly. "He is."

Reston cocked his head a moment, but said nothing more to the subject. "Good night, sir."

"Good night, Reston." Tristan waited until his valet had gone, then drank his tea quickly, setting the cup on the nightstand and blowing out the candle. It wasn't that he wasn't tired—he tired far too easily these days, and in truth, the brandy was less about helping him sleep than numbing him so he didn't remember his dreams. He lay in the dark, not daring to move, praying for sleep to come quickly, and that, for once, he wouldn't dream.

"Ho'sies, Papa! Ho'sies!"

"Yes, love, I see them." Tristan laughed, shifting Jamie from his hip to his shoulders, where he promptly knocked Tristan's hat off into the dust of the Horse Guards' parade grounds. Charlotte started to bend over to retrieve it, but a gentleman standing a few feet away picked it up and handed it to her with a bow. She smiled her thanks.

They had braved the January chill since the entire cavalry corps presently billeted in London was on review for the Prince of Wales. Charles, being still an active cavalry officer, had put on his uniform for the first time in weeks and joined those of his regiment not still in America. He was riding Paragon, Tris noted, admiring the way he looked on the horse, the gold facings on his dark blue uniform glittering in echo of the decorative trappings of his mount. "Do you see Uncle Charlie out there, Jamie?" he asked his excited son.

"Unca Cholly!" Jamie shrieked, waving his arms and bouncing madly. "Ho'sies!"

Charlotte fretted, "Is he safe up there, Tris?"

"Safer than on the ground, Lottie," Tris said absently, his attention on the parade. *The Royals might be the flashier troop*, he thought, with their horsehair-tailed helmets and scarlet coats, but there was a powerful elegance to the gold-braided shakos and darker colors of the dragoons. It suited Charles: power and elegance, rather than flash.

"He does look lovely, doesn't he, Tris?" Lottie asked at his elbow.

He glanced down at her, schooling his features to show only mild interest. "The blue uniforms are more elegant than the red," he said coolly. "And of course, he does have an excellent seat—which he should after twelve years in the cavalry. One is only surprised that he is not bowlegged."

"Good heavens," Charlotte said. "I hope not!"

She watched the review. Tristan watched Charles.

It was moments like this that Tristan could understand the appeal of the military. It wasn't so much the spectacle of the review, the flash and polish, but the way they all moved together, parts of an entity, each element belonging to the whole. He could almost feel it, in a secondhand sort of way: how the individual could take pride in the regiment, in the control and ritual and obedience to the ones in charge. *It must be lovely*, he thought, *to have orders to follow, and to follow willingly; to have a shared goal and the will to achieve it.*

He wondered if he hadn't made the wrong decision four years ago; if he should have taken his father's offer of a commission in the cavalry. Would he still feel as he did, that he had no future, no reason to go on? Or would the shared goals of these officers and soldiers have been enough to keep him going?

Wryly, he shook his head. It was just a spell cast by the spectacle and panoply before him. He would have been no happier in the military than he was now. He'd never been one to blindly follow orders; his relationship with his father was certainly proof of that. And at least he had Jamie to show for it. The military would not have kept him happy.

What did it do to keep Charles happy?

AFTER the review was over, they bought some chestnuts from a vendor and Tristan broke them up, feeding them carefully to Jamie so that he didn't choke. "Chew," he said sternly, and Jamie chewed until Tristan gave him permission to swallow. Then he pointed over Tristan's shoulder. "Ho'sie!"

They turned to see Charles standing behind them, his hand on Paragon's bridle. "Did you enjoy the show, Jamie?"

"Ho'sies!" Jamie chortled. "So'jers an' ho'sies!"

"Of which the far more important are the ho'sies, correct, James?" Tristan asked his son.

"Ho'sies!" Jamie pointed at Paragon. "Unca Cholly ho'sie!"

"Yes, it is. This is Paragon. Can you say 'Paragon', Jamie?"

"Pahgon," Jamie said obediently. "Pat ho'sie, Unca Cholly!"

"Is it safe?" Charlotte asked again.

"Oh, Paragon is well-named," Charles said. "Jamie will come to no harm. Here." He held his arms out to Tris, who surrendered Jamie to him. Jamie patted the horse's cheek gently and laughed when the horse quivered its skin.

Charles said, "Might I take him up before me?"

Lottie looked anxious, but Tris nodded. "Of course," he said. "He'll be getting his own pony soon enough. I've had him up before—although generally in the country, on one of the milder-mannered hacks."

"Not on the Brat, I hope?" Charles smiled.

"Heavens, no!" Lottie exclaimed. "That horse is beastly. It *bit* my Jenny last week."

"Your Jenny will flirt with him," Tristan said, "and he thinks he's still intact, not a gelding. She's lucky she got away with just a nip." He took Jamie from Charles until his brother-in-law was back in the saddle, then handed him up.

"Oh, be careful, Charlie!" Charlotte said.

Jamie was beatific. When Charles had completed his careful circuit of the parade grounds, he insisted on giving "Pahgon" a kiss to thank him for the ride. Then Charles handed him back to Tristan and promised to see them later after he was finished here.

Tristan and Charlotte made their way back to their carriage. The crowd had dissipated while they waited for Jamie's return, so they were able to get through the few streets around the Horse Guards without difficulty. Jamie chattered the whole time about the ho'sies and Pahgon and Unca Cholly.

"It was kind of your brother to take Jamie up with him," Tristan said diffidently when Jamie's prattle eased.

"Charlie is a very kind person," Lottie agreed. "I find it so difficult to comprehend what kept him in the military this long. I certainly wouldn't like to go through what they must, and to kill people."

"No," Tristan said. "I understand that even for an officer, it's a difficult life. But I suppose it must have its compensations. Camaraderie, a sense of purpose, a sense of being a part of something."

"Mm, perhaps." Lottie fed Jamie more pieces of roasted chestnut. "And after all, he's been doing it so long. And he's not your average officer, of course, being on Lord Wellington's staff and Lord Castlereagh's and working as liaison with the Germans and all that. I suppose that would be interesting work."

"I suppose," Tristan said doubtfully. "I've heard that Wellington is not easy to work for. Charles is a very patient person."

"Oh, Charlie's about as patient as one can be," Lottie said. "He used to drive Daniel insane. We're both just—what's the word?—phlegmatic. Like our mother."

"Well, Daniel's certainly not that," Tristan said. They had arrived at the carriage; the footman George held the door for Lottie. Tristan handed Jamie up, and then jumped into the carriage, settling in the backward-facing seat across from Lottie. George closed the door and a moment later the carriage moved off.

"Speaking of relatives," Charlotte said, "my great-aunt Callista has invited us to visit next Thursday. She lives out at Richmond. If you've other plans, Charlie has said he'll be happy to escort myself and Ellen."

"Thursday? I suppose...."

"It isn't necessary, Tris," Charlotte assured him. "I know you'd be bored, so if you'd prefer not to go, it's not a problem. Aunt Callista really wants to see Charlie, anyway."

"And she doesn't like me," Tristan said with a twisted grin.

"Well—no. She thinks you're a flibbertigibbet."

"And who am I to argue?" Tristan said lightly. He turned to gaze out the window at the gray January sky.

CHAPTER 10

TRISTAN opened the door to the library and was disappointed to find the room empty and dim, lit only by the fire in the hearth. Right—Charles had taken Charlotte and Ellen to visit some old relative who lived out in Richmond. The past few nights, he'd come home to find Charles in residence, poring over his strange books after a day of following his mentor around or observing patients or whatever it was he did in his physician training. It had been wonderful to sit and talk to him, to discuss what Charles was reading, or pick up whatever book he himself had been reading the night before, or look at whatever it was Charles had set aside for him. He rubbed his head tiredly. He would miss Charles tonight, but perhaps that was for the best. He slept better when he was drunk, and though the conversation was invigorating to the intellect, it wasn't conducive to relaxation. Too often he laid awake, going over in his head what he'd said, what Charles had said, thinking about both the topics of conversation and the unspoken topics that haunted him. And then when he did sleep, it was to dream, and the nightmares were growing worse.

Last night he'd torn himself away from Charles's company at midnight to go upstairs, where he had had Reston leave a bottle of brandy. He'd drunk himself to sleep, anesthetized by the alcohol to the point that at least the dreams didn't wake him.

He'd been no less tired when he'd woken this morning, though.

Charles had never said anything about his drinking, though Tristan knew that he disapproved. Not by any overt expression, but by a faint look of sadness in his eyes whenever Tristan lifted a glass. He supposed he should be angry—how dare Charles judge him—but he wasn't. It made him sad too. And he didn't feel like Charles was really judging him, not the way his father always had. The look had more of a sense of grief, as if Charles really cared about Tristan.

Right.

Tris poured himself a glass of brandy and brought it and the bottle to the desk, and settled behind it in the big chair that Charles usually co-opted. The lamp wick needed trimming, and he did so, then lit the lamp. Using the key on his watch fob, he opened the lower desk drawer and took out his current journal from the set in the deep drawer. He'd always kept a journal. His mother had given him the first, and he remembered how excited he had been to see the blank pages waiting for his pencil. He still had that small, battered leather book, buried deep in the bottom of the pile.

He sat for a moment, his hand on the leather cover of the journal, then opened it to where the piece of blotting paper marked the last entry. It was dated five days ago, and was brief.

Obsession getting worse. Damn'd if I can write about it here; can't leave evidence to hang me. Enough to say my dreams are too vivid. What can I do?

What, indeed?

He leaned his head on his fist, longing to write all that he was feeling, just as he had for the last twenty-some years. In those journals he'd poured out all the grief from the loss of his mother, his anger at his father, his loneliness at being sent away to school; his first fight, his first drink, his first lover. The names of all the subsequent ones, with detailed notes about what each particularly liked, and, eventually, what about each of them he disliked enough to end the relationship. He'd found it easy enough to chronicle those obsessions—why not this one?

Why not?

He laughed, the sound harsh and bitter in his ears. God, why not? For the past six months, he'd been carefully preparing his finances with the intention of ending his life. His plans were set; once Charlotte and the children were comfortably settled in the country, he would return to London and blow his brains out. *That* had never been in question; still wasn't. His lust for Charles—his *doomed* lust for Charles—was only another reason why his plans needn't change. Why shouldn't he pour out his longing, his yearning, for this unattainable paragon? He'd just have to be sure never to mention him by name, so that his reputation would remain unsullied, in case the journal was discovered before he could put his plans into action. And in the end, it would be simple enough to burn the journal before he put the barrel into his mouth.

He opened the inkwell, dipped his pen, and began to write.

IT WAS quite late when Charles and the ladies returned to the townhouse; the footman who opened the door was yawning and his wig was askew. "Go to bed, George, as soon as you've locked up," Lottie said. "We shan't be needing anything else this evening."

"Ma'am," he said, tugging his forelock, and turned back to the door to throw the heavy bolts. "Just as soon as I fetch Mr. Reston and Will."

"George, is Mr. Northwood still up?" Charles asked casually, hiding his dismay. If George was calling on Reston and the other footman, that could mean only that Tristan was drinking again. Damn; but then again it had only been a few days—certainly too soon to break Tristan's habit.

"Aye, sir. In the library, as usual."

Charlotte sighed faintly. "Oh, dear," she said.

"Go on up, Lottie," Charles instructed, then turned to George. "There's no point in disturbing Mr. Reston. You and I should be sufficient to get Mr. Northwood to bed. Lottie, light the candles in the upper hall; I'll snuff them after we get Tristan tucked up."

"Certainly," Lottie acquiesced.

Charles rapped lightly on the library door, then opened it. The lamp on the desk guttered low, illuminating Tristan's dark head as he sprawled half-on the desk, his fingers curled around an empty glass. The equally empty bottle lay on the floor beside the desk.

Tristan opened his eyes and said blearily, "Bloody brandy's gone."

"I see that," Charles said.

"You weren't here to talk to," his brother-in-law went on, his voice accusing. He raised his head and glared at Charles.

"No, I wasn't. But I'm here now."

"I'm drunk," Tristan retorted. "Bloody buggering good that does now."

"I suppose it doesn't."

"Still, I'll sleep tonight, I s'pose."

"I s'pose you will."

"Don't bloody fucking mock me, you arrogant prick!" Tristan roared.

Charles felt more than heard George, behind him, step back further out into the hall. "I beg your pardon," he said coolly.

Tristan stared at him a long moment, then said in a low voice, "Ballocks." Shaking his head, he sat back in the chair and stared at the desk a moment. No, not at the desk, but at a small book lying there. With an audible sigh, he reached down and opened a drawer in the desk, setting the book inside before closing it, and with the overly careful movements of the inebriated, locked the drawer. Then he rose from the chair, leaning heavily on the desk a moment before stumbling toward the door.

Charles caught his arm as he fumbled past him. "Tris," was all he said, but Tristan froze, not looking at him, but staring bitterly out into the hall. Then something, some tension, some repressed tautness, drained out of him and he slumped against the wall. "Ballocks," he muttered again, then rubbed his hand over his eyes. "Sorry, Charlie. I didn't—you weren't—sorry."

He closed his fingers around Tristan's elbow, and drew it over his shoulder. "Come on, lad, let's get you upstairs." He nodded at George, who took his other arm and guided them to the stairs.

In Tristan's room, he dismissed George with a smile and closed the door, turning back to where Tristan sat on the edge of the bed, his hands limp in his lap and his face expressionless. "Let's get you to bed," he said softly.

A deep shudder wracked Tristan's lean frame, and he covered his face with his hands. Concerned, Charles murmured "Tris?" and crouched beside him, his hand on Tristan's knee. "Are you all right?"

"I'm drunk," Tristan said, the words muffled.

"I know."

"I'm always bloody drunk. Do you know that? Ale for breakfast, wine with dinner, brandy before bed. Last night I went drunk to bed again. It was the only way…."

"Only way what?"

"Only way to sleep."

"Tris…."

Tristan laughed, the sound harsh. "In the words of the Bard: 'I have bad dreams'."

"What about?"

This time the laugh was very nearly a sob. "Oh, I can't tell you about that. Least of all you."

"What can you tell me?"

The other man rubbed his face again. "I have forty thousand pounds in the Funds," he said matter-of-factly. "Not specifically me: they're in a trust held for Charlotte and Jamie. I have the interest from it during my lifetime."

"Was this something your father set up?" Charles probed. Was this what made Tristan so bitter? That his wealth was not his own, but locked into a trust, as if he could not be trusted to manage it like a man?

"My father?" Tristan laughed. "Oh, hardly. I don't know what his financial arrangements for Jamie are, although as long-headed as he is, I'm sure he has some. No, *I* built this for them. Once Lottie and I married we had more than enough income for our living expenses so I invested the excess. I was lucky. And in the last few years I've sold off whatever assets that weren't necessary, and invested that. So I wanted you to know: Lottie will never be left bankrupt by me."

"I never thought it could happen," Charles said gently.

"I wanted you to know. I'm not as useless as all that." Tristan hiccoughed quietly. "I'm a sad, pathetic excuse for a man but I'm not completely useless."

"Who says?" Charles demanded, his ire rising.

"Everyone. It's a fact. I'm surprised you haven't heard." Tristan began unwrapping his cravat. "Everyone knows it—Tristan Northwood, womanizer, drunk, fool. Don't trust him with your women, your liquor or your money." He dropped the cravat on the floor and began on the buttons of his waistcoat.

Charles tugged on Tristan's boot. "Pull your foot up," he instructed, then he went on, "I've heard nothing of the sort. Most people speak well of you, at least nowadays. Of course I can't deny that I've heard stories of your antics when you were single, but you've steadied since Jamie was born." One Hessian off, he reached for the other.

"'Antics'." Tristan snorted, and pulled off his waistcoat. "That's a generous term."

"They weren't much more than that," Charles pointed out. "Games you played. No one but you was ever hurt by them."

"Pure luck, I assure you," Tristan sneered. He leaned back on his hands as Charles pulled off his stockings. "Well, Mountjoy, if you're ever in need of a position as a valet, I shall be happy to write you a reference."

"Thank you," Charles said mildly. "If you'd kindly get up?"

Tristan obeyed, hanging onto the bedpost for balance. Charles turned down the bed and helped him get into it, still in shirt and trousers, and folded the blankets over him. Tristan lay back on the pillows, his expression suddenly lost and lonely. "Charlie?" he whispered.

Charles smoothed his tumble of hair back off his forehead. "Go to sleep, Tris. Sweet dreams."

Tris caught Charles's hand and held it a moment, then jerked it to his mouth for a quick kiss on the fingers. Then he thrust it away as if it offended him. "Not likely," he said grumpily, then he rolled over, his back to Charles.

Obviously dismissed, Charles went to the connecting door. "Good night, Tris."

There was no response. Charles opened the door and went into his room.

Tristan woke with his usual aching head and a vague memory of speaking to Charles last night—in the library? In his bedroom? His vision seemed to flicker between the two locations. Had Charles helped him to bed last night? God, had he *said* anything? Why did he seem to remember the touch, the taste of Charles's skin against his lips? He groaned aloud. Could he possibly have been so *stupid* as to actually *touch* Charles?

He sat up abruptly, startling Reston and sending his head to pounding. "Reston," he said curtly. "Is Major Mountjoy in his room?"

"No, sir," Reston said in puzzlement. "He went down to breakfast an hour or so ago, and I believe he was going down to his regimental headquarters. Something about a letter from his old company commander. He did not share the details." He lifted Tristan's dressing gown for Tristan to slide his arms into. "Do you wish me to shave you now, sir?"

"Yes," Tristan said, and went to sit in the chair. Reston lathered him up and started shaving; Tristan closed his eyes and let the daily ritual soothe him. He couldn't have said anything to Charles; he was apparently unhurt, which he was sure he would not have been had he accosted Charles as he suspected he might have. Surely even calm Charles would have reacted violently to overtures from another man? He was a soldier, and used to physical force, and such a thing would impinge upon his honor, wouldn't it? He groaned again.

"Nearly done, sir," Reston said softly. "When I am finished, would you like something for your headache?"

"Do we have any of that tea stuff Major Mountjoy supplied?" Tristan asked.

"Yes, sir. In fact, the major gave me some more this morning. He said he thought you might rise with another headache."

Tristan frowned. "He did?"

"Yes, sir." Reston hesitated, then said, "I was not awakened by either of the footman to assist you last night. I apologize for not being here when you went to bed."

Tristan snorted. "Major Mountjoy and George tucked me in, Reston, so I was well tended. Aside from sleeping in my clothes again." He glanced down at his wrinkled trousers.

"We'll take care of that, sir." Reston left him to go lay out fresh clothing for Tristan.

Tris stared at himself in the mirror over the dressing table. Nothing new there; same old face, same old hair. Same old Tris. No outward sign of perversion, of sodomy, of unnatural lusts.

Why did these emotions not feel perverse at all, but natural and *right*? He'd always thought that sodomy was the worst of the sins, but he longed for Charles in a way he'd never wanted any of the women he'd had.

He'd always wanted to fall in love. What mockery it was that when he did, it was with a *man*.

The thought stunned him. Was it love, not just lust? Was he truly in love with Charles? In love with the one person he could never be with, could never share a life with, could never even admit his feelings for?

God, Fate was a bloody *bastard*.

CHARLES still hadn't returned when Tristan left for his appointment at Angelo's, nor did he show up there or at Jackson's later, as he sometimes did. After his bout, Tristan washed up and joined Gibson at Jackson's fireside, taking the pint of ale his friend had kept for him and settling in one of the big armchairs. "You're still quick enough," Gibson observed, "but you tire more easily. You need to put on some weight. Jackson thinks you don't eat enough beef."

The very thought made Tris nauseous, and he sipped at his ale. "I eat enough," he said shortly. "Just because you and our host tip the scales at sixteen stone…."

"I don't weigh sixteen stone," Gibson said, snorting.

"Bloody hell you don't," Tris retorted. "And at least he has the excuse of most of it being muscle."

"Yes, well, you can't weigh much more than twelve or thirteen, and you're bloody near six foot, Tris. It's just not healthy. Not in a man your build. It ain't... manly."

"P'raps I should take myself off to a madge house, then," Tristan said angrily. "*If* I knew where one was, which I *don't*."

"No reason you should," Gibson said, startled. "And I'm not making accusations, Tris. Just worried about you. God knows you're no molly. Not like...."

"'Like'?" Tris echoed.

Gibson leaned closer and dropped his voice. "Willoughby," he whispered. "There's a madge house on King Street, and I'll *swear* I saw him going in there."

Gibson's mistress had a house on King Street, so it was likely. "King Street?" Tris said, schooling his voice to a deliberately lazy drawl. "Slumming, was he?"

"Bloody bastard," Gibs said, laughing. "Nothing wrong with King Street!"

"Just the neighbors." Tris drained his ale. "Well, if you and Jackson are so concerned about my weight, you can buy me that beefsteak. And you can tell me more about Willoughby while you're at it. I thought he was betrothed to Lady Simpkin's niece?" And a good pair they were, the niece being as pallid and uninteresting as Willoughby was. He considered it. Yes, he could imagine Willoughby in a madge house. He had only had a vague idea what went on in one, but Willoughby struck him as the kind that would let a man do *that* to him, let another man take him over and command him. The thought should have disgusted him, did disgust him when he thought of Willoughby. But if the tables were turned and it was *Charles* commanding, taking.... He shuddered in sudden, fierce desire.

"Yes, pretty horrifyin', ain't it?" Gibs said. "Of course, if it were a choice between a sweet molly-boy and Miss Simpkin? Don't know that I wouldn't run off to the place myself."

They laughed loudly and changed the subject until they were sitting at a corner table in a nearby pub. After the waiter had taken their order, Tris said casually, "So which house is the madge house? I hope it's not too close to Sukey's—otherwise casual passersby might think *you* were the one attending."

"Oh, it's down the street, four or five houses. The one with the blue shutters?"

"That? I thought that old retired general or admiral or something lived there." Tris took a sip of ale.

"He did, but he died about two years ago. The house stood empty for a six-month, but a couple bought it after that. I had the misfortune to meet them once; they've no presence at all. Cits, no better. It's supposed to be a private residence, and the visitors their guests, but they have the most rum sorts for friends, if so. And then Willoughby—the man won't acknowledge anyone not of the ton, let alone a rum pair like that. I'd thought of reporting it to the authorities, but they're quiet enough, and we've never had problems with them. No business of mine what a man does with his drawers down." He glanced up as the waiter produced plates of beef swimming in juice and garnished with red potatoes. "Here you are, Tris. This will put meat on your bones."

Tris regarded his plate dubiously, then shook his head and speared a potato with his fork. "Most people would report it," he said, and bit into the potato. It was delicious, cooked to perfection, with a savory note from the beef juice. Too bad he wasn't that hungry.

Gibson shrugged. "Not sayin' I approve. Church says it's wrong, it's wrong. But it's also none of my business. Not any more than a man addicted to the drink, or to laudanum—it's a perversion just like those. As long as no one gets hurt by it, it's none of my business." He waved his knife at Tris. "I wouldn't have said anything to anyone except you or Berks, you know. Those poor sods have enough trouble as it is. And I'm too softhearted to want deaths on my conscience."

"I know," Tris said. "Poor sods."

THE street was quiet in the midnight dark, but there were lights ablaze in the house with the blue shutters. Tris had the hackney driver pull up two houses down and pretended to watch the house they'd stopped at, though its windows were dark. "Lookin' for somethin' specific, guv'nor?" the hackney driver asked from above.

"No," Tristan said, his voice muffled by the scarf wrapped around his face and neck. "Just—observing."

"Right," the jarvey snorted, but shut the trap door anyway.

They'd only sat there a few minutes when a slim figure turned the corner, tapping casually along the sidewalk with a jaunty swing of his cane. He slowed as he approached the carriage, then studied the side panel and the open window a moment before approaching. In the flicker of the hackney's sidelights, Tris saw a young, handsome face above a fashionably tied cravat, slender hands in faultless gloves, and a form swathed in an expensive greatcoat. All the hallmarks of a member of the ton, but Tris was familiar with most of them, and this was no gentleman he knew.

The man came up to the carriage and rested his gloved hand next to where Tris gripped the sill nervously. "Are you waiting for someone, sir?" The voice was low, silky, and unmistakably Cockney.

"No. Thank you."

In the dim light, Tris couldn't tell the color of the man's eyes, only that they were light and lustrous. The dark lashes flicked downward, and the man withdrew his hand, only to draw his glove off slowly, and return the hand to the window, settling gently on Tris's kid-covered one. "Are you certain?" the man said softly, and his naked fingers slid up Tristan's hand to brush gently over the bare skin of his wrist. "I might be one you didn't even know you was lookin' for. Why don't you step down from there and come wif me? I knows a place as is quite comfortable." The curious mixture of polite language and obvious lower-class antecedents only added to the man's appeal. Tristan shivered.

"No, thank you," he said again, but his voice shook. He knew he should order the jarvey to drive on, but something kept him pinned in place. It was as if the light touch of the man's fingers were a vise holding his hand to the edge of the window.

"It's a cold night to be sitting out here what when there's a warm spot just a few feet away," the man purred. "A warm spot and seems like I could p'raps make it warmer."

"I am quite warm enough," Tristan choked out.

The fingers stroked the skin of his forearm again. "Aye, sir," the man murmured. "I can feel it. So warm. A fire in you. Like to 'eat myself at that fire, I would."

"How would you do that?" Tristan whispered unwillingly, his voice hoarse.

"Well, that's a question, innit?" A flash of teeth in the shadows and a low rumble of laughter. Tristan shuddered as the blood left his head to pool somewhere south. He shifted awkwardly.

The man noticed and his grin widened. "Like me to tell you, would you, then?"

Tristan swallowed, then whispered, "Yes...."

"First thing I'd do, is I'd climb up into that 'ack with you," the man said, lowering his voice so that the jarvey couldn't hear and stepping close to Tristan's fingers. Tris could feel his breath through the kid; it curled in gilded mist in the dim flickering light. "I'd open up that lovely greatcoat of yours and snuggle in close. When me fingers was warm enough, I'd start on the buttons of your trousers—so many buttons, might take me a long time. Then I'd put my 'ands in there, under the buttons. Nice warm 'ands, nice warm fingers. But you—ah, you'd be 'ot, then, wouldn'tcha? Thick, 'ard, 'ot. But my mouf? It's 'otter, I swan." He met Tristan's dazed eyes and licked his lips. They shone wet. "I'd show you," the man went on. "Put my mouf on that 'ot prick of yours, take you down while my nice warm fingers was warmin' up your stones."

Tristan had thought it was freezing outside, but in the hack it was anything but cold. Sweat beaded on Tristan's forehead, and he fumbled with his free hand at his cravat to loosen it. His trousers were suddenly too tight, his legs trembling, his breath sharp and quick.

The demon at the door smiled wickedly and kept talking, telling Tristan all the evil, delicious things he would do. Although he touched nothing but the back of Tristan's wrist, it was as if he were in the carriage, running his hands over Tristan's body, touching him intimately. Tristan closed his eyes.

That was worse. With his eyes closed, he imagined that Charles was there, sitting beside him, doing all the things that wicked Cockney voice was saying.

"And then when we was both all toasty, then I'd do me own buttons," the wicked voice said, soft and irresistible. "Slide me trousers down to me knees and lean over that facin' seat, and guide that 'ot prick right in. You'd like that, wouldn'tcha, guv? I'm tighter than any woman. 'Otter, too. And stronger—you can fuck me just as 'ard as you like, and never worry. I likes a good 'ard fuck, I do."

Tristan's arse tightened at his words, and a fresh rush of arousal flushed his cheeks and neck. He didn't want to fuck this stranger. He didn't want to fuck anyone. He wanted—oh, *God*, what he wanted... Charles. "No," he said involuntarily, and the stranger grinned again.

"Oh, so's like that, then?" he said in that wicked, husky-smooth voice.

"No!" Tristan jerked his hand away from the window. He fumbled in his greatcoat pocket and pulled out a crown, thrusting it at the man outside.

"For your time," he gasped, then he pounded on the roof of the hack with his cane. "Drive on!" he shouted, flinging himself back against the battered squabs. He was panting wildly, as if he'd been running. Behind him he heard the man laughing as the hack trundled away.

The roof trap flipped open. "Where to, guv'nor?" the jarvey asked.

"Hyde Park," Tristan said, giving him the first destination his tumbled thoughts came up with.

"Aye, sir," the jarvey said, and flipped the trap door closed, leaving Tristan alone. He curled up over his aching cock, half-terrified, half-mad with lust, not for the stranger that had just been speaking to him, but for the man he knew he couldn't have. "God," he whispered, and the stranger's last words came back to him: *"Oh, so's like that, then...."*

Yes. Exactly like that. Charles's hands, Charles's mouth, Charles's prick, Charles holding him down on the opposite seat, his own trousers down around his knees, Charles holding him, thrusting into him, Charles's weight on him, holding him down.

Involuntarily his hand closed over his trousers, over the hard, aching ridge of his erection; closed, squeezed, his movements frantic, blind and desperate. He jerked back against the filthy cushions, crying out as he spent, still buttoned up. "Charles," he wept. "Charles."

By the time the hack had rattled through the dark streets to Hyde Park, Tristan was mopping the tears from his face with his woolen scarf and struggling to put his mind equally at rights. Finally, he rapped again at the roof and asked to be set down at Piccadilly and Park Lane. The jarvey obliged and Tristan paid his shot, careful to keep the scarf around his face so that the jarvey wouldn't be able to identify him later.

Shame. It wasn't a feeling he was used to. All the mischief he'd got up to before and since his marriage had been marked by anger or boredom, not shame, and this time he hadn't even *done* anything—nothing except spend, and God knew he'd done plenty of that in the past, and at least this time he'd been alone and how bad was that, coming like a schoolboy in his first pair of long trousers?—and he'd never felt shame like this, for what had just happened. Because in the end, it was Charles, and he didn't deserve this, didn't deserve to be thought of in the same sentence as that, that whore who'd just been speaking to him, but God was he any better, thinking of Charles taking him that way, just the way that man had described. Was he any better?

He walked down Park Lane past his turning and kept going, walking several blocks out of his way before finally finding his way back to his own door. He stared up at it. There was a light in the library, Charles no doubt still sitting over his books, and he felt a deep, heartbreaking longing to go to him, to sit at his feet and let him pat his hair and then take him up, and kiss him, and love him.

Who was he fooling? Charles would *flatten* him if he had any inkling of the tenor of Tristan's thoughts.

He went up the steps and the footman opened the door. Tris nodded at his "Good evening, sir," and went straight up the stairs without even looking at the closed library door.

CHARLES glanced up from his book at the sound of the footman's voice and the subsequent closing of the front door. He waited a moment, expecting Tris to come into the library, but heard instead his footsteps on the stairs. He frowned, rose, and went to the library door. "George?" he said.

The footman glanced over at Charles. "Sir?"

"Was that Mr. Northwood?"

"Yes, sir."

"Was he all right, George?"

"Well, sir." George looked uncomfortable. "No, sir, not really. Looked like he'd had a shock. Pasty, like."

"Yes. Thank you." Charles nodded and closed the door again, leaning back against it and thinking. What had happened? Tristan usually at least glanced in if Charles was still up, and it was barely past midnight, hardly late by Tristan's standards. He was torn between wanting to see what was wrong and wanting to abide by Tristan's apparent wish to be alone—his concern battled with his courtesy.

Courtesy won out, keeping him in the library for another half hour, but he found it impossible to concentrate on his studies and closed up shop before the clock struck the half-hour. When he stopped at Tristan's door, he heard nothing, but there were voices in the little sitting room at the end of the hall. He scratched gently on the door.

"Come in," Charlotte's voice called.

He obeyed. His sister and Ellen were playing cards. "You're up late," he observed.

"I wanted to get Tristan's opinion on the dinner we're hosting Tuesday next," Charlotte said absently, discarding.

"Didn't you hear him come up?" Charles asked curiously.

"Oh, yes, twenty minutes ago or so," Lottie said. She waited until Ellen had drawn a new card, then said, "He wasn't feeling well so he went to bed early."

"I don't think he's at all well, Lottie."

"No, I don't think so either." She studied her cards, then drew another. "Do you think he should see a physician? Other than you, I mean?"

Her casual dismissal of Tristan's condition irked Charles. "Don't you even care that your husband is ill, Charlotte?"

She glanced up in surprise. "Oh, I have angered you!" she said, startled.

"Yes, you have," he retorted. "This is your husband we're talking about! Don't you care that he is unwell?"

"Well, of course," she said. "But it's rather late to be calling a physician, isn't it? And I'm not at all sure he's *physically* unwell, anyway, Charlie. It's probably just another one of his headaches."

"Now, Lottie, you know we discussed that perhaps his headaches have a physical cause," Ellen said anxiously. "Charles is right to be concerned."

"Well, it's quite half-past twelve, if not later. I hardly think we should be sending George or whatever-his-name-is out for a physician at this hour. Perhaps your friend MacQuarrie would be willing to examine Tris in the morning. Assuming he permits it, which knowing Tris, I doubt."

"I sometimes wonder how you can be my sister," Charles said sharply.

She quirked an eyebrow. "You got all the sensibility, Charlie. You know that. Mama always said so." She laid down her cards and hoisted herself to her feet to give him a hug. "Darling Charlie, of course I care about Tristan. He's my husband, and my very good friend. I just don't *worry* about him the way you do. I don't see the point. He's been suffering from some malaise or other the past six-month, but it never seems to be *serious*." She studied Charles's eyes frankly. "I think he's just unhappy, Charlie. When he's happy again, he'll be fine. And I can't help him with that."

"You won't even try," Charles said bitterly.

"Charlie, Tris doesn't want me to...."

"Of course he does. Did you ever think that if you had paid the least bit of attention to Tris, that he wouldn't be this unhappy? Did you ever consider *his* feelings instead of your own?"

"Charles, that's not fair." Ellen began.

"No, Ellen," Charlotte said calmly, "Charlie is right. I don't pay Tris enough attention. But he doesn't pay me any attention, either. He and I have little in common at the best of times, but we have worked out a comfortable compromise, I believe. At least, it always worked before. If I knew what it was that happened six months ago, I would be happy to help Tris resolve it. But he won't talk to me about that. And I have asked him. He said it was nothing." She tilted her head and gave Charles that birdlike look. "I hoped he would talk to you about it, but apparently he doesn't feel comfortable enough with you to do so."

That hurt. It was true, but it hurt. "I have tried to be a good friend to Tristan, Charlotte," Charles said stiffly.

"I am not saying anything other," Charlotte replied. "I know you have. But it's rather up to Tristan, isn't it?" She patted his chest gently. "Go to bed, Charlie. Go riding with Tristan in the morning and see if you can get him to talk to you. Then you'll both feel better."

Charles closed his eyes, letting his head sag. Then he sighed. "What am I to do, Lottie?"

It was a rhetorical question, but she answered it anyway. "Go to bed, Charlie."

He nodded and left them, going to his room. The fire was banked, but the room was warm enough; he shed coat and boots and set them aside for Reid to deal with in the morning. He'd long ago trained his batman-cum-valet to retire at a reasonable hour; the day that Charles needed help undressing was the day he had an arm in a sling or something equivalent. But tonight he almost wished Reid were here, and talking the way he'd often heard Reston chatting with Tristan: it would be something to distract him from his worry. He peeled off his shirt and drew a nightshirt over his head, and just before he shed his trousers, he went to the connecting door and turned the knob, drawing the door open. The room was dark, the curtained bed a solid black square in the scant illumination from the banked fire in the fireplace.

"Tris?" he said in a low voice.

There was silence a moment, then Tristan responded, "What is it, Charles?" His voice sounded drained and weary.

"Charlotte said you were unwell. I was wondering if there is anything I could do?"

"No," Tristan said. "Just go to bed. I'll be better in the morning."

"Shall we ride tomorrow? Red sky tonight says it will be fair."

A long moment of silence, then the tired voice again. "If you like."

"Good," Charles said. "Goodnight, Tris."

"Goodnight, Charles."

He hesitated a long moment, then quietly shut the door.

CHAPTER 11

CHARLES knocked the snow off his feet before stepping into the foyer of the house that had become home in the last six weeks. Will, the footman, shivered as he closed the door behind him. "Foul night out, sir," he said.

"No question," Charles said, nodding. It was—cold, the snow mixed with rain and a stiff wind to drive the stuff into heretofore-unsuspected gaps in one's outerwear. And he'd had to walk a mile through the filthy streets of Spitalfields before he could find a hack; fortunately the foul weather had kept the criminal elements indoors tonight.

The hospital had been more crowded than usual, of course; not only with more ill people in the bloody belly of February, but with those simply looking for a sheltered place to spend the night. Sorting them out wasn't easy; almost all of them had some sort of catarrh or cough, but not all of them were interested in having a doctor look at them. Suspicion of the medical profession was in full flower as usual, despite the nasty weather.

He shrugged out of his greatcoat and scarf and handed them and his hat and gloves to Will. "Mr. Northwood still out?"

"No, sir. He's been in the library most of the evening; I think he just went up to say goodnight to Master Jamie."

"Ah, then he'll likely be down again. I hope there's a fire there?"

"Yes, sir, nice and hot, and I brought tea in not a half hour past."

"Good."

"Shall I go up and light the fire in your room after I've locked up, sir?"

"Yes, thank you." Charles took the cloth Will handed him and wiped his boots, then gave the cloth back and went into the library while Will locked up. It was as warm in there as advertised, the candelabra on the mantel blazing with light and the oil lamp on the desk casting a fine clear glow on the blotter.

There was a small leather-bound book open there, the kind that would fit into a man's pocket, with a folded sheet of paper stuck in it as a sort of bookmark. Curious, Charles set his cup on the blotter and turned the book around to glance down at the page. It was a journal entry in Tris's hand, dated with the day's date. He caught only a glimpse of the first words beneath the date, then turned the book away, not wishing to invade Tristan's privacy. Then the words he'd glanced at sank in, and his blood went cold. He turned the book again, gripping the front edge of the desk in shock and pain.

I can bear it no longer. I can't live like this anymore. It must be tonight.

Everything is ready; the trust is solid, all loose ends have been taken care of. I will not be leaving my family with nothing. I trust my father and Charlotte's and Charles to guard them and to look out for their future. The trust will support them comfortably and leave a legacy for my children, even above that which awaits Jamie as my father's heir.

It's been so long since I first crafted this plan, so many months of preparations. I wish that I could have stuck with the original; that Charlotte and the children were safely home at Lilac Cottage, far away from the ton, far away from the scandal that will follow my death.

I wish I knew if she carried a girl or a boy. But I cannot wait any longer. The dreams are worse, when I dare sleep, and even brandy does not help me sleep. I am going mad.

Charlotte deserves better than I can give her. The best I can do for her is to remove myself from her life.

My hesitancy about abandoning Charlotte so close to her time is assuaged by the fact that Charles is here. He will shield her from the worst of the scandal and his presence will calm her so that her health and the health of the child will not be endangered. She has never needed me, *but he is a different story. I can depend on Charles.*

Charlie.

My Charlie.

My God, why? What is it about the man that so destroys any sense of calm I might once have had? Foolish question. It is not right that I should feel these strange emotions when I think of him. He is a man, not a woman, a man who would be horrified if he knew of the feelings I hide. This book comes with me tonight to Boodle's and I will burn it before I take up my pistol. No one must ever know of the shame, lest it reflect on him, and that is nothing I would wish upon him. He has never been anything but a true, honest friend to me and to my wife. It is not his fault that I feel this lust. Not his fault. Only mine.

The list of my sins is so long

The entry ended there. Charles reread it, sick and hoping that he'd misread it the first time. The words were unchanged, so with trembling hands he lifted the folded sheet. It was a penciled draft of a letter, addressed to Charlotte.

My dear Lottie,

I regret that I have put you in such an untenable situation. Please know that if I had seen any other alternative, I would not have embarrassed you so terribly. It is only knowing that you have Charles to guard you that gives me the strength to set you free.

The documents you will need are in the top drawer of my desk in the library, in a folder marked "Charlotte." This will give you all the information you need about the trust I have set up for you and the children, and contains a copy of my will, which is in the hands of my solicitor. His name and address are also in that folder. I have named Charles executor; I trust him to have your and the children's best interests at heart. Please convey my deepest apologies to him for foisting such responsibility on him; if I were not convinced of his sincere affection for you I would have made other arrangements.

Please understand that what I have chosen to do does not reflect on you in any way. You have been the best wife I could have asked for. My respect and affection for you are boundless. I only wish I could have been a better husband to you, and a better father to Jamie. You both deserve so much more than I have given you, more than I would ever be able to give you. If there is one good thing I have ever done, it is my contribution to the wonder that is Jamie. I love him dearly, and take solace in the fact that he is too young to be distressed at my absence. Please, when he is older, tell him that his father loved him too well to inflict himself on him.

I trust that my father will accept Jamie far better than he ever did me. He will not find him *a disappointment. Nevertheless, I pray that you will guard against any inadvertent cruelty my father may visit on him; I absolve him of deliberate evil, but know too well how sharp words can cut. I would protect Jamie from unkindness, as far as is possible.*

Forgive me.
Your loving,
Tristan

He folded the letter and put it back into the journal, his mind numb and his gut roiling with horror. He stood holding the little book a moment, then shoved it into his coat pocket and turned to go after Tris. But Tristan was standing in the doorway, his face black with rage.

"What the *devil* do you think you're doing?" He slammed the door and had Charles's cravat in his fist before Charles had a chance to blink. "How *dare* you read my private correspondence?"

"How dare *you* contemplate this travesty?" Charles jerked loose, equally furious. "How dare *you*?"

"It's none of your business." Tristan was shaking. "Give me back my journal, you bastard!"

"No," Charles snapped.

Tristan hit him, the well-trained blow knocking Charles back against the desk. Charles grabbed his fist as he drew it back for another shot, and Tristan kicked Charles's feet out from under him. He went sprawling, his shoulder striking the edge of the desk, with Tristan atop him, his hands around Charles's throat. "You bastard," Tris snarled in fury, "you *bloody* bastard!"

Charles fought back, and it was the dirty fighting he'd learned in Spain, not the boxing skills he'd picked up at Jackson's, breaking Tristan's grip, shoving him off him and aiming a furious fist at Tristan's solar plexus. But Tristan had apparently learned some dirty moves of his own; he dodged Charles's blow and twisted out of range. Charles barely evaded a knee to the groin, and his head rang with a sneaky blow to the ear. They grappled in silence, the only sounds the grunts as a blow hit home or the scrape of furniture pushed across the oak floorboards as they rolled around, determined to hurt each other. At least Charles wanted to hurt Tristan. He suspected, in the corner of his mind that was not irrational with fear and rage, that Tristan fully intended to kill him.

They knocked over a small table and a bowl of potpourri went crashing to the carpet and rolling away, leaving rose petals and scented leaves strewn on the rug. Charles managed to get Tristan pinned underneath him, his arms dragged up over his head and held in place, Charles's shins straddling Tristan's thighs and holding him down. "Damn it, Tristan!" Charles roared. "What the bloody hell is the matter with you?"

Tristan didn't answer, just squirmed, trying to break Charles's hold. But he was tiring, Charles could see; his breath came in quick, shallow pants, his limbs trembling with strain, his face pale and sweaty. "Let me go, God damn you," he gasped.

"So you can kill me?" Charles retorted.

"Yes, damn you!" That outburst seemed to take the last of Tristan's strength; he sagged under Charles, going limp against the carpet. Charles shifted off him so that his knees rested on the carpet on either side of Tristan's legs instead of directly on Tris. He didn't release Tristan's hands until he was sure Tristan wasn't going to hit him again, then sat back on his heels.

"Damn you," Tristan whispered bleakly, turning his head so his cheek rested against the wool rug and throwing an arm over his head.

"Why, Tris?" Charles asked, his voice rough with pain, his hands clenched on his thighs.

"Why what? Why did I hit you?"

"No. You know what I'm talking about."

Tristan turned to look at him, his eyes glittering silver, his fine mouth drawn into an aristocratic sneer. "I hit you," he said bitterly, as if deliberately misunderstanding Charles, "because you were nosing about in matters that don't concern you. I thought you would prefer it to my calling you out, though I'm perfectly willing to settle it that way as well, if you have the courage."

"Suicide by brother-in-law?" Charles asked. "I don't think so, Tris."

"Bugger you," Tristan said harshly.

Charles reached down and laid his palm on Tristan's groin, feeling him already half-hard and stiffening. Tristan panted shallowly, his sneer gone, his eyes wide and shocked. "Now we get to it," Charles said quietly.

Tristan shoved at his shoulders, trying to scramble away. Charles caught his wrists. "Tristan," he said, his voice firm, as if he were dealing with a recalcitrant horse or dog, "Tristan."

"Let me go," Tristan muttered, his color high. He wouldn't meet Charles's eyes. "For God's sake, Charlie, let me go."

"No," Charles replied. "Not until I'm certain you won't—" He was going to say, "Hurt yourself," but Tristan had lunged forward to kiss him, his mouth bruising on Charles's. Charles felt a sting and tang of blood on his lip, then Tristan's tongue was sweeping into his mouth and he was lost in the heat and hunger of Tristan's kiss.

He didn't remember releasing Tristan's wrists but he must have, because Tristan's hands were in his hair, and his own were running up and down Tristan's back, dragging him close against him.

Tristan tasted of brandy and licorice and Tris; he was warm in Charles's arms and hot in Charles's mouth. He pushed at Charles, and Charles went down on the carpeting, Tristan sprawled over him, his hips against Charles's and his lean thighs between Charles's own. He rocked his groin into Charles's, then dragged his mouth away, staring down at him with shocked eyes. "You've got a cockstand," he accused.

Charles slid his hands down to cup Tristan's arse and pull him hard against him, shifting to rub their erections together. "Of course I bloody do," he growled. "I usually do around you," and he moved one hand to the back of Tristan's head to pull him down into another kiss. This time he took control, exploring the sweet recesses of Tristan's mouth thoroughly before moving to claim the side of Tristan's jaw. He fumbled with the linen cravat binding Tristan's shirt points, pulling the knot loose and dragging the cravat off so that he could explore the long lines of his neck and throat with lips and tongue.

He was just reaching for the buttons on Tristan's trousers when a soft scratching came at the door. "Sir? Major Mountjoy?"

Tristan shoved Charles off him and scrambled to his feet, his eyes wild. Charles stood up and said aloud, "Yes, Will?" moving to stand behind the desk.

The door creaked open and Will peeked in. His eyes widened when he saw the table knocked over and the petals strewn on the floor; he turned to look at Charles and his eyes got even wider. "Sir? Major? Are you all right?"

Tristan had turned his back to Will and was staring down into the fire. Charles raised a hand to his face and winced as his fingers made contact with a swelling jaw. "Fine," he said heartily. "I just walked into a fist. Mr. Northwood is quite handy with his fives."

Tristan barked a laugh. Will looked from Charles to Tristan and said guardedly, "Well, sir, so I understand from what George says about Mr. Northwood's sessions with Mr. Jackson. I've locked up, and lit the fire in your room. I'll be right back with a broom for the potpourri."

"Fine," Charles said. He waited until Will had bowed himself back out the door and closed it behind him, then walked across the room to Tristan and laid his hands on his shoulders. "Are you all right?" he asked quietly.

Again a laugh, this one half sob. "No, of course not. I don't know. I don't know what to think."

Charles rubbed his shoulders gently, his cheek against Tristan's hair. "Well, he'll be back momentarily, so while I think we need to talk, here is probably not the best place. Why don't you go upstairs and get ready for bed? I'll close up shop here and come to you when I'm done."

"No," Tristan said, and Charles's heart stuttered. But then he went on, "Reston is in the habit of dropping in and out of my room, unlike your Reid. I'll come to you." His voice shook.

Charles nodded and turned his head to lay his lips gently on the side of Tristan's throat, breathing in the brandy and licorice scent of his skin. He felt him swallow nervously. "You don't have to," he said softly. "We can leave it at this and just forget it ever happened."

"No," Tristan said. He turned in Charles's arms. "No. Charlie. This... this...." He trailed off, his expression uncertain.

"Yes, I know. Go on. I'll see you upstairs."

He walked to the door to watch Tristan climb the stairs, his head bowed, his fingers clutching the banister. *Wrong*, he thought unhappily. This was wrong. He loved Tristan, wanted Tristan, but not like this. Not, not *broken*. He wanted the arrogant, challenging Tris, the one who raced his horse in Hyde Park, who chased swans, who took punishing blows at Jackson's with a grin on his face. Not this fragile, broken thing.

No, what was wrong was that he *did* want him like this. Wanted the other, true, wanted that for Tristan's sake, but he wanted this Tristan, too. Wanted Tristan however he could have him. He leaned his head against the doorframe and closed his eyes.

"Is Mr. Northwood all right, sir?"

It was Will, his face anxious and embarrassed. Charles stared at him blankly a moment. "He's... tired, Will. I think perhaps he's not feeling well."

"I hope it's not a fever," Will said anxiously. "Lot of fevers goin' about these days, with the cold wet weather and all. Make a man act out of character, they do." He eyed Charles's bruised face.

"I'm sure he'll be fine," Charles said. "I'll check on him in a few minutes, after he's had a chance to get ready for bed. He'll feel better once Reston has him tucked up, I'm sure." He gave Will a brief smile.

"Sir," Will said, with a tug on his forelock, and went into the library, broom and dustpan in hand.

Charles followed him, and while he cleaned up, Charles banked the fire, covered the inkwells, arranged the papers neatly on the desk, and blew out the candles and the oil lamp. Will finished up and bade him good night; Charles responded absently, lost in thought. It was just as he was straightening the papers again in the near darkness that he realized that he was dragging his feet, and shook himself. He'd never been a coward, had faced down charging cuirassiers and irate Wellingtons, but this—this *possibility*—had him terrified.

With a muttered curse, he went upstairs to his bedroom.

THE stairs seemed endless but Tris climbed them doggedly, as shaky as he had ever been after a night of drinking. When he went into his bedroom, Reston was turning down the bed. "Sir?" he said in surprise. "I was under the impression you were going out tonight…?"

"I don't feel well, Reston," Tristan said. His voice was hoarse, as if he'd been crying. He felt like crying. He felt like singing. What was wrong with him? Why was he so frightened when he was so close to getting something he'd wanted for so long? And why wasn't he *more* frightened of facing something so foreign to his experience, instead of this giddy combination of fear and exhilaration?

"If Mr. Northwood will pardon my saying so, you don't look well, either," Reston said. He crossed the room to assist Tristan out of his coat, then helped him out of his clothes and into his nightshirt and banyan. "Shall I send up a pot of tea, or some soup for your supper, sir?"

"No," Tristan said nervously. "No, I don't want anything. I'm just going to read for a few minutes, then I'm going to bed. I shan't be needing you again tonight."

"Thank you, sir," Reston said with a slight bow. "I trust you will feel better in the morning."

"God, I hope so," Tristan muttered. When Reston had left the room, he went to the door and turned the key quietly, then leaned his forehead on the door. *What am I doing?* he wondered. *Do I dare take what comfort Charles is offering? And what exactly* was *he offering?* He shivered with fear—or was it anticipation? Was he ready for this? Did he *dare*?

Of course he did. He drew himself up unsteadily. He was Tristan Northwood. He'd never turned down a dare in his life.

He squared his shoulders and walked into Charles's room, closing the door behind him.

Charles was already in the room, on one knee before the fireplace, adding coals from the scuttle. His coat was over the back of the armchair, and his boots beside the door, but he was otherwise still fully dressed. For a moment Tristan wondered if he should say anything, alert Charles to his presence, but then Charles said over his shoulder, "It's a bit cold in here. I don't want you to take a chill." Then he got up, put the scuttle back in its place on the hearth, and went to the washstand to wash the coal dust from his hands. Only then did he turn and look at Tristan, a faint smile on his face. "I'm glad you decided to come," he said softly, and he crossed the room to stand before him, reaching out to brush his fingers over Tristan's cheek.

Tris leaned into the touch, thinking about all the nights he'd fantasized about this happening, dreaming about Charles touching him gently, lovingly like this. If this were all he could have from Charles it would be all right—just knowing that Charles knew about him and didn't hate him, didn't despise him. Or if he did, that he was still willing to treat Tristan with kindness. "You're too kind to me," he said huskily. "I don't deserve it."

Charles shook his head. "If we only ever received what we deserved, Tris, we'd all be damned to hell in short order."

Tristan laughed humorlessly. "Oh, it's far too late for me," he said. "I'll seek what comfort I can on this earth." He reached up and folded his hands around Charles's face, finding the rasp of beard underneath his palms unbearably erotic. "I want this, Charlie. But I don't know what I'm doing," he confessed unsteadily.

"Don't worry," Charles said. "I do. Do you trust me?"

Tristan laughed, the laugh as shaky as the rest of him. "Usually when people ask that, it's because they're about to do something you won't like," he said. "But—yes, I trust you."

Charles just smiled. His hand slipped from Tristan's cheek to behind his head, cupping his skull and drawing him forward into Charles's embrace. Charles kissed him slowly, carefully, exploring his mouth with tender, licking strokes that warmed like the summer sun on an upturned face. Tristan let out a small sigh, a shudder of desire and hunger and surrender. "I hope you'll like this," Charles murmured, finding Tristan's mouth again. His fingers moved between them, unbuttoning Tristan's banyan, then drawing it and the nightshirt off and tossing them over the chair with his own coat and pulling Tristan back into his arms. Tristan's skin rasped against linen and wool and the brocade and the buttons of Charles's waistcoat, his nakedness against Charles's clothing, and for the first time in a long, long time, he felt small and helpless and *safe*—though he was no smaller than Charles, no weaker than he, and on the verge of exploring something so frightening and alien he should have been frantic with fear.

But like that long ago morning on the balustrade of the balcony four stories above the street, he had moved way past fear... and into *peace*. Charles was the one in control now; he had nothing to do, no decisions to make—it was all in Charles's hands.

Charles moved then, guiding him to the bed without releasing his mouth, until Tristan's thighs bumped against the edge of the mattress, then he stepped back and helped Tris up onto the bed and crawled up beside him. "I promise not to hurt you, and if you tell me to stop, I will stop. We'll just end it there. No regrets, no shame. But I need your trust, Tristan. I need you to have faith that I will not hurt you. Please don't be afraid."

Tristan looked up into those dark, warm eyes and felt something shift inside him. The fear was, if not completely gone, at least diminished to tolerable levels. He essayed a grin. He knew Charles wouldn't expect more than he was capable of giving—his friendship with the man over the last month had shown him that. "Whatever you want, Charlie. I'm yours."

"By God," Charles said, and his eyes went strangely bright, "by God, Tris, you *are* mine, and I *will* take care of you."

"I trust you," Tristan said, "but you're going to have to be patient with me. I've never done this, you see."

"Of course you haven't," Charles said, frowning. "Why would you?"

"Well, there were boys at school who did, who, who *forced* it on other boys, but I always had Gibs and Berks with me, and it never happened to me. And I fought a lot too." He grinned up at Charles. "I still fight a lot."

"Don't fight me tonight, all right, Tris?"

"I won't. I want this, Charlie. I *want* it." It didn't matter any longer if it was wrong, or if it was illegal, or if it was against everything he'd ever been taught. It was what he wanted, and what Charles wanted. And that was enough.

Charles kissed him. "Trust me," he said against Tristan's mouth. He drew Tristan's arms up again, pressing his hands against the spiraled posts of the headboard. "Put your hands around the posts and hold on. Don't let go."

"All right," Tristan said cautiously. "Why?"

"I want you to feel safe, to give you something to hold onto. Besides," he said, his voice turning dark and sweetly wicked, "this way I get to touch you all I want, and you can't stop me unless you make the effort."

Tristan shuddered, not in fear, but in arousal. "My God," he whispered raggedly.

"Do you trust me?" Charles asked again.

"I do."

Charles picked up a length of black silk and bound it around Tristan's head, blindfolding him. The silk smelled like Charles, that warm and strange woodsy-herbal scent, and Tristan, who'd tensed at the beginning of the blindfolding, relaxed again.

"Are you all right?" Charles asked, his voice close to Tristan's ear.

"Yes." He was. It was so strange; he was blind, and even though he could move his hands easily enough, he didn't *want* to; he wanted to do what Charles told him, wanted to be helpless under his hands, and that should have frightened him but it didn't. The fear was gone completely. It was as if he'd given it over to Charles, trusting that those strong, competent hands would hold him safe. "This is odd. Why are you doing this?"

"I don't want you distracted," Charles said. "I don't want you to think. You think far too much, Tris." Then Charles kissed him again, a soft, warm kiss; undemanding, but Tristan felt himself rising, yearning toward that invisible mouth. He caught Charles's lip in his teeth, tugging gently; Charles laughed and pressed him down into the pillows, the warm mouth turned suddenly hot, the searching tongue demanding. Tristan pulled hard against the headboard, needing desperately to touch Charles, to hold him, but subconsciously obeying Charles's instructions not to let go.

Charles broke away, his breath harsh and loud. "You try my will, love. You don't know what you do to me."

"Is it anything like what you do to me?" Tristan shot back, frustrated by his own restraint and the blindfold. "Damn it, Charlie, let me *see*."

Charles laughed, but the sound was joyous, not mocking. "Oh, no, love. Not yet. Tonight is all for you. Just remember—if it gets too much, if you get uncomfortable or frightened—just tell me to stop."

Heart pounding, Tristan lay still in the darkness, his other senses straining. He heard the faint rustle of cloth, then the soft *clink* of a bottle being opened, and suddenly smelled the woodsy scent he associated with Charles. The mattress sank as Charles sat at the foot; then warm, slippery hands settled on his right foot, the fingers strong and gentle as they worked the oil into the sole. "This is eucalyptus oil," Charles said softly as he rubbed. "From Australia. And rosemary oil. An old woman in Portugal told me that the combination relaxes the body and clears the mind. I just like the scent. Do you?"

"It smells like you," Tristan said.

Charles chuckled. "I hope that's a good thing."

"You smell good," Tristan admitted. "I like it. It's… warm, somehow. It makes me feel…."

"Feel?" Charles prompted gently when it became apparent Tristan wasn't going to finish the statement.

"Safe," Tristan whispered.

Charles was silent a moment, then said in a husky voice, "You're safe with me, Tris. You know that, don't you?"

"Yes." Tris let his tension go in a long sigh, letting his body lay limp on the sheets. It was the strangest feeling, being blind; it was as if suddenly all his other senses were that much more acute. His attention focused on where Charles's fingers kneaded his foot, then moved up to gently caress his ankle before working their way up his calf. When he reached Tristan's knee he released him; then Tristan felt his hands on his left foot. The silky warmth of the oil, the gentle strength of Charles's hands: he felt as though each touch reached far beyond the place where Charles's fingers made contact, so that when Charles rubbed his calf, Tristan felt it in his fingers and throat and groin, and when he stroked his knee, he felt it in his toes and shoulders and neck.

Charles kissed the inside of his knee, and the brush of lips startled Tristan, the brief warm, damp pressure shooting directly to his gut. He gasped faintly, and Charles chuckled but said nothing. Instead, he smoothed his hands up Tristan's thighs, sliding down around his hips and over the curve of his buttocks to slip down the backs of his thighs to his knees again. His hands passed so close to Tristan's erect shaft that Tristan felt their warmth and arched his back, anticipating the touch of those warm hands, but it never came. Then the hands went away, a brief kiss touched his hip, and then the sound of the bottle again.

This time it was Tristan's arms that got the attention, from his forearms down to his shoulders. Charles took each hand, one at a time, and gently rubbed the oil into his palms and fingers and wrists, then he lifted and stroked Tristan's arms thoroughly, but again, no farther than his shoulder, first one, then the other, so that his hands and fingers were limp when Charles put them back and closed them again around the posts of the headboard.

Then Charles kissed him, one slick hand curving along Tristan's jaw and slipping down his neck, his fingers stroking, teasing sensation from Tristan's skin. He smoothed along the curve of Tristan's shoulder, then down over his pectoral muscle and paused. Drawing back, he whispered, "Do you like it when you're touched here…?" and his fingers brushed Tristan's nipple.

Tristan's body arched in response. The touch was gentle, but the sensation of the warm, slick fingers was too much. He cried out softly, then went limp again as Charles's hand moved away. "I've never... no one ever...."

There was a moment of stillness, then Charles said in disbelief, "No one's ever touched you there? No one?"

His face burning, Tristan shook his head, his hair scrubbing against the linen of the pillowcase. "Sometimes, when I'm making love, they rub against the woman's skin... it feels good."

"Then why don't you let them touch you there, if it feels good?"

Tristan let out a long sighing breath. "No one ever offered. Besides— my responsibility is their pleasure—it's just a bonus that I take my own."

"My God," Charles said flatly.

Tristan's face grew hotter. "Let me go," he said dully, embarrassed. This wasn't what he wanted. He'd looked for oblivion, not having all his failings thrown in his face. He didn't feel safe anymore; he felt humiliated and trapped. He released the spindles of the headboard and reached for the blindfold.

A pair of hands caught his, and the fingers were each kissed gently before Charles placed them back on the headboard. "Not yet, Tris. Please." Then Charles's palm came down gently on his breast, and his mouth settled on Tristan's again, licking into his and stroking in rhythm with Charles's palm against Tristan's nipple, and he sobbed softly, confused and hurt and hungry.

Charles drew back, resting his cheek against Tristan's. "I'm sorry, love. I didn't mean to bring up anything uncomfortable. I just wanted to please you, not hurt you. But it hurts *me* to know that you've missed out on such a simple, pleasant thing." His palm slid away and his fingers toyed with the stiffened nub, circling it, teasing it.

Then he shifted again and his hand was gone and his cheek; and then Tristan felt the warmth of Charles's breath on his chest and Charles's mouth took the place of his fingers, and this time he wasn't content with stroking, though he was doing that, with his *tongue*, for God's sake. But then his lips closed on the nub, sucking gently, and Tristan bucked again, moaning in pleasure.

Charles's mouth shifted to the other side, playing and suckling there, too, a moment before moving away. "Did you like that?"

"Oh, God...," Tristan moaned helplessly.

Charles chuckled, and bent his head again, his mouth traveling over Tristan's chest and abdomen, tasting his skin. Tristan lay with his hands fisted around the spindles, his body quivering as Charles explored him with hands and mouth and tongue. "So beautiful," Charles murmured, "my Tris, so beautiful...."

His hand trailed down Tristan's hip and over his thigh, curling up to brush between Tristan's legs and cup his ballocks gently. Tristan hissed softly and Charles chuckled. "Never tell me you've never been touched there?"

"No—I mean, yes, of course, but only"—he hesitated—"never by *ladies*. Only...."

"Only whores?" Charles supplied. "Tristan, love, you can say it. I know you don't mean anything by it."

"I don't. I mean, I know I don't, but I don't know what you would think I meant. I don't mean to, to, to say anything to make you think I think...."

Charles chuckled again. "I'm not a whore, Tristan, and I know it, so don't worry about what you say. I'm not going to take anything wrong, and if you say something that *is* wrong, I'm sure enough of myself that I'm not going to be hurt by it. I'll just correct you. Besides, didn't I say this was about you, not me? Don't think about what you say. Just say it. I won't be hurt." His fingers moved over Tristan's testicles and stroked the skin behind them. "So soft," he mused, before shifting his attention back the other direction and taking Tristan's cock in his hand, curling his fingers around it gently. Tristan hissed again in pleasure.

"Wait," he gasped as Charles's hand started to move. Charles stopped, just holding him, and Tristan breathed rapidly, trying to stave off the desire to spend. After a moment, he let out a long, slow breath and said, "Sorry."

"Nothing to be sorry for," Charles said softly. "Are you all right?"

"Yes. It's just... this blindfold makes everything so much more intense."

"That's the point of it, but we haven't even got to the intense part, yet," Charles said in amusement.

"What do you—" Tristan started to ask, but then his cock was surrounded by wet warmth and a stroking tongue and the faintest brush of teeth, and he drove his head back into the pillows in pleasure. "Oh, my God...."

He gave himself over to the luxury, focused only on the feel of Charles's mouth around him and fighting the urge to seek release. He barely realized it when Charles's warm, slick fingers stroked over his nether entrance—it was just another sensation added to the litany—and when those fingers pressed lightly inside, that was just another sensation too. He relaxed automatically, the pleasure outweighing the faint burn of resistant tissue.

And then Charles's fingers brushed over a spot that sent lightning flashing down his spine, and he arched, crying, "Stop! Stop!"

Charles froze, drew back, but only from Tristan's cock. His fingers stopped moving but stayed inside Tristan. "Stop?" he rasped.

Tristan panted, but his hands still obediently clutched the headboard spindles. "Wait," he amended. "Wait."

"I'm not hurting you?"

"No. No. It's just—it's just too much."

Charles leaned forward and brushed a kiss on Tristan's forehead. "You're sweating," he said.

"I don't know why," Tristan gasped. "You're doing all the work."

"Not work," Charles corrected. "Pleasure…," he said and bent to draw Tristan back into his mouth, stroking and sucking as his fingers drew more lightning, a steady series of soft shocks. Tristan was sobbing now, trying to catch his breath, wound up as tight as a watch spring, pulling on the wood posts, arching his hips in rhythm with Charles's mouth and fingers.

Charles released his cock and that helped, but now the discomfort in his arse was gone and the fingers were twisting and rubbing against *that spot*, and Tristan was sure he was going to explode. "I can't," he sobbed, "I can't…."

"You can," Charles whispered in his ear. "You can." And suddenly Tristan was past speaking, past the almost painful urgency, and flying, lost to everything. That strange sense of peace was back, but now it was tied up with his need for release and his trust that Charles would take care of him, that his pleasure was in Charles's hands, and all he waited for was Charles's word….

And it came, soft, against his mouth as Charles bent to kiss him: "Let go," Charles whispered. "Let go."

Tristan screamed into Charles's mouth, and spent, his body bowing under Charles's hands. His orgasm seemed to go on forever, more fierce, more intense than any he ever remembered, a high, wild release that spun him out of control and then crashed him back into his drained, exhausted body. He lay limp a moment; then, overwhelmed, began to weep.

CHARLES slid the blindfold off, then gathered Tristan into his arms, holding him while he wept. He knew that being deprived of any sense during a sensual experience made the experience more intense; his first lover had been a master at games-playing, and he'd tried the blindfolding with Gregory once, and the other man had loved it. He also knew that it would give Tristan the feeling that Charles was in control, and if he later had regrets, it would be easier on Tristan to blame Charles than himself. He didn't want Tristan to blame himself for anything they did together—he only wanted Tristan to relish the experience, but understood that Tristan's upbringing made what they'd done together unacceptable. He sighed. It was so much easier coming from a less structured household the way he and Lottie did; the Mountjoys were rather notorious.

But he hadn't expected Tristan to react so strongly. It was as if everything that had been tied so tightly together had exploded, like canister shot.

He stroked the bowed back gently, noting the prominent shoulder blades, the knobs of the spine, the defined ribs. Tristan was too thin, too frail, pared down to bare essentials like this; he was considerably more fragile than he had been when Charles had arrived. Had he been on this downward track since before then, or had Charles's presence set him sliding? Charles swallowed hard to stave off his own tears and bent to kiss Tristan's hair. "Shh," he whispered lovingly. "Shh… I've got you, love."

Slowly the weeping eased, and Tristan sank bonelessly into sleep. Charles laid him back down on the bed and slipped the nightshirt back over his thin frame, then went to make up the herbal tea he had waiting. When it had steeped long enough, he brought it back and set it on the nightstand, shaking Tris gently awake. "Love?"

Tristan's eyes blinked open and he gazed blankly up at Charles. "My head aches," he said thickly.

"I know. I've brought something to help with that." Charles helped him sit up and cupped his hand around Tristan's to hold the mug. "Drink up."

"This stuff tastes foul," Tristan complained.

"I know. You say that every time, but you know it works. I've added honey to it so it shouldn't be so bad."

Tristan took a sip. "Doesn't help," he growled, but he finished the contents anyway.

"All right," Charles said. "Now I'm going to take you back to your bed, and you're going to sleep. Sleep as long as you like—sleep as long as you have to. You're exhausted, Tris. You've had months of being exhausted."

"It feels like forever," Tris said tiredly. "But Charlie—I dream…."

"You won't dream," Charles assured him. "Not now. Not tonight. I promise."

"I trust you, Charlie." Tris let him help him to his feet, but his legs nearly gave out when he tried to stand. "I don't know what's wrong with me," he complained.

"You're tired, that's all. Put your arm over my shoulder, and I'll hold you up…. There."

Once tucked into his own bed, Tristan let out a long, worn-out sigh. "I'm so tired," he said. "I'm just so tired, Charlie."

"I know, love. Sleep. I'll be here when you wake up."

Tristan froze. "No," he said sharply, all sleepiness gone. "Don't say that. Just—don't. Be here or not, I don't care. Just don't *promise*. Just—don't."

"All right," Charles said in a placating tone. "I won't promise anything of the sort. But is it all right if I sit with you while you sleep?"

Tristan nodded, and closed his eyes.

Charles smoothed a tumble of hair back from Tristan's forehead and frowned. He was warm—warmer than the temperature of the room warranted. A fever wasn't unexpected with the state of nervous exhaustion Tris was in—he was likely fighting off some infection his worn body had let in. Charles might only have begun his physician training, but he'd seen this often enough in the army, the susceptibility of the human body to illness after physical or emotional stress. Fortunately, the herbal tea wasn't only effective for nervousness or sleeplessness, but was a useful febrifuge. Mostly what Tris needed was rest—not only physical rest, but surcease from the nervous exhaustion that plagued him. Charles smoothed the tangle of curls off Tristan's damp forehead. *Rest*, he thought at his lover. *Rest.*

As Tris settled back into sleep, Charles pulled a chair over beside the bed to sit and watch over him a little while. He didn't think he could sleep, anyway; his fierce hunger for Tris had been overridden by his concern for his lover's state. There was time, he thought, time for patience. He'd waited this long to make Tristan his; another night wouldn't matter. He bent and dropped a gentle kiss on Tristan's brow, then settled back in his chair.

CHAPTER 12

CHARLES wrung out the flannel in the bowl of cold water and wiped Tristan's brow gently. Sometime during the night Tristan had developed a fever; Charles, who had been dozing in a chair by Tristan's bed, waiting for him to wake, had been wakened himself by Tristan's restless tossing and muttering. He never quite woke up; exhaustion had him tight in its grip.

In the flickering candlelight, Tristan's face looked drawn and haunted. Charles cursed himself for the thousandth time since his vigil began, for letting his desire for Tris push him into seduction of a man hovering on the edge of nervous collapse. Small wonder he was ill; in the space of a few hours Charles had fought with him, seduced him, forced him to acknowledge feelings he'd probably denied his whole life, turned him upside down, and left him helpless. Tristan Northwood, the consummate Corinthian, competent and independent, a man who from all reports never asked for help from anyone, had surrendered to Charles, turned his life and his body over into Charles's hands. If he had been well, it would have shaken him, but it appeared Tristan had been skating on very thin ice for a very long time now, hiding his fear and his loneliness behind that fearless façade.

He hoped Tristan's surrender to him wasn't just another dare Tristan had had to take.

The cool cloth seemed to calm him; his head stopped its restless thrashing and he lay still, though his breath was labored. Charles reached under Tristan's jaw to finger the glands there; they were hard but only slightly swollen. Some kind of infection, then, not just exhaustion; although he had never read any documentation on it, he'd observed that people who were tired or worn down had less resistance to infection. Tristan had probably been exposed to someone with an illness in one of those low dives he frequented. His fingers rasped along the jawline, against the dark bristles, then up to gently stroke the fierce cheekbones.

He'd been intrigued by Tristan just from Lottie's letters, but Tristan in the flesh was devastating. The first sight of him in the drawing room still haunted Charles: the lean, broad-shouldered, athletic body, the tousled, silky dark hair, the arrogantly handsome face—and those eyes. They'd struck him dumb, seeming to see right through him; silvery pewter and cold as stormclouds, a fierce contrast to that lush, sulky mouth. He traced a finger along that mouth now; it was soft and lax in sleep, but still kept that sweet lushness; not plump or thick, but just full enough, just sculptured enough. The kiss in the library had been everything Charles had dreamed of, wild and hot and hungry, and those in his bedroom fierce and desperate, but Charles longed for different kisses from Tris now. He wanted slow, lazy kisses, smiling kisses, warm and loving. He wanted them to make love not out of need and longing, but out of love and desire; to explore Tristan and let Tris explore him. Tonight he had made love to Tristan, not asking for him to reciprocate; he wanted Tristan to be able to say that he had done nothing to feel guilty about, if he woke so inclined. He didn't want a repeat of the Gregory situation. He prayed desperately that Tris would still want him when he woke, but if not, he wouldn't press it.

Tristan murmured something in his sleep; it sounded like "Charlie," but Charles wasn't sure. Then he said clearly, "Please," and Charles touched his temple. "Tris?" he whispered, but it seemed his lover had fallen asleep again.

There was a scratching on the door; Charles glanced over at the clock to see that it was six in the morning. It was still dark out. "Come," he called in a low voice.

Reston peeked in and blinked to see Charles. "Major?" he asked in a puzzled voice.

"Yes. I'm afraid Mr. Northwood is quite ill. I woke to hear him tossing about and found he had a fever. He's sleeping now, but he's had a restless night." He kept his voice low, not wanting to wake Tris.

"Oh, sir, you should have rung for me!" Reston came in, wringing his hands. "He mentioned not feeling well last evening, and I should have checked on him!"

"Nonsense," Charles said. "I was awake; why should you have been? I would not say 'no' to a cup of tea, however."

"I shall have tea and toast sent up immediately," Reston said, "and then I will be happy to sit with the master a while."

"I may take you up on it—I'm feeling a bit grimy 'round the edges," Charles said frankly. "If Reid is awake, can you ask him to lay out some fresh clothes for me?"

"Certainly," Reston said. He came closer to the bed. "Does the master have a fever?"

"He does," Charles said. "His neck glands are slightly swollen, so it seems he has an infection, probably one he picked up somewhere. We should probably limit the number of people that come in contact with him, but I suppose it would be safe enough for people to be in the same room. Lottie should not nurse him, but she could sit with him if she stays far enough away. The same for you—I should not wish you to be taken ill. Reid, however, never gets sick, and I've been exposed to far worse at the hospital, so both of us should manage nursing him. If the fever has not gone down by later this morning, I shall send for Dr. MacQuarrie. Fevers frequently are worse at night, for some reason, and ease during the day. Something to do with sunshine or something, I suppose." Tristan was starting to toss again; Charles wet the flannel again and wiped his sweaty forehead. Over his shoulder, he said, "You can send up the tea, and sit with Mr. Northwood while I wash and change, but tell Reid I shall be requiring his services. And let Mrs. Northwood know her husband is unwell but that she is under no circumstances to expect to nurse him."

"Certainly," Reston said, and he left the room.

Tristan muttered something unintelligibly, and Charles stroked his forehead gently with the flannel. "Poor, foolish Tristan," he said affectionately, "you should have said you were unwell. But no, my stubborn, fierce love, you had to pretend that all was well, just as you always do." He leaned forward and kissed Tristan's damp hair. "We're going to have to have a talk, you and I," he said against the tangled strands. "A long talk. But in the meantime, sleep, love. Sleep."

THE room was dark and quiet when Tristan woke, only the faint sounds of the fire crackling in the hearth and a stray feather of sunlight through drawn drapes. He raised his aching head to see Charlotte dozing in the armchair by the fire. Confused, he laid his head back on the crisp linen pillowcase and stared up into the darkness.

Inventory: One head, aching. Not unusual for him. Two pair limbs, both pair feeling limp and wrung-out as overdone string beans. Slightly less usual, but still not outside the realm of experience. Scent: warm, herbal; familiar but not his own, although he was alone in the bed. He raised a hand to his nose and sniffed. Yes, the scent was coming from him. It was faintly woodsy, and soothing; he sniffed again, breathing it in. Charles. Yes, that was the scent. Charles.

Charles.

Memory crashed in, and he tensed, drawing his knees up and rolling onto his side into a fetal position, tight and tense and unhappy. Not, he realized to his surprise, because of what Charles had done to him—no, that had been wonderful, the most amazing experience of his life. No—for what *he* had done—or rather, failed to do. Charles had made love to him gently, beautifully, generously—the first time anyone had ever done so. And Tristan had done... nothing. Nothing but weep like a deflowered virgin on Charles's lap. Done nothing to reciprocate, to show Charles his gratitude for Charles's patient, loving consideration; done nothing to ease Charles's tension, fill Charles's need. He'd been as selfish and self-centered as every other lover he himself had ever had. Been just like them, only concerned with their own pleasure.

The one true, important thing Ware had ever told him was that a gentleman never took his pleasure before his lover did. It had been Tristan's touchstone through his long years of womanizing, a point of pride; never had he left a lover wanting.

Until now. When it really mattered, when his lover *meant* something, Tristan had failed. He'd proved himself self-absorbed and worthless, in the one area he had always felt worthy.

There was nothing more. If Charles hadn't minded, if he'd just been waiting for Tristan to wake, wouldn't it have been him in the chair instead of Lottie? Or more likely, in this bed, his arms around Tristan, his warm scent more than just lingering on Tristan's skin? No, he'd wrecked whatever chance they'd had with his tears and his whining and his selfishness.

He pushed aside the bedclothes and slid out of bed onto legs that shook with weakness. Lottie still dozed, her needlework limp in her lap. She didn't stir as he stumbled across to the windows, but as he pulled back the drapes and let the sunlight in, he heard her wake behind him. "Tris?" she mumbled sleepily.

He ignored her and unfastened the latch, throwing the casement wide. Three floors below, the street was quiet; he looked straight down and saw that the areaway to the lower floor was directly below him. That added another story. Good. If he went headfirst, he was sure to break his neck cleanly.

As he climbed into the window, crouching so that he would pitch forward onto his head, he felt Lottie's hands in the back of his nightshirt and heard her screaming, "Reston! Charlie!!" as if from very far away. He hesitated, afraid for a moment that his weight would pull Lottie along with him. That wouldn't be good. Jamie needed her. "Let go," he snarled over his shoulder. "Lottie, for God's sake, let go!"

Then a second pair of hands were pulling him back. He lost his balance and slid back into the room, but onto his feet; with a jerk and a curse he was freed of Lottie's and Reston's hands and turning back to the window. Reston was crying, "Sir, oh sir, please, sir...!" and Lottie was still calling out for Charlie as they grabbed at him again.

The door to Charles's room slammed open and he came in at a run, his shirt loose over half-buttoned trousers, his feet bare. He took one look at Tristan fighting off the restraining hands and dove for him, tossing him onto the bed, and flinging himself on top of him to hold him down. "Tris, damn it!" he hissed in Tristan's ear. "What the *devil* do you think you're doing?"

The weight and warmth of Charles's body pinioned him and he let out a long, shuddering breath as he went limp.

CHARLES felt him collapse and went weak himself with relief. He'd stayed awake all night watching Tristan's fevered sleep; when Charlotte had come in around dawn and heard that Tristan was ill and offered to sit with him instead, he'd updated Reston about Tristan's fever, then taken himself off for a brief nap. Very brief—he glanced at the clock on the mantle—he'd been asleep barely an hour. "What happened?"

"I don't know," Lottie said. "He was sleeping, and I suppose I dozed off. The next thing I knew he was opening the window and trying to climb out."

"Poor, dear master," Reston said, wringing his hands miserably. "Is it the fever, Major? Or...." The tone of his voice was ripe with dread.

"He's not mad," Charles said over his shoulder. Tristan was weeping again, this time quietly, hopelessly. "It's the fever. He's delirious. He doesn't know what he's doing."

Softly, so that only Charles could hear, Tristan wept, "Yes, I do."

"No, you don't. Shut up," Charles whispered back. "Reston," he said aloud, "fetch some tea. We'll try that feverfew. Lottie, will you get it from my medicine case? It's in the box marked 'Brazil'."

"I thought that was snuff," Lottie said.

"That was the purpose of the box, but I don't take snuff. Go. Please." He glanced at Reston, who nodded and vanished out the door, closing it quietly behind him.

"How long do you want me to look for it?" Lottie asked thoughtfully.

"A few minutes. I don't care. Until Reston comes back. Go. I need to talk to Tris."

She sketched a mocking curtsey, then went through the door into Charles's room.

Charles rolled off to lie beside Tris, his hand smoothing the tangle of brown curls. "Are you all right, Tris?"

"Fine," Tris said bitterly. "Go away."

"And let you dive out the window?"

"That was the general intent, yes." He sat up, his back to Charles. "What do you want, Charles?"

"Ah, it's back to Charles," Charles said. "You're angry. Why? Because of what I did to you last night?"

"No," Tris said flatly. "You know damn well I enjoyed that."

"That doesn't matter," Charles said. "Someone with a strong feeling about relations between men might enjoy the experience, but hate himself—or his partner—afterward. Is that what's going on in your head, Tris?"

"I don't hate you," Tris said.

"Oh, all right. It's yourself you hate—thus the interrupted swan dive from the window." Charles sighed and stroked Tris's shoulder. "Why? Because you enjoyed it?"

"No." Tristan covered his eyes with one shaking hand. "I did enjoy it. It was… it was wonderful, Charlie. It's not about the, the sodomy. God, what an ugly word. It just doesn't fit the reality of it; it makes it sound sordid and shallow instead of beautiful."

"Then what is it about?"

Tristan lowered his hand and looked at him through watery, bloodshot eyes. "I didn't *do* anything!"

Charles frowned. "Of course not. How could you? What did you expect to do?"

"You let me go. You made love to me, and I did nothing but bloody weep."

Charles went up on his knees behind Tristan and slid his forearm around the front of Tristan's chest, pulling him back against him and onto Charles's lap as he sat back on his heels. "Tris, love, what I did to you was intense—very intense. You were wound up like a spring, and when I let you let go, you, well, unwound. The crying was a catharsis, and not unexpected. In fact—it was flattering."

"Flattering? Having a grown man sobbing in your lap?"

"Yes." Charles leaned down and nuzzled Tristan's neck. Tris tilted his head automatically to give Charles better access. "Because it was I that brought you to that. You broke down because of me, because of what I did for you. It was intense for both of us, Tris; you don't know what it felt like to hold you like that, balanced in my hands, knowing that all it would take would be a word from me to send you spiraling into pleasure."

Tris's heart was pounding under the palm Charles had pressed to Tristan's breast.

"And it was pleasure, wasn't it, Tris, my love?"

"God, yes…" Tris breathed, remembering.

Charles slid his hand down and under the loose fabric of the nightshirt, finding Tris's cock and curling his fingers around the warm, limp shaft. Tris arched at the touch. "God, you feel so good," he breathed into Tris's ear. "I could make love to you again right now, you know that? Except that Lottie's about to walk into the room, and Reston's on his way back with tea, and I'm exhausted, and you're worse, you're drained and feverish and you need sleep. I beg you, love, don't frighten my poor sister again like that." He released Tris and wrapped his arms around his chest instead.

"I'm sorry," Tristan began, but Charles shook his head, his hair brushing against Tristan's cheek.

"I'm not looking for an apology," he said firmly. "I just don't want you to do it again."

Tristan sighed and leaned his head back against Charles's shoulder. "I don't know what to do," he said wearily. "Everything is just so— overwhelming. Frightening. I'm not a coward, Charlie, but I'm so bloody scared I don't know what to do. Not of you. Not of this. But of everything else. It's all so… huge."

"It's not, really," Charles said softly. "It seems that way because you're so tired, physically and emotionally. I've seen this in soldiers when they've been pushed beyond their tolerance. The perspective gets skewed, and everything seems more important than it is." He added wryly, "Fortunately, at the military level, just about then is when the guns start, and you can't think at all anymore about anything after that." He smoothed Tristan's hair back from his forehead. "After you've rested, we'll do that talking I promised you, and maybe things won't seem so bad. Just remember that you're not alone. I'm here. I'll take care of you."

Tristan turned his face into Charles's neck and sighed, his eyes closing. His lips moved, and Charles thought they might have shaped "Thanks," but by then Tris was asleep, his body lax and heavy on Charles's.

He shifted back and let Tris slide down onto the pillows, then drew the blanket up over the sleeping man. Charlotte said from the doorway, "Will he be all right?"

"I expect so," Charles said. He got up and took the box from her hands just as Reston came back in carrying the tea tray.

Reston glanced over at the bed. "Oh, the master is asleep again?"

"Yes, for now. I'll stay with him 'til he wakes and I can get some of this tea into him."

"If you'll pardon me, sir, Mr. Reid has expressed his concern that you have not slept," Reston said.

Charles gave him a faint smile. "It's not the first time I've been up all night, nor the last. I'll just curl up beside Mr. Northwood for a while," he said, "and that way we needn't worry about him waking disoriented as he did just now. You and Reid can go about your normal duties." He set the pot of water on the hearth to keep warm, took the tray from Reston, and placed it on the small table beneath the pier glass.

"Sir," Reston said, hesitating. "Major?"

"Yes, Reston?"

"I just wanted to say… I'm grateful for your care for the master." He met Charles's eyes levelly. "I've known him, boy and man, a good many years, and he—well, he's like a son to me, if I may be so bold as to say so. He's a good man. He deserves people who care for him, like you and Mrs. Northwood."

Charles put a hand on the older man's shoulder. "Thank you, Reston. I'll take care of him for you. I promise."

When the valet had gone, Charles dropped into the chair opposite Lottie's. "I'll be damned," he said.

"About what?" Lottie asked curiously. "Reston? What was so strange about him?"

"I think he knows, Lottie. About me—about what I feel for Tristan. And if I'm not mistaken—he's just given us his blessing."

"I hope you're right," Lottie said doubtfully, "but it's best we don't make assumptions." She walked over to the door and turned the key firmly.

"Lottie—does this bother you at all? I mean, me and Tris?"

She came quickly back across the room and kissed his cheek firmly. "Of course not. You two are quite my favorite gentlemen. I've hated that Tristan has been unhappy, and if you can change that, I am quite content." Her voice turned anxious. "You *do* think you can make him happy, Charlie? He is quite conventional in a number of ways—I'm so afraid for you both."

"I believe I can, *Liebchen*," Charles said soberly. "I believe I can."

She patted his cheek. "I hope you're right. Now, you just curl up and rest, and I'll be in the sitting room next door guarding your flank. Isn't that how they say it in the army?"

"Yes, just like that," Charles said in amusement.

She patted his cheek again and left the room, closing the door quietly behind her. Charles shook his head and climbed up on the bed next to Tristan.

THERE was someone large and warm next to Tris when he next woke; a heavy arm draped over his waist, and the steady thud of a heartbeat in his ear. He breathed in the scent of rosemary and eucalyptus and smiled to himself. "Charlie," he whispered, more to himself than aloud, and rolled over to face his lover.

"Hello, love," Charles said softly.

"I thought maybe I dreamed you," Tristan said.

"No. How are you feeling?"

"Tired. Confused." He took a breath. "I don't know what I'm feeling, but I think I just might be happy."

That beautiful smile blossomed on Charles's face. "Are you?"

"I think so. I'm not sure. I don't think I've ever been happy before, so I can't be positive. But I've never felt quite like this before. Oh, God, did I really just say that?" Tristan made a face. "So trite."

"It's not trite if it's true. No second thoughts?"

"I've been through the second thoughts, and the third thoughts, and every other thoughts there might be. I know I'm damned to hell for this but I don't bloody care. Being with you—being in your arms right now is more than I'd ever expected out of life."

"Ah, damn, Tris," Charles said, his voice raw, "I love you."

Tristan froze, his heart pounding. "What?" he rasped.

"I said I love you." Charles was calm, but certain. "I'm *in* love with you."

"No one's ever said that to me before," Tristan whispered.

"Well, it's true now."

"What happens next?"

"What do you want to happen?"

Tristan was quiet a long moment, then said, "Well, it isn't anything we can exactly go shouting from rooftops, can we?"

Charles chuckled. "Is that what you want to do?"

"God, yes." Tristan put his hand on Charles's shirt, bunching the fabric in his fist. "I want to send it to the Times: 'Mr. Tristan Northwood is pleased to announce that he is betrothed to the Honorable Major Charles Mountjoy, late of Lord Castlereagh and his Grace the Duke of Wellington's personal staff. The happy couple are At Home to visitors at Number 8 Cavendish Street.' But I think that will create quite a furor if it were to be published."

"That it would."

Tristan kept hold of the shirt. "Charlie?"

"Yes, love?"

"You knew, didn't you? How I felt about you?"

"Before you did, I think," Charles said. "But I didn't know how you would respond if I approached you. I had to let you work it out on your own."

"Don't you think that we're damned to hell for this?" Tris worried his bottom lip with his teeth. "It says so in the Bible."

"The Bible damns many things," Charles said agreeably, "including eating bacon, and wearing linen with wool. But people do." He cocked his head. "And then there's adultery," he added gently.

"Yes, but that's more socially acceptable," Tristan said.

"We aren't talking society," Charles said. "We're talking the Bible." He shook his head. "Well, I'm sure I'm damned for working on the Sabbath, anyway; as a soldier you can't quite avoid it. Tris, love, sometimes you just have to know when something's right and when it's wrong, and neither the Bible nor society nor someone else's opinion matters in the end. It's what *you* think is right. And this—this is *right*."

"I think so," Tris said. "God, I feel like a child again. I'm so… lost. I don't know what to do next."

"I told you not to worry about that," Charles said. "I told you I would take care of you."

"But I'm not a child. I don't need to be taken care of. I just—I want to take care of you, too, Charlie. I want to give you everything." He kissed Charles fiercely. "I want to be what you want. What do you want, Charlie? What can I do for you?"

Charles disengaged him, holding his hands in both of his. "Tris, you don't even know what you're asking."

"Yes, I do," Tris said recklessly. "I want to lie with you. To have carnal relations. To fuck." He kissed Charles again. "I know what that is. I want that. I want *you*."

Charles was quiet a moment, then said "Not yet, Tris."

"Why not? I want you. I love you. I'm ready."

"I'm not." Charles lowered his head to rest against Tris's. "I'm not ready, Tris. You're ill, and you're so fragile right now—emotionally, physically. Your nerves are shattered. My God, you're a good three stone underweight—even Jackson mentioned it to me the last time you had a bout at his place. And you're emotionally raw—you just tried to kill yourself! I'm terrified for you, Tris, and I'm terrified that something I do will send you right over the edge again. Just as my touching you last night nearly killed you this morning. I'm scared to death, Tris. Scared to *death*."

"It wasn't you that sent me to the window, Charlie. It was me."

"That's what I mean. Until I know for sure that it won't happen again— that you won't shatter the way you just did—I can't take this to the next level with you. I'm too frightened."

"I thought nothing scared you," Tris said softly.

"Nothing did—until I met you. Then suddenly there was this other person I needed to be there for, and the world became a dangerous place."

Tristan went still. Charles noticed instantly. "What is it?" he demanded.

"It—what you just said. It's how I felt when I realized that Jamie knew who I was. That he *recognized* me, that my being with him made him happy.

It was like the world shifted, and suddenly I was in this position of being responsible for him, for his happiness. It's a horrible feeling."

"Is it?"

Tristan thought, then amended, "No, not horrible. Just—overwhelming."

"Exactly. I wouldn't change it for the world. But it's still frightening." Charles kissed him gently.

Tristan wound his arms around Charles's shoulders, leaning into the kiss, feeling the soft, firm mouth on his, the warm, wet stroke of Charles's tongue against his. He tasted sweet, of tea and mint. Charles drew him against his chest, holding him in arms that were hard and strong, not soft and clinging; arms that could hold him steady instead of leaning on him, pulling him down until he drowned in helplessness. There was nothing helpless about Charles's embrace.

The thought eased something inside Tris, something that had been a hard, painful knot for longer than he could remember—so long that he'd not even realized it was there. The last thought he had before drifting into sleep was that he wasn't alone anymore....

CHAPTER 13

CHARLES was pacing the sitting room, prowling like a caged cat, back and forth, back and forth. Charlotte watched him a while, then finally said, "Oh, Charlie, will you *stop*? You're driving me mad."

"How much longer..." he began, but just then the door to Tristan's bedroom opened and Dr. MacQuarrie came out, his bag in hand. He closed the door quietly, then turned to the two anxious faces watching him.

"Your diagnosis was quite correct, Charlie," he said in his dry fashion. "Nervous exhaustion, leading to a fever. The skullcap and feverfew were good choices; I'd also recommend willow bark or another febrifuge like butterbur to help keep the fever down; that and beef tea for a day, then get him back on a normal diet. Plenty of beefsteak; he needs building up. And rest. Keep him in bed for at least two more days."

Charles sighed in relief and sank down onto the sofa beside Charlotte. "Thank God," he breathed. "I had visions of it being something serious."

"It is serious." MacQuarrie set his bag down and sat in the chair opposite the twins. "I had the chance to speak with Northwood. I'm very concerned."

"About Tristan?" Charlotte asked.

"About you," MacQuarrie said to Charles. "Charlie, you're a bright lad, and I think you'll make an excellent physician, but there's something you need to learn. Something all physicians need to learn. And that is that you're not God, and you can't save everyone."

Charles's eyes widened and he stared at MacQuarrie in a panic. "But you just said Tris would be all right!"

"I'm not talking about Tris. Well, in a sense, I am, but not about his fever." The doctor fixed his gaze firmly on Charles. "Do you know what I see when I look at him? Not Tristan Northwood. I see Gregory Winstead."

Charles fell back in his chair, covering his face with one hand. Charlotte looked confused. "Gregory Winstead? Wasn't he the one that ran berserk and attacked an officer? What has Tristan to do with him?"

"Gregory Winstead was a very troubled young man that Charles tried to help. Unfortunately, he was beyond either Charles's or anyone else's aid. From what little Mr. Northwood told me, I get the impression that his nervous exhaustion is quite severe. And I'm concerned that Charles will take it on himself to save Mr. Northwood, and will be devastated if he fails. Charlie...."

"I'm not trying to save Tris," Charles said, agitated. "Well, yes, but only in giving him the help he needs. I know I couldn't have saved Greg. I *know* that. Yes, I spent a lot of time thinking that I could have done more...."

"But you couldn't have," Lottie assured him, patting his hand gently. He turned his hand so that it clutched hers. "We talked about this in our correspondence, and I thought you had realized that."

"I did. I do." Charles rubbed his eyes with his free hand. "I know that I did whatever I could for Greg, but sometimes I don't *feel* that way. Does that make any sense?"

"Of course," the doctor said. "Charlie, I'm not telling you not to help Mr. Northwood. I know you want to help—that's part and parcel of being a doctor of medicine. I'm just... concerned that...." He blew out his breath in frustration.

Lottie patted Charles's hand again and lurched to her feet. "I think that perhaps you and Dr. MacQuarrie need to speak privately," she said placidly. "I shall go in and sit with Tris." She dropped a curtsey to the doctor, then went back through the door into her husband's bedroom.

The doctor blinked, then turned to Charles, his expression puzzled. Charles smiled briefly. "She's odd that way," he said by way of explanation. "It's almost as if she reads minds. I've never seen her at a loss to know what to do. I'm not saying she's never wrong—she's just never uncertain. I've always envied her that."

"She doesn't seem to be very concerned about your relationship with her husband," MacQuarrie said.

Charles blinked. "Tristan is my friend...," he said slowly.

"Come, Charles. Your feelings for Tristan, like his for you, are more than just friendly. He made that quite clear after I assured him that his secrets—and yours—are quite safe with me."

Charles felt the blood drain from his face. "Mac," he began, then trailed off helplessly.

"Charles," Mac said gently, "I knew about you and Winstead. I know that he broke off his relationship with you and that that left you helpless to aid him when he went through all that nonsense with Warren. I've served in the South Seas, and the Indies, and other places where sodomy is not the crime it is in England, and it seems to me that it has no deleterious effect on any other element of life, despite what Europeans, particularly the English, believe. Europeans don't have a monopoly on culture; far older ones than ours accept the differences in men more graciously. I respect our religion, but as a physician and a scientist, I don't always believe what Christianity preaches. As I told Tristan, whatever is told to me is as safe as if it were said to a papist priest in the confessional. And I'd have to be blind not to see the way you look at him—and he looks at you." He rubbed his jaw thoughtfully. "To be honest, it doesn't surprise me as much as I would have thought. You, I knew about. Him—with all his womanizing reputation and his wild antics, it makes sense to me now."

"You've lost me," Charles said.

"Sometimes, acting so—*extremely*—is an attempt to hide in plain sight. A terribly shy man might act boisterous to hide his shyness; a man who is melancholic may laugh louder than anyone else. And a man who is uncertain of his own masculinity may feel the need to act twice as manly. Sometimes, it takes the form of bullying, like Warren, and the boys you knew in school, as we discussed once before. And sometimes, it takes the form of reckless, daredevil behavior—proving how much of a man you are by bravery and fearlessness. Northwood needed to prove his masculinity to himself, and thus to others. Because sometimes one knows things without knowing them." He shook his head. "There is so much we don't know or understand about why people behave the way they do. Why is your sister so confident, so uninterested in other people's opinions, when her husband is so opposite? You and she are twins, born the same hour, and the superstitious nonsense of our ancestors would have you identical in nature. But that is patently not so—your personalities are vastly different. There is more to know about our minds than we can even begin to suspect, and behavior like Tristan's, behavior like Warren's, behavior like poor Winstead's. What makes such men do what they do?"

"That falls into the realm of philosophy and is thus beyond my poor perspective," Charles said.

MacQuarrie snorted. "Be that as it may, I know that the two of you have something between you. I pray that it doesn't result in one of you being harmed. But more than that—Northwood's problems may turn out to be more than you can handle. I'm asking you to take a good hard look at him, and at what it is you feel for him. Is he worth risking your life for? Is there any real hope for the two of you? I should hate to see him drag you down with him."

"I think—I believe—that much of what troubles Tris is related to what you described, his need to be a man. He just needs to understand that loving someone doesn't make him less than manly." Charles rubbed his face again wearily. "I don't know if he can learn that. I don't know if I can help him. All I know is that I have to try. You asked if he was worth it. I have to say yes. He is."

"Then you have no choice but to try," MacQuarrie said heavily. "Just realize that he is the one who will have to take charge of his life. All you can do is help him realize it, and pray he doesn't react like Winstead. At least Winstead did not betray you to the authorities. You can only believe that Northwood will not."

"I know." Charles nodded, then rose as MacQuarrie did. "Thank you, Mac."

"Just don't let him wreck you, Charlie. You've too much to offer to throw your life away on one man." He shook Charles's hand. "I'll call on you tomorrow to see how he does; I won't expect you back at the hospital for another three or four days, but certainly by then you should see signs of improvement."

"Thank you, Mac," Charles said again, and escorted him to the door.

"SLEEPING again?" Charlotte asked quietly.

Charles looked up from his post at Tristan's bedside. It was the second day of Tristan's illness, and Charles was exhausted, but reassured by his slow progress. "Yes. But the fever's gone, so I'm hopeful he'll be hungry when he wakes. Reston brought up some broth; I'm keeping it warm on the hearth for him. I'm concerned about his lack of appetite—some of that's due to the fever, of course, but I've noticed over the last month that he doesn't eat very well."

"No," Lottie agreed. "And he drinks too much. Papa and Daniel are the same way, but I don't think Tris is addicted to the drink the way they are. I've known him to go weeks without becoming inebriated or drinking more than anyone else does. It's only been in the last few months that he's made a habit of it." She leaned back against the door, shaking off Charles's offer of the chair. "No, thank you, I've been sitting all afternoon and I need to stand a bit."

"After Tris wakes up and has something to eat, I'll take you for a walk," Charles promised. "It seems to be quite pleasant this afternoon."

"I wouldn't say no," Lottie said. "As for Tris's appetite: he's never been a big eater, but lately he doesn't eat much at all. I've asked him about it but he just says something about not being hungry or having had a sandwich earlier or some such nonsense. I think the drinking has killed his appetite. Still, he'd only lost a little weight until recently. He's much worse in the last few weeks."

"Since I've come," Charles said softly.

"Yes," Lottie agreed.

He snorted. "I can always rely on you for honesty," he said curtly.

"Yes, you can," his twin retorted. "I don't believe in playing games, Charlie. He *is* worse since you've come. I'm not saying it's because of you, but it might be."

"I think it is," Charles said. "I just need to find out what to do about it."

"Well, in my opinion, you've made a start."

He snorted again. "Right. By sending him into a decline to the point of him being ill. That's *very* helpful."

"You've said yourself that sometimes one has to get sicker before one gets better," she pointed out logically. "Tristan just needs to decide if he's going to get better or keep on going the way he has. That's something you can help with, more than I."

"She's right," a quiet voice said from the bed. "I can't do this without you, Charlie. I can't go on without you."

"That's not really true, Tris," Charles said gently. "It feels that way right now because you're still weak—and trust me, I'll be here to help you. But you'll get past this, I promise."

"Just get me past the wanting to put a bullet in my brain part, and that will help."

"Do you still feel that way?"

Tristan was silent a moment, then sighed. "No. Not so much anymore. I want to get up and try and get my life back together. But right now I'll settle for that soup you mentioned."

"Are you hungry?"

"Devil a bit! Starving."

Charles grinned at him. "That's a good start." He rose and leaned over the bed, lifting Tris into a sitting position with his back against the pile of pillows. Charlotte tucked the blankets around him, and he smiled his thanks.

"Did you need help with it?" she asked in concern. "It's in a mug so it should be easier for you to hold."

"Whose idea was that?" Tris asked.

"Charlie's, of course. I think he'll make a wonderful physician, don't you?"

"Yes," Tristan said, smiling at her. "You'd make a quite good nurse too, you know."

"Oh, that's too much work." She shook her head. "I'll only nurse my family."

"Thank you." Tristan's voice was very soft.

She patted his hand affectionately and said, "Eat your soup. Charles has promised me a walk in the park this afternoon, but he won't go until you're settled." Then she glanced up at her brother. "Come fetch me when you're ready, Charlie," and she went back through the sitting room door.

Charles set the tray on Tristan's lap and sat on the bed beside him. "How are you feeling?" he asked.

Tristan made a face. "Are you asking as my physician or my brother-in-law?"

"As your lover," Charles said calmly.

Tristan's eyes flashed to his, wide and startled. "Are we lovers?" he asked.

"In my mind," Charles said. "What about yours?"

Lifting the mug to his lips in shaking hands, Tristan took a sip. "I suppose we are, if that's what you'd call it. I'm still so confused about it—aren't you?"

"Not in the slightest," Charles said. "I know what I want, but if you need more time, or even don't want to pursue this, just tell me."

"No. No, I want this." Tris set the mug down on the tray. "God, Charlie, I want this. But I'm terrified. Is that stupid?"

"No, of course not." Charles chuckled. "You've had your life turned upside down. And you've spent the last half-year focused on one ambition, and now that's changed—I hope!"

"It has, I think." Tris raised his eyes to meet Charles's. "I'm no less frightened now than I was before, but there's not the, the despair I felt before. I felt so alone, so lost. But when I'm with you—I don't feel like it's so overwhelming. That maybe I can handle the things that scare me so much."

"What scares you, Tris?"

Tris took another sip of broth. "I don't know. Sometimes I'm just afraid of everything. Sometimes it's more specific. Sometimes it's just knowing that people have expectations of me that I can never meet." He swallowed hard, his fingers white around the mug. "That they will be disappointed in me, like my father is."

"Who are 'they'?" Charles asked quietly.

"My friends, acquaintances." He hesitated, then went on, "Jamie. The new child."

"I notice you don't include Charlotte."

Tristan snorted. "I can't disappoint Charlotte because she already has no expectations. She knows me too well. Besides, she doesn't really care. Oh, I think she's fond of me, but she doesn't care what I do. Anything I do just amuses her. She's very restful that way. But others—Jamie, Gibs, Berks, the rest of the ton—they have expectations."

"I think," Charles said reassuringly, "that you'll find that they actually don't. That you're imposing your own expectations of yourself on them. Jamie will love you simply because you're you. Gibson and Berkeley aren't that critical—sometimes I wonder if they have any critical faculties between them whatsoever. And why should you give a good goddamn about the rest of the ton? For Charlotte's sake? She couldn't care less what people think of her." He regarded Tristan thoughtfully, then reached out and pushed the lock of dark hair off his forehead. "I think that the only one who has expectations of you is you."

"God knows my father doesn't," Tristan said bitterly. "Or if he did, they're entirely negative."

"I don't know your father, so I can't say."

Tristan was silent a long moment, then said, "You've read the journal you took from me."

"Of course I haven't!" Charles said indignantly. "Not more than the one page I read. I don't pry." Then he thought about it, and added with a tinge of embarrassment, "Not usually, anyway."

Tristan laughed humorlessly. "Just the once, and I have to admit I'm glad you did. So much would never have happened—and so much might well have. But it's all right. Aside from a few pages chronicling my obsession with a certain officer of the 14th, my journals are mostly just appointments and observations. I don't care if you read them."

"'Journals'? Have you always kept one?"

Tristan shrugged. "Since I was a boy. They're all in the drawer in my desk; the key's on my watch chain. Read them if you've a mind to; they're hardly exciting."

"The one entry I read was quite exciting enough," Charles said dryly.

"Well, if you want to know my father better—at least from my perspective, which I admit may be a little skewed, as he is quite respected by those who don't know him—you may read about him in my journal," Tristan said carelessly.

Charles glanced at him and saw a brief, anxious expression flicker across his face before he settled it into his usual Tristan casualness. "Now," Tristan went on, "your sister is waiting for her walk. I'm sure Reston is hovering in the corridor waiting to come sit with me—no doubt it's the highlight of his afternoon. Go away and come back when you and Lottie are all breathless and exhausted. I like when you come straight here from outside; the air smells so fresh and cold." He gave Charles a quick smile. "I promise to be good for Reston. In fact, I think I may go back to sleep."

"I'll take your word on that, Tris."

"You have it. Go. Walk."

Charles brushed his hand over Tristan's head, smoothing his hair, then bent and kissed him briefly before taking the tray from his lap. "Go back to sleep," he commanded.

"Aye, sir," Tristan said, saluting.

Charles laughed.

RESTON came in, looking anxious, and Charles nodded at them both before exiting through the sitting room door. "Sit down, Reston," Tristan ordered, "and tell me what I've missed sleeping through the last two days."

"Nothing of consequence, sir," Reston said, settling into the chair beside the bed that Charles had just vacated. "Mr. Franklin sends his regards and hopes for a speedy recovery. Messieurs Berkeley and Gibson have visited to inquire about your health, and Mr. Gibson asked if you would appreciate flowers. I thought not."

Tristan chuckled. "You think correctly. Gad. I can just imagine the sort of flowers Gibs would consider appropriate for a man's sickroom."

"Indeed, sir. Mrs. Northwood and I reviewed your appointments and sent excuses as necessary. I trust that was acceptable?"

"Of course. I really ought to think about getting a new valet and promoting you to butler; you perform both tasks excellently, and I should really be paying you a butler's wages."

"That's kind of you, sir, but I am quite content to continue as we are for the time being." Reston smiled kindly at him. "We can reconsider the situation once you are back on your feet."

"I wish I knew when that would be," Tristan said grumpily.

"Major Mountjoy seems to think another day or two resting, from what he said to myself and Mrs. Northwood this morning. But he said he thinks your fever has passed the worst and you should start feeling better soon. Particularly if you start eating better." He frowned at Tristan.

Tristan chuckled again. "Yes, sir, Mr. Reston!" he said, and sketched a salute. "Major Mountjoy's military ways rubbing off on you?"

"He is a very commanding presence, is he not? I quite feel like one of his troops sometimes."

"Sometimes I do too," Tristan admitted. "But it's not a bad thing to be. He's very considerate."

"He'll make an excellent physician," Reston said. "I should be afraid not to follow his medical instructions."

"No doubt he'd have you drawn and quartered, or whatever it is they do in the army," Tristan murmured. "Well, if it assuages your worry, I'll tell you I drank the beef broth you left for me, and am ready for the real thing now. A nice beefsteak would hit the spot."

"We'll start you with chicken, I think," Reston said sternly. "Stewed, with carrots and peas. And Cook's biscuits."

Tristan's stomach rumbled, and he grinned at Reston. "I think my belly agrees with you," he said.

Chapter 14

Baron Ware was standing by the fireplace, gazing down at the flames, when Charles came into the library. At the sound of his footsteps, Ware looked up, his expression thunderous. "Who the devil are you, sir?" he demanded.

"Charles Mountjoy," Charles said, advancing with his hand extended. "Lottie's brother."

Ware shook his hand automatically. "Where the devil is my son? I come to town only to be met with the news that he's dying or some such rot." His words were harsh and dismissive, but there was something in his face that spoke more of fear than disdain.

"Not quite. He *has* been quite ill—a brain fever—but I trust he is out of danger."

Ware swallowed hard and looked up at the ceiling a moment, then back at Charles, his brows drawn together, his lips thinned. "And no one thought to notify me that my son was ill?"

"It was quite sudden," Charles said, "and we thought you fixed in the country."

"Has a physician seen him?"

"Dr. MacQuarrie, of the Horse Guards...."

"An army surgeon?" Ware demanded. "You called in a bloody army surgeon for my son?"

"Not a surgeon, a physician," Charles replied coldly. "The Duke of Wellington's personal physician while he was in Portugal, now serving the Horse Guards in London. And a specialist in the type of fever Tristan suffered. I trust that someone recommended by the Duke of Wellington is acceptable to you?"

Mollified, Ware backed down. "Well. That's different. As to my being fixed in the country, don't you think I would have come up if someone had had the decency to send a message as to Tristan's condition?"

"In truth, sir," Charles said flatly, "it was not expected that you would have any interest in—what was it?—a 'loose, degenerate, disappointing excuse for a human being'. After all, you have your heir in Jamie. What does Tristan matter to you?"

The baron went white and staggered back against the mantle as if he'd been struck. "How *dare* you, sir, say such a thing to me?"

"Only repeating your own words, my lord," Charles shot back.

If possible, the baron went whiter still. "Who the devil says?"

"Tristan," Charles said.

Ware opened his mouth as if to say something, then closed it. He ran a shaking hand over his forehead. "My son said that to you."

"Not exactly. I read the entry in his journal for the day you said that. It was only one of a number of your comments that he recorded. He seemed to need to keep a history of your insults." Charles smiled thinly, without any humor at all. "Some of them were quite inventive, I must say." He waited a moment, but the baron was speechless, so he went on. "Needless to say, my conclusion that you would not be interested in Tristan's condition should not be unexpected—after all, this fever is not contagious, so you needn't worry about Jamie. I trust your mind has been set at ease?"

"Stop," Ware said in an undertone.

Charles obliged, simply standing with his hands clasped behind his back, rocking back and forth on his heels. He half expected Ware to strike him. It was harsh, hitting the man with his own words like that, but the more he'd read of Tris's journal, the angrier he'd got with Tris's father. It was satisfying on one level to see the man so shaken, but at the same time he began to doubt Tris's allegations that his father hated him. That white face and shaking hands did not belong to someone who didn't care. He could have said more, but waited instead—sometimes silence drew more than questions did.

Finally, Ware said, "Tristan and I have had our difficulties. He—after his mother died, I—we always seemed to be at cross-purposes. But that does not mean that I don't love my son, Mr. Mountjoy. I have always tried to do what is best for him, but he refuses to see that. He thinks I try to control him." He looked up, finally meeting Charles's eyes. "I only want what's best for him. I could never make him understand that."

Charles only nodded. After another long moment, Ware said humbly, "May I see him?"

"I don't guarantee that he's awake—or if he is, that he's lucid," Charles warned. "He's mostly been sleeping these last few days. The worst of the fever is gone, but he's exhausted, and sometimes it comes back, though not nearly as bad as before."

"But he's out of danger?"

"Dr. MacQuarrie says so, as long as the fever stays out of his lungs. Which it has, so far." Charles opened the library door again and held it for the baron. "Do you know which room he is in?"

"No," Ware said dully. "I've never been here before."

"Ah," Charles said. "Then follow me." He led the way upstairs to the sickroom and, rapping lightly on the door, went in, the baron at his heels.

He smiled to himself in amusement. Lottie sat at Tristan's bedside in the pose of the devoted wife, wiping Tristan's clammy, pale brow. Both of Tristan's wrists were bound to the bedposts. "What the devil?" Ware gasped, then at Charlotte's scandalized look, he flushed in embarrassment. "I beg your pardon, Charlotte," he said hastily. "But why is my son *bound*?"

"It's only when neither I nor a footman are in the room with him," Charles said, and went to release Tristan. He pinched Tristan's hand as he slid the linen off. "The last time we left him alone with Charlotte he nearly got out the window."

"Out the *window*?" Ware said in confusion. "Where did he think he was going?"

"Down," Tristan said hoarsely, then added in a sing-song, "Down, down to the ground; splat! Jam on the cobbles." He then giggled.

"Oh dear," Charlotte said. "Are you sure you should release him, Charlie?"

"Of course, Lottie," Charles said. "He's not mad, are you, Tris?"

"I know a hawk from a handsaw," he replied. "Hullo, Papa. Come to gaze upon the wreck of love's young dream?"

"I came to see how you were feeling," Ware said uncomfortably.

"Tired, mostly. They said I was ill. I suppose I am. Maybe I'm dead. Maybe I'm on my deathbed and that's why you're here." He turned worried eyes on Charlotte. "Am I on my deathbed, Lottie? Am I going to die?"

"No," she said, patting his face with her damp flannel. "That would be very silly of you, wouldn't it?"

"People do," he argued, then he closed his eyes and seemed to go to sleep.

Charlotte turned to look up at Ware. "He is mostly just tired," she assured him. "He talks like this when he's worn out. I suppose he must have been like this when he was ill when he was a child?"

"Tristan was never ill as a child," Ware said. "Just once...."

"Scarlet fever," Tristan said, without opening his eyes. "I brought it home from the vicar's when I was playing with his children. I wasn't supposed to be there. It killed Mama and the baby, didn't it, Papa? I murdered them, didn't I, Papa?" He giggled again. "And now it's got me."

"You didn't murder your mother," Ware said, scandalized. "It wasn't your fault."

Tristan opened his eyes and sat up, startling them all. "Then why the *hell* have you blamed me for it all these years?" He was trembling all over.

Charles sat on the bed beside him and put his arm around his shoulders. "Tris," he said urgently. "Tris, no one is blaming you for anything. Come, lie down again. You're overtired, and need to rest."

"Make him go away," Tris said, turning his face into Charles's shoulder. "Make him stop looking at me. It hurts when he looks at me."

Over Tristan's head, Charles met Ware's appalled gaze. "Perhaps you and Charlotte should go downstairs and have some tea. I'll sit with Tristan a while, and try and get him back to sleep. Lottie?"

"Of course," Lottie said, and taking Ware by the sleeve, she led him from the bedroom.

Charles waited until he no longer heard their footsteps on the stairs, then went and closed the bedroom door. Then he came back to the bed and cuffed Tristan lightly on the head. "Whose idea was that little farce?"

"I don't know what you mean," Tris said sullenly. He rolled over and buried his face in the pillow.

"And how did she get you all pasty and clammy like that?"

"The water in the bowl was damned cold!" Tristan complained, his voice muffled. "And that was her idea. Mine was to be tied up."

"You wanted to shock him, didn't you?"

Tris turned his head and regarded Charles dully. "And why not? I've never missed the opportunity to before, and I shan't give up the habit now."

"If you really wanted to shock him, you could tell him about us," Charles said quietly.

"It's still a hanging offense in Britain," Tristan growled, "and even the hint of a rumor of it would scotch your career—either the military or the medical one."

"Still," Charles said, "that was unkind, Tris. I've never known you to be deliberately unkind, let alone mean-spirited."

"How can it be unkind when he doesn't give a damn?" Tristan asked bitterly. He rolled back over onto the pillow again.

Charles stroked his damp hair gently. "I think he does," he said. "We spoke for a few minutes, and I think he was truly frightened for you, even before your little charade."

"It wasn't wholly a charade," Tristan said into the linens. "It does hurt when he looks at me. It's always hurt."

"And so you lash out at him, and he at you, and the whole thing starts over again."

"And he *does* blame me for Mama's death. He's always blamed me. He wasn't very kind even before she died, but afterwards...." Tristan shook his head and jerked away when Charles would have put his hand on his shoulder. "Oh, it doesn't matter. Go away. I'm tired."

"And leave you alone to splat on the cobbles? I don't think so."

"Tie me up again, then, if you think I'll be that stupid."

"I don't think you're stupid. I think you're... sad."

Tristan sobbed faintly, but jerked away from his touch again.

"And about the unkindness—Tris, when you're unkind to someone, it doesn't only matter to them. It hurts you too. And if the other person really *doesn't* care—the only one you're hurting is yourself."

Tristan rolled over and regarded him with sodden eyes. "Charlie—it doesn't matter. I tried for so long to be what he wanted and I never could be. I gave up. Now I'm what he doesn't want. And that suits me."

No, it doesn't, Charles thought sadly. He bent to kiss Tristan, his mouth tender, his hand gentle as he stroked the damp forehead.

Tris sobbed again and threw his arms around Charles. "I'm sorry, I'm sorry," he wept against Charles's mouth.

"Shh," Charles said. He sat on the edge of the bed and drew Tristan up against him, kissing him. "Shh," he said again.

Tristan pulled on Charles's waistcoat. "Charlie, I need you. Please. Come to bed. I don't care that it's the middle of the day or that my father is downstairs or anything. I need you."

Charles shucked his coat and waistcoat and Hessians and lay on the bed beside Tris. His lover fumbled with his trouser buttons, but Charles put his hand on Tristan's fingers to stop him. "Tris. Calm down. You're overwrought and overtired. I'm not making love to you like this."

Tristan burst into tears. Charles gathered him up in his arms and held him until the wracking sobs eased. "Now," he said gently, "I think you need to eat. You barely touched your breakfast."

"I ate last night," Tristan said tiredly. He pushed Charles away and lay on his back. "I'm not hungry."

"You need to eat," Charles repeated. "You've been in bed for three days and if you ever plan on getting out of it, you need to eat. I know the fever's made you lose your appetite, but the fever's been gone for a full day, and you won't get better without eating."

Tristan blew out a breath, then said, "I imagine you think I'm acting like a child."

"No. Just a very tired, ill man." Charles grinned at him. "We'll blame your crankiness on that."

"Well, *I* think I'm acting like a child. Petty revenge on my father, crying like an infant, making demands of you. I'm sick of me, even if you're not. Bring on the lunch tray, I'll eat."

"There's my reasonable Tris."

"I suppose I have to be reasonable if I'm to ever get my hands on you," Tristan pointed out.

Charles grinned. "Means that much to you, does it?"

"You know it does." Tristan shook his head. "Oh, I don't mean that that is all there is, Charlie. I'm very fond of you. And I would love being with you."

"I know." Charles slid out of the bed, helped Tris sit up, well-propped with pillows, and fetched the lunch tray where Reston had left it before the baron's arrival. "I'm afraid it's probably gone cold," he said as he settled it on Tristan's knees, "but it's mostly sandwiches and cheese, so it shouldn't be too bad. I wouldn't drink the soup, though." He handed Tris a sandwich and watched in contentment as Tris began to eat.

Lottie had never much cared for Tristan's father, but she felt distinctly sympathetic as she led him back into the library and ordered tea from the footman. She settled the shaken man in Tris's favorite wing chair and eased her bulk into a chair opposite. "He really is on the road to recovery," she said reassuringly. "He's worn out and sometimes talks a little wildly, but he's *much* better than he was even a day ago. The fever is mostly gone; it sometimes comes back for a while, but it's not as high as it was in the beginning. And the cravats—tying him up, you know—is just preventative. He hasn't tried anything foolish in *days*."

The baron lowered the hand that had been covering his eyes and looked at her, his expression haunted. "I don't know what I'd do if I lost him," he said in a broken voice. "I almost lost him once. I never want to go through anything like that—like this—again. I know he dislikes me but I'd hoped that someday we'd move past that—that he'd understand why I did what I've done over the years, and we could reach some accommodation. But to come so close to losing him...."

"You won't lose him," Lottie said confidently. "He's recovering quite well; Dr. MacQuarrie says he'll be his old self in no time at all. He just needs rest, and we're seeing to that. And food. He's too thin."

"Do they know what caused the fever?"

Lottie shook her head. "He's been suffering from nervous excitability for a while now, and Dr. MacQuarrie thinks it just led to exhaustive collapse. Charles knows a great deal about medical conditions from his years in the army, and has been treating Tristan with an infusion of different plants and some North American herb. It seems to be helping. Charles is studying to be a physician with Dr. MacQuarrie, and Dr. MacQuarrie concurs with the treatment, since Tris shows no sign of any other malady."

"I suppose we can be grateful for that," the baron muttered.

"*Do* you blame Tris for the death of his mother?" Lottie asked pleasantly.

Ware jerked in shock. "I beg your pardon?"

"Do you blame Tris for the death of his mother?" she repeated patiently. "He said you did."

"Of course I don't!"

"Well, it seems to me you must have given Tris that impression," Lottie mused, "because he certainly thinks you do. How did she die? Tris never speaks of her—well, I never speak of mine, either, so I suppose he doesn't feel he can, and I don't feel I can ask."

"She died of scarlet fever. There was an epidemic in the village, and several people died of it besides Alice. Emily, Tristan's baby sister, also died, as did the vicar and his three children. Tristan had been playing with them the day he contracted the illness."

"So Tristan brought the fever home with him?"

"Yes, but I never taxed him with that!"

"Oh, Tristan is quite capable of coming up with that on his own," Lottie said serenely. She rose, went to the door, and exchanged a few words with the footman in the hall. A moment later the other footman returned with the tea tray, and she indicated he was to set it on the low table between their two chairs.

Settling back in her chair, she poured out.

"You don't maintain a butler?" the baron asked curiously.

"Oh, no. It isn't really necessary and the expense would be foolish, Tris says. We don't entertain so much that a butler is really essential. Ellen—my cousin and companion; I believe you met at our wedding—is more than capable as a housekeeper, and we have several maids and footmen, so we are comfortably staffed."

"Tristan? Avoiding expense? That's a change. He was always rather extravagant."

"I don't know about extravagant—he never seemed so to me, but I never paid much attention to his expenses. But if so, after Jamie was born he decided to become more sensible. I'm surprised his man of business has not mentioned it—wasn't he also yours?"

"He was at one time, but as he grew older, he asked to be replaced by a younger man. My business interests are very extensive, and he did not feel as though he was keeping up with them. So I suggested he take over Tris's instead. Although I see him occasionally, he generally does not confide in me."

"Hmm," Lottie said. She sipped her tea, then added, "When Tris was taken ill, I had the opportunity to both speak to Franklin and to review some documents Tris had left in case of such an occurrence. Well, to be honest, in case of his death, but I stretched the meaning. He has been most careful with his funds, and both Jamie and I are well-protected in the case of his death."

"That is more sensible than I would have expected from any young man, let alone Tristan," the baron said. "I'm surprised. Most men his age think of themselves as immortal."

"Oh," Lottie said in a soft voice, "Tristan is *very* aware of his mortality."

"That incident—when he tried to climb out the window—he was delirious, wasn't he? It wasn't really intentional?"

Lottie raised her head and met his eyes levelly. "He was dead serious, Lord Ware. And while we have convinced the servants that he was delirious, I can tell you honestly that he was not. In fact, Tristan's initial collapse came about when Charles discovered that he was intending to destroy himself and charged him with it."

The baron went white, and the hands that lowered the cup and saucer to the table shook so that the china rang. "My God," he breathed. "*Tris?*"

"Yes," she said. "I hope that it was simply depression caused by his nervous exhaustion, but I can tell you that despite appearances, Tristan has been unhappy for a very long time—well before our marriage, in fact. Sadly, it has not been in my power to improve his state. That was why I was so grateful that Charlie was able to stay with us. He has a lot of experience dealing with people and I hoped that he would be a friend to Tris."

"And has he?"

"Oh, yes," Charlotte smiled. "Tristan has become rather fond of Charles since he became ill. I do believe that Charles's friendship will be just the thing for Tris. He is a very lonely man. Tris, I mean. Charles is never lonely." She turned in her chair as the door opened. "Ah, here he is," she said delightedly. "Our little man."

The nurse came in the door, leading Jamie, who was stumping along on his short little legs. "Mama!" he cried and let go Nurse's hand to toddle over to clutch at Charlotte's skirts.

"He's grown so much since last summer," Baron Ware marveled. "And walking, too! He is the very picture of Tristan at his age—except for the dark eyes."

Jamie turned and studied his grandfather, still clutching Lottie's skirt. "Hello," the baron said warily.

"H'wo," Jamie replied politely.

"Do you remember your grandfather, Jamie?" Lottie asked.

"No," Jamie said. He stuck his fist in his mouth and chewed on it a moment, then said, "I ha boo."

Baron Ware looked up at Lottie, panic-stricken. "He means he has a boo-hoo," she said. "He fell yesterday and scraped his knee. Show Grandfather your boo-hoo." To the baron, she said, "He cried when he fell, and so we call it a boo-hoo, don't we, love? Because he cried 'boo-hoo'."

"He should call it a scrape," the baron said, "shouldn't he?"

"He should call it whatever he likes," Lottie said amiably.

Jamie looked at her, then back at the baron. Then he picked up the skirts of his little dress and displayed his knee. There was a tiny scratch on the kneecap.

"I see," the baron said solemnly. "Does it hurt?"

"No," Jamie said. He dropped his skirts and leaned against Lottie.

"I don't know what to do with children," the baron confessed. "I never knew what to do with Tris; his mother handled everything. Then she died and I sent Tris to school, and after that we were constantly at loggerheads. No matter what I did, it never mattered. He seemed to take delight in annoying me or making me angry. When he did so well at Cambridge, I thought perhaps he had changed, but then he came down to Town instead of staying on there as I'd hoped. I thought perhaps he'd take a lecturer's position and then when he was a little older he could begin taking over some of my duties. But he came down and seemed to have no interests in anything except drinking and whor... drinking and things." He looked down at Jamie, who was watching him thoughtfully. "I don't know what happened. I never expected him to hate me. Why does he hate me?"

"Because he hates himself," Lottie said. To Jamie, she said, "Fetch the stool over there, Jamie, love, and you can climb in my lap. I can't pick you up anymore."

"Let me," Ware said and rose, bending to lift Jamie up into Lottie's lap. "There. Is that comfortable?"

Lottie bent her head to whisper, "Tell him 'thank you'," and Jamie's head rose to look at his grandfather. "Fanku," he said solemnly.

"You're welcome," the baron said, equally solemnly, then he turned back to Charlotte. "What should I do about Tris?"

CHAPTER 15

BY THE fourth day of Tristan's illness, he was feeling better and his temper had turned irascible from his enforced inactivity. To placate him, Charles had hauled his medical books up from the library and settled on the sofa next to him, poring over the volumes in English with him, translating aloud the ones in German. Tristan took the ones in Latin and Greek and did the same for Charles; although Charles had had some of the classical languages at Eton, Tristan was much better at translating those.

When he tired, as he inevitably did, he made Charles talk about the hospital and his activities there. He was especially interested in the descriptions of the more physical elements of his experiences, rather than the treatment for illnesses that Charles found fascinating. Charles supposed it made sense; Tristan had always been far more interested in the physical. "No, seriously," he said, "what do you do with a broken bone?"

"Call a surgeon," Charles laughed.

Tris hit him with a pillow. "Seriously, Charlie!"

"Well, if a surgeon's not handy, there are some things you can do," and he proceeded to explain the process for setting a bone, followed by how to manage broken ribs, how to wrap a sprain properly, and the importance of cleanliness when stitching a wound. "It's especially important when something is embedded in the wound, such as with a ball from a pistol," he said. "Embedded elements can lead to putrefaction. Oddly enough, boiling water on the wound and on the knife can sometimes prevent the putrefaction. I don't know why. MacQuarrie has a theory that it has something to do with animalcules."

"The invisible creatures Van Leeuwenhoek discovered with the microscope," Tristan acknowledged. "I read his research at Trinity. It wasn't my field, but I found it interesting nonetheless."

"Well, Mac thinks they cause the putrefaction, and that the boiling water kills them. All I know is that clean equipment and boiling water seem to make a difference in treating wounded soldiers."

"Well, I knew about wrapping sprains from fisticuffs," Tristan observed. "Jackson showed some of us how to manage that since they're pretty common. I watched him stitch up a man's cheek once."

"Didn't make you sick?"

Tristan snorted. "A little thing like that? Ballocks. I've been stitched up myself much worse. Fell out of a tree onto a fence."

"Is that the scar on your back? I felt it the other evening when I was giving you the rub down."

"That's it."

"How old were you?"

Tristan thought a moment, then said, "Twenty-eight—no, twenty-seven. It was the year before I married Lottie."

"You were a grown man and you were climbing a *tree*?"

Tristan grinned. "It was the only way to get into the house; the lady's husband had footmen posted at the door to keep me out. Well, not me specifically; just whoever it was he suspected of cuckolding him. Good thing Gibson was there; he and a couple other friends spirited me away before the footmen found me. Got quite a lecture from the surgeon who stitched me up. Never did understand why surgeons aren't thought of just as highly as physicians; their work's just as important, if not more so."

Charles shrugged. "Just as the barrister is more highly thought of than a mere solicitor; it's all in the perception. God knows the solicitor does most of the work. Now, that's enough mental work for you; we've got to give that brain of yours a rest as well as your body. And speaking of your body, here's your supper." That was to the soft knock on the bedroom door. Charles rose and let Reston in with the tray.

"Oh, God, not more of that beef tea. I swear it's worse than that evil American potion you make up."

"It's not that bad—either of them. And they're both good for you."

"Bunk," Tris replied. "They're both just nasty, but the skullcap tea is the worst."

"It isn't," his lover snorted. "It's your imagination. You think that because it's medicinal, it should taste bad. It tastes no worse than brandy."

"Yes, but brandy has the advantage of bringing on a nice drunk," Tris said.

He set the beef tea aside while he ate what Reston had brought: roast chicken, new potatoes, and bread pudding. When he was done, Charles handed him the cup again and he made a face, but finished it off, setting the cup back on the tray. "There. I've eaten my dinner and drunk my tea. What reward do I get?"

Charles took the tray from his lap and set it on the floor by the door, then sat on the sofa beside Tristan. "A kiss," he said, and his mouth settled on Tris's, warm and steady. Tris sighed happily and opened to Charles's questing tongue, welcoming it with his own. His hands slid over Charles's shirtfront and to the buttons at the collar, working them undone, then pulling the shirt from Charles's trousers. "Off," he said, his voice muffled by Charles's lips.

"Bossy," Charles said, drawing back and pulling the shirt over his head. "You must be feeling better."

Tris smiled, running his fingers over Charles's smooth chest. "I would have thought you to be more hairy," he said, leaning forward to lick at one flat nipple.

"And why is that?"

"Because you're so fierce and masculine."

"And blond," Charles pointed out. "Blonds have less body hair in general. I'm sorry to disappoint you."

"You don't. I like it." Tristan's tongue flicked over the solid planes of his chest. "I can see your skin clearly, taste it. You taste so different from a woman."

"Tris—are you sure this is what you want? I don't want to be pressing you. This—this is important to me and I don't want you regretting it later."

"'Pressing me'? I've been trying to get you in bed for days now. Besides, I never regret anything," Tris said absently. His hands traveled down that beautifully sculpted torso to the edge of Charles's trousers. "Least of all sex."

Charles caught his hands and held them still. "This isn't just sex," he said harshly.

Startled, Tris looked up. Charles's eyes were dark and hard, and Tris felt a thrill of fear and something unidentifiable race through him. "No," he said, swallowing. "No, it isn't."

"Just so you know that."

"What are you worried about?" Tris asked, reaching up to rub away the line between Charles's brows. He hadn't lost that hard look and it made Tristan uncomfortable. "What's wrong?"

"I'm just...." Charles caught Tristan's hands again and rested his forehead on Tris's knuckles. "Not sure."

"Not sure of what?" Tristan asked, feeling that shiver of fear again, but this time it wasn't so pleasant. "Not sure of *me*?" He jerked his hands away and shifted away, sliding off the sofa. His legs trembled a little, but held him; he reached for the banyan on the chair and drew it on, then went to look out the window.

"I love you," Charles said.

"So you've said." Tristan's voice sounded flat even to his own ears.

Down on the lamp-lit street, a couple of draymen were arguing over their carts. A large carriage with a crest on the side went by, splashing the pair; they turned as one to find common cause in cursing the carriage driver. A handful of militia in red coats trotted by, slowing to watch as a pair of shop girls hurried past on their way home.

The silence in the room was deafening. Finally, Tristan said tiredly, "I don't know what you want, Charlie. This is all new to me. I'd made up my mind that I wanted you a long time ago, but now it seems that you're shoving me away. You say you love me, and I think I love you, but I don't really know what that all means. I don't know what love is, or what it means in this situation. At least with the physical, I know what I'm asking. I don't know all the details, I don't even know *how* you want me, or how I want you, but I know that what I feel for you I never felt for any of the women I've fornicated with in the last fifteen years. *Never*. I don't know if it's love or just finally realizing that I'm not the man I thought I was." He laughed humorlessly. "Not that that's any great loss."

"It's when you speak like that that I can find it in myself to be angry with you," Charles said.

Tristan waved a dismissive hand. "I'm not looking for kindness, Charlie."

"I'm not being kind, Tristan."

Tris turned, frowning at the bitterness in Charles's voice. "I don't mean to make you angry. I'm just trying to understand what it is you want from me. You talk about love as if it were something natural, something normal...."

"It is," Charles growled.

"But I have never heard of anything like this. Oh, I went to public school and was aware of the silliness that went on there, I know all about madge houses, and even know a few men who frequent them, though of course that's never discussed in public, but I've never heard of two men actually having a, a *connection* as though it were *normal*."

"That," Charles said harshly, "is exactly what the problem is, Tris. You seem to think that this isn't normal. Isn't natural."

"Well, it isn't," Tris said reasonably. "It's not the way men are meant to be. It might be just lust, not love. I want you, but when you say you love me, is it just because you're fond of me, you know me from Charlotte's letters, you desire me as I desire you? That isn't what love is."

"What is love, then?" Charles stood, running his hand through his hair agitatedly. "What would you describe love as, then, if not knowledge and fondness and desire?"

Tristan stared at him blankly. "I don't know," he admitted.

"Then isn't that enough?"

"No," Tristan said. "Not if it's going to stop you from taking me to bed and rogering me until I scream." He gave Charles a smile he'd practiced far too often on bored wives.

Charles turned and left the room, closing the adjoining door with a decided click.

"*Bloody* hell!" Tristan swore and went after him.

When he came into Charles's bedroom, Charles was sitting on the end of his bed, tugging off his boots. He looked up, startled, when Tris came in. His face was bleak.

"You didn't think I was going to let this go, did you?" Tris demanded, yanking the boot from Charles's hand and throwing it across the room.

"I'm not one of your inamoratas." Charles's teeth were clenched. "I'm not going to treat you like a man-whore, Tristan. Either you want to lie with me because it matters or you don't."

"I have *never* met a man like you before," Tristan said. "If any of my friends were in this position with a woman, they'd already be in bed with her skirts up around her ears. You—well, what I'd like is to box your ears until they ring. Pray explain to me what is the difficulty? Do you want me or not?"

"Of course I want you," Charles snarled. "My *God*, I've wanted you from the beginning."

"You want me. So if loving me is what's stopping you from fucking me, then stop loving me, for God's sake. You have me confused, Charlie. All I know is that I want you and you want me, and for some reason you're keeping me from acting on it."

"I'm sorry," Charles said and lay back on the bed, running his hands through his hair. "It's just that, well, this is the first time in years that I've wanted to go to bed with someone I care about. And I remember what happened the last time, and, bugger, Tris, I'm terrified."

"What happened last time?"

"He changed his mind. He said he loved me, but then just a few days after our affair started, he changed his mind. Said he'd had a crisis of conscience and that the feelings he had for me were *unnatural*, that he had to stop for both our sakes. Asked to be transferred to another company so we wouldn't be together so much. So I could see him occasionally, pass him on sentry duty, even speak to him once in a while, but never touch him, never kiss him, never know what it was like to hold him again."

"And you think that will happen with me," Tris surmised. "So you don't trust me."

"And when you say things like it's just lust, or sex, or fucking, it makes it sound so shallow and cold. I've had those kinds of encounters, Tris. I've had to: the furtive coupling that eases nothing but physical need. I don't want that from you. So if that's all it is for you, then I'd rather go back to my regiment." Charles's voice was hoarse from unshed tears.

"You don't trust me." Tristan thought he might cry himself.

"I do trust you," Charles said. "I'm just… afraid."

"The brave soldier." Tristan sat down on the bed beside him, laying his hand on Charles's belly. "I'm supposed to be the one who's afraid. And I am. But not of lying with you. Not of taking you, even though I can't quite figure out how it's not going to hurt. I'm afraid of losing you."

Charles reached up and took Tristan's hand, drawing him down on the bed beside him. They lay across the coverlet on their backs, gazing up at the canopy, their only physical contact their intertwined fingers. Finally Charles said, "But that's exactly what I'm afraid of, Tris. Losing you. Of you deciding that this isn't what you want. Because maybe it will hurt, and nothing I do will give you pleasure, and you'll decide it's not worth it. That I'm not worth it."

Tristan shifted to his side, resting his head on his hand and studying Charles with faint amusement. "I could say the same," he pointed out.

"Perhaps I won't give you pleasure, and you'll decide to run away with one of the footmen. It's a risk you take, Charlie." He gave him a wry grin. "I dare you."

"You and your dares." Charles lay still a moment, then rolled over in a rush, taking Tris with him and under him. He sank his teeth gently into Tristan's shoulder, not hard enough to break the skin, but firm enough to hold him. Tris gasped and his heart started pounding wildly. Charles shifted his weight so that his legs pressed Tristan's thighs apart and he settled into the space, rocking gently against Tristan. Heat flooded Tristan's veins and he groaned, raising his legs and wrapping them around Charles's hips, locking his ankles to hold Charles to him forever.

Charles made a noise against Tristan's shoulder and his mouth turned gentle, kissing up the curve of his shoulder and throat, suckling his earlobe and then flicking his tongue into Tristan's ear. Tristan shuddered and reached for Charles's head, pulling him up so that he could kiss him again, hungrily, then twisted his body, rolling them back the other way until he was pinning Charles, straddling him. Then he broke the kiss and sat up, settling on those strong thighs, and pulled his banyan and nightshirt over his head and tossed them onto the floor. "I hope your door is locked," he said, bending to kiss Charles's chest.

Charles groaned and buried his hands in Tristan's hair. The feel of those long, powerful fingers against his skull made Tris shiver in delight. Charles's skin was warm and salty; Tristan licked him, tasting him, even as his hands slid down that muscled abdomen to the fastenings of his trousers, finding and dispatching the multiplicity of buttons.

And then, for the first time, he lay hands on another man's cock.

He knew what it should feel like; he'd handled his own often enough. But somehow, the hard, velvety shaft in his hands roused him even more than Charles's hands on his own had; he felt the rush of blood to his own staff, felt the surge of heat to his face and lips and breast. He glanced up to see Charles's back arched, his head thrown back, heard the rasp of harsh breaths and thought, *This—this is what I want. What I've always wanted....*

The last of the fear bled away and it was with nothing but desire and love that he bent to lick the little pearl of fluid from the tip of Charles's cock. It tasted of salt and spice, faintly bitter and addictive as the best brandy. Tris licked the round head, the edge of foreskin, the drop that eased from the tiny slit to replace the one he'd already tasted, then set about exploring Charles intently with his lips and tongue. He licked along the shaft, tasted the warm, furry weight of Charles's ballocks, nuzzled up Charles's groin into the musky warmth of the nest of hair there. His fingers played alongside as he licked back up to the tip again, then took Charles into his mouth, sliding down deep as he could without gagging, his fingers closing around the base. He drew back, his lips tight over his teeth and his tongue and cheeks sucking hard, all the way back up to the head, then back down again.

"Oh, *God*," Charles groaned.

Tris released him long enough to say, "I bloody *love* the way you taste, Charlie," before closing his mouth over Charles's cock again. He recalled the times he'd had whores take him like this and tried to remember the things they'd done that felt especially good; it became a game for him to see what ones made Charles whimper, what ones made him groan. Charles's hands had fallen away from his head and were clenched in the coverlet beside him, hanging on as if he thought he was going to fly off the bed. His fingers felt Charles's balls tighten even before Charles's strangled "Tris!" and he went down deep again, his other hand pulling up on the loose velvety skin as he took Charles in and swallowed the hot seed that burst against his throat. Then he licked the remnants from Charles's shaft until it went soft, and then, only then, did he raise his head to meet Charles's dazed eyes. The sight made a slow, deep warmth begin to glow in his chest, a warmth that was like, yet unlike, the feeling he had the first time he'd seen Jamie.

Oh.

He smiled and said honestly, rawly, "I love you, Charlie."

He eased up next to Charles on the bed, curling up against the solid, sweat-streaked chest and resting his head on Charles's shoulder. Charles said, "That wasn't supposed to be how it went."

"Oh?"

"Yes. I was supposed to make love to you, not the other way around."

"You did that once, a few days ago, as I recall. Turnabout's fair play, don't you think?" Tristan turned his head to look at Charles. "Did you like it?" he asked, suddenly uncertain.

"Oh, love," Charles said fervently, "it was *astounding*."

"No running off with the footmen?"

"Well," Charles said thoughtfully, "they are bruisers, aren't they? You did hire them for their looks, I'm sure."

Tristan dug his fingers into Charles's ribs and Charles yelped, then wrapped his arms around Tris and rolled over, covering him, enveloping him, encasing him in warm flesh. Tristan sighed and ran his hands up Charles's muscular back. "Charlie," he said in contentment. "*My* Charlie."

"Yours," Charles said agreeably and kissed him, his mouth soft, with the odd but wonderful contrast of bristly whiskers on Tristan's cheek. Tristan closed his eyes and returned the kiss, feeling like at last—at *last*—he'd found home.

THE clock on the mantel chimed softly; Tristan lay in the darkness of the drawn bedcurtains and counted to himself. At five, the chiming stopped. Early, then.

He turned his head into the warm shelter of Charles's shoulder. It was too dark to see his lover, but the lack of light only made his other senses stronger: he could hear Charles's quiet, regular breathing, smell the warm herbal scent of his skin and the stronger, more pungent smell of their lovemaking. And felt the rough, sandy stubble of Charles's cheek against his forehead. Soon, too soon, he'd have to creep back into his own room. Last night, after Reston had finished tidying up, Tristan had drawn the bedcurtains on his own bed, to give the illusion that he was still there, and come here, into Charles's arms.

They'd spent the night exploring each other, finding out what made each other respond. Tristan had discovered that Charles was quite ticklish and took advantage of it; Charles, for his part, had found out that the soles of Tristan's feet were amazingly sensitive and that licking them made Tristan insane with lust. Despite Charles's determined exploration of every inch of Tristan's skin, and Tristan's of Charles, they'd kept it simple. They'd sated their desire with hands and mouths, stifling their cries in the bedclothes and each other's skin. Then they'd both fallen asleep, exhausted and content.

He'd never slept with a lover before, except Charlotte—and then only during their honeymoon. Even when they were benighted when traveling back and forth from their country house, he'd always arranged separate rooms at whatever inn they'd ended up.

He'd dozed in a lover's bed every once in a while, but never for more than a few minutes. And yet here he was, after a good six hours of steady, dreamless sleep. Dreamless. Sleep. He smiled to himself. Was this all it took? To lie in the arms of a man? Or just *this* man? Because he felt relatively sure that it was this man who made the difference. While he'd admitted to himself that he'd found other men attractive, it was men in general, not anyone specific. Charles was different. It wasn't just attraction; he *liked* Charles as well as loved him.

There was a faint scraping sound in the room. Curious, he crawled to the foot of the bed and peeked out through the curtains, careful not to reveal himself. It was just one of the scullery maids, come to build up the banked fire and warm the room before Charles would rise. He smiled to himself, wondering if she'd already done the fire in his own room, thinking the master was deep in his usual drunken repose behind the blue velvet curtains.

Then the bed shifted and a warm pair of lips dropped a kiss in the small of Tristan's back. He jerked in startlement and bit back a gasp; it seemed that he'd been quiet enough, though, as the maid kept on with her work, undisturbed.

Then the chaste lips turned wicked, hot and wet; a tongue flicked over the dimples of his arse, and hands settled on his hips to raise him to his knees and hold him immobile. He clenched the curtains in his fist until he realized that if the maid turned around, she'd see him; then he released them and grabbed instead for the bedcovers, drawing them up and into his mouth to bite down on them, stifling a cry as those wicked lips moved lower, the hands moving to part his cheeks and the sweet, wet tongue sliding between to flick over his opening before dropping to lick at his ballocks. *Oh, God*, he thought helplessly as Charles nuzzled there, and at the insides of his thighs, and then back again at his entrance, pushing at it with his wet tongue. The sensation was indescribable; he thought perhaps his eyes rolled back in his head, and he *knew* he felt dizzy. They hadn't done *that* last night.

The tongue and hands were withdrawn and he breathed easier, though he had to admit disappointment, until he heard the faint squeak of a cork being drawn and the enclosed darkness of the bed was suddenly rich with the scent of eucalyptus and rosemary. If the naughty kisses hadn't been enough to arouse him, just the smell of the oil was. He bit back a moan as he felt warm, slick fingers on his arse, and then in him, stroking and stretching; he stuffed more of the blankets in his mouth as Charles's fingers found *that spot* and coaxed shivers from him. He'd touched him there last night, stroking until Tristan was mad with it, then whispered wickedly, "Next time it will be my cock there," and Tristan had spent just from the words. He now started rocking back against the rhythm of those fingers, wild for their touch and eager for Charles's promise.

Charles leaned over him, his mouth at Tristan's ear, and whispered, "*Ssshh*," then withdrew his fingers. Tristan felt something larger, blunter, press against him, and thought, *Oh, my God...* as Charles pushed into him.

It hurt for a moment, burning, but then something happened in Tristan's head, and he thought, *Oh*, just as he had when he realized he was in love with Charles. It was as if a tiny portion of the universe suddenly shifted into something that made sense. He relaxed, letting Charles into his body as easily as he'd let him into his heart. And it felt *good*.

He let Charles set the rhythm, and when he figured it out, he started rocking back and forth again, this time in response to Charles's movements. Charles's chuckle was inaudible, but he felt the rumble inside and out and smiled to himself in the darkness, feeling the tide of desire rising. Charles kissed his back, his shoulders, the nape of his neck; he twisted around to meet Charles's mouth and hooked an arm around his neck to hold him. The angle was awkward but he didn't care; he needed to feel and taste Charles even as Charles felt and tasted him. "Charles," he whispered, and Charles murmured, "Yes...."

And then he was biting the bedclothes again to stifle his cries until he heard the soft click of the door latch, and saw through the folds of bedcurtains that the room was empty. He moaned *"Charlie...!"* and Charles laughed and closed his fingers around Tristan's prick, stroking and pulling, his digits strong and sure. With a deep, heartrending groan, Tristan spent in Charles's fingers, and Charles bit Tristan in the fleshy part of the shoulder as he plunged into Tristan over and over again. Tristan thought of the whore outside the madge house saying "I likes a good 'ard fuck, I do...," and he laughed as Charles cried out and Tristan felt the heat of his spend deep inside, all the way to his heart, he thought.

"Something funny?" Charles gasped out when he could talk again. He rolled over onto his side and pulled Tris close in, their feet tangled together on the pillows, their heads resting on the bundle of blankets that Tristan had been chewing on. "I've had you crying in extremis, and now laughing. Have you nothing between?"

"I don't seem to," Tris said. He kissed Charles lingeringly, his hands moving over Charles's sweaty body. "Not where you're concerned, at any rate. I'm mad for you, Charles, so you must expect emotional extremes."

"Mm-hmm," Charles said and kissed him, then rested his head on Tristan's shoulder. "You did quite well, you know, keeping quiet until that girl was gone."

"You!" Tristan poked him in the belly. "I thought I was going to lose my mind, trying to keep from crying out and being discovered in your bed. You madman, don't you think she'd run to tell the nearest constable?"

"I don't know," Charles mused. "You seem to have the knack for breeding loyalty in your servants. I don't know that she would run and tell. I think at the worst she would go to Reston, who'd reassure her that there was nothing wrong."

"You have more faith in my servants than I do," Tristan said.

Charles said, "This is a risky way of life, Tris. You will have to trust your servants to keep your secrets—they will find them out, and they are your last line of defense against those who don't understand." He smoothed his hand over Tristan's stubbled cheek. "I think you have good servants; I think Reston knows, and I know Reid does. Between them, they will guard you."

"And you?"

Charles smiled. "I've been taking care of myself longer than I care to remember, but yes, I trust them to guard my flank."

"And Lottie. Them and Lottie."

"Oh, I'm not forgetting Lottie," Charles chuckled. "She is passionate about few things—letter-writing, and loyalty. She's a bit of a bulldog."

"What about Ellen?"

"Ellen is all right," Charles said. "She's known about me since I was a boy. But for your sake, we'll keep it secret from her as long as we can. It's always safer."

"'Safer'," Tristan snorted. "Since when do I play safe?"

"Well, love," Charles said, kissing him again, "you've picked a wondrous way to thumb your nose at the world."

"That isn't why," Tristan said, feeling a sudden anxiousness. "It isn't why, Charlie."

"Oh, I know," Charles replied, a note of surprise in his voice. "I know. It's all right, Tris."

"I just need you to know."

Charles laughed. "I do know. I know all I need to about you, love, and it's all good."

Tristan looked up at him, and in the light through the parted bedcurtains, saw truth. And love. He smiled and closed his eyes again, nestling into the warmth and safety of his lover.

CHARLES woke him a while later, so that he could creep back into his own bedroom in time to ring for Reston as usual. It was full morning, the winter sun bright through the drapes, and Tristan blinked as he opened the bedcurtains. "What time is it?" he rasped, then he cleared his throat.

"Rising eight," Charles said after a glance at the clock on the nightstand. "Are you meeting with Franklin this morning?"

"Yes; it's been nearly a week, and I sent a message to him yesterday to come 'round." Tristan stretched, then laughed as his flung nightshirt hit him in the face. "Dare I take that as a hint?"

"You don't want to scandalize poor Reid," Charles said, yawning. "He'll be along momentarily."

"I doubt if much scandalizes 'poor Reid'," Tristan said. "After how many years as your batman?"

"Too many, I think."

"Are you going to the hospital this afternoon?"

"Yes—just as you're getting back to your regular schedule, so must I." Charles pulled on his banyan and went to the nightstand to wash up. "You should stay quiet today, though; see Franklin if you must, and Jamie, of course, but you shouldn't go back to your usual activities for a few days. Drink has a deleterious effect on one under the best of circumstances; recovery from a fever will only be slowed by a liberal application of gin."

Tristan went to him and put his arms around his waist, leaning his cheek against Charles's from behind. "My usual activities hold very little interest for me these days," he murmured. "I wonder why?"

Charles snorted. "No doubt because you fear you won't be able to keep up with your friends," he said dryly.

Tristan pinched his arse. He jumped. Tris said, "They need to keep up with me, not arsey-varsey. No, it's because I'm far more interested in these *unusual* activities I've discovered."

Charles turned in his arms and kissed him. Drawing away, he said, "In truth, Tris, I'd rather spend the day in bed with you than tending to the undeserving poor, but I've made a commitment to something and must fulfill it."

"What's that like?" Tristan asked, "making a commitment? The only one I've ever made is to Charlotte and that wasn't really me doing it. I can't imagine what it must be like, to be part of something that's even remotely important, like what you're doing. Like what you did, in the cavalry and as ADC to Wellington and all."

"I can't imagine any other way to live," Charles said frankly. "The way you do, just drifting through life—God, Tris, no wonder you were ready to end it. The few weeks I spent following you around before Mac rescued me were unbearable. How have you stood it for so long?"

"It's what I'm used to," Tristan said in surprise. "I never thought of it as drifting. It's just… it's just what I do. It's what any man of my class does."

"Thank God my father doesn't expect me to live like that. He doesn't much care what I do, but he doesn't demand I behave that way."

"Your brother does. He's not in my set, but I've seen him around enough."

"More reason to live differently." Charles handed Tristan his banyan and smoothed his hair back from his forehead before kissing him there. "You're as much a prisoner of your life as anyone I know. Isn't there anything you'd like to do—aside from the obvious?"

"I never really thought there was anything *to* do," Tristan said, pulling on the banyan and shaking out the sleeves. "I've no talents: can't write, or draw, or play an instrument any better than any other person of my acquaintance. I've no head for business—"

"Now, that's not true," Charles interrupted. "What about the funds you've invested for Charlotte and Jamie? Do you think just anyone could have built that nest egg so large in the space of just a few months? That took talent."

Tristan waved a hand. "Blame that on Franklin. I just provided the seed money. And he keeps making noises about me learning more so that I'm prepared to take over from my father, but it bores me to death. Oh, the investing is interesting, but I have the attention span of a gnat."

"That sounds like your father speaking," Charles said quietly.

Tristan shrugged. "No one ever said my father was either dishonest or less than perspicacious. I don't argue with what he says; he's usually right."

"Not about you."

He shrugged again. "It doesn't matter—I still have no interest in his businesses. I have no interest in anything, in fact, except Jamie—and you." It was painful to admit, but it was true enough.

"What about medicine?"

Nonplused, Tristan said, "What?"

"Anatomy, in specific. Medical anatomy. When you've joined me in the library in the evenings, you've seemed fascinated by it. You have a much better memory for the various systems than I do."

"It isn't anything. I do think…." Tristan strode to the connecting door. "I'd best ring Reston and get dressed. Franklin will be along any moment."

"Tris."

He paused and looked over his shoulder. "What?"

"For what it's worth, I think you would have made an excellent surgeon. You have an instinctive understanding of the way the human body works—I've seen it when you're fencing or coaching others at Jackson's. Would you like to accompany me to the hospital one day soon, and see what it's like?"

"I couldn't be a surgeon," Tristan said stiffly. "It's not appropriate for one of my station."

"No one says you have to practice," Charles said, "but wouldn't you like to *know*?"

Tristan stared at him, a deep thudding in his ears. He realized after a moment that it was his heartbeat. "Yes," he said, finally, feeling as though he were saying something else, something far more meaningful. "Yes, I'd like that."

Charles smiled. "Go get dressed. We'll talk later."

Dazed, Tristan obeyed.

CHAPTER 16

IT WAS a full week before Tristan was able to take Charles up on his offer. A week of slowly dissipating weariness as his muscles recovered from their enforced idleness; a week of sobriety, obeying Charles's dictates about drink slowing his recovery; a week of domesticity, playing with Jamie, talking to Ellen, listening to Charlotte reading from her copious correspondence. And a week of evenings with Charles, first in the library, poring over their books, and later, poring over something far more interesting, learning what pleased his lover.

It seemed to be true, what Charles had said about having an understanding of the human body. He did know it, both from his carnal experiences with women, and from his lessons with Jackson and Angelo. He knew the way muscles moved, where damage was most easily done, and most easily mended. He knew where a body was most or least sensitive, where it was strongest, and where it needed to be touched with the utmost delicacy. He used those lessons when exploring Charles, and helping Charles to explore him. Before long, they were equals in bed; both sure, both giving, both knowing how to coax the most pleasure out of each other. And the rightness of it dispelled Tristan's old doubts about its morality: how could anything that brought such joy to both of them and hurt no one else be evil?

Reston took his new instructions—not to disturb Tristan in the mornings until he was rung for—with equanimity and said only that he would relay them to the rest of the household staff as well. "You do need your rest, sir," he said understandingly. "May I be permitted to express the entire staff's congratulations on your return to health?"

"I imagine they're grateful I'm not still a demanding invalid," Tristan said with a grin.

He grinned more easily these days. The dark cloud that had seemed to hover over him this past six-month was gone. He still had his dark moments, when Charles was at the hospital or in the depths of the small hours, or when the craving for brandy was at its worst, but they were moments, not the continuous feeling of grief and despair that had plagued him so long. For the first time in his life he began to think that perhaps his father was wrong; that it wasn't so much that he was a failure as that he'd never really tried. Charles made him want to try.

Try what, he still wasn't sure.

He lunched with Gibson and Berkeley one afternoon at a restaurant in the City, a place more than a few steps above their usual haunts. "What?" he said defensively at their disbelieving stares when he ordered coffee for himself.

"Coffee? *Coffee?*" Berkeley stuttered. He glanced at Gibson. "It's not Woodsy," he said confidingly to his friend. "He's been abducted by fairies and replaced with a changeling."

Tristan hit him with a bun. "Shut up, idiot," he said cheerfully. "It's my brother-in-law's doing; he says I need to teetotal for a few weeks to get my blood back to its usual shape."

"Didn't know blood had a shape," Gibs mused. "Thought it was just sort of liquid."

Tris hit him with a bun, too.

"Aim's not suffered," Gibs said, picking it up off the table where it had bounced and eating it. "So when are you coming back to Jackson's? He was askin' about you the other day."

"A few more days," Tristan said. "I'll need to get back into shape."

"Why not tomorrow?" Berkeley bent over and fished around on the floor until he found the bun Tristan had thrown. He picked a few strands of carpet off it and ate it absently.

"I'm going to the hospital with Charles tomorrow."

"Why? Is he sick?"

Tristan laughed. "No, he's studying to become a physician, and he attends Dr. MacQuarrie at St. Joseph's in Spitalfields. He invited me to come along with him and see what it's all about."

"Depressin', I should think," Gibs said. "Can't imagine anything else. Blood and guts and whatnot."

"Ah, we see plenty of that in the odd pub fight," Berks opined. "Nothin' new there."

"I imagine it will be depressing," Tristan acknowledged. "But I think it will be interesting, too. St. Joseph's has been experimenting with some new surgical procedures and has had some success with them, and Charles has promised to introduce me to the Chief of Surgery there."

His friends stared, Berks blinking like a fish. Tristan gave a laugh. "I'm done now," he said. "Anyone for the eel pie?"

THE excursion was a success, at least as far as Tristan was concerned. St. Joseph's might have been in one of the poorer areas of London, but it was well-endowed and had an excellent staff, overseen by MacQuarrie and the Chief of Surgery, a man named Crosby who was a physician by training, but had switched professions and become a member of the College of Surgeons instead. He had a strong opinion on the present division between surgery and medicine that he expounded on at length as he worked. "Learn more from actual cuttin' than you ever do from *books*!" he roared as he surged through the halls of the hospital, Tristan and Charles and a half dozen students at his heels.

Tristan was able to witness an operation for the removal of a tumor, several bonesettings, the lancing of an abscess, and the amputation of an arm. Charles, who although he was in the physician program had battlefield surgery experience, assisted with the last, and came out of the operating theater unrolling the sleeves of his shirt. He pulled the blood-spattered apron over his head and tossed it into a basket waiting beside the door. "Well, that went better than I expected," he said, sliding his arms into the waistcoat Tristan held for him. "It was the left arm, and he's right-handed, and he swooned before we even got to the cauterization. That's the worst part, I think."

"It can't be as bad as the sound of the bone saw," Tristan said, grimacing. "That was dreadful."

"I suppose there's nothing good about amputation," Charles acknowledged, "except the alternative—blood poisoning and death. That's the last of the scheduled surgeries for today. Thank God. I don't think I'm cut out to be a surgeon. Takes a steadier hand than I've got. And a steadier stomach. I'm to make the rounds with Mac in the wards. Are you ready to go home, or would you like to tag along?"

"I'd rather like to come with you, if you don't mind," Tristan said.

"I would have thought you would be disgusted by all of this." Charles cocked his head. "But you're not, are you?"

"Not in the slightest. It's fascinating. Oh, the surgeries were gruesome, no doubt. But it's amazing the way it all works; how a man can know precisely what to do with another person's body to make it respond...." He realized that his words could be taken two ways and blushed scarlet, laughing. "You know what I mean," he said.

"Oddly enough, I do. Come along, then."

IT WASN'T the last trip of its kind. As the days went on, the staff and patients at St. Joseph's gradually forgot that Tristan was only an observer and began accepting him as a fixture there. Perpetually shorthanded, they quickly found out that he had a steady hand, a stomach of cast-iron, and, once he'd built his strength back up from his illness, the muscles to manage—or sometimes manhandle—both twisted limbs and recalcitrant patients. The doctors, busy and distracted, paid no attention to his fashionable coats or quality boots; he was a strong hand when they needed one, and they seemed to always need one, and he was quick to respond to even the least courteous, harried demands. By early March, he'd unofficially joined the ranks of the students that followed Dr. Crosby on his rounds and in the operating theater, learning to set limbs and stitch wounds and draw teeth, and even, sometimes, to observe real surgeries. Although the hospital was a teaching one and affiliated with one of the schools that licensed physicians, the rules were often ignored in trauma situations, and willing hands meant more than official status at a place that treated the poor more than the affluent. He found it absorbing, if sometimes disturbing, and the hours flew. Charles, whose interest was leaning toward medicine rather than surgery, was usually off with MacQuarrie, but Tristan found his own niche among the surgical apprentices. Some days, he didn't rejoin Charles until late in the evening as they climbed wearily into Tristan's carriage for the ride home.

To his surprise, Tristan discovered a serenity, a quiet pleasure in working with the irascible surgeon and the dozens of people under his supervision. It was hard, bloody, exhausting work, but the sense of accomplishment over a well-set limb or a neat job of stitches was its own reward. Tristan was amazed at his delight when Crosby looked over a dislocated arm he'd just fixed (with the aid of two large orderlies) and grunted approval. He, son of the great Baron Ware, was pleased by the approval of a petit bourgeois? He was, and said so to Charlie.

Who only grinned, and said, "I told you that you would make an excellent surgeon."

He didn't spend every waking hour at the hospital. He still made time for the odd hour at Jackson's and Angelo's, and still went out with his friends to social events, but those were hours taken away from the hospital, and therefore, in his eyes, wasted. He drank very little, so that he would be clear-eyed and clearheaded the next day. Gibson and Berkeley and his other friends shook their heads over him, but Gibson took him aside and told him that whatever it was that had made him so happy, he was fully in support of it. When he told Gibs about the surgery and the fascination it had for him, Gibs had only patted his shoulder and said lugubriously, "Whatever makes you happy, Woods."

And it did make him happy. He understood now what drove Charles to this, the sense of achievement, the desire to learn, the need to *know* and to *help*.

Oddly, this new undertaking meant that he and Charles actually saw less of each other even than they had before, when their lives and interests diverged. The comradely evenings in the library were shortened by the need for an early retiring, or by Tristan's social calendar, even pared down as it was, but they still managed to find a little time to be together outside the bedroom, whether it was the hour at Jackson's or a quick luncheon before heading off to the hospital. Once or twice, they'd made hurried love in the carriage as it was stuck in City traffic, but it was still winter, after all, and too cold for that sort of activity on a regular basis.

At night, though, they slept in each other's arms, even if most nights it was only sleep. Sometimes, they would lie with each other, but instead of sleeping afterward, would talk about something that happened during the day at the hospital, or something one of them had heard that the other hadn't. All in all, Tristan thought more than once, it was rather like the vision of domesticity that he'd once had before his marriage, only then, it had been an imaginary wife he'd envisioned sharing pillow talk with. Not a... what was Charles? A sort of husband? Was he a wife, then, or was Charles? True, more often than not it was Charles taking him, but they'd traded places on more than one occasion. Or was it just that it didn't matter? Charles was his, and he was Charles's, and that was it.

The thought was satisfactory enough.

CHAPTER 17

SETTLING onto the side of the bed, Charles smiled at the elderly woman looking nervously up at him. "I'm just going to listen to your heart, if that is acceptable to you, Mrs. Sharpe?"

She nodded. He rolled up the sheet of parchment and set one end to her chest and his ear to the other. The thump that he heard was steady and strong, and he smiled again. "Perfect," he said. "A nice, steady beat."

"That's good?" she asked, her Cockney accent strong. "I've nuffin' wrong wif me 'eart?"

"Not a thing that I can tell. Now, tell me—the pain you had in your chest. Was it burning?"

"Oh, awful. Thought I was gon' to drop right there on the street. Come over all flushed and 'ot and dizzy, and I remembered my da bein' took that way just before he dropt dead. Scared me silly."

"Hmm. Was this after or before your dinner?"

"After. Had a nice bit of pork chitterlin's and suet puddin' for dessert."

Charles regarded her carefully. She was a typical London matron, a good four stone overweight, with the round, shiny face of a much younger woman. *Well-preserved*, he thought and chuckled to himself. *Aye, well-preserved with mutton fat and suet, not so much youthful as well-greased. No wonder she had heartburn.* "Well," he said, frowning faintly, "that may be the problem. Too much fat in the diet can cause not only heart problems, but the sort of pain you're experiencing." He'd read about this—a herniation of the esophagus, the book had described it, common in overweight individuals and the symptoms mimicking a heart attack. At least he hoped it was that and not gallstones. Gallstones would require surgery and continuous care—an expense he was certain Mrs. Sharpe had not the wherewithal to bear—or a slow and painful death from peritonitis.

Well, there was one way to investigate, at any rate. "The pain. Can you show me exactly where it occurred?"

She replied, "Well, I'll tell ye—it felt like all over me chest. But mostly, 'ere." She tapped herself between her voluminous breasts. "Right 'ere, where me 'eart is."

"Not on the right side at all?"

She shook her head. Charles grinned in relief. "Well, then, I think what you have is a small wound on the tube that goes into your stomach. Greasy, fatty and spicy foods can irritate your stomach and cause the pain. For such a little thing it can cause a *great* deal of pain, which I'm sure you can attest to."

"Will it get worse?" she asked anxiously.

"If you don't tend it properly, it can ulcerate and cause severe problems." He looked stern and doctor-like. "And the only way to treat it is for you to watch what you eat. No spicy food; eat plenty of fresh vegetables; cook your meat in water or broth instead of fats or oils. No more suet pudding. A little milk is all right, but no cheese. Eat lots of fruit—apples, pears, peaches. Until you feel better, stay away from oranges or lemons." Well, it might not cure the hernia, but it would probably make her lose weight and feel better, anyway.

With a heavy sigh, she said, "Well, if you say so, Doctor. But veg is so dear, and there's nothin' so good as a nice fry-up."

"If you wish to have that pain happen again, keep eating fry-up," he said dryly. "Now, is there someone waiting for you?"

"Aye, me son Dickon."

"I'll fetch him along, and you can go home." He helped her off the cot and into the small chair. "Wait right here."

MacQuarrie, who'd been observing him as he worked his way down the ward, said, "I take it your diagnosis was an esophageal hernia?"

"It seems likely, from the symptoms. What is your opinion?"

"The same. Good work, Mountjoy. We'll make a physician of you yet. Go fetch the son, and I'll see you back at my office."

HE KNEW Dickon as soon as he saw him: a middle-aged man with the same cheerful round face and plump physique as his mother, perched nervously on the edge of a chair in the shabby waiting room of the free hospital. "Mr.

Sharpe?" Charles said. "Your mother can go home now. Fortunately, it wasn't a heart attack at all, although if she doesn't lose about four stone, it could very well be next time. She needs to watch what she eats—I've told her the details."

"Thank ye, sir," Dickon said humbly, clutching his cap. He rose from the chair.

"Right there," Charles gestured down the short hall. "Second door on the right. Your mam's about halfway down the ward on the right. You can go straight out the back at the other end and be on the street without having to go through the main hospital again." He nodded his goodbye to the man as he shambled past, then glanced around the waiting room. There were two women, younger than Mrs. Sharpe, their heads together as they chatted, apparently in no hurry, probably waiting for another patient, and a morose-looking man holding a cloth to his jaw. "What ails you, sir?" Charles asked briskly.

"Toof," the man mumbled.

Charles crouched by the side of the chair and pulled the cloth away. "Open," he said, and the man obeyed. Ouch. It looked like one of his molars was abscessed. "That will have to be drawn," he said to the man. "Hold on a moment," he said and went down the hall to Bertie's surgery. "Got a bad tooth in the waiting room," he said to the surgeon, who shook his head.

"Anyone attached to it, or is it just sitting on the floor?"

"Ha ha," Charles said.

Bertie lumbered out of his office, buttoning up his vest as he followed Charles. He echoed Charles's previous movements, crouching to have a look inside the man's mouth. "Ugly," he commented. "Well, up with you. I've the tools in my office."

They were no sooner out of the waiting room when the door from the hospital opened and a well-dressed man came in. Charles raised an eyebrow, and the two women tittered. "Can I help you, sir?"

"You can if you're Charles Mountjoy," the man said.

"I am."

"I'm from Lord Castlereagh's office. His Lordship sent me to fetch you. Says it's urgent."

Charles frowned. "Just let me get my coat and tell my supervisor I'm leaving."

"Aye, sir."

Mac was just finishing up with a hugely pregnant woman dressed in the same over-frilled but shabby style as the women in the waiting room. "Aye, Charlie?"

"There's a man from Castlereagh come to fetch me," he said. "I know we've rounds yet to finish, but Castlereagh...."

"Needs must when the devil drives, lad. The Empire comes first." He patted the woman on the shoulder and ushered her out of the examining room.

Charles paused at the office to grab his coat and hat and went to meet the messenger. "Did you come by cab?" he asked the man.

"No, sir, by Lord Castlereagh's coach." They left the hospital and walked to the end of the narrow street where the coach waited. An armed guard sat beside the driver.

Raising an eyebrow, Charles said, "It must be important."

"Aye, sir," the man said, shaking his head. "Very." But he said no more, only commenting that Lord Castlereagh had the whole of it when Charles pressed him for more information.

CASTLEREAGH did have the whole of it. Charles stared at him blankly. *"What?"*

"Escaped. A few days before the first of March, when he landed on the French coast. The French Fifth Regiment was sent to intercept him and instead went over to his side. That was just a day or two ago, but reports are that he's continuing to march on Paris, and that more troops are joining him. We're looking at a resumption of the war."

"Bloody *hell*," Charles said, and he dropped into the chair Castlereagh indicated.

"We're in a terrible situation," his lordship said. "Most of our best troops are still in America. Wellington's in Vienna, which is the best place for him right now, as he can coordinate the Allies' counter. He will need to eventually take command of the army; we're just not sure when or where yet."

"No chance the French will refuse to support Napoleon, is there?"

"None. Even Talleyrand doesn't think we have a chance of that. Popular feeling is against the King, and Bonaparte still has fanatical admirers in France. Particularly among the military." Castlereagh rustled through the dispatches on his desk. "I need you to go to Belgium."

"Belgium?"

"Yes. Brussels, specifically. I don't think that Arthur Wellesley will be able to make it from Vienna before the beginning of April, but that's where the army will be forming. It's less than three hundred miles from there to Paris, and if Bonaparte takes back his capital, that's where we'll need to strike. Ultimately, it will be us, the Germans, and the Dutch. The northern Army of Occupation is already headquartered there, and there is a strong British civilian presence, what with all the hoopla over the return of William of the Netherlands."

"Has he made up his mind about calling himself 'king' yet, or is he still insisting on delaying his coronation?" Charles asked. "Half the world thinks of Slender Billy as the Prince of Orange, not his father."

"He made the announcement a few days ago according to the latest dispatch," Castlereagh said, "and he's agreed to be crowned sometime this summer—assuming that we're able to cut Napoleon off at the knees. That's another reason I want you in Brussels: I'm sending General Hill out to run herd on the young prince, else we'll have him invading France on his own. The prince knows you and respects you, and you'll be able to back up Hill's orders."

"Daddy Hill would do fine on his own," Charles objected.

Castlereagh narrowed his eyes at him. "You *are* still a commissioned officer of His Majesty's Cavalry, are you not?"

"Yes, sir," Charles said, "but only because I've yet to receive a response to my letter to my former colonel. He's still in the Caribbean with the rest of the 14th, and I'm honor-bound to offer my commission to one of the remaining captains before I can search for another purchaser."

Castlereagh sighed. "I know you're eager to sell out, Charles, and I also know you're eager to start your new career, but Britain's needs take priority. When the Duke released you to my service in Paris, he made it very clear that it was a temporary assignment and that he eventually expected you back on his staff if he requested it. When he arrives in Brussels, he's going to want his officers around him. Your assignment to General Hill's staff will also be temporary, with the understanding that Wellington has the option of co-opting you if he chooses. Which he will; as I said, the Germans will make up a large part—if not the majority—of the forces to stand against Bonaparte. He'll need you as liaison; translator, if nothing else."

My God, Charles thought unhappily, *Tris will not be happy.* Aloud, he said, "Yes, sir. Of course."

Castlereagh handed him a sheaf of papers. "Here. Go report to General Hill; he'll give you the details on your transportation. It should be a fairly easy assignment, but I'll feel better if I know you're there to keep an eye on things."

"Thank you, sir," Charles said. He took the papers and put them in his greatcoat pocket, then shook Castlereagh's hand and turned to leave.

"Charles?"

He stopped and turned back to his lordship. "Sir?"

"Don't let the word get out, please. You may tell your nearest and dearest, but we're trying to keep this under wraps as long as we can. It'll probably only be a few days before it becomes public knowledge, but we're trying to avoid hysteria."

"I understand, sir." Charles nodded, bowed, and let himself out.

"HOW did Castlereagh seem to you?" General Hill asked as he perused the papers Charles had handed him.

"Resigned," Charles said promptly. "Tired. Depressed. Understandably so."

"Yes, sadly enough." Hill gestured at the chair before his desk. "Sit down, Major. I'll need to look at these and then write up some orders of my own before I let you go."

"Sir," Charles said and sat. He watched Hill's face as he read through the documents, then met his eyes candidly when the general raised his head. "This will be difficult for him," he said, "after the relative successes of the Congress."

"Just being back in London has been hard on him," Hill acknowledged. "But he shines under pressure, like his friend Wellington. We are damned fortunate to have two such men on our side, Mountjoy. France can have her Talleyrand; I'll stand Castlereagh and Wellington against a dozen such."

"Talleyrand is a genius," Charles agreed, "and Castlereagh and Wellington much less flamboyant, but I have to agree with you. That kind of steady determination is what we need now."

"Precisely," Hill said. "And that's why I'm glad Castlereagh is sending you with me. You'll be a steadying influence on that young firebrand of a prince. I've already got reports of his enthusiasm that terrify me."

Charles regarded the calm, phlegmatic face of the man before him. "Aye, sir, I can see that it does."

"Young mackerel," Hill growled in amusement.

"Who else from the staff is in Belgium?" Charles asked.

"March is there—of course he would be; his papa is in charge of the army, and the whole bloody family's tagged along, sisters, hangers-on and all. If he doesn't manage to marry off all the Lennox girls with all the northern army there, he's no great shakes of an older brother. Slender Billy, of course. The 95th's already on its way back from America, thank God, so Harry Smith will be there. I'm sure most of the Great Man's surviving staff will find their way to Belgium, one way or another. They'll not miss this."

"I wish I could," Charles muttered.

"You and I both, Major, but we're a little more sensible than the other rabble."

"The Duke's permitted to refer to us as rabble, but he'll take you to task for it," Charles said with an unwilling grin.

"Oh, no fears," Hill shot back, "he agrees with me. But he did give you a compliment, once. Said that for cavalry you were an intelligent man."

"I'm well aware of his Grace's preference for the infantry," Charles said, snorting. "He and I have had discussions on the matter."

"Which he wins, of course."

"Of course. He's Wellington."

"Yes, he is. Well. Let's take a look at these and make some plans, shall we?"

"MUCH better, sir, much better," "Gentleman" Jackson said heartily, slapping Tristan's bare shoulder and handing him a much-needed towel. "Thought Chesleigh had you there, once or twice, but you're a bit faster these days. Glad to see the fire's back. You were getting a mite peaky for a while there."

"I was," Tristan agreed with a grin, wiping the sweat from his face. "I'm happy to see that I haven't quite forgot everything since I was here last."

"On the cont'ry, sir," Jackson said, "I think your little time away was good for you. You've put some weight back on and got the energy to go with it—somethin' I ain't seen in quite some time."

"Thanks to my live-in physician," Tristan said. "You haven't seen him yet today, have you?"

"Physician? Oh, your brother-in-law?" The former boxer thought a moment, then shook his head. "He was here yesterday afternoon as usual, but I haven't seen him today. Briggs!" he shouted at another man, "you seen Mountjoy today?"

Briggs shook his head and went back to trying to explain whatever it was to an intent student.

"No matter," Tristan said and pulled his shirt back on, tucking it into his trousers and adding the waistcoat. Jackson signaled for one of his employees to come over and retie Tristan's cravat for him, then invited him into the parlor for a drink.

"No, thank you," Tristan replied, smiling. "I've a few errands to run, and then we've a dinner party tonight, so I'm pressed for time."

"Errands?" Jackson snorted in amusement. "Thought you toffs had footmen to run about for you."

"I wouldn't trust a footman with either my haberdasher or my tobacconist," Tristan said wryly, shaking Jackson's hand. "I'll see you in a day or two."

"Aye, sir," Jackson said, pocketing the vail Tristan had slipped him.

HIS HABERDASHER and tobacconist taken care of, Tristan went home and upstairs to prepare for dinner. They were dining with another of Charlotte's longtime correspondents, a Lady Cowan and her baronet husband, who had arrived early for the Season. Tristan didn't know them well; he'd met Sir Henry once or twice, but they had few friends in common.

Charlotte came in while he was tying a fresh cravat around his neck, a letter in her hand and a perturbed look on her face. "Tris?"

"Yes, Lottie?"

"Have you heard any rumors about Napoleon?"

"No, why?"

"I just got a letter from Liesl. You know she and her husband are with King Ferdinand, the king of Naples, in Sicily."

"The one Napoleon kicked out and replaced with his brother-in-law? Yes."

"Well, she sent me a letter along with the diplomatic pouch to Whitehall; they're always so kind about forwarding her mail as a courtesy to Ferdinand." She held up the letter. A neat rectangle had been cut out of the middle. "This has never happened before! They always open her letters and reseal them under a government seal, but they've never *wrecked* them before!"

Tristan took the letter, frowning. The letter was in German so he handed it back to Lottie. "She must have said something politically sensitive," he observed. "What does she say around it?"

"The sentence before starts, 'Rumor has it that Napoleon…' and then it picks up again '…there is nothing more to be said.' How vexatious! We could have had the most current gossip about Bonaparte to share tonight!"

Tristan chuckled and patted her cheek. "You will just have to settle for being amusing, love. Are you ready to go down?"

"Yes."

He went to the adjoining door and knocked. "Charlie? Are you ready to go?"

Charles's voice came back muffled. "I'll meet you downstairs."

"All right." Tristan turned to Lottie. "Come along then; we'll have a cup of tea while we wait for Charlie."

In the drawing room, Tristan poured Lottie a cup of tea and sat beside her on the couch. "How are you feeling?" he asked conversationally.

"Quite well," she said, "if fat. I don't remember being this uncomfortable with Jamie. Ellen says that that means it's a girl. What shall we name her if it is? I had quite made up my mind that it would be another boy and had settled on 'William', but if it's a girl that sets my plans quite awry. I don't care for 'Wilhelmina'."

Tristan laughed. "I should think not!"

"And not after either of us, I think," Lottie said. "I don't like it when parents name their children after themselves. It's too much like gloating."

"Just be glad you're not married to the future King of the Netherlands, then," Tristan pointed out. "His boys are all 'Wilhelm Friedrich' and his girls are all 'Wilhelmina Frederika'."

Charlotte burst out laughing. "You're joking!"

"And his wife's name is Wilhelmina, which excuses the girls, but seriously!"

"Another mark against 'Wilhelmina' for this one, then," Lottie said, patting her enlarged abdomen.

"Have you given it any thought?" Tristan asked.

"I was thinking Caroline Ellen Liselotte," Charlotte mused. "After Charles and Ellen and Liesl."

"That's quite accept...." Tristan trailed off as Charles came into the drawing room.

He was dressed in his full dress dragoons uniform: white satin breeches, dark blue uniform coat laced with gold, a chapeau bras under his arm. His expression was somber.

"What the *devil*—" Tris began, but Charlotte interrupted him.

"Oh, *Charlie*," she cried in dismay, "why are you wearing that? I thought you were quite decided on wearing your new coat."

"Lottie," Charles said quietly, "I've bad news, but it mustn't leave this room."

Tristan glanced at George the footman, who nodded and stepped out into the hall, closing the door quietly behind him. "What is it, Charlie?"

"I'm being sent to Belgium with General Hill." Charles hesitated, then went on, "Napoleon Bonaparte has escaped from Elba and is raising France. The French King has already left Paris and is on his way to Ghent."

Tristan felt the blood drain from his face and his fingers went cold. "We're back at war."

"Yes. Or we will be, soon. Wellington's being called back from Vienna, but until then, General Hill will be with the Army of Occupation in Belgium, and Lord Castlereagh's asked me to go with him to liaise with the German forces there."

"Oh, Charlie," Lottie said.

"No," Tristan said bleakly. "No, Charlie, *please*."

"Tris—I don't have a choice. I'm still an officer of His Majesty's Army. I have to follow orders."

"*Bugger* orders! You're retiring! You're selling your commission. They don't need you anymore. We need you. *I* need you! Christ, Charlie, don't *do* this!"

"Tris." Charles came across the room swiftly, dropping his hat on the sofa and taking Tristan's hands in his, holding tightly. "I made this choice when I joined twelve years ago. I took an oath to serve where asked and I have never gone back on that oath. I *can't* go back on it." He put a hand to Tristan's cheek. "I can't," he whispered.

Tris reached up and closed his fingers around Charles's wrist, holding him there, feeling the callused palm warm against his skin. "You promised to take care of me, Charlie. I need you." He felt as if he were going to weep; it took an effort to keep from outright tears.

"You don't need me, Tris. You're strong enough to manage on your own—you've proved that over and over. And besides, I'm only a liaison. It's nothing. Chances are we'll take Paris without firing a shot."

"Ballocks," Tristan said savagely.

Charles rested his forehead against Tristan's. "I don't want to go," he admitted. "I argued with both Castlereagh and Hill, but Tris, they need me."

"Ballocks," Tristan said again, but less angrily. He closed his eyes, holding Charles's hand against his cheek a long moment, then pulled it away. "When do you leave?"

"In two days' time." He glanced up at Charlotte. "I'm sorry, Lottie. I promised to be here when you were brought to bed but I'm afraid I'll have to renege on that promise as well. I'm sorry."

"Nonsense," Charlotte said. "I managed to birth Jamie just fine without you, so I see no reason to expect your help with this one." She patted her abdomen. "Little Caroline will just have to wait to meet her uncle." She studied Tristan, then added, "And besides, once *that's* all over, there's no reason to keep Tris here. He could easily go over to Brussels. So many of our friends are already there. Even the Lennoxes—but then, the Duke of Richmond's there with the army, and Lord March. But lots of other people are too—I get letters from them all the time. It would be quite like London. Only without the speaking-English part. You could take a house there, and when I was feeling more the thing, I could come and visit Charlie too."

"I don't know. It's a possibility, I suppose." Tristan turned and walked across to the hearth, staring down into the flames a long moment, but his thoughts wouldn't organize. Finally, he sighed, turned back to the room, and said, "Well. You'll be quite the beau of the ball tonight, Charlie. The women will be falling all over themselves to draw your attention."

"I don't want their attention," Charles said fiercely. "You know what I want, Tris."

"Yes." Tris essayed a smile. It felt awkward on his lips. "I know. Well." He swallowed hard, then held his arm out to Charlotte. "We'd best be going. We don't want to be late for supper."

Charlotte gave him an anxious look. "Are you all right, Tris?"

"I'll be fine," he said. He glanced at Charles. "Charlie says I'll be fine, so I'll be fine."

"I'm never wrong," Charles said with an attempt at humor.

"Not yet," Tristan said. "And I hope never. Come on, then. Let's go pretend."

CHAPTER 18

TRISTAN woke early and lay quietly in the darkness of the drawn bedcurtains. Charles slept behind him, his arm thrown carelessly over Tristan's side and his breath warm on Tristan's neck. Odd, Tristan thought contentedly, that he'd never realized how enjoyable waking up sober could be. No headache, no nausea, no discomfort at all, just the warmth of linen and lover. He laced his fingers gently through Charles's and let out a soft sigh.

"Awake already?" He felt more than heard Charles's voice, rumbling against his skin. It was scratchy with sleep.

"I thought you were still unconscious," Tristan murmured. "Did I wake you?"

"No." Warm lips pressed his shoulder, and his fingers curled against Tristan's belly. Tristan's cock stirred and Charles chuckled. "Good morning, love," he said.

Tristan turned his head and smiled at Charles in the darkness. "God, I'm going to miss this," he said.

"It's just for a few weeks," Charles said.

Tristan fumbled for Charles's cheek to guide himself in for a kiss; light, at first, but then Charles's tongue took possession of Tristan's mouth, and they shifted so that Charles sprawled over Tristan. Tris drew his legs up and wrapped them around Charles's back, sliding his hands down to cup Charles's muscular arse. He rocked against Charles, loving the solidity, the stability, the strength of his lover's body. "Love me, Charlie," he murmured, and took Charles's mouth again, his hands and tongue eager. He felt Charles's rumbling laughter and drew back. "What's so funny?"

"You, love," Charles said, dipping his head to lick at Tristan's throat. "Love you? As if I had any choice in the matter."

"You know what I mean," Tristan said, digging his fingers into Charles's ribs.

"You're as big a brat as that horse of yours," Charles said, smacking his hands away and catching him by the wrists.

Tristan gasped in surprise at the sensations that being restrained triggered. His heart sped up, his pulse raced, and his cock grew harder. At first he thought it was fear, but it wasn't. It was… excitement. "Like that, do you?" Charles murmured wickedly. "I should have known, after your little performance for your father, that you would enjoy the odd bit of binding. I should have left you tied up like that and taken you then and there, shouldn't I?"

"Yes," Tristan moaned.

Charles laughed again. "Oh, my love, you are an endless source of surprise and delight. Why didn't you ever say anything?"

"I didn't know." Tristan arched up to kiss Charles. "I liked it that first night, when you told me what to do, made me hold onto the bed and all. And when you told me to let go… God, Charlie, I've never *felt* anything like that before. I don't understand. I never do what anyone tells me to do. It's just not my nature."

"Not true," Charles said lazily. "I've seen you listen to Jackson or Henry Angelo, and you're quick enough to jump when Mac or Crosby or one of the other doctors snaps their fingers." His fingers tightened on Tristan's wrists, not hard enough to bruise, but certainly hard enough to make their presence felt. Tristan's breath came quickly. "Well," Charles said, his lazy tones changed to interest. "Well. This is something we should explore in more detail sometime when we have a few hours to play. But for now—turn over." He released Tristan and shifted to the side. "On your belly—grab hold of the headboard as you did that other night."

Panting, Tristan obeyed, feeling his cock already seeping in excitement. "Oh, God," he whispered.

"Shh," Charles said. "I'd spank you, but it would be too noisy. Later."

The words sent a shiver through Tristan. He bit his lip, barely able to contain himself, then clenched his teeth, determined not to make a sound as Charles's hands moved over his back, his arse, cupping his cheeks and sliding between to stroke the opening there. He shifted over Tristan to reach beneath the pillow and draw out the little bottle they'd taken to keeping there. The scent of the oil had Tristan moaning low, and when Charles's fingers breached him, sliding slickly into his entrance, he could barely bite back the cry. "Shh," Charles said again, and then in that low voice said, "You're not to spend until I say so, do you understand? You don't spend. You take what I give you—*all* I give you—but you don't spend until I give you permission."

Tristan turned his head to bite at the pillow. He heard Charles's low chuckle, but it was far away; he was focused on the hands at his gate, the fingers rising inside to stretch the tight channel. It was nothing different from what they'd done before, but having Charles controlling him the way he was made everything so much more intense, pushing Tristan into a state of need he didn't think he'd ever experienced. He moved slightly, but Charles's free hand settled on Tristan's arse, holding him down. "Not yet," Charles murmured in his ear. "You're not to move."

He couldn't have moved if he'd tried. His whole being was centered on the fingers in him, the voice above him, the scent all around him. The scent of sex. The scent of Charles.

And then, somehow, he slid into that *place* again, the one where he was free and floating and still. He was aware of his body responding to Charles but it was an intellectual awareness, a peaceful acceptance of his desire, his *need* for Charles. Charles was in command here. He only had to do what Charles told him to do. Nothing else. No demands, no expectations. Just Charles.

Just Tristan. Just who he was. And for the first time he could remember, that was enough.

Time treacled past, slow and thick and golden. Charles coaxed him higher and higher into that state, separate yet part of his body, at peace and thoroughly aroused at the same time. He welcomed Charles when he slid inside, felt the thick cock rocking into him, the full head bumping gently against the spot inside him that teased him so. It felt so good. He floated in that feeling, only sighing gently when Charles's hand curled around his cock, smearing the shed drops of liquid around him. "God, you're all wet and you haven't even spent yet," Charles said softly.

Tristan only sighed again. "Charles…." It was barely more than a breath.

Charles's hand and cock sped up, driving harder into Tristan. Tristan roused ever higher, higher and higher, until finally Charles gasped, "Now, Tris! Now!" and Tristan came out of his daze with a shock, back into his body, which was arching and climaxing and pouring his heat and his heart out in an enormous wash of lust and love. It was amazing. It was transcendent. It was… perfect.

Charles fell back, rolling over onto the bed with Tristan clamped to his chest, himself still buried deep inside him. "God, Tris! That was…."

"Perfect," Tristan said. He laid his head back on Charles's shoulder and regarded his lover peacefully. "Perfect. Like you, Charlie."

"God, no," Charles said with a half-laugh. "That would be you. My perfect Tris."

"If we can't make love again before you go," Tristan said, "at least this time was memorable."

"And we can't," Charles said. "Our ship sails on the morrow's morning tide; this evening Hill and I leave for Dover. We've only today left, and I've too much to do today to spend it in bed with you, Tris." He stroked Tristan's hair gently. "My beautiful Tris."

"My beautiful Charlie," Tristan said, and echoed the gesture, laughing. Their lips met in a soft kiss, and Tris ran his hands over Charles's face, memorizing his touch, his skin, his shape. "I love you so and it breaks my heart to say goodbye to you, but you'll come back to me, won't you?"

"Always," Charles promised. "And you'll come to Brussels, as soon as Charlotte's settled? Assuming the French haven't come to their senses by then?"

"As soon as I can." He rolled off Charles and got to his feet, stretching. "What a way to wake up in the morning," he said. "I'll miss that." He gave Charles a cocky grin. "So will you."

Charles laughed. "I will," he said. "But not for long. Promise me that?"

"Not for long," Tris said. "Never for long."

IN THE end, their leave-taking was public and more formal than either would have liked. Charles stood in the hall, great-coated and scarved and hatted, his dispatch case under one arm and Jamie in the other. Tristan stood with his arms around Charlotte, who was weeping, something he'd never seen her do before. He felt like weeping himself, but clenched his jaw and only nodded curtly at Charles's farewells.

Charles turned and murmured something to Jamie, who nodded solemnly, then he handed the toddler back to Tristan. Jamie put his arms around Tristan's neck and buried his face in Tristan's shoulder, not quite sure what was amiss, but picking up on the grief and fear around him. "You'll take care?" Tristan said in a low voice.

"Of course," Charles said. "I'll write you both as soon as I'm settled in Brussels. I don't need to tell Lottie to write back, I know."

His sister gave him a watery smile. Ellen, standing to Charlotte's other side, patted her shoulder gently. "I'll see that you get all the news, Charlie," she said, and wiped her eyes with a damp handkerchief.

"I rely on you to take care of my Lottie, Ellen. You and Tris." He bent and kissed her cheek, then kissed Lottie, who squeezed his hand hard as she kissed him back.

Then he turned to Tristan. "Northwood," he said coolly.

"Mountjoy," Tristan replied in the same tone.

Charles nodded curtly and turned toward the door, where General Hill's footman waited with his luggage. He stopped, his back toward them, a long, still moment; then he turned and walked the few steps back to Tristan and Jamie, and gathered them both into his arms. They stood there, just holding each other, until Tristan let out a faint sob and pulled away. "Go," he said in a low voice.

Another curt nod, and Charles was gone, a swirl of wet March wind blowing in through the open door. George hurried to close it behind him.

"Well," Tristan said in his usual cool fashion, "that's that. Tea, Lottie?"

She looked up at him blankly. He'd surprised her for once, and it was in a small, helpless voice that she replied, "If you wish, Tristan."

"I do. Ellen? Will you mind if Jamie joins us?"

"Not at all, Tristan." The look she gave him was approving. "I think that would be most enjoyable."

"Well, demon," Tristan said to Jamie, "will you behave yourself for tea?"

"Jam!" Jamie caroled, and the piping sound broke the tension in the hall. Tristan took Lottie's arm, and they went in for tea.

"SO," MACQUARRIE said when Tristan walked into the hospital the next day, "you're back. Mountjoy leave for Brussels?"

"Last evening," Tristan said coolly. He set his hat on the shelf in the cloakroom and hung his greatcoat on the hook underneath. "They were to have left Dover on the morning tide."

"I half expected you to vanish back into your social life, without Mountjoy to drag you here daily."

"Did you?" Tristan checked his pocket watch, then said indifferently, "If you'll excuse me, Dr. Crosby is about to start his rounds."

"Stiff-necked young cub," MacQuarrie said in amusement. "How's Lottie holding up?"

"*Mrs. Northwood*," Tristan snapped, "is fine. *If* you'll excuse me?" He turned and stalked off down the corridor toward Crosby's office.

He didn't know why he was so short-tempered with MacQuarrie. The physician had always been friendly to both him and Charles. But the casual, offhand comments irked Tristan, touching as they did on a subject that was still painful.

He'd cried himself to sleep last night like a child, huddled in his cold, empty bed with only the blankets for comfort. He'd sprinkled his pillow with drops of the rosemary and eucalyptus oil to remind him of Charles, but that only made him miss him more. He knew he was acting like a small spoiled child, but he felt lost and lonely and alone. Only knowing that Charles was out there, loving him, missing him.... At least he *hoped* Charles was missing him. Was he? Or was he only grateful to be shut of Tristan's clinging, whining presence? That brought on another spate of tears.

When he awoke in the morning, tired and drained, he considered just staying in bed for the day, pleading illness and indulging in selfish misery. But Charles would have frowned at such behavior, so he'd got up, washed his face, and set about the day as usual. His grief and the lack of sleep made him snappish, so he skipped his usual visits to his Bond Street haunts and went directly to the hospital. Here, at least, he would be distracted by the demands of people whose problems were far worse than just missing a lover.

Crosby and his phalanx of students were just gathering in the corridor outside his office; he eyed Tristan narrowly, but said only, "Glad you could join us, Mr. Northwood" in his sarcastic way. Tristan grinned and tipped an imaginary hat at the surgeon, then joined the other students in following him down the hall to the first ward.

CHAPTER 19

"YOUR father's invited us to go to the theater on Wednesday," Charlotte said. She took a bite of the sole amandine Cook had produced for lunch. "It's Kean, doing something Shakespearean. It's been well received."

Tristan swallowed the piece of fish he was chewing and said in surprise, "What difference does it make what's playing?"

"I told him we'd be happy to attend."

Her husband froze, his fork halfway to his mouth. Slowly he set it down and asked sharply, "And why would you do something so abysmally stupid?"

Ellen took in a breath of dismay. Charlotte narrowed her eyes. "Oh, my," she said coolly, "are we about to have a quarrel? I'd wondered what that was like."

"We're not about to have a quarrel," Tristan snapped. "We're not about to have even so much as a discussion. I'm not going. End of conversation."

She pointed her fork at him. "Conversation's not ended until I say it's ended. You *are* going, and so am I. And so is Ellen. *And* we're having supper afterwards at Grillon's."

"I have other plans."

"No, you don't. I checked with Reston, *and* with Mr. Gibson. He said you'd cried off from meeting him at Boodle's because you wanted to spend an evening with me. And *I* am going to the play, so, so are you." She ate another piece of fish.

"Perhaps I lied to Gibs," Tristan said. "Perhaps I'm spending the evening with my mistress."

"You don't *have* a mistress," Charlotte said complacently. "At least"—a forkful of green beans followed the fish and was chewed thoroughly before being swallowed—"not on England's green shores."

Tristan flushed angrily. "Much you know," he spat. "And whether I want to spend the evening with my drunkard friends or not, you had no right to make, make *arrangements* for me specifically against my wishes."

She blinked wide brown eyes at him. "Why, Tristan, you never *specifically* said you didn't wish to go to the theater with your Papa."

His jaw dropped. "Lottie! You are well aware of my feelings about my father! It's disingenuous to say that you didn't know what my wishes would be in regards to that!"

She smiled faintly. "Well, Tris, you're right. I did know what you would have said, but I've decided it's silly for you to go on with this chip on your shoulder about your father."

"'Chip on my shoulder'?" Tristan couldn't believe his ears. "My father hates me, and I him. Why in *God's* name would I want to go to the *theater* with him?"

"Don't curse," Lottie said placidly. "It upsets Ellen."

He turned furious eyes on his wife's companion, who squeaked in dismay. "No, it doesn't," he snapped, returning his gaze to his wife. "She's sensible. Unlike you."

"Oh, Tristan," Charlotte said, chuckling, "that's ridiculous. Not about Ellen. About me. You won't find a more sensible woman—even Charlie says so."

The mention of his lover's name cut him. He rose, flinging his napkin down on the table beside his dish. "If you will excuse me," he said icily.

"No,' Lottie said. "Sit down, Tristan, and be reasonable."

"I don't *choose* to be reasonable," he said in a low, fierce voice.

"Oh, dear. It appears we are going to quarrel after all. Ellen, if you would be so kind? I hate to disturb your lunch…."

"Oh, I am quite finished," Ellen said, and she beat a hasty retreat.

Tristan remained standing, glowering down at his wife, who gazed back up at him and said thoughtfully, "You know, I believe that is the first time you've ever really been angry with me. Been anything at all, really. It's an interesting change. You're always so collected. Being with Charlie seems to have loosened something inside you."

"Do *not*," Tristan gritted out, "mention that, if you please."

"Mention what?" she asked innocently. "Charlie? Charlie, Charlie, Charlie? My beloved brother Charlie? Charles Edward Mountjoy, major of the 14th, staff officer? The Honorable Charles Mountjoy, second son of the

Earl of Chilson? Mount. Joy. There's something… suggestive about my family name, don't you think?"

"Why are you doing this to me?" Tristan shouted.

"Because it's so refreshing to see you *feeling* something for a change!"

He stared at her, shocked. She looked up at him from her chair, her face composed, but something fierce and angry in her eyes. "Sit down," she said, the quietness of her voice belying the message in those eyes.

He sat. Wordlessly, he picked up his fork and ate some green beans.

Charlotte watched him. Finally, she said, "While you were ill, your father and I had a long talk about you. Since then, I have had supper with him on several occasions when you were otherwise engaged. I'd always accepted your interpretation of your relationship with him, and his behavior certainly never suggested otherwise. Our conversation on the day of your little performance was eye-opening, to say the least."

"I suppose," Tristan said bitterly, "you're about to tell me that all these years he's loved me and only wanted the best for me."

"Actually, yes," she said.

"If that isn't like a woman," he sneered.

"And if that isn't like a man, to refuse to see beyond the nose on his face!"

"Oh, have we reached the insults stage of our quarrel?" he sniped. "I should like to know, not having had this experience before."

"You began it," she said dryly. "Now it's your turn to say, 'No, *you* started it.' That's how quarrels go, you know. They quickly devolve into meaningless posturing."

"Listening to you speak one might think you were educated," Tristan said. "Too bad spelling wasn't part of your education."

"Oh, *very* good," she said approvingly. "We're exchanging personal insults. One would think you *had* done this before."

Despite his anger, this struck him as immensely funny, and he broke into an unwilling laugh. "Perhaps I might have," he said, "if my sister had lived. We would have been like you and Daniel, perhaps, exchanging insults at every opportunity."

"You would have been a much happier person," she mused, "if you'd had someone to fight with on a regular basis. And I don't really *argue* with Daniel; I just *annoy* him. He's far too foolish to have a successful argument with." She took another bite of fish. "And I am a perfectly good speller—in

German. English spelling isn't *sensible*. Besides, I do it on purpose. I got into the habit to annoy my governess and Papa, and now I do it to annoy the Army censors and you. I admit to not being a *good* speller, but my regular correspondence is quite comprehensible."

"Well, not understanding German, I can't verify that claim," Tristan said with a grin. "So you can say anything you like on the subject without refutation."

"I know," she said smugly. "Now. About the theater."

He felt the grin slide from his face. "An entire evening in my father's company?" he said bitterly. "What evil have I ever done you, Charlotte?"

"That is a leading question, Tris, and I won't deign to answer," she said, smiling back at him. "Seriously, I'm not saying you should fall into each other's embrace and let bygones be bygones and all that nonsense. I just think you should attempt some level of courtesy for Jamie's sake; he should learn to know his grandfather."

Tristan looked down at his plate and stirred his vegetables uneasily. He remembered too well the letter he'd written to Charlotte the night he'd planned his death, and the concern he'd had that his father would intimidate and hurt Jamie the way he had hurt Tristan. If Jamie was familiar with his grandfather, and Charlotte were there to buffer his comments, it might be better for Jamie than it had been for himself. Jamie might even grow used to his grandfather's gruff ways and not take them as seriously as Tristan always had. He swallowed hard, then said, "For Jamie."

"And the new baby," Lottie said, reaching over to pat his hand. "It will be quite all right, you'll see."

IT WASN'T quite "all right," but it was tolerable. Tristan greeted his father politely, as strangers do; his father reciprocated. They sat beside each other on the rear-facing seat in the carriage, conversing individually with Lottie and Ellen; they sat separated by the ladies and thus excused from conversation during the play. At Grillon's, however, they sat at a table for four, with Tristan and his father opposite, in a private alcove off the main restaurant. They settled the ladies, ordered their supper, and then Lottie said brightly to Tristan, "Tris, tell your papa what you said during the courtroom scene. It was so amusing."

"I doubt the baron would find it so, my dear," Tristan said politely. "Ellen, are you sure you want the filet? I've heard that the chicken is quite superior."

"The filet will be fine, Tristan," Ellen said.

"I should like to hear what you said, Tristan," the baron said quietly.

Tristan didn't look up. He stared at his plate a long moment, then took a drink of water. "It was nothing," he said. "I've forgotten."

His father didn't respond, but a moment later said, "Lottie tells me you have begun studying medicine with her brother."

"No," Tristan said, "I've begun studying surgery, not medicine. And it's nothing. Just another current interest that will die as quickly as the rest of them, no doubt." He took another drink, wishing it were brandy. "It will come in handy when I need to stitch up one of my friends after another pub brawl."

"Tristan," Lottie said in a low voice.

"Well, Lottie, what would you have me say? It doesn't matter, anyway." He looked up then and met his father's eye. "I was not happy with Lottie when she informed me she had accepted this invitation. I'm sure neither of us really wants to be here, so let's just not pretend, hey?"

"You're quite mistaken," the baron said. "I was most eager for this evening."

Tristan laughed, a short, bitter snort. "I'll wager you were. Eager for it to be done with." He stared at his plate a moment, then said, "This is pointless. Sir, I would appreciate it if you would see the ladies home. I find that I have lost my appetite." He laid his napkin on the table beside his plate.

"Tristan," Lottie said.

"Tristan," the baron echoed, "please. Have I fallen so low in your estimation that you cannot bear to be in the same room as me?"

Tristan's fingers tightened on the cloth of his napkin. "Neither of us has so high an opinion of the other as to judge," he said. "My estimation of you is quite the same as yours of me."

"Then it is quite high enough," the baron said. "I...."

"Liar," Tristan said, surprising himself. "Filthy, *bloody* liar!" He didn't raise his voice, although at this moment there was no one in the restaurant, no one in the world, but him and his father. "You've never made any secret of the fact that you despise me, and this, this *nonsense*, this travesty of a supper party—good God, man, what is it you want from me? Absolution of some kind? You suddenly want to be friends? You've nothing to offer me, and I've nothing to offer you. We're just bound by law, and if you saw fit to disinherit me I would thank God fasting. Why don't you? You have your heir in Jamie. You don't need me any longer. Isn't that why you arranged my marriage to Lottie? To get you a substitute?"

"You owe your wife an apology," the baron said, "for both your language and for your insult to her about your marriage."

"Fine," Tristan said, his breath harsh. "Lottie, pray accept my apologies. Ellen, my dear, I am sorry to drag you into this. This should never have happened." He rose, setting his chair under the table carefully, as if it mattered. "Sir, I shall be in contact with my solicitor in the morning. There must be some way for us to dissolve this legal connection, at least."

"Tristan!" It was a cry of despair, and Tristan was shocked when his father raised his face to see tears streaming down his cheeks. "My God, son, have I so destroyed us?" He put his face in his hands and sobbed.

Dazed, Tristan closed his fingers on the chair back and stared at the stranger wearing his father's body. Lottie was patting her father-in-law's arm consolingly. "There, there," she murmured. "Oh, sir, I would never have agreed to this if I had thought you would be so hurt by it."

If she thought *he* would be hurt by it? Tristan's gut wrenched. So Lottie's loyalty was so easily bought? He had thought they were friends, at least.

"No," Ware said, pushing her hand away. "It is not about my feelings, Lottie." He looked at Tristan, his face bleak. "I had hoped that we had not gone quite past the point of no return, Tristan. That somehow we would be able to put the past aside and learn to be at least cordial to each other. But I...." He fished in his pocket for his handkerchief, wiping his eyes and blowing his nose soundly.

A woman's voice sounded in Tristan's ears: not Lottie's, or Ellen's. "You have hurt your papa, Tristan. Give him a kiss and say you're sorry." Only it wasn't "Papa" the woman's voice had said, it had been "little sister." Eight-year-old Tristan had obeyed, hugging his beloved little Emily and whispering in her tiny ear, "I'm so sorry, Emmy. I won't do it again."

He didn't remember what it was he had done, just remembered the voice, soft and sweet and loving. "I'm sorry," he said abruptly. His fingers on the chair were white-knuckled.

"No," Ware said again, "it is entirely my fault. I thought you needed guidance. I knew nothing about raising children—I never even expected to wed! But I met Alice, and then my brother died, and all this was thrust upon me. I did my best—I *thought* I was doing my best, but I've failed. I failed her, and I've failed you, and thus doubly her. Please. Sit. If you prefer, I will leave...."

"No, stay," Tristan said. He felt unutterably weary. "We've already ordered. But I think we should leave this discussion to a more private moment."

The baron nodded and patted Lottie's hand gently. "Thank you, my dear. Ellen, I apologize for my poor behavior."

"No need," Ellen said softly. "It is difficult to maintain one's composure when one is upset, I have found. One either gets emotional, or chilly, as Tristan does. But Tristan is right; you need to discuss this in private, without either Lottie or me there to interfere."

"Thank you," Ware said somberly.

Tristan drew out his chair and sat down, placing his napkin back in his lap. "Well," he said, "and what did *you* think of Kean's performance, sir?"

The baron looked at him and laughed softly. "I think he could take lessons from you, son. But he was quite adequate for the role."

The waiters returned with their first course, and further conversation was light and casual. It was the first time in his life that Tristan had had the opportunity to interact on a social level with his father in so intimate a setting, and to his very great surprise discovered a droll sense of humor not unlike his own, a common sense attitude toward society, and a thorough understanding of the events leading up to Napoleon's abdication and current return. Rumors of the Emperor's escape from Elba had already begun circulating, and it gave Tristan an odd sense of accomplishment to be able to quietly confirm the rumors to his father.

"The Exchange is in a panic, of course," Ware said, "and I think that it could be no worse if the government would just come out and acknowledge that Napoleon is back in France. Still, once Wellesley is in Brussels, the panic should ease. 'Change has a great deal of faith in the general."

"We should really call him 'Wellington', sir," Lottie opined. "Or 'His Grace'—he is now a duke, after all."

"Bah," the baron said, with all the disdain of a lesser but ancient title for a johnny-come-lately, "I knew him when he was a lieutenant—and not a very good one, from all reports."

"Some people are better generals than they are lieutenants," Ellen said. "I've often observed that some people are much better at giving orders than at taking them."

"And sometimes it just depends on who's giving the orders," Tristan said.

"What do your correspondents say on the status in Brussels, Lottie?"

"Well," Lottie said, pleased to be given the floor, "mail is quite heavily censored these days, to prevent Napoleon's spies—which are many in Brussels, as I understand—from discovering troop movements and so forth, so actual details are very few. But Baronne D'Hooghvoorst says that most of the cowhearted have already left for home, and the rest are quite merry and excited about the Duke arriving. He is quite a favorite among hostesses—even if his manners can sometimes be a bit stiff with his underlings, he's quite charming in company. And of course his staff are very well liked."

"Heard from your brother yet?"

"Just a short note to say he had arrived," Lottie said placidly, "and to ask us to send on one of his books that he had forgotten. I'm sure he will write more later, when he has time. The Comtesse de Luiny has invited us to join them there, and for Charlie's sake I would, but under the circumstances I think we can safely say no." She patted the swell of her abdomen cheerfully. "She did give me the name of a gentleman who can arrange a house for when Tristan goes over there in the summer."

"Tristan?" Ware glanced over at his son. "Are you planning on going to Brussels?"

"After Lottie and the children are safely settled in the country for the summer, I thought I would take a jaunt over," Tristan said casually. "Just to see how Major Mountjoy does, so I can let his sister know that he is fine, of course. I have some acquaintance there, at any rate."

"Hm," the baron said.

Tristan thought there was a faint note of disapproval in the sound, but the baron didn't elaborate, simply changed the subject. *Well*, he thought, *It could have been worse, given their history*. He could have made a stink about Tristan leaving so soon after the baby's birth, but he seemed to be on his best behavior. Tristan rubbed his aching head and wished for brandy rather than the wine they'd been served with dinner.

AFTER dinner they returned home, and Tristan, to his own great surprise, invited the baron in for a drink. They bade the ladies good night and retired to the library.

Baron Ware took a sip of the brandy and nodded approvingly. "You keep a good cellar, I understand."

"A few bottles of good stuff," Tristan said carelessly. "We're not entertaining much these days, so when we do we mostly get it from Berry's. Brandy, of course, is a little trickier."

He waited for his father's disapproval, but the baron only said, "Run, of course. It's a shame that Britain and France can't manage to keep a business relationship even when they're *not* at war. Tariffs on goods the British don't produce are foolish; taxes should only protect British-made goods." At Tristan's look of surprise, his father said dryly, "I'm a businessman, Tristan, for all intents and purposes, though of course I don't admit it socially. I know you think all I do is pore over dusty ledgers, but my interests are rather farther-ranging than that."

"Shall I call you a 'cit', then, sir?"

Ware chuckled. "Perhaps not quite that bad, but I do more than just manage my properties." He sipped his brandy, then said, "A few months ago I made you an offer regarding your string of hunters. I was disappointed that you did not see fit to take me up on it."

"It wasn't necessary," Tristan said.

"You shouldn't have had to sell your horses to settle a gaming debt," Ware persisted. "Not when I have funds aplenty...."

"I sold them because I didn't want them any longer, and thought it was foolish to maintain the expense," Tristan said, "not because of any imaginary gaming debt! I don't know who told you that I gamble to excess, but they are at best wrong, and at worst, lying to you."

Ware frowned. "But I've heard that you play at parties...."

"At *parties*," Tristan emphasized. "Card games, for penny points. I've been to hells, yes, and played there too—for the amount of cash I've carried in my pockets. I go if my friends wish to. When I am out of cash, I stop. I admit to being addicted to drink—I am not stupid enough to complicate that with an addiction to gambling as well. I like playing cards with friends; that's a matter of skill. But faro, or roulette, or dicing? Those are just games of chance, and are boring to boot. The only kind of gambling that interests me is on the Exchange—and then, only when I've done my research."

Ware sat back in his chair and regarded his son blankly. "You don't gamble."

"I have said so," Tristan replied, irked.

"Then what could you have possibly spent the money on? I know your household expenses nearly to the penny, and neither you nor Charlotte are extravagant enough to account for the excess."

Tristan sighed. "I have nearly forty thousand pounds in the Funds, in a trust for Charlotte and Jamie. And the new baby. Combined with Charlotte's settlement, and whatever you have in trust for the children—you see, I at least give you the dignity of believing that you do have such a trust—they should want for nothing should something happen to me."

"Tristan, you're thirty-two years old," Ware said, frowning. "A man your age doesn't think about his mortality. Men your age think you're immortal."

"I came very close to my own mortality," Tristan said, and he drained his glass, rising to refill it. He was still at the sideboard when his father's voice came again.

"You mean your intent to commit suicide."

The glass clinked against the side of the decanter. Tristan steadied it, then turned back to his guest. "Charlotte?"

"Yes. When I came to see you. When you were ill." Ware raised his eyes to his son's. "It was then I knew that I had failed you and had to see if there was any way to make recompense. Charlotte counseled me to wait a few weeks, then try again." He sipped his brandy, his hand shaking. "I can't believe that you were serious. Oh, I don't doubt you were, but Tristan...."

"I had gone to fetch my pistols," Tristan said, his voice flat. "I had written a draft of a letter to Charlotte and left it on my desk. I was going to go to my club and do it there. While I was gone, Charles came in and read the letter. We fought. He convinced me to wait. And as it turned out, I was merely suffering from nervous exhaustion, so once I'd recovered from that, my spirits improved and I no longer felt the need to commit self-murder."

"I don't understand why you felt that need to begin with."

Tristan turned the glass in his hand, studying the play of firelight on the amber liquid. "I had no wish to be an embarrassment to my son," he said finally. "He didn't deserve a father who was a useless, drunken fool, a waste of time and energy, a worthless, feckless idiot."

"You are none of those things!"

Tristan only looked at him. His father's face was indignant, but as Tristan stared, a slow flush built up in his cheeks and he sagged, looking old. "I said those things?" he whispered.

"At one time or another," Tristan said.

"I *beg* your pardon," Ware said, scarlet.

"Oh, it's true enough," Tristan said, his voice careless, "it's just not comfortable to *hear*, you understand. More brandy?"

"Just bring the whole decanter," Ware said.

Tristan obeyed, pouring his father another glass and settling back in his own chair.

"It isn't true, you know," Ware said. "The useless, worthless stuff. It isn't true. I don't even know why I said it."

"Because it was what you believed," Tristan replied. "It doesn't matter."

"It does matter! Because of my careless words, my son chose to destroy himself rather than go on, believing what I said in a fit of pique? God!" Ware flung his head back against the padded back of the wing chair. "I cannot believe I was so stupid! I told her, over and over again, I said, 'Alice, I don't know the first thing about children,' and she always said, 'It doesn't matter; I'll take care of that part.' But she didn't. She *left* me, and I didn't know what to do, didn't know the first thing about being a father! I didn't know my own father; he spent all his time with Albert, teaching him about the estate, and I was happy enough with my mathematics, so I didn't miss him. But then there I was, alone with you, and I didn't know what to do! Alice was supposed to know. But she *left* me." His eyes when they met Tristan's were stark and haunted and grief-stricken. "I didn't know what to do. And so I did it all wrong."

He took a drink. "And so here we are. All wrong. I wanted the best for you. I wanted you to *be* the best. You were so bright—brilliant. Redding, the vicar you had lessons with, said you were the most intelligent boy he'd ever tutored; you learned fast and you remembered things, and that you had an amazingly mathematical mind. I was so proud of you. You did so well in school, and I thought that I wouldn't make the same mistake and take you out of Cambridge until you were ready, that you could stay on and find a place there, and I could train someone else to manage the estate, and you could stay and be a Cambridge Fellow, and be happy there, the way I couldn't. But you didn't stay there. Why didn't you stay there?"

"I wasn't good enough!"

"You had *first-class honors*!" Ware roared. "You ranked *twelfth* in the Mathematical Tripos! You could have had a research scholarship!"

"I was *twelfth*!" Tristan roared back. "Not good enough!"

Ware fell back in his chair. "My *God*," he gasped, "what the devil do you mean 'not good enough'? What kind of expectations did you think I had?"

"Perfection," Tristan said flatly.

His father only stared at him. Finally he said, "Is that what you thought? That I required you to be perfect?"

"That is certainly the impression you gave," Tristan said. He sighed and leaned his head back against the chair, echoing his father's earlier move. Odd how they had some of the same mannerisms, he thought absently, when they spent so little time together. "As I said, it doesn't matter."

"I never wanted you to be perfect," Ware said. "I only wanted the best for you. I wanted you to be *happy*."

Closing his eyes, Tristan said, "Then it looks like we both failed."

The fire in the hearth crackled loudly, the pop of resin sounding like gunshots in the silence. Finally Ware said, "What would make you happy, Tristan?"

Tristan thought. Finally, he said, "I don't know what *would* make me happy, but there are a few things that *do* make me happy. Jamie, for one thing. It was part of the reason why I… why I had made the decision I had. Jamie is so beautiful, so perfect, that I couldn't bear to see the love he has for me turn into disdain. As it will. But I think I can accept that, now that—" He stopped, too close to self-betrayal.

"Now that what?"

Oh, hell. "Now that I've found someone who loves me the way I am," Tristan said. "Someone who doesn't care how flawed I am. Someone I can love with a full heart."

"Oh." Ware studied his glass, then looked up at Tristan. "Does Charlotte know? About this… other person?"

Tristan barked a short laugh. "I should say so, considering it was she who introduced us."

"Well. That's… interesting. Have you, um, settled her locally?"

Again the long period of silence. Tristan considered his options carefully, but he was tired. "No. He's currently in Brussels."

Ware blinked, then said slowly, "I could have sworn you just said…."

"'He'." Tristan was unequivocal. "Yes. You heard correctly. So you see, Papa, all your predictions came true. I am not only worthless and feckless and an idiot, I'm a sodomite as well. I'm in love with a man." He watched as the baron rose, his glass in his trembling hand. Absently, as though watching a play, he wondered if his father would strike him, or merely throw the brandy in his face. He hoped he would strike him; it would be a shame to waste such expensive liquor.

"This is my fault," Ware rasped.

It was Tristan's turn to blink. This wasn't what he expected. "I beg your pardon?"

"It's my fault. I failed as your father, drove you to excesses with whores, and drinking, and now you're looking for something worse, something more degrading, something…. Oh, God." Ware put his hand to his forehead and swayed.

Tristan shot to his feet, grabbing his elbow. "Please, sir! Sit down!"

Ware obeyed, slumping back into his chair. "Oh, God forgive me," he moaned.

Tristan crouched before him, taking the glass from him and setting it on the side table, then chafing his hands gently. They were ice cold. "This is not your fault, sir, trust me on that," he said earnestly. "Forgive me, but please do not blame yourself!"

"Who shall I blame, then? You? No, I cannot see it. You're confused, Tris, you're mistaking kindness for something more, and I'm sure the man cannot be reciprocating… Brussels? It cannot be Major Mountjoy? But he is a soldier—a *staff officer*! He cannot be what you describe." He shook his head firmly. "You are mistaken. You admire him, that's understandable, he's an admirable man, and you need to look up to someone who is admirable and reliable and all the things I am not. This is not love, Tristan. It is liking, and respect, and fondness. These things are all acceptable. I am sure you have not had any acquaintance before that engendered these feelings, and so you have mistaken them." He gave Tristan a quavery smile, and Tristan was shocked to realize that his father had somehow, during the last dozen years, grown old.

"No, sir, I am sure you are right," he said gently, regretting his rash decision to admit to his feelings for Charles. His father looked not angry, but ill. "I am just being foolish."

The baron looked down at their entwined hands. "Tristan," he said brokenly, "my beloved boy, *can* you forgive me?"

"I think we need to forgive each other," Tristan said. "That is what Lottie would say. And you know I always listen to what she says, for she is eminently sensible."

The baron lowered his head to rest his brow on their hands. Tristan, after a moment, leaned forward to rest his own on his father's grizzled head. "We will try," he said to Ware. "We can but try."

"DID you manage not to kill each other?" Charlotte asked from the doorway to the hall.

Tristan drew his cravat off before answering. "No thanks to you, Miss Mischief," he said dryly. "We did manage to reach a sort of accommodation, and have agreed to attempt to forgive each other. I invited him to dinner Sunday." He started to wriggle out of his coat; Charlotte came into the bedroom to tug on his sleeves. Laying it on the chair for Reston to deal with in the morning, Tristan went on, "He seems genuinely apologetic for his mishandling of me and equally desirous of improved relations. It seems to have come as a shock to him that he actually said all the things he has to me over the years. I suppose they were uttered without thought, but assumed they reflected his true feelings, not the frustration they apparently did. I don't know, Lottie." He sat down on the bed and regarded his wife with eyes that ached. "I told him about my feelings for Charles."

Lottie sat down on his coat with a thump. "You did what?" she asked faintly.

"I told him I was in love with Charles. He informed me that I was mistaken; that it was merely respect and affection, and that it was his fault for not providing me with someone I could relate to appropriately, so that I misunderstood my feelings for another man." He shook his head. "I think Charles has got to him somehow."

"What did you do?"

"Told him he was right, of course. What else could I do? Go into detail about our amorous activities?"

Charlotte shuddered. "Good heavens, no. I suppose it is for the best if he thinks it platonic. I shall remember to let Ellen know that we will continue to ignore the situation."

"How can a woman so wise be such an execrable speller?" Tristan teased.

"Wisdom and spelling do not necessarily go hand in hand," Charlotte said, snorting in amusement. "Well, it will be more comfortable this summer if he feels accepted at our home in the country; Wareham is quite close, and it will be pleasant to have a man near at hand while you are in Brussels with

Charles. The baron does seem to like Ellen; perhaps I shall engineer a romance between the two of them. She is not yet forty and still capable of carrying a child—would you mind a younger brother or sister?"

He laughed. "Lottie! My father is old!"

"He can't be much past sixty, if that," she said reasonably. "I should like to see Ellen comfortably settled; she is of course welcome to stay with us forever, but I sometimes think she would like a home of her own."

"I'm sure if my father had ever given thought to remarriage he might have done so any time in the last twenty-five years," Tristan pointed out.

"Hmm," Lottie said. "Still. It will be a way to pass the time while you and Charlie are gone."

He laughed again. "Miss Mischief strikes again. If you keep up your matchmaking, we shall have to see about making you one of the Patronesses of Almack's."

She shuddered. "Good heavens, no, please! Dry cake and weak lemonade. No, thank you. It was bad enough when I had to attend there as a debutante."

"Well, then, we'll have to find you some bucolic farmers and milkmaids for you to matchmake for near the Cottage, if only to keep you from trouble."

She patted her burgeoning belly. "I'm sure I will have plenty to do to keep me from trouble."

"Only a few more weeks," he said.

She smiled at him. "I know. Are you quite tired or would you be up for a game of whist?"

"I'm tired, but I'll play a hand. I take it your addendum there is keeping you up?"

"As usual. Well, if you're tired, at least I'll have a chance of winning." She tucked her hand in his shirt-sleeved arm and they went into the sitting room.

BOOK THREE

BRUSSELS, 1815

CHAPTER 20

THE carriage rattled to a stop, and a moment later Will the footman opened the door. Tristan rose from the seat, stiff from the hours immobile in the carriage, and stepped down onto clean-swept pavement, straightened, and looked around.

The house was on the small side, but all of those in this street were. That did not prevent them from looking well-tended and elegant, and substantial enough for Charlotte, if she and the children, now ensconced at Lilac Cottage, chose to visit. "The rue de Valois is one of the most exclusive in Brussels," a faintly accented voice said behind Tris. He turned to see a small, dapper Belgian at his elbow. "*M'sieur* Nort'wood?" he inquired. "I am Etienne Bellocq. I 'ired this 'ouse for you at your lady's request. I am sure you will find it all that you require. It is *petite bijou*—a little gem."

Tristan shook his hand. "Mr. Bellocq," he acknowledged. "Very kind of you to meet me. How did you know I would be arriving today?"

"I did not," the man said with a smile, and led the way to the front door, where he fished a handful of keys out of his pocket and started trying them in the lock. "But I 'ave a boy watching on the Antwerp gate, and he come and runs to me when you arrive. The soldiers there are very thorough with the checking of the documents, no?"

"Very thorough," Tristan agreed.

"This is good—we are too close to Paris to be casual, no? But now that *M'sieur le Duc* 'as arrived, we 'ave no fear of the Napoleons of this world."

"I have no fear of any Napoleons, myself," Tristan said with a faint grin. "I'll wager I could best him in a brawl."

Monsieur Bellocq looked confused, but rallied gamely. "I am sure of that too." He found the right key, pushed the door open and escorted Tristan inside. "I 'ad my 'ousekeeper come and make sure all is clean for you. 'Ave you brought your servants with you or do you need to 'ire them? I warned milady Nort'wood that with all the British people here there are few decent servants to 'ire."

"I've brought my own," Tristan assured him. "My valet and a footman and a cook-maid. I shan't be entertaining very much, so they should be enough for my comfort."

"*Bien, bien*," the Belgian said. "Good, good. Here is the drawing room—not so large, but not so small, either, and very comfortable. She looks out upon the garden on the side, see? No looking at walls or in other people's windows. The chambers upstairs above here the same. There are chambers on the other side above the dining room, but they look upon the walls. Not so nice. But we give those rooms to people we do not like, no?"

Tristan laughed. "I hope I do not have to put up people I do not like," he said with a snort. "Is there a study or bookroom here I can use for an office?"

"Be'ind the dining room. It was once the butler's pantry but that 'as been moved to the old kitchen. The new kitchen is in the back; it was added only last year. The servants', how you say, *quartiers*? No, that cannot be correct."

"Quarters," Tristan said. "*Quartier* is 'district' or 'neighborhood' in English."

"*Merci*. Yes. The quarters are above the kitchen, but separate from the rest of the 'ouse. Their stairs go up from the kitchen."

Will came in with valises under both arms. "Sir?"

"Upstairs, Will—the front bedroom, hopefully on the side overlooking the garden," Tristan said, stepping out of the way so that he could climb the narrow stairs.

Reston, following Will into the house, said in concern, "The *front* bedroom, sir? On the street?"

"It's a quiet enough street," Tristan said carelessly.

Will went noisily up the stairs with Reston on his heels.

"It *is* a quiet street," Monsieur Bellocq assured him. "The front bedroom will be fine, and you can see who comes to the calling, no?"

"Yes," Tristan said. And, he thought complacently, with the servants in the back of the house, there would be no witnesses if he, perhaps, chose to have company in that front bedroom. He smiled to himself. "I have a friend on the Duke's staff," he said to Monsieur Bellocq. "He has a billet in the rue du Marais...."

"Oh, that is not so far! A few streets away only. But if he is on the staff of *M'sieur le Duc*, you may see him tonight. Lady Passingwell holds a little rout but the Duc will be there and he likes to see his young officers enjoying themselves. Your friend will no doubt be there."

"But I don't have an invitation," Tristan pointed out.

Monsieur Bellocq tapped the side of his nose. "You leave such things to Etienne Bellocq. Lady Passingwell is well known to me, and I shall see that you receive an invitation to the little rout."

"My thanks, but I think I'll still send a note round to his billet," Tristan said in amusement.

"But of course you should," Monsieur Bellocq rubbed his hands together in satisfaction. "So! I leave you to, how you say, ess-plore?"

"Explore."

"Yes, yes. You settle in and I will see to the invitation. Oh! Yes!" He took a card case from his pocket and handed Tristan his card. "Here is my direction, should you have questions. And welcome to Brussels, *M'sieur* Nort'wood."

"Thank you, *M'sieur* Bellocq." They shook hands, and Tristan watched him go, a smile on his face. He was exactly as Charles had described him, and a relief it was to have someone make all the arrangements for this visit.

The house was as promised, a little gem, but the front bedroom took up the whole width of the house and featured an enormous bed with heavy brocade drapes. He tugged on the fabric, pleased to see them sturdy and dust-free, and imagining himself and Charles tucked up there, the curtains drawn around the bed, together in a dark, sheltered cave of silk and linen. God, he missed Charles. The ache was as physical as it was emotional; a need for the touch of his hand, the scent of his skin, his warmth, his strength, the sound of his voice rumbling in Tristan's ear. His hand turned gentle on the silk brocade, his fingers stroking it without thinking. Soon, he promised himself. Soon he would see Charles again, and as soon after that as he could arrange it, he would hold him, and kiss him, and love him the way he'd longed to these dreadful, lonely weeks. Soon.

CHARLES snagged a glass of champagne off the tray of a passing waiter and turned back to Randall. "I didn't have time to stop back at my billet," he explained, "since I went straight to His Grace when I got back from Namur, but fortunately Griffin's my size and had spare pantaloons and a waistcoat at his. His jackets were all too narrow in the shoulders, but his valet kindly brushed out my coat for me. It's not what I would have chosen to wear here, but the Duke wanted me to accompany him so that I could finish my report." He tugged on the hem of the black waistcoat. He was a little taller than Griffin, too, but fortunately his Hessians hid the fault in the pantaloons.

Randall said, "You were to Namur and back this afternoon? That's sixty miles."

"That's His Grace," Charles said dryly. "And it was where Blucher was today. It would be easier if Blucher were headquartered closer, but he's been ensconced here longer than we have."

"The Duke's not happy lately, is he?"

"Have you ever known him to be?" Charles asked rhetorically. "No, but he's happier now that he has his own Quartermaster again. What possessed those idiots at Whitehall? And then to saddle him with Uxbridge as his second. His Grace is fit to be tied."

"Can you blame him? The man ran off with his sister-in-law."

Charles snorted. "He's a damn good commander."

"Of cavalry. And you know the Duke's opinion of cavalry."

That brought a laugh. "I hear it often enough. I wonder if Uxbridge is the reason. God, I hope they serve supper soon; I missed dinner. I'd kill for a sandwich."

"Come along, old boy," Randall said, catching hold of his sleeve and dragging him across the crowded room. "I'll do you one better. I've an acquaintance with the chef here; he's the son of our old butler. He'll find something for you to gnaw on while you're waiting for the real thing. I assume the Duke's done with you?"

"For now," Charles said darkly. "Until he thinks of another question or wants me off to Moscow to visit the Tsar."

Randall laughed. "Your own fault for bein' so damned efficient, Monty. Mess something up next time."

"And have to face him with his temper up? No, thank you. I've seen him turn that cold gaze on too many hapless underlings to want it focused on me. I'd *rather* be off to visit the Tsar." Charles grinned unwillingly. "Though frankly, it's exciting, being one of his lads. You never know what he's going to throw at you. And him perfectly confident you'll manage it. Makes you want to excel, Randy."

"Thanks—I'll stick to the Young Frog."

"Don't let the Duke hear you referring to Slender Billy that way," Charles warned.

Randall held up his hands. "Not on your life, Monty. Come on, the kitchen's this way. We'll be back in plenty of time for His Grace to send you off to Moscow."

"MR. NORTHWOOD, how good to see you!" Lady Passingwell greeted him, stretching out both hands. "If I had known you were going to be in Brussels, I would have sent you a card. How remiss of Charlotte not to write me."

"It was a rather spontaneous decision," Tristan said, taking her hands and bowing low over them. "She was fussing about her brother, and I said I would be happy to make a quick trip over to check on him. Although I believe she receives a letter from him daily, she won't be content until I have seen him and confirmed that he is indeed well."

"Was he the one who recommended Mr. Bellocq? Such a delightful little man, for a Belgian. I was quite astonished when he told me today you were here. He's an old friend of the Richmonds' solicitor, you know. But quite unexceptionable, and of an excellent character." She tucked her hand in Tristan's arm and guided him around the drawing room. "The Richmonds will be here later; Her Grace has sent a message that they are waiting on His Grace's return from some review or other. You know of course that the Duke of Richmond is in charge of the defense of Brussels in the event of a French attack? Such a responsibility, but if anyone is capable, it's Charles Lennox. You do know that his son March is ADC to the Prince of Orange?"

Tristan laughed. "If I did not, I know now. *Pace*, Lady P. I need not be brought immediately up to date on all the activities of the good residents of Brussels. I'm not leaving for at least a fortnight."

"Oh, good. There will be quite a lot of enjoyable activities, now that the weather has improved. Lady Alvanley is in town, with Kitty and Fanny; I am sure they will be hosting something, and I will be certain to get you a ticket to that. And the Richmonds, of course, and oh, a dozen other people!"

Tristan gave the crowded drawing room a quick glance and said dryly, "Yes, just a dozen or so."

She laughed and thumped his arm with her fan. "Oh, hush," she said. "May I say, Mr. Northwood, how *good* it is to see you smiling again! You seem quite your old self. Charlotte told me that you were quite ill this winter, but you seem quite recovered! I must tell you that I have been worried over the last year; the last time I saw you, you seemed not at all your usual gay self." She smiled delightedly up at him. "But I see the old Tristan Northwood again."

"Thank you for your concern," he said soberly, but smiling with his eyes down at her. "Now, much as I have enjoyed getting caught up on the entertainment awaiting me here, I did really come to see my brother-in-law, and was told he would be here. I sent him a message at his quarters, but have not heard from him yet."

"Oh, the Duke has him running about," Lady Passingwell said. "He is here, somewhere. He came with the Duke an hour since. Let's go find him." She patted his arm and steered him off into the crowd.

HUNGER abated by a roast beef sandwich and a tankard of ale shared with Randall in the warmth of the busy kitchen, Charles checked back with His Grace and when told to "go off and enjoy" himself, wandered out of the overheated drawing room and onto the terrace. He took a cheroot from the breast pocket of his uniform coat, lit it at one of the flambeaux illuminating the terrace and gardens below, and leaned on the balustrade, gazing sightlessly out over the quiet scene and smoking. Behind him a quartet began playing a sprightly Bach piece, and he listened to the music absently.

He was tired. Not just from the sixty-mile round trip out to Blucher's headquarters; he'd done longer rides in less time under more stressful conditions in the Peninsula. But the endless rounds of meetings and reviews and messages back and forth along the long line of Wellington's troop spread from here to Ostend, followed by the intense social demands of his position and then, finally, at the end of a very long day, a late retiring to a cold, empty bed and the promise of an early rising—all these were wearing on him.

He hadn't expected to be back at this. A year ago he'd made up his mind that the military no longer needed him, and that he no longer needed them, that he was ready for a peaceful life spent helping others instead of figuring out how to kill them. Three months ago he thought he'd found what he wanted: days at the hospital, nights in Tristan's arms. And then it was all taken away from him and he was forced back into the life he'd happily given up.

Temporarily, he reminded himself savagely. *Temporarily*. Soon this would all be over, Bonaparte back on Elba or wherever they'd decided to put him—some of the men at the Congress had been agitating for a safer spot even before the disastrous escape, someplace like the barren volcanic island of St. Helena in the middle of the Atlantic, or the South Seas somewhere—and he'd be able to finally sell out and settle down.

Always before, in moments like this, he'd just assumed there would be an afterward. That he'd come through unscathed—or very minorly scathed, he thought wryly, thinking of a few of the scars he'd acquired—and ready to move on to the next challenge, the next adventure. So why was it that this time he wasn't so sure? No, more than that. This time he was *afraid*. Was it because he'd got out of the habit of thinking of himself as a soldier? Was it the hours he'd spent in the hospital, sometimes doing nothing more for some poor patient than trying to make him comfortable? He'd seen death aplenty before, had dished it out, had held the hand of some comrade until the eyes had glazed over, had picked up pieces of men who'd been standing beside him only minutes before. He'd always known intellectually that it could easily have been him, but it wasn't until now that he felt it in his gut. He could be hurt. He could *die*. And leave Tristan alone again.

He dragged in a deep mouthful of cigar smoke and let it out in a slow steady stream. Tris had been such a mess when he'd left. Charlotte had reassured him in her regular letters that he'd recovered quickly afterward, was still pursuing his surgical studies, and had in fact seemed more like his old self, only less brittle. Happier, she'd said. Missing Charles, of course, but happier with himself and full of plans for when Charles came home. He'd even begun a tentative relationship with Baron Ware. Charlotte had said they were like two dogs sniffing around each other, but still, it was more than it was before. Charles was glad of that. Perhaps if he didn't return, Tris would be all right, with the support of his wife and his father.

It was odd, thinking of Tris like this. His presence was so strong in Charles's mind that he almost felt that his lover was present, was a shadow at his back....

"Charlie?"

He jumped and spun around in shock, the cheroot falling from his fingers. Tristan grinned uncertainly and bent and picked up the cigar, holding it out to him. "I'm sorry. I didn't mean to startle you."

Charles took the cheroot unthinkingly and said in disbelief, "Tris? What the devil are you doing here?"

The grin faded. "You sent the name of that businessman, Bellocq, to Charlotte. She arranged it." Tristan cocked his head and said quietly, "You aren't pleased to see me?"

"Oh, God, Tris!" Charles wrapped his arms around him and squeezed. "Not pleased? The devil I'm not! I just didn't expect you for weeks yet! Is Charlotte all right?"

"Of course. I wouldn't have left her if she weren't. I took her down to the country more than a week ago. She and your new niece and Jamie are fine."

Charles released him and held him at arms' length, studying him critically. "You look well." He glanced over Tristan's shoulder at the brightly lit French windows and let his hand slide down Tristan's arm, brushing his fingers gently before letting go. "When did you arrive?"

"A few hours ago. I sent a message to your billet but didn't get an answer. Your landlord said you'd left earlier."

"Rode to Namur on the Duke's business," Charles said. "Got back this evening and came nearly straight here. Haven't been back to my rooms yet today. God, you're a sight for sore eyes. Come on." He cocked his head in the direction of the end of the terrace, away from the lights and the windows. "I need a proper greeting."

The light in Tristan's face was nearly enough to illuminate the darkest shadows in the garden. He followed Charles down the terrace to the end, and when they were safe in the dark, Charles drew him into his arms, finding his mouth with his own. Tristan's lips were warm and soft and welcoming; Charles groaned in relief and suppressed hunger. He felt Tristan's hands in his hair, digging in to hold him; he slid his own arms down around his lover's hips, pulling him in hard against him, feeling Tristan's desire against his own. Half-laughing, half-groaning, he pulled away, clutching Tristan's waist and holding him apart. "God, Tris," he gasped, "this had better not be a dream. Where are you staying?"

"Number 4, rue de Valois," Tris said. "Do you know it?"

"No. I've had a little time to explore the city outside the immediate area around headquarters, but not the residential areas. Mostly scouting out entertainment opportunities for Wellington and his coterie."

"Not a problem." Tristan drew out his card case and a pencil. On the back of one of his cards, he wrote the address, then a rough map. "Here's the rue du Marais, here's Richmond's, here's rue de Valois. Not difficult." He tucked it into Charles's inside breast pocket. "Keep it with you always."

"Sentimentalist," Charles jeered, but he patted Tristan's hand where it lay on the coat, then reached up to cup Tristan's cheek. "Damn," he breathed, "you're here. I've been dreaming of you, you know."

"Which part of me?" Tristan teased, rubbing his fingers over the lacings of Charles's coat.

Charles groaned. "God. Your mouth. Your hands. Your bloody beautiful arse." He leaned forward, his lips brushing Tristan's ear. "Your stiff prick," he whispered, and licked the whorl of his ear, laughing softly as Tris shuddered in his arms. Then he drew back and regarded Tris soberly. "Your laughter. Your eyes. Your voice. The way you think, the way you talk, the words you use, the smile you give me just before you drop off to sleep.... God, Tristan, there isn't anything about you I don't miss, including the way that you look when you're quashing some mushroom: the sardonic eyebrow, the sneering lip. The insufferable drawl."

"Ballocks," Tristan said, embarrassed. "I don't drawl."

"You do. You've got the role of the disdainful aristocrat down. I see that and all I can think is that worldly, bored aristocrat is *mine*, and I can wipe that disdain from his face with a touch."

"You can," Tristan whispered. "Will you come to me tonight?"

Charles sighed and shook his head. "I doubt it. I'm in His Grace's train tonight and there are a few more stops on his progress. He won't bed down 'til four, if I know him, and we've a meeting with the Prince of Orange and some of his less-than-happy Belgian subjects at eight. We're trying to stave off a repeat of the disaster with the Saxons under Blucher."

"What disaster?"

"Mutiny," Charles said grimly, releasing Tristan. "The Saxon king was a satellite of Napoleon, and the Congress divided the country between Prussia and Russia. What a mess. There were almost fourteen thousand Saxon troops conscripted for this campaign, and a fortnight ago a handful of them nearly murdered Blucher in his bed. He had to execute a couple of them, and he hates having to do things like that. The old bastard has a temper like the devil and hates the French with a passion, but he loves his men like children. But there's no way we can trust the Saxon contingent now, despite the fact that the vast majority of them are loyal to Blucher—or at least to their officers. It doesn't make anyone happy, but it looks like we're sending them all home. The meeting tomorrow's to discuss that and how we can keep it from happening with the Belgians—there's a strong pro-French faction here as well; a good percentage of the Belgian-Dutch contingent cut their teeth as French troops. And most of them are under the Prince of Orange—who is less than fond of his father's new subjects, let alone the French." He shook his head. "They don't like him. He's a decent enough lad, though a bit too... enthusiastic. Eager to prove his worth, and too damned inexperienced to boot." He took a draw on his almost-forgotten cheroot and blew the smoke out impatiently. "Half of our troops are inexperienced, half of them pro-Bonaparte, and would to God they were the same half—we could tuck them in an out-of-the-way spot and ignore them. But the problem is that the pro-Bonaparte half are some of the best soldiers in the corps. Say what you will about the French—their system of advancement beats the British advancement-by-purchase method, hands down, when it comes to turning out decent officers."

"Careful," Tristan murmured, "that sounds almost treasonous."

Charles let out a sharp bark of laughter. "Add it to the list of things that can hang me," he said bitterly.

He looked up to see Tristan's face. "Ah, God," he groaned. "I didn't mean to say all that to you, Tris. I should have just kept my mouth shut and been happy you're here. But I haven't been able to talk to anyone about this and it's driving me mad."

"And you're exhausted, and you don't want to be here any more than I want you to be," Tristan said.

"That's true enough. Well. Let me take you to His Grace. He'll like you—he's a snob, and you're wellborn. I warn you, though, he's even better than you with the disdainful expression. I think it's the nose. Come on, then." He stubbed his cigar out on the balustrade and dropped the end into a nearby flowerpot. "Let's find him before he decides to move on to his next event without telling me."

"I *have* met him before, you know," Tristan said as they wended their way through the crowd. "Last year, at the Honours."

"That's right; I was in Vienna with Castlereagh by then and quite forgot that he was in London," Charles acknowledged. "Of course you would have met him; you two move in the same circles."

"I doubt he would remember me, at any rate."

"Oh, you'd be surprised," Charles said. "You're just the type of young nobleman whose company he enjoys. I think he's always been very conscious of his dignity, as the mere second son of an Irish peer, and he enjoys having the respect of the very class he'd grown up envying."

"You and your theories!" Tristan laughed as they negotiated a crush near the door. "No one is safe from Charlie Mountjoy's pokings and pryings."

"I like to figure out why people do what they do," Charles said mildly. "It's interesting."

"Lottie does, too, but she's more, I don't know, *abstract* about it. It's a game for her. You take it much more seriously."

"Blame it on the German side of the family," Charles said with a chuckle. "The brooding and romantic Germans rather than the coldly analytical Prussians. Lottie got the Prussian blood, I think. Too bad she was born female; she would have made an excellent officer."

"She's certainly good at managing staff—and sometimes me," Tristan shot back.

"Oh, she's managed all of us since we lost Mama," his lover said dryly. "Here's the Duke."

There was a crowd around His Grace, but by virtue of their superior height, they managed to catch his attention, and he beckoned them forward. "Mountjoy." He nodded, then turned to Tristan. "Northwood. Welcome to Brussels. Come to see the fun?"

"Hardly," Tristan said, shaking his hand. "My wife sent me to check on her brother's welfare; I can't convince her that he hasn't completely forgot how to take care of himself. A few months under her roof and he's her responsibility again."

"Well, if he won't get himself a wife, a sister will do. A man needs a woman to look out for him," said the man who avoided his own wife at every opportunity. "Where are you situated?"

"Rue de Valois," Tristan said.

"Pleasant prospect there. Quiet. I imagine Mountjoy will find it a refuge from the noise of his billet."

"He is, of course, always welcome there. As are you, Duke. I don't entertain largely, with Lottie in Leicestershire, but I've plans for a card party—gentlemen only. May I send you a card?"

"Certainly. I may not be able to stay, but I'll look in on you."

They chatted a few more minutes, then His Grace's attention was drawn away, and with a casual, "Don't go far, Mountjoy—I'm leaving in a quarter hour and require your attendance," he left them. Charles made a wry face.

"The story of my life in Brussels, I'm afraid. I imagine we're off to placate some terrified ally or other. I doubt we shall see much of each other, Tris."

"I expected half as much," Tristan said. He drew a key from his waistcoat pocket. "Here's a key to the garden door. The stairs on the left go up to the front of the house; the servants' quarters have a separate entrance. Come when you can." He dropped his voice and said, "Whenever you can."

Charles took the key, his fingers lingering a moment on Tristan's palm. "It may be late," he warned, "and only for a short while."

"Whenever you can," Tristan said again. They turned to watch the dancers in silence, shoulder to shoulder.

Captain Randall came up a few minutes later and said, "Mountjoy, Himself is looking for you; he's ready to leave. Hullo." He nodded at Tristan.

"Tris, this is my friend Captain Francis Randall. Randy, Mr. Tristan Northwood, my brother-in-law."

"Oh, you're the brother-in-law," Randall said, and shook his hand. "How's Mrs. Northwood?"

"Quite well, thank you. In the country for the summer."

"Good. Welcome to Brussels, Northwood. Mountjoy?"

"Coming, Randy. Tris—I'll see you later."

Tristan watched them leave, following Wellington out like skiffs circling a merchantman; then, with no other real reason to stay, took his own leave of his hostess, and went back to the silent house on the rue de Valois.

A SOFT sound woke Tristan in the black of the night; he lay still a moment, then heard it again, the thump of a boot hitting the floor. Grinning, he drew back the bed curtain to see Charles sitting in the armchair in the room in his shirtsleeves; as he watched, his lover carefully set the boots beside the chair.

Then, to Tristan's consternation, he put his hands over his face and sat hunched in upon himself.

The posture was so unlike Charles that Tristan was out of bed and crouched at his side before he'd even consciously made the decision to move. "Charlie?" he asked in a low, concerned voice.

Charles glanced up and the expression on his face was so bleak, so exhausted, that Tristan sucked in a breath, then drew him into his arms, Charles's head on his breast. Charles gave a great, heavy shudder. "What's wrong?"

"I can't do this anymore," Charles said in a thin, strained voice. "I'd forgot what it was like. I've become a coward in the last two years, Tris. I can't bear this, seeing all these men and knowing that in a few days they'll all be so much meat for worms. I've become wedded to the idea of healing them, not sending them out to die. Oh, God, Tris—he's talking about giving me a command!"

"Is he serious?"

"I don't know. Sometimes I think so; but he does this sometimes, throws out ideas as if he's thinking out loud. We're low on officers in the King's German Legion; they're mostly Hanoverians and having a commander that speaks German would be an asset, I can see that. And it comes with a promotion to colonel."

"Does that matter?"

"God, no. I just don't want to command any longer. A few years ago I would have fought for it, but I can't do it, Tris. I can't send them to their deaths. We're outnumbered, outmanned and outgunned, from all reports; half the men in both the Dutch and the German armies are French sympathizers, and too many of our best troops are still in America." He drew back and looked up at Tristan's face. "I'm not afraid for myself," he said wearily. "I'll be fine; I'm always fine, so don't look so aghast. But the men...."

Tristan smoothed a lock of hair back from his forehead. "Come to bed, Charlie. It will look different in the morning."

"I'm too tired to do you much good tonight," Charles said miserably.

"The only thing I want is for you to sleep beside me. There will be time later for everything else." He glanced up at the clock on the mantel, illuminated by the lamp he'd left burning there for Charles's anticipated arrival. "Good Lord, it's nearly four. No wonder you're tired."

"And we're to meet at nine," Charles said. "It was supposed to be eight, but March talked him out of it."

"Good for March." He drew Charles to his feet and stripped him of his dirty clothes. "You'll need to allow time in the morning to go back to your billet to change, unless you want to borrow a shirt from me. Not regulation, I'm sure."

"Better quality. That would do."

Tris drew back the bedclothes and pushed Charles onto his belly. "I've got the bottle of oil that you left for me," he said, "and it's my turn to take care of you for a change. So lie still and I'll see if I can't put you in better form before you drop off."

Charles said nothing, just turned his head on the pillow and gave another great, shuddering sigh. Tristan warmed the oil in his hands and set about giving Charles a massage as Charles had done more than once for him.

As he did, he named the muscles he rubbed, "Trapezius. Deltoid. Teres Major. Latissimus Dorsi…." He felt the faint rumble of Charles's chuckle, then the laughter faded and Charles slept. Tristan kept working until he felt the muscles completely relax, knowing that Charles's sleep was that of exhaustion, and that unless he was fully at ease, the sleep would not bring rest.

When there was no tension left in Charles's body, Tristan eased over to lie beside him, drawing Charles's limp arm over his waist and resting his head against Charles's shoulder.

HE'D planned on staying awake through the night, to let Charles sleep soundly and wake him when he needed to make his meeting, but it seemed it had only been a moment and he was opening his eyes to drawn bedcurtains and Charles at the washstand, shaving. "You're awake," he said stupidly, blinking.

Charles turned to him, flashing a quick grin. "I am, and after a most comfortable sleep. Thank you, love. Your kindness last night is making it easier for me to face the day."

"What will you do?" Tristan asked, sliding off the bed and reaching for his banyan.

Charles shrugged. "Meet with the Duke and whatever nervous noble he's placating this morning. Follow him around and take notes and run errands, same as I always do."

"About the command."

His lover's face went still. "It's not an offer, yet."

"But when it is?"

"I don't know. I suppose it will depend on the tenor of the offer; if he's determined, there's no point in refusing him. If I do, he'll just send me back to one of the regiments as a major, and I'll be no better than before. Worse; I'll have less control, following the orders of men I don't know and can't trust. If it's just speculation, I'll let him know tactfully that I prefer being one of his ADCs to command. It's a compliment, really; he doesn't do field promotions often. It's one of the things we've argued about; he decries the quality of the officers he gets, but adheres to the promotion-by-purchase rules. The French system is better, but I suppose it's some kind of patriotism on his part to stick with the British way." He dried his face on a towel. "I just hope the British way is enough to stop Bonaparte."

"You'll do it," Tristan said confidently.

"I hope you're right. Did you bring the Brat to Brussels?"

"I did. This house shares a stables with its neighbors."

"Good. The Duke's got a tête-à-tête with one of his inamoratas this afternoon and has released us from durance vile for the nonce. Care to take a ride around one? I can show you the city."

"Are you sure you wouldn't rather come back here for a rest?"

"I'll rest when I'm dead," Charles said with another grin. "Isn't that one of your sayings?"

"Yes, and a bloody stupid one at that," Tris shot back.

"Well, Paragon needs some exercise, since I rode Patch and Betsy yesterday, and so will Brat by this afternoon. We'll take care of the horses first. That's the way of the cavalry. Horses first, riders later." He closed up his shirt and tied his cravat before turning back to Tristan and taking him in his arms. Kissing him tenderly, he said in a low voice, "The Duke's tryst will go on into the evening; he's already said he won't need us until tomorrow. On the other hand, he's just as likely to be late to his tryst, so I may be later than one. But there's a fine restaurant in town; we'll stop for lunch there on our travels."

Tristan smoothed back a lock of blond hair and kissed the broad forehead revealed. In a low, sultry voice, he said, "We'll ride this afternoon, and then this evening, it will be I doing the riding."

"You wicked thing," Charles said, laughing, and he kissed him. "Save it for when I can act on it and don't have to meet my general sporting a cockstand."

"Go on, then," Tristan said. "I've already warned the household that you'll be stopping here some nights as your billet is noisy— I got that idea from your Duke—so they won't be surprised to see you downstairs. In the meantime, I'll go mess up the bed you allegedly slept in."

"Wicked, wicked Tris," Charles said in amusement.

"All those years of criminal conversation must be good for something, if only a conspiratorial mind," he retorted, giving Charles a little push.

Charles dropped a kiss on Tristan's cheek and was gone.

He took the light from the room, though the morning sun was already shining through the drapes. Tristan sighed and went to the guest bedroom he'd chosen for Charles, bringing along the damp towel for verisimilitude. There he hooked the towel on the washstand, then mussed up the bed, lying down on the pillows for a moment to give the illusion that someone had slept there.

Finally, he went back to his own bed, climbed back in to linens still redolent of the scent of Charles, and fell back to sleep.

CHAPTER 21

THE late May sun was warm on Tristan's face as he sprawled on the blanket thrown down on the hillside. Beside him, Charles sat with his chin on his knees, looking out over the countryside. "It's a pretty place," he mused absently. "Too bad it's destined to be a battlefield."

"You're that sure?" Tristan asked sleepily. "That it will be here?"

"The French border's only a short way away, and this is the main route to Brussels, and the army's here. Napoleon's best chance is to crush the Northern Coalition; none of the other allies are strong enough to stand against him. As long as he stays that side of the border, we can do nothing, but he won't stay. His Grace has already worked out some of the logistics based on the spies we have in the French camp. Of course, I'm sure Boney has done the same with his."

"What's that in the distance?"

"Place called Hougoumont. 'Chateau de Hougoumont', formally, but it's really just a big farm. Nobody lives there except the tenant farmer."

"Mm," Tristan said.

Charles lay back and threw his arm over his eyes. "So. What's wrong?"

"What makes you think anything's wrong?"

"You've been here four days. We've talked about Charlotte, Caroline, Jamie, Ellen, your father, London, Lilac Cottage, Brussels, the upcoming battles, Napoleon, and Wellington. We've talked about Blucher and Gneisenau and Wilhelm Friedrich. But not once have you mentioned anything about medicine or your studies with Crosby. What happened? Was he angry about you leaving London?"

"No." It was Tristan's turn to sit up and rest his forehead on his knees. "He didn't need to be. I'm not studying with him any longer."

"Whyever not?" Charles lowered his arm and gazed up at him.

"Because." Tristan swallowed and raised his head to stare out at the distance. "He told me that I was wasting my time."

"*What*? That's insane. Just before I left, MacQuarrie said that he was quite pleased with your progress. What happened?" Rolling onto his side, Charles propped his head up on one elbow.

"I assisted him in a surgery. A tumor removal. It was successful and the patient was doing well. I thought Crosby was happy with my performance. But afterwards he called me into his office and told me that I would never make a good surgeon." Tristan swallowed. "He said that I was adequate as far as the rougher forms of surgery—like bonesetting and blood-letting—were concerned, but that more complex surgeries like cutting for stone would forever be beyond me. It seems as though my hands aren't steady enough. He says that the drink has ruined me for finer surgery. He suggested I switch studies to medicine, and that under MacQuarrie I would learn enough that I could set up as a country doctor if I wished, or work under another physician. But I'd never make a really competent surgeon." He held his hands out in front of him. They looked steady. Far steadier than Tristan's heart right now. He'd held off on telling Charles because he knew how disappointed he'd be, but Charles had asked, and so he'd answered. "It doesn't matter that I've barely drunk a drop since starting at St. Joseph's months ago. Apparently the damage was done."

"What did you do?" Charles asked quietly.

Tristan swallowed. "What do you think I did? I went straight home and got stinking drunk. Then the next morning I packed up Charlotte, the children, and my hangover and went home to Lilac Cottage."

"Are you still drinking?" The voice was still quiet, not accusing, not anything but inquiring.

"No. I've found I don't have the taste for it any longer, and I'm sick of waking with a headache and nausea. So apparently I'm not only not a good surgeon, I'm not a good drunk anymore, either. I suppose I'll have to stay in the country and see if I can not be a good landowner too."

"That sounds like self-pity," Charles said.

"Of course it does," Tristan replied, forcing lightness into his voice. "That's what it is. So. Once Charlotte and the children were settled, I packed up and came here. I'm warning you, though—Charlotte has it in her mind to match your cousin Ellen with my father. I think Brussels on the eve of battle is a safer place for me than Lilac Cottage."

"It's all right to be disappointed, Tris. I wish you would have told me sooner."

"I didn't want you to know. I knew you'd be more disappointed than I."

"I doubt it. Well, if Napoleon wins this battle, Europe will be back at war, and the army is always looking for surgeons. Shall I introduce you to Dr. Grant?"

Tristan gave him a wry grin. "Charlotte would *murder* you," he said. He lay down on his side, mirroring Charles's posture.

"Seriously, Tris—what are you thinking of doing?"

"I don't know." Tristan pulled up a blade of grass and chewed on it thoughtfully. "I've considered Crosby's suggestion that I study medicine instead, and that's a possibility. I sent them each a polite note just before I left for Leicestershire, thanking Crosby and mentioning to MacQuarrie what Crosby said and telling him I'd be in contact with him on my return to London, if he was interested and able to take me on as a student. I also added that I thought you might vouch for me."

"Of course I will," Charles said promptly. He leaned forward and kissed Tristan softly.

"Lottie thinks the battle will be terrible," Tristan murmured against Charles's mouth. "She says I need to be prepared to do real work, and sent a huge box of medical supplies. It just arrived yesterday."

"She's probably not wrong," his lover said, his fingers moving to loosen Tristan's cravat. "You know her correspondents always keep her informed. They'll bring the wounded back to the city, most likely. Will you help?"

"Of course I will," Tristan echoed Charles's words. He sighed as Charles's mouth settled on his throat. "Charlie—dare we? Here?"

"There's no one for miles, we're on the highest point in the area, and the grass is over our heads here," Charles said, and he scraped his teeth along Tristan's jaw. Tristan shivered. "We're safe as houses."

"Good," Tristan said, and pushed him over onto his back, climbing on top of him. Charles laughed and rolled them over in the grass, his hands turning rough and wild. Tristan matched him as they tore at each other's clothing, desperate to be skin to skin. "Ah," Tristan gasped as Charles slid into him, his cock slick with spit, "that's so good, Charlie."

"You're so beautiful," Charles said against his chest, licking and sucking as Tristan wrapped his legs around Charles's waist. "I've waited my whole life for you, I swear. Mine, Tris. Mine."

"Yours, Charlie, love…."

Charles crested first, arching against the pull of Tristan's legs with a deep groan, then his hand found Tristan and coaxed him into release. Spent, he rolled off Tristan and lay beside him in the grass, both of them breathing hard.

The light and sky blurred in Tristan's eyes, and he realized he was weeping. Not sobbing, not crying, just quietly weeping, and he wasn't sure why. "Tris?" Charles asked softly from beside him.

He shook his head and rolled over onto his belly, pressing his face into the smell of earth and crushed grass, a warm, healthy smell. A deep shudder wracked his body and then he *was* crying, harsh, fierce sobs. He was marginally aware of Charles moving, of his laying his arm across his back and pressing his face to Tristan's shoulder, but he was too wrapped up in this strange, frightening despair to acknowledge him.

When he'd exhausted himself, he said into the ground, "I never used to cry. You've turned me into a watering pot."

"My sincerest apologies," Charles said wryly. "Care to tell me what that was about?"

"I think that I thought that if I never mentioned it to you, it wouldn't be real," Tristan said, looking up and meeting Charles's eyes. Charles immediately reached over and rubbed a streak of dirt off his cheek. "The thing with Crosby, I mean. I was just pretending that it hadn't happened, that I would be going back to London and picking up where I left off with him, and nothing would have changed. Telling you made it real, somehow. I'm sorry to be so lachrymose, Charlie. I never used to be."

"It's all right." Charles drew him into his arms and they lay there in the sunlight, the scent of the grass surrounding them. "It's strange. You've an ancient name, a beautiful face, a strong body, a lovely wife, two wonderful children, and plenty of cash, not to mention a devastatingly handsome lover. But they're bars to you, aren't they. Just bars of a cage. You're like a skylark, bashing your wings against the cage wire, unable to sing unless you're free."

"Well, not so much the devastatingly handsome lover," Tristan said. "You're more the door to the cage, Charlie, but you're right. I feel trapped. I've always felt trapped. It's foolish and ungrateful, but I've never wanted all that. I don't care about the name, the looks are meaningless, and while I adore my children and am fond of Lottie, I never asked for them, never needed them. Even my friends—I love them, but in so many ways they bore me. I've always felt as if I were playing a role I hadn't auditioned for. But I didn't realize it until I met you. I need *more*. I need… *different*.

"And then I started working with Crosby and the others and I felt as if I had come home. That *this* was what I was meant to be doing. And now it's gone, lost to me, because of my *own damned fault*." He tensed, his hands fisting. "My own foolishness, my own *stupidity*. And nothing I can do will change that."

"Tris, Crosby is not the only surgeon in the world—or even in London. Someone else might think differently. And maybe even if he's right, and you'll never be able to do the finer forms of surgery, what's wrong with doing what he said, and studying medicine? You could still study surgery; it's part of what we'll be learning, even if we're not permitted to actually practice it. You'll just learn more than that. Perhaps you'll find a way that you could combine them, something more than just a 'country doctor'." He drew him close and kissed his forehead. "Perhaps go into practice with another physician, focusing on the diseases of the body while he focuses on things like beastly tasting South American herbs?"

Tristan let out a watery chuckle. "I see the plot," he said. "You want to go into partnership and let me do all the work while you spend all your time with your precious books."

"You've struck it," Charles said with a grin. "But the important word there was partnership, Tris. Study with me. Learn with me. Work with me." He kissed him again. "Live with me. Love me."

"I do. God, what you're suggesting—I never even considered it possible. A partnership as physicians? You and I?"

"Why not? I'm happiest when I'm working with a partner."

Tristan leaned against Charles's shoulder and let his thoughts wander. After a moment something occurred to him and he asked, "Who was he, Charlie? A partner?"

"Who?"

"The one you said you loved, that was afraid and shut you out. That you lost."

"Ah. Gregory. Gregory Winstead. We were cornets together, back at the beginning of our careers. He was about my age." Charles fell silent, then added quietly, "We were friends, once."

"But no longer?"

"He's dead. Died in Spain, oh, nearly five years ago now." Charles drew Tristan's head down onto his shoulder and rubbed his cheek against the tousled dark hair. "He was… sweet. A good soldier, a good officer; solid in the saddle and well-liked by his men. Firm, but fair, as the good ones try to be."

"Was he killed in battle?"

"No." Charles took a breath and rubbed his cheek against Tristan's hair again, as if the gesture gave him courage. "I'm not sure I can talk about this."

"You don't have to."

There was a faint rumble beneath Tristan's ear, a wry chuckle that was less about humor and more about surrender. "No, I suppose not. But you want to hear."

"I want to understand. I know that he broke it off with you because he was frightened; I suppose I can understand that, it being a hanging offense and all."

"I don't know what it was that frightened him." Charles was quiet for a few minutes, then said, "We were in the same company from the beginning. The regiment spent most of the beginning of the century in England; we didn't ship for the Peninsula until 1808. That was the last time I was home until this past January.

"There wasn't much opportunity for advancement while we were still posted in England, but that changed once we arrived in Portugal. We made lieutenant within days of each other, right after Talavera, on the spoils of that battle.

"We'd been friends since we met in Trowbridge, and I always knew that what I felt for him was more than just liking, and suspected he felt the same. But we didn't act on it; we both knew the consequences of being caught. But Spain was different. I don't know if it was because we felt so lost—it was the first time away from England for both of us—or if it was the fact that we were really fighting now, not just performing maneuvers, or what it was. But whatever it was, being in Spain changed things. Made everything feel so much more urgent. And it was—we never knew whether we'd survive a battle. I suppose it was inevitable that we would end up...."

He trailed off. His fingers stroked Tristan's shoulder, gently, endlessly, but when Tristan glanced up, he saw that Charles's eyes were seeing something far different from the tall grasses shifting in the breeze, or the faint puffs of white cloud far overhead. When he resumed, his voice was rough. "Two days of leave, spent together in bed. I'd never known such bliss, and thought Greg felt the same. Then I left to lead a reconnaissance mission for Craufurd's Light Division, to whom we were attached. When I got back it was to find that Greg had transferred to another cavalry regiment. It was one we'd always felt sorry for; their colonel was a brute, not a gentleman like Hawker.

It took me a couple of days to get the opportunity to find Greg, and when I did, he only said that our… connection had been a mistake, and that he no longer wished to be associated with me.

"I won my captaincy in the same action at Ciudad Rodrigo that killed Lieutenant Colonel Talbot—a great loss for the regiment, though Hervey did a fine enough job as his second. Greg wasn't with me that time; his colonel, a bastard named Warren, wasn't so generous with promotions. And if he had been, it wouldn't have been given to Greg; he hated Greg passionately. I sometimes wonder if he didn't hate him so badly because he wanted him, and didn't have the guts to act on it. Whatever the reason, he was a colonel, and Greg a mere lieutenant, and under his command. And I was nothing to Greg any more. I could only stand by and watch while Warren did everything in his power to undermine Greg with his men and other officers, and in general make his life a misery.

"It was perhaps a year later that we were billeted in this beastly little village in Extremadura—if you ever go to Spain, Tris, avoid that region like you'd avoid a leper. It's miserable. I don't know what happened. Greg was sitting outside this horrible little shack mending some harness, I think, and Warren passed by and said something to him. I don't even know what he said. Greg went…. All I could think of was the berserkers from the old German tales my nanny told us. He wasn't quite foaming at the mouth, but I'd never seen him so enraged. He attacked Warren and tried to strangle him with the piece of harness. It took four men to pull him off, and he was fighting them still as they dragged him off to the one building in the pathetic place that would hold a man as strong and determined as Greg. The local madhouse."

He snorted humorlessly. "That tiny village didn't even have a church, but it had a madhouse. That was the reason for the village, apparently; it had been built to serve the managers of the place. Apparently some bureaucrat or other determined that the best place to put crazy people was in the most godforsaken spot in that godforsaken country. As it was, it was where they put Greg until they'd decided when to hang him for mutiny. Mutiny. Greg!"

Tristan put his hand on Charles's chest, feeling the sweat-damp linen and the solid warmth of the skin beneath.

"They didn't have to hang him," Charles said heavily. "He did that himself."

Tristan froze. "He killed himself?"

"He was there three days. I went to Hervey and Warren and tried to intercede for him. Warren was impossible, of course; I was merely a captain and not even of the same company. Hervey was more sympathetic, but there were witnesses and a clear case against him. Even Mac interceded; he was a staff physician at the time. But it didn't matter in the end. Three days after the incident, they went to fetch him, and he was dead, hung by his own belt in the cell."

"My God," Tristan breathed. "Oh, Charlie."

"I should have done more," Charles said. "I keep wracking my brain trying to think of what I could have done, but there's always this feeling in the back of my skull that I should have done more. If I had only had the courage to walk across the street, I would have been talking to Greg when Warren went by, and nothing would have happened. Or if I'd been faster, I could have caught Greg when he went after Warren, and stopped him. But I was slow off the mark."

"And if you had stopped him that time, there would have been another time," Tristan said. "Bullies like Warren don't stop, Charlie. I saw enough of that at school. I was lucky to have met Gibson the first day, but Berkeley was hazed mercilessly for the whole first term. Bullies only back down from a greater show of force. Neither you nor Winstead were in the position to stand up to him."

"Perhaps," Charles said. He was quiet a long moment, then said, "But you see why it distressed me so much when you were contemplating suicide? I had just found you, was just learning to love you, and hoping that perhaps you weren't indifferent to me, and then I find out you're in the same position as poor Greg—at the end of your rope. When I read that letter to Lottie I thought I would go mad myself. I couldn't bear to lose you when I'd just found you, Tris."

"I'm sorry," Tristan said.

"I need to know that I can depend on you. That you'll *be* my partner, my lover, my friend. That you'll be there for me. I swear I will be there for you."

"After the war," Tristan said. "After the war, I will swear anything you like. But for now, Charlie, I just want you to love me."

"I think," Charles said, "I can manage that."

CHAPTER 22

THERE was a pawnshop across the street from the bookstore; Tristan tucked his purchase beneath his arm and wandered over. He thought Charles would be amused by his find: an old copy of Walter Scott's translations of German fairy tales. He was sure Charles was familiar with the originals from his old German nurse, and it would be interesting to see if Scott's translations were true to the tales. But he wanted to get Charles something else; the fifteenth was his birthday, and if their evening was to be tied up with the Duchess of Richmond's ball, afterward they would be able to have their own private celebration.

The shop had the usual in the window: brass vases, the odd watch, enameled snuffboxes, a silver-backed hairbrush, a miniature of a bilious-looking woman…. Tristan pushed open the door and went in. A small, dark-haired man looked up from his assiduous polishing of a set of silver serving utensils and welcomed him in French; Tristan responded politely and went back to looking at the glass cases. The offerings might have seen better days, but the shop was scrupulously clean, the glass polished, bright and clear. He looked over the arrays of pocketknives, quizzing glasses, rings, watch fobs, and silver toothpicks, in among larger items: footstools, boots, reticules, even a sword or two. A case set back behind the counter held open boxes displaying pistols of all types: dueling, horse, even a dainty set that might have been made for a lady's hand. Charles had his own pistols, as did Tris; each had a nice pair of Manton's that Lottie had ordered for them at one time or another, Charles had his horse-pistols as a cavalryman, and Tris had several other pairs for traveling. So his interest in the pistols was academic; he glanced over them and found none that compared to the ones they already owned.

He went back to the case that held the knives; he'd only given them a cursory glance but had the feeling he'd seen something that hadn't quite registered. He had: a slim blade of perhaps nine inches in length, the hilt wrapped in brass wire but lacking a crosspiece. It was tucked in a black leather sheath with a clip on the back, as if it were to be worn....

"In a boot-top," a voice said from the other side of the counter. Tristan glanced up, frowning faintly. It was the shopkeeper, who had put down his polishing rag to attend his customer. "The knife goes in the boot and the clip outside, so that the knife is not seen, *n'est ce pas*? Only the little bit of the hilt, so the person can pull it out in dangerous moments." He cocked his head. "It is very good for the dangerous places a man may go—they may take his sword or his pistol, but no one thinks to look at the boots." He opened the case and withdrew the knife, laying it on the counter.

Tristan picked it up, noting the good quality of the leather. The clip was sturdy, bent metal covered with leather and stitched with suede inside so as not to scar the boot. He curled his fingers around the hilt and withdrew the blade.

"Steel," the shopkeeper said. "Good steel." And it was; Tristan tilted the blade and noted the telltale swirls of damascened metal illuminated in the sunlight from the shop window. The knife was well-balanced, too, the hilt small, but still large enough to feel comfortable in Tristan's grip. Charles's hands were a little bigger than Tristan's, but not by enough to make a difference. "How much?" he asked.

The shopkeeper named a price; they haggled a bit and ended up with Tristan walking away with the knife and both of them feeling pleased. Especially Tris. It was a nice birthday gift for Charles, and it went a little ways toward easing some of the fear he was living with. *Tomorrow*, he thought, and tucked the knife in his pocket.

HE'D meant to wrap them both and give them to Charles before the ball, but Charles sent a hastily scribbled note around that afternoon to say that the Duke had word of a French advance on Mons, and that troops had been dispatched to deal with it. Charles was sent to assess the situation and report back; he would see Tristan later at the ball. Disappointed, Tristan left the book at home but put the knife back in his pocket.

He arrived timely at the ball, danced with several comtesses, Lady Elizabeth Conyngham, Miss Seymour, and Miss Arden, flirted with his hostess and her daughters, and glanced up, heart in his throat, every time a new arrival came through the door. Wellington arrived late and seemed distracted, but flirted and danced as was his habit at such events.

Later in the evening, he ended up at Tristan's side after one set, and Tristan took the opportunity to say lightly, "So you have sent my brother-in-law off on one of his hey-go-mad errands again, have you, sir?"

Wellington laughed, but there was a strain behind his eyes. "I have, Northwood, and trust he will bring back nothing but good news. There was a bit of a to-do out on the Mons road this afternoon, but I expect it is nothing more than a few skirmishers out to see what they may find. We shall soon send them to the right-about."

"I pray you're right," Tristan said, still in that light voice. "It would be a shame should Her Grace's party be interrupted."

"She would never forgive me," Wellington replied with a strained smile, then he looked across the room. "Ah, there's our wandering boy now. If you will excuse me, Northwood—I'll get his report and turn him loose to enjoy what's left of his birthday." He nodded at Tristan, then moved purposefully across the room.

Tristan looked past him to see Charles at the door to the long building the Richmonds had turned into a ballroom for the evening. He was dusty, dirty, and exhausted-looking; as soon as he had seen the Duke coming his way, he stepped back out of the chamber, out of the sight of the rest of the guests. Tristan followed the Duke to the door, but he and Charles had already vanished.

He stood in the antechamber a moment, uncertain whether to pursue them outside, but His Grace reappeared in the door and went back into the ballroom alone. A moment later, Charles stuck his head inside the door. "There you are," he rasped, his voice hoarse. "The Duke said you were here."

"I am. Charlie...."

"Not here, Tris. Come on." He gestured and Tristan obeyed.

He led Tris around the building to a shadowed part of the garden. "I've only a few minutes," he said tiredly. "The attack on Mons was a feint. The French are moving on Quatre Bras; Perponcher and the Prince of Saxe-Weimar have been holding them for hours. I've just come from there. If they take the crossroads, they'll split us off from Blucher."

"Dear God," Tristan whispered. "We'll not be able to stand without the Germans."

"Wellington was expecting a pincers movement, but Napoleon's foxed him. Damn it, Tris!" Charles was shaking with exhaustion and frustration.

"He can't expect you to go back out there," Tristan said in disbelief.

"No—he said for me to go back to my billet, that now was the time for infantry. Him and his damn infantry! He said he won't be going out there himself for hours, so I'll have time for a nap."

"Come home with me. You need more than a nap…."

"Can't." Charles gave him a weary smile. "Have to be close to the Duke; when he goes, he'll want me there with him. I just wanted to let you know I'm sorry for ruining your plans."

"It's your birthday," Tristan said numbly. "You've got gifts waiting at home…."

"I'll get them tomorrow, after this is all over," Charles said. He smoothed a finger over Tristan's cheek. "They'll wait." He leaned forward and rested his head on Tristan's shoulder. Tristan put his arms around him, stroking his back and shoulder muscles gently. Charles's arms came up and wrapped around Tristan tightly, as if he were an anchor in a storm. "Tomorrow," he said hoarsely. "It will all be over tomorrow." Then he released Tris and stepped back. Again, the tired smile. "I'd best be off; I've no time to waste."

"I'll walk with you," Tristan said. "Where's your mount?"

"Out front." Charles had begun to walk toward the street, but paused and looked back at Tris. "It's Paragon; he's as exhausted as I am, but needs more than a few hours of sleep. I'll ride Patch or Betsy tomorrow; it's a battle, not a parade, and both of them are as wily as they are ugly. But I want you to take Paragon with you back to your stable and put him in with Brat. They'll be trying to conscript extra horses, and once the word gets out that the French are on the move, there'll be a rush to get out of the city. I don't want to take the risk of losing him as I will if I leave him in with the other regimental cattle. I don't care as much about the others. But Paragon… he's only seven, Tris. He'll make a good mount for Jamie when he's older. I want Jamie to have him."

"Don't talk like that," Tristan said fiercely. "Don't talk so."

"I'm not worried," Charles said with a grin that more closely approximated his usual one. "Wellington's not steered us wrong yet, and it's not like I'm in a line regiment. I'm just an aide."

"Yes, one he has riding all over God's creation," Tristan said. "And in that blue uniform you're as likely to be shot by our own men as the French. Can't you at least borrow a red jacket?"

Charles laughed and draped an arm over Tristan's shoulder. "What, and be mistaken for one of the lobsterbacks? Not on your life, old man."

"It's more likely to be on yours."

"'Fess up—you're jealous. You'd like to be out there as much as anyone else, riding hell for leather from company to company, dodging skirmishers and cannonades, racing time to get the messages through, to come back to Wellington's 'well done's and another mission. I'm exhausted, Tris, but even after a year of peace, there's something in me that rises to that challenge. I don't want another command position, but being one of the Duke's errand boys...." His grin turned into a rueful, wry expression. "You'd love it as much as I do. I'm as right about that as I was about you and medicine. You're all wrong for society, Tris. It's most of your problems rolled into one."

Tristan found one of the Richmonds' grooms, giving him instructions to take Paragon to the house on the rue de Valois, and to tell his own grooms to guard the horses in the stables carefully, under the circumstances. Then, Paragon seen to, the two men walked off toward Charles's billet. "You don't have to escort me, Tris," Charles said. "I'll be all right."

"I'm not escorting you," Tristan said, "and I know you'll be all right. I just want to spend a few more minutes with you."

Charles nudged him gently with his shoulder, and Tristan nudged back. Then they went on in silence.

At the building that was housing Charles and a few of his fellow officers, Charles drew Tristan again into the shadows alongside the building. Unlike the Richmonds', this made no attempt to appear as a garden or anything else; it was just a narrow alley between two houses, their walls windowless and blind. Behind the house in the mews came the sound of men and the jingle of harness as they prepared to move out. "They've got their orders already," Charles said hoarsely, his voice fading from weariness. "We've got to get reinforcements out to Ligny and Quatre Bras."

"God, Charlie," Tristan groaned. "To be stuck here while you're out there... I don't know how I will bear it 'til you come home."

"You'll be fine. I'll wager it's all over before you rise tomorrow, you slugabed. I'm the one who's missing his birthday—but I'll share yours in September, all right?"

"Of course. I…. Oh, wait. I do have a gift for you; I don't know why I stuck it in my pocket. I must be prescient. Perhaps you'll find it useful." Tristan pulled the little knife out and pressed it into Charles's hand. "It's a boot knife."

"Clever," Charles said, and he pulled it from the sheath, admiring it in the fickle moonlight. "Thanks, Tris."

"Here." Tristan took the knife from him and crouched to slide the sheath into Charles's right boot. He curled his fingers a moment around Charles's strong calf, then slid his hands up, caressing the muscled thigh. Charles reached down and stroked Tristan's hair. "Tristan," he said, his voice thick with tears.

Tris rose, pushing Charles back against the wall of the house, taking advantage of the cloud that slid across the face of the moon to kiss him in sheltering darkness. Charles's mouth welcomed him. Tristan sank his fingers into Charles's hair, finding it stiff with the salt of sweat, but he paid no mind, holding him steady as he ravaged his mouth, ground against Charles's hips with his pelvis, determined to imprint the taste and feel of Charles in his mind and memory.

"Oh, my God!"

Tristan jerked back from Charles and stared blankly down the alley at the silhouette there. The voice was faintly familiar, but the face was invisible.

Not so theirs; there was the sound of breath being sucked in, then, "Northwood? And… oh, my God—*Mountjoy*?"

"Randy." Charles's voice was quiet, sounding frozen.

Captain Randall lunged down the alley toward them. The cloud slid from the moon, and Tristan could now see his face, his expression furious and his eyes on Tristan. "You filthy sodomite!" he spat, giving Tristan a shove. "How *dare* you assault him this way? I knew you were a libertine, but this is outside all bounds of decency!"

"*Randy!*" Charles's voice was louder now and edged with anger. "Stop it. There was no assault!"

"Ballocks!" Randall hissed. "I saw the way he pushed you against the wall and forced his filthy kisses on you. I'll see him *hanged* for that."

Tristan stumbled back, feeling the blood drain from his face. He reached behind him, found the wall of the opposite house, and leaned on it, his legs suddenly weak. "Charlie?" he whispered.

"Randy—it's not like that. Tris didn't assault me."

The captain stiffened and stared at Charles, aghast. "You didn't *welcome* his advances, Monty?"

"No," Tristan said, his skin suddenly cold. He drew on all the aristocratic hauteur that Charles had so often teased him about, and went on, "Major Mountjoy is innocent of everything but exhaustion. I took advantage of that. Major, I apologize, deeply. Perhaps it's best you go on to your quarters."

"Damn you, Tris," Charles said. He rubbed his face wearily. "Randy— it wasn't Tristan's fault. We had—have—a, an involvement...."

"Don't be ridiculous, Major," Tristan said. "It's not necessary to protect me for your sister's sake. Captain Randall is not a fool; he knows that I am what he called me. It is what others will also believe. Besides, it's not necessary to protect me. Captain Randall knows that a single accusation against a nobleman is hardly enough to hang one. Even one as"—he paused and shot his cuffs for effect—"as *notorious* as I am." He glanced at Randall. "However, such an accusation would destroy the career of an officer. I trust Captain Randall respects your abilities far too much to take that risk?"

The captain glared at him, then glanced at Charles. "Monty? Have you nothing to say for yourself?"

Charles rubbed his face again. He opened his mouth to speak, but Tristan overrode him. "Our forces are besieged, and his Grace wishes the major to accompany him when he rides out. He's given the major a short time to rest before then. For the love of God, man, let him rest. Let him attend the Duke. Arrest me, if you like; I've nothing better to do." He held out his wrists.

"Oh, for God's sake," Randall said irritably, "stop acting like Kemble onstage at Covent Garden."

"Kemble? No less than Kean, my dear boy," Tristan said loftily. "Kemble is a technician, Kean an artist."

"Don't know—haven't seen 'im," Randall shot back. "Good God— you're talking *theater*; I'm talking *crime*!"

"Some of the theater I've seen should be classified as crime," Tristan said recklessly. He had no idea where this was coming from; something wild inside, the thing that spoke for him when challenged, when dared, when on the verge of discovery or danger. And at this moment, he was all of them.

"This really means nothing to you?" The captain's voice was heavy with disbelief. "That you can destroy an honorable officer, an honorable *man*...."

"Why not?" Tristan shot back. "I've already disgraced all the honorable women in London; I've had to switch countries and genders to keep up with my libertine ways."

"That's *enough!*" Charles's voice was harsh. "Randy, Tris—stop it!" He caught Randall's sleeve. "Randy, leave him alone. He's not the one who instigated it."

"Monty, I won't believe that of you," the captain said firmly.

"Fine. Don't. But don't believe it of Tris, either." Charles ran his fingers through his rumpled hair. "Look—I was selling out. Will sell out, after all of this. I'm not staying in the army, Randy, you know that, not after this battle. I'm done. All I want is to go home. I am *begging* you, Randy—don't report this. Leave Tris alone. I beg you, Randy—for the friendship we shared. If nothing else—for Keighley."

The captain had opened his mouth to speak, but Charles's last words made him hesitate. Then he shook his head. "It's filthy. It's disgusting, and it's illegal *and* immoral. But damn it, Monty, *you* I don't want to see hanged. Damn it."

"If you bring Tristan up on charges, it's bound to come out," Charles said. "It'll tar everyone, me, Lottie, my nephew.... Please, Randy."

Randall stood a moment, then said, "*Damn* it, Monty." He gave Tristan a vicious glare and said to him, "If I ever set eyes on you again, I'll kill you. I know where the blame belongs, even if he denies it. But for now.... For Mountjoy's sake. Besides, I've no time for this now; I'm called to attend the prince. Go, Monty—I'll see you in a couple of hours. You," he said, turning to Tristan, "can go to hell." He turned on his heel and strode back down the alley.

"Well," Tristan said, "that was interesting. You'd better go, Charles, before he changes his mind."

"Tris—oh, God, Tris, this isn't how I wanted to leave you."

"It's all right, Charlie." Tristan gave him a thin smile and an awkward pat on the shoulder.

Charles stared at him a long moment, then reached out and dragged him into his arms, kissing him fiercely. Tris resisted a moment, then collapsed against him, clutching his coat and weeping helplessly. "God," he sobbed, "I am such a *woman.*"

"If you were," Charles said with a half-laugh, "we wouldn't be in this fix."

"I've lost you your friend," Tristan said, resting his forehead against Charles's shoulder. "I've put you in even more danger than you already are."

"What is this 'I' nonsense?" Charles said harshly. "You've done nothing but what I've asked of you, Tris. And this is nothing. Randy won't say anything. He's honorable."

Tristan snorted. "And you're naïve, Charlie. He won't be able to resist the gossip. Or perhaps one day he'll be drunk as a lord and someone will mention your name, or mine, and he won't even be aware of what he's saying." He turned his face into Charles's neck. "It doesn't matter," he said tiredly. "Go rest, Charles. Come to me tomorrow when it's all over. When you can. We'll deal more with this later. You haven't much time. Go."

"I don't like to leave you like this."

Tristan drew himself up and gave Charles *The Look*. "I beg your pardon?" he said, arching a brow. "You think me *incapable* of coping, perhaps?"

Charles gave a bark of graveyard laughter. "I begin to think there is nothing you can't cope with. You don't lack courage, Tris. I'll go, then. You too. Go home and go to bed."

"I shall be returning to the Richmonds'," Tristan said. "There to prove that I have never left the building, and thus diffuse any gossip. Leave it in my hands, Charles; I'm an old hand at dissembling."

"There's my brilliant Tris," Charles said, kissing him briefly, then he moved off toward the back of the house, to the lights and voices and hubbub.

Tristan watched him go, his heart breaking, then straightened himself up and went back to the Richmonds' in time for supper. There, he dropped careful comments that, if put together, would make it clear that Tristan had never left the ball.

He might as well have been silent. By the time he returned the rumors had begun to spread, not about Tristan Northwood, but about Napoleon Bonaparte. Especially when, one by one, in pairs, or small groups, the officers that had been present excused themselves. The Duke of Wellington made his farewells to his host and hostess to the faint distant sounds of the troops mobilizing, but not before sending the Prince of Orange unceremoniously off to bed, like the unruly child he so often resembled. The dance floor cleared with officers taking leave of their friends and flirts. There was a sotto voce argument between Georgianna Lennox and Lord Hay. The Gay Gordons, who'd done some Scottish dances for the crowd earlier in the evening, had all gone, the forward guard on their way to the crossroads at Quatre Bras. The

Black Brunswickers, with their distinctive black uniforms and death's-head insignia, had also vanished. Some of the women had broken down in tears, but the Duchess of Richmond was still in full sail, sweeping around the room, sorting out confusion and getting things set to rights. Tristan had always admired her for her presence; he admired her for her composure even more now.

He saw Hume, the Duke's physician, and crossed the corner of the room. "Dr. Hume, sir?"

The doctor glanced up curiously. "Sir?"

"Tristan Northwood," Tris began, but Hume nodded, giving him a strained smile.

"Major Mountjoy's brother, of course. How d'ye do, sir? Monty's spoken of you often. Says you're studying surgery under Crosby. Fine surgeon. A bit daft, but they mostly all are."

"Yes, sir, so I'm given to understand."

"I hope you've come to offer your services," Hume said. "We'll need all the steady hands we can get in the next few days."

"I don't know how steady they are," Tris replied, "but yes, I'm offering them. How can I help?"

"Let me introduce you to James Grant—he's principal medical officer, and in charge of coordinating efforts." Hume led the way across the room to a serious-looking man talking to several others in quiet tones. He looked up at Hume's approach, then fixed gimlet eyes on Tristan. Hume made the introductions.

"Studying under Crosby, eh? Man's a crackpot, but a good surgeon." He drilled Tristan for a few minutes on various surgical procedures, then said, "We've got preparations set in a handful of general hospitals, but only one in Brussels. The general hospital here is well staffed with Belgian physicians and surgeons; they're prepared to handle the casualties that can be sent here. The regimental medical officers will handle the bulk of the battlefield injuries whenever possible. You've not got the experience of a surgeon, but we may need you as an assistant here, under the locals. Working in a poor hospital like St. Joseph's, you've probably got more trauma experience than some of the surgeons here, but they won't like you stepping on their toes. Politics," he said in disgust. "Still, we'll have use for you."

"I'll be happy to help where I can." Tristan said. "Can you even estimate how many wounded we'll be dealing with?"

"God only knows. Whatever He sees fit to send us, I suppose. I'll put you in touch with a couple of others who'll be in the city," Grant promised. "Have you lodgings in town?"

"The rue de Valois," Tristan said. "Number 4."

"Good," Grant said absently. "Close. We'll have work for you by noon, I imagine. I'll send someone over in the morning to give you an update, let you know where you'll be needed. Because you will be needed, Mr. Northwood. You will be needed."

CHAPTER 23

TRISTAN woke late on the seventeenth from a troubled sleep, after falling into an exhausted slumber some time before dawn. Reston, bringing his breakfast, filled him in on what he'd missed: the panic engendered by a troop of artillery moving through the streets thought to be in retreat, when they were actually on their way to the battlefield, and the actual retreat of a squad of Belgian cavalry that had set the town into a frenzy. Those events had been closer to dawn; the town had been quiet for the last hour. He dressed quickly, not waiting for Reston to attend him, and went out into the street to see what was happening.

Wounded had been stumbling into the city since afternoon yesterday; Grant had filled the promise made at the Richmonds' the night before and sent a Dr. Maartens to Tristan's door in the morning. The doctor had introduced Tris to some of the other regimental army surgeons, but by late afternoon most of them had gone out to the battlefield near Quatre Bras to their posts. Maartens, who was not, he informed Tristan in a superior manner, an *army surgeon*, but an Important Local Physician, remained in charge. Tristan didn't like him, but he had to admit he seemed to know what he was doing and was competent as well at organizing the rest of the Belgian doctors who'd appeared like manna from heaven. They sorted through the new arrivals as they came in, mostly on foot, weeding out the ones who required immediate care from the ones who could wait and the ones, God help them, who had walked the miles from the battlefield only to die on the cobbles of the Brussels streets.

Today was different. Here was a scene of complete and appalling chaos. Literally staggering at the sight of scores of men lying or sitting on the pavement, burnt and torn and bloody, Tristan stared in stunned disbelief. *Good God*, he thought. Perhaps it was a rout, a total loss, and Napoleon ascendant again… but then, from deeper in the city, the clatter of hooves heralded some other troop headed for the Gate. It was a cavalry regiment, in their bright red jackets and horsehair-topped helmets; heavy dragoons with their muskets and swords shining, fresh troops from Ostend or somewhere else up the line. And they were headed out the Namur road, toward the fighting, not away. If it was a rout, they would have been going the other way, wouldn't they?

The troop slowed as they approached the wounded men, and a ragged cheer went up from the bodies on the ground. As one, the dragoons raised their swords in salute to the wounded, and they cheered again. The Gate swallowed them up, but Tristan heard the pounding of hooves as the troop broke into a canter on the more open road beyond.

It was a moment of grace in a scene of particular gracelessness. Tristan blinked and looked down at the crowds of wounded, then at the people moving among them, men, women, even some children, some in the tidy working-dress of the bourgeois, some in the shabbier garb of the serving class; nuns in their stiff black habits; even some in the silks and muslins of the aristocracy. They carried buckets with dippers of water, rags to wipe sweat or blood from skin, bundles of bandages. A few men were loading men on stretchers and carrying them to carts standing nearby. Dr. Maartens was nowhere in sight.

Tristan went to join the men loading carts. "Where are they going?"

"Some to the hospital," one of the men said, "some to the church; they've set up a sort of hospital there, the nuns have, at any rate. I've heard the priests aren't too happy having 'goddamns' in their church." The man chuckled. "That's what they call the British soldiers, you know. 'Goddamns', because of their foul language. But I don't think the nuns even blink. They're a tough race. Here, give us a hand." He and Tris went to lift the wounded man onto the cart, but he screamed pathetically and a fresh gout of blood soaked Tristan's sleeve. The other man looked at Tristan, his gaze significant; Tristan realized the wounded man didn't have much of a chance unless he could get stitched quickly. "Here," he said, "let me see." He climbed into the cart and eased the man over on his side. He pulled his shirt out of his trousers and tore off a strip, folding it into a pad and placing it over the wound and tying it tightly in place. "It won't help much," he said, "but it might slow the bleeding until he gets more attention." As they turned to help another man onto the cart, Tristan said, "I need my kit." He called over a boy who was giving water to soldiers and sent him off to tell Reston to pack up and deliver the bag he kept his medical kit in.

The other man was looking at him strangely. "Are you a doctor? A surgeon?"

"Not really. I've been studying surgery, but I have some little experience with wounds," Tristan said.

"That's more than most of us have. I'm Derek Chamberlain, by the way. Solicitor to the Seymours. Came in with some papers to sign two days ago. They're still waiting."

"Tristan Northwood." They shook bloody hands.

"Northwood? Isn't that the Wares?"

"It is. My brother-in-law's with Wellington; my wife sent me over to keep an eye on him. Not that I'd be able to find him in this mess if he did get hurt." Tristan swallowed fear and turned to look over the sea of red and blue jackets, most of them muddied to dirt color.

"It'll get worse before it gets better," Chamberlain said ruefully.

"What's the word? I worked with the medical teams yesterday, but it wasn't nearly as bad as this."

"They were slow moving the wounded out after the battles yesterday," Chamberlain said as they moved to help another from a litter. "And word came late that the Germans were badly broken along their line. Most of them just came in overnight."

"And they've been lying here since?" Tristan felt sick. "It wasn't this bad in the small hours when I went home! Why did no one enlist help?"

"They have been, but a good many people left Brussels yesterday. Wellington was fit to be tied, with them clogging up the Ostend road and him trying to keep communications open."

"I spent yesterday trying to get information, but it's scattered. I know that the attack on Mons was only a feint, and that the bulk of the fighting was at Quatre Bras, but not much more than that." The cart, full, rumbled off, and they picked up the litter and carried it through the wounded to where another man waved for it.

"Thanks, Chamberlain," the man said, and Tristan and he lifted the wounded soldier onto the litter. "It's a bad break but the surgeons are all busy. Hullo, Northwood."

"Bellingham? Good God, what are you doing here?"

"Came in with the Conynghams but caught a catarrh and been in bed for a week."

Tristan looked at the twisted wreck of the soldier's arm. "I think I could set this if I had something to splint it," he said.

"Use this," Chamberlain said, handing him what looked like a broken piece of lance. "It's mad what they'll hang onto, even unconscious; there's dreck like this everywhere."

Tristan dug out his pocketknife and cut off the sleeve of the uniform jacket, afraid to put him through the torture of removing it. Then he cut away his shirt sleeve.

"Oh, *Christus*," Chamberlain swore. The bone pressed against the skin of the man's upper arm, purple and grotesquely misshapen.

Tristan worked his fingers around the injury. It looked bad, but he didn't feel a lot of pieces of bone, and the skin wasn't broken. "It's not as bad as it looks," he said to the men, and to the patient, who stared up at him with pain-deadened eyes, uncomprehending. "I think we can save it." With Chamberlain's help, and Bellingham holding the man still, Tristan drew the arm out straight, pulling on the elbow to ease the bone back into place. Then with Chamberlain still holding the arm immobile, Tristan used the man's shirtsleeve and another strip from his own shirt hem to lash the arm to the piece of broken lance. "It didn't break the skin, and that's a blessing," he said absently as he worked. "Minimizes the risk of infection. If it heals clean, he'll use it again."

"Where did you learn that, Northwood?" Bellingham asked curiously. "Setting up as a surgeon?"

"Following my benighted brother-in-law around a hospital," Tristan said. "You learn fast when you're overwhelmed like that. He's studying to be a physician." He tied off the last of the linen. "But I'm good at pitching in like Chamberlain here, so I got some experience." He wasn't about to talk about his aborted career; the pain was still too fresh. He rose from his crouching position and surveyed the scene, not seeing details, but aware of all of it. "Is anyone coordinating things here? We need to move the less seriously injured out of the way and try and get more of them under cover. The sun will be high soon; it's early yet but it will be hot and we don't need them baking any more than they have. Even some canvas. We'll need water. And bandages. And we'll need housing for them; Bellingham, you've got an aristocratic name— use it to get some doors open to us. It's Brussels and it's June, so it's either going to be raining or hot. Chamberlain, let's see if we can't get some of this lot sorted out...."

WHEN he got Tristan's message, Reston sent the boy back with the kit, and a little later, Will to find out what happened. The footman found his master in the midst of blood and chaos, kneeling beside a bare-chested soldier, stitching an ugly gash in the man's side. He was saying cheerfully, "You're a lucky man, Sergeant! It's a clean cut, went straight in and out and never touched a thing. Better than a musket ball stuck in you, that's for certain. Let me finish stitching the front and then we'll flip you over and I'll do the back and you'll be right as rain." But Will saw the worried look he gave the stranger kneeling at the man's shoulder who was holding him down.

"Sir?" Will said hesitantly. He had to repeat it louder over the moans and screams around him for his master to hear him.

"A moment, Will." Tristan finished tying off the thread and placed a pad of lint on the wound. Then he said, "Will, lend a hand here?" and the footman found himself turning the wounded man over while Tristan held the lint clamped to the stitched wound. The injury on the back was worse, but his master set to work immediately, as if it were nothing. "Will, I'm glad you're here," Tristan said, his eyes on his stitchery. "Go home and tell Reston to give you enough funds to buy as much in the way of bandages and brandy as you can find. And to prepare the spare bedrooms and the common rooms on the ground floor for visitors. We'll need pallets of some kind. Have the grooms move the furniture out and into whatever space there is in the stables. There will be a dozen or so coming straightaway; they'll need tea and tending. See that lady over there in the blue bonnet?"

Will glanced up. "Yes, sir," he said numbly.

"That's Mrs. Ethan. Go ask her what else will be needed, and see that she gets it. I won't say cost is no object; there will be gouging, no doubt, but you're a bright lad; you should be able to dicker a more reasonable price. But we need these things, quickly. Go."

"Sir!" Will leapt into action.

Tristan glanced up and saw his footman speak earnestly with the woman in the modest bonnet, then take off at a run back toward the rue de Valois. *A good boy*, he thought absently, then turned back to his work.

"CAREFUL!" Tristan shouted to the men in the first-floor window as they levered the man bound to the stretcher through the opening. They'd built a block and tackle arrangement in the overhanging eaves that allowed them to raise the less-wounded up to the bedrooms on the upper story; it was easier than maneuvering up the narrow stairs and less traumatic on the patients. Several other households who were able to shelter the wounded had experimented with similar arrangements. It was risky, but if the wounded were able to be secured to the stretchers and the stretchers carefully attached to the lift ropes, it was faster and simpler to get them into the rooms upstairs. The more seriously wounded were kept on the ground floor; it was a matter there of only a few steps up, and so the dining room and drawing room furniture was carefully stored in the stables. The floors of the two large main rooms were paved with pallets with injured men on them.

Chamberlain said, "That's the last of the ones for you. There are a few more that the Conynghams will take, and then the rest will have to suffer with tarpaulin cover if it rains."

Tristan looked up at the sky. "It will," he said tiredly. "I just hope it doesn't turn into a flood; the men still in the streets will drown. To survive a battle only to drown in the city would be an embarrassment."

His friend's voice was hoarse as he chuckled. "Well, it's a good sign, rain before a battle. The soldiers call it 'Wellington weather'—apparently he's never lost a battle if it's rained the night before."

"He should win this one at a walk, then," Tris said dryly, "considering it looks like those clouds are going to provide us with rain of Ark-like proportions."

Chamberlain laughed. "Go deal with your patients. I'm off to round up some more tarpaulins for the stragglers. And try and get some rest if you can; you'll have your work cut out for you tomorrow. How are your supplies holding up?"

"Don't worry," Tristan said, "if we need to rip up the contents of the linen closets for bandages, I can afford to replace them."

"Good thing," Chamberlain replied. "I'll have the less-well-off send their bills to you too."

"Do," Tristan invited him. "My father has more money than the king; it will do him good to spend some of it." He saluted Chamberlain, then went indoors to deal with his patients.

IT BEING June, the day had been hot, but a thunderstorm rolled in shortly thereafter. By then, thankfully, they had gotten the majority of the wounded under some kind of shelter, either in the houses the local residents had generously opened up, or under a huge tent in the street near the Gate. After his guests had been settled, Tristan had returned to the Gate to work with new arrivals, but the incoming volume had died to a trickle, and word had come that there had been little or no activity on the front lines most of the day. With the storm, that quiet state would likely continue through the night. Most of the ambulatory injured had already reached the city or died along the way; there would be few more arrivals until long after the resumption of hostilities on the morrow. Tristan took the opportunity to see about acquiring more medical supplies, pleasantly surprised to discover that the Bruxellois apothecaries had all opened their shops and were providing the Belgian and British physicians with all they had in the way of lint for bandages and medicines. Tristan stocked up on feverfew, butterbur, willowbark, and Charles's favorite, skullcap, as well, figuring that once the soldiers made it here, fever would be their greatest enemy.

Caught up in his own concerns and fears, he was startled to discover that for the vast majority of the Bruxellois, life went on quite as if nothing were happening. There were couples on the streets strolling among the shops underneath huge umbrellas; the restaurants were full and brightly lit against the dark afternoon; a theater owner in an oilskin coat was pasting up a bill for that evening's performance; and a waiter in an enormous apron was sweeping the water off the pavement before his café. Tristan walked down the street in a daze, Will behind him carrying his purchases in two enormous sacks. "Are they mad?" he said over his shoulder to Will. "Napoleon not ten miles distant, and they drink and laugh as if it were an ordinary day?"

"Maybe for them 't is," Will said practicably. "Boney's been here before, I heard tell. Mayhap they don't care who's in charge. Some of 'em don't much like the Dutch king, when all's said and done."

Tristan stopped and stared at Will. "You've got a brain," he accused.

Will blinked. "Well… yes, sir. Allus did."

"Huh," Tristan said. "Well, you're probably right. Still. It seems… I don't know. Something."

"Jenny say kwah," Will supplied.

"What?"

"Jenny say kwah," Will repeated. "It's what Jean-Baptiste the groom from next door says when he don't know what to say."

"Oh!" Tristan bit back a laugh. "You mean '*je ne sais quoi*'."

"Yes, sir. That." Will thought a moment. "Though I might describe 'em as rude, myself."

"Rude," Tristan nodded.

"The booj-wah, anyway, most of 'em. The apothecaries seem to be all right, what with givin' us the supplies and all."

"Right," Tristan said, oddly charmed by his footman's sudden erudition.

They arrived back at the house just as another storm front rolled through and opened up. Tristan opened his umbrella again, and they ran under its dubious shelter to the front door, where Tris ushered Will through unceremoniously. The footman carried the heavy sacks back through to the kitchen to sort out, while Tristan went into his bookroom in search of something to drink.

There was a man sitting there; he leapt to his feet as Tris entered. "Reid?" Tris said uncertainly.

"Sir. I've a note for you, sir. From the major."

"Is he all right?"

"Fine as fivepence, sir."

"Oh, good. Have you had tea or anything?"

"No, sir. Just arrived."

"Well, you can go on back to the kitchen when I've read this. Is the major expecting a reply?"

"Don't know, sir. I came to fetch Patch; Betsy's plumb wore out from yesterday. Major asked me to drop that here but Mr. Reston asked me to wait for you. I've got to get back with Patch *pronto*."

"'*Pronto*'?" Tris took the note from Reid and opened it.

"Means 'soonest' in Spanish, sir."

The note was brief, scrawled in pencil. "Am well. Thinking of you. Love, C." Tristan folded it and tucked it into his pocket. "No need for a reply. Just give him my regards. Is he all right?"

"Aye, sir, never a scratch on him. Been back and forth out to Wavre where Blucher retreated to—you'll have heard that the French broke the Prussians at Ligny? Damn near killed old 'Marshal Forwards'. Got pinned under his mount and rode over by his own troops before they found him. Back in the saddle again today and just raging about the Frenchies killing his favorite horse."

"As if Blucher needs another excuse to hate the French," Tristan said dryly. "Well, tell the major to watch his back and that all is well here. Go down to the kitchen and tell the girl to make you up a bottle of tea to take back with you. And some sandwiches."

"Won't turn it down," Reid said. "It's going to be a long, wet, hungry night for us. The major's snug enough for now at headquarters, but the

Duke'll be calling for him soon enough. That's why I'm in such a bleedin' hurry—beggin' your pardon, sir."

"What the hell for?" Tristan joked, then sent him on his way before collapsing into the cushions of his chair. Charles was all right, and safe. This battle couldn't last much more than another day, could it? Then that would be all. Another day, and surely Charles could survive another day—he'd survived so many.

Just one more day.

HE WAS proud of his little household. Parks, the little cook-maid, apparently had a slew of younger siblings at home and when she wasn't brewing up beef tea and possets, was efficiently acquiring supplies from mysterious sources and stockpiling them for tomorrow's injured. She'd even found a couple of young assistants who'd lost positions when their employers had fled Brussels on the eve of battle. Will was a willing pair of hands, strong and dependable, and equally adept at finding food as well as medical gear—Tristan suspected him of breaking into abandoned houses and raiding their larders. The grooms Tris had hired locally pitched in just as willingly, dividing their time between helping in the house and guarding assiduously the horses and furniture residing in the stables. And Reston—poor old Reston—managed them all patiently and kept close watch on their condition. If any of them looked the slightest bit weary, he'd cut them out of the herd like a professional border collie, ushering them down to the kitchen for tea and a rest. Even Tristan wasn't exempt from his eagle eye.

But it was Tristan who, at midnight, sent all of them to bed while he dossed down in the drawing room with his most serious cases. "It will be a long day tomorrow," he said to them, "and if today is any indication, a longer one the day after. I'll need you all rested and ready to take on whatever Boney presents to us. Parks, you make sure you and your girls are barricaded in well and the house is locked up; there will be stragglers and deserters wandering the city. Michaels, I want you and Ferrers to sleep in the stables with the horses for the same reason. Sleep late, all of you; I'll call for you when you're needed. Get as much rest as you can. That goes for you too, Parks; I can make my own tea and toast my own bread if I'm so inclined, and if I need you, I'll wake you. Reston!"

"Sir!"

"That goes double for you. Sleep. Will, you'll bunk in the dining room, if you don't mind, and keep an ear out for any fussing in there. Call me if any of the men need me. I'll be in here." He glanced around at his "troops" and felt a glow of accomplishment, of satisfaction, even through the haze of weariness. "Good men. Good night!"

"Night, sir." "Good night to you, sir!" "Bonne nuit!" He grinned, then turned to lie, fully dressed, on the pallet waiting for him beneath the window.

Chapter 24

It HAD been merely a ditch full of water earlier that day when Charles had jumped Patch across it on his way out to the Prussians at Wavre, but who knew how many troops had fought back and forth across it since then, and the ground was torn up and muddy, the water swirling brown and red from churned-up earth and shed blood. Although the action seemed to have moved away for the time being, there were bodies strewn here and there, the action still too fierce to allow for retrieval of the dead and wounded. Smoke from the artillery and Whinyate's rockets still swirled in patches, making it difficult for Charles to see far enough ahead to mark a safe path through to British lines. At any moment the tide of battle could shift and overrun the stream again, and Charles with it. It wouldn't be the first time, but it would delay Charles, and he needed to get back to the Duke, to let him know that Blucher was on his way with badly needed reinforcements.

There. A little ways north of where he was now, behind the flash of gunfire and sword blades and the smoke of the guns, the colors of one of the line regiments. He couldn't make out which, but it didn't matter. He set Patch at a canter along the stream bank toward the spot; he could cross the stream there behind the front line and given that there was action going on, the chances were as good as any the Duke was somewhere nearby.

He was a bare twenty yards from his chosen crossing point when a shell, off course and spinning wildly, came at them from across the creek. He jerked Patch's head around to avoid it, but it struck his mount just as Patch rose on his back legs, shearing off the front and sending him over backward with the impact. Years of training betrayed Charles; he automatically stayed in the saddle, and Patch came down hard on his left side. He heard the snap of bone as he and the horse crashed into the mud on the stream bank. Blood fountained up over him as he struggled to get his broken left leg out from under the thrashing horse, but Patch's dying convulsions only drove him deeper into the mud and closer to the embankment. His chest seized with pain and panic; if Patch went over the edge, he'd slide into the water, his weight dragging Charles with him to a watery death. He threw his upper body across Patch's withers as far up as he could, to counterbalance the weight; fortunately he'd been leaning forward into Patch's shoulders as the horse had gone backward, and so he was already half out of the small cavalry saddle. The horse threw his head back, screaming horribly in pain; it was as much to protect himself from being brained by the horse as any other reason that Charles grabbed the thick leather headstall at the top of the bridle. The leather bit at his fingers; but he hung on as Patch convulsed. He was dying, but not fast enough.

Charles's sword, buckled to the saddle for a cross-draw, was buried, inaccessible in the mud beneath Patch's left side, alongside Charles's broken leg. He fumbled for the long knife in its sheath on the right side, but the sheath was empty; he recalled in despair leaving it in the throat of a French cuirassier in a melee on his way out to Wavre hours ago. He clung to the bridle, hoping to still the horse's movements, but the bank beneath them was already crumbling, clods of earth breaking off to splash in the water below.

Odd how the world was suddenly so silent, the clash of swords and the roar of the guns sounding faint and distant, the only clear sounds the rush of water and Patch's thin, horrible screams. The ground shifted and Patch seemed to slide, dragging Charles's useless leg further underneath him; Charles braced himself for the fall, but then they were still again, except for Patch's frenzied thrashing.

He was going to die. The thought came quietly, dispassionately, from somewhere in the back of his head. Not for him the miraculous survival that Blucher had experienced, pinned for hours beneath his dead horse, ridden over by troops, and still alive, still healthy, full of gin and spit. Not for him even the dignity of death in battle. No, he was going to be drowned—by *his own horse*. The absurdity of it almost made him grin, wishing he could share it with Tris.

Tris.

A flash of memory in among the throbbing pain from his leg, of Tris kneeling at his feet, looking up at him with that peculiarly Tris expression of lust and love and trust. Kneeling at his feet, sliding *something* into his boot.... The knife. Tris's birthday present to him.

Twisting, he managed to drag his uninjured right leg up over Patch's belly, close enough for him to reach for the little knife set in its sheath. His hands were slick with blood, but the hilt was wrapped with blessed wire, the grip sure even in his slippery fingers. He pulled the knife from the sheath.

Holding it between his forefinger and thumb, he used his other fingers to find the jugular groove in the side of Patch's neck. "Sorry, old boy," he whispered, then he shifted his grip, his fist closing around the wire-wrapped hilt. Bracing himself against the leather headstall, he drove the little blade into Patch's carotid artery.

Blood spurted, a single great gout; Patch jerked once more, then the big head flopped to the side and he lay blessedly still. Charles managed to shift a little more, sliding his good leg back to brace against the muddy ground behind him. He released the headstall and dug his fingers under the cheek strap, pulling himself as far over his mount's shoulder as he could, then started trying again to work his leg out from beneath Patch's belly.

He heard a faint whine, and then something punched him hard in the shoulder, driving him face forward into Patch's shoulder and knocking the breath out of him. He sucked in air, gasping at the shock; pain blossomed in his chest and back, and there was a patch of blood on the one unbloodied spot of coarse hair on his mount's shoulder. *A patch on Patch*, he thought, laughing hilariously in his mind, even as his body gasped for breath.

The cheek strap under his fingers grew slippery; he tightened them automatically, his fingers sliding on the leather. Greg's fingers had slid along the leather on the reins he'd been mending, Charles remembered dreamily, smoothing the wax into the newly stitched repair and along the long strap. The scene was almost as clear now as it had been all those years ago: Greg sitting in the sun, his graceful hands sliding, stroking as he'd once stroked Charles. Charles had stood in the shadow of one of the houses, watching longingly, remembering the touch of those hands on his body; and then Warren had walked by and the world ended. The grief and guilt had haunted Charles ever since.

Now Tris would face the same grief. At least he was spared the guilt. The hand still holding the knife hilt tightened. He couldn't lose the knife. Tris would want it back.

Tristan. He seemed to feel a touch, a kiss, to smell the brandy and licorice and leather smell that was Tris, to hear the soft, drawling voice murmuring wordlessly. And then it all went away.

SOMETIMES there were words, but speaking a language he wasn't familiar with, and that in itself was odd since he was fluent in Spanish, French, and several of the German dialects, and sometimes there were wordless sounds. Sometimes he heard screaming, and wished irritably that it would stop, but then it would stop and for some reason he then wanted to weep. Sometimes he felt as if he were floating, flying effortlessly, and then other times he was jostled quite unbearably, bounced from pillar to post, banged up against solid objects, pawed and manhandled by unseen hands. And always, always, there was pain: sharp, fierce burning pain in his shoulder and head, piercing pain when he drew breath, and the horrible, deep, dull, throbbing misery in his hip and leg. He lashed out once and heard a grunt of pain from someone else, and was glad someone else was suffering, even though he knew that was wrong. He didn't care. He *hurt*, damn it, and someone was going to know about it.

And sometimes he'd close his eyes, and when he opened them he would be somewhere else. Sometimes the sky was blue above him, and sometimes gray, and sometimes there wouldn't be sky, but would be dirty thatch or canvas.

And then, at last, a voice that spoke words he recognized, even if the voice belonged to a stranger. "I've patched him up but there's nothing else to do for him, the poor bastard. The bullet went through his shoulder and I've bandaged that, but the rest—there's nothing for it. The leg needs to come off but if you won't let me, that's that. Send him back to Brussels; I've other patients to see."

He wondered who the poor bastard was. He knew the tone, though; when the army surgeons said there was nothing more to do, then it meant they were leaving it up to God, and that, any good soldier knew, was not good news. "Has he a billet in the city?" Again, the dry, weary voice of the surgeon.

"Aye, sir. And better, relatives to care for him."

That voice he knew. He didn't remember the name, but it didn't matter; he knew the voice, and it comforted him. That voice would take care of him.

Thankfully, he sank back into darkness.

SOMEONE had gone around lighting lanterns hours ago, then just a little while ago had come back around and refilled them. The yellow light flickered over the ranks of bodies laid out like cards in some cosmic game of Patience. Some of the army doctors had ridden in with the carts of wounded when they could, but they were exhausted and barely standing themselves. Dawn wasn't far off, but Tris knew the morning would bring no respite; the carts and wagons continued to roll in, and the dead and wounded continued to pile up. Sometimes he couldn't tell which was which.

"Go home," a voice said behind him.

Tristan turned to see a gray-faced Bellingham leaning on one of his footmen. "Go home," the nobleman said again. "You're swaying on your feet. You'll do none of them any good if you fall on them."

"There's too many of them still need help," Tristan objected.

A man lying at his feet looked up at him with eyes like great black holes. "This is nothing," he said in Belgian-accented French. "The fields are piled with bodies, thick with them. Hell has been unleashed, and we cannot stand against it. Piles of bodies. Mountains of bodies." He coughed, and blood spilled from his mouth. Tristan bent quickly, but the man was already dead.

"Piles of bodies?" Tristan looked up at Bellingham, horrified. "*Mountains?*"

"Go home," Bellingham said again. "Get some rest. You'll do more good tomorrow than you will tonight. And you've wounded there, as well; they need you too. Go."

Tristan rose from his crouch and staggered a little; the footman reached out and steadied him. Tris nodded his thanks. "You're right," he said, choking back tears of exhaustion and horror. "I'll do no one good this way. But I shan't sleep. I don't think I'll ever sleep again."

Bellingham nodded. "I feel the same way. Good night, then. Rest, at least."

"I'll try. Good night."

HE STUMBLED once or twice on the short walk home, the second time landing hard on his hands and knees and staying a moment, too exhausted to rise. Finally he managed to get to his feet and stumbled to his own door. Will, bless him, opened the door and caught him as he fell in; between the two of them they managed to get him to the pallet in the drawing room. "You should sleep in your own bed, sir," Will said worriedly, but Tristan waved him away.

"I've just got to lie down for a bit," he said. "I couldn't manage the stairs."

"Yes, sir," Will said doubtfully.

"Like old times, ain't it, Will? You helping me to bed because I can't walk any longer?"

"No, sir. This is different."

Tristan considered, lowering himself gingerly to the pallet. "I suppose so," he said. "Is the house locked up?"

"Yes, sir. You were the last to come in. The women are locked up in their room, and Mr. Reston is in bed. He was fretting, sir, but he's asleep now."

"Fretting about me," Tristan said. He lay his head on the pillow and looked up at Will. "You're tired, Will. Go to bed."

"Yes, sir. Gratefully."

"All our guests tended and quiet?"

"Yes, sir. Fed and washed and sleeping."

"Good. Rest up. There will be plenty of work for us tomorrow." He was almost asleep now, the rough pallet as comfortable as the deepest of feather ticks. "Plenty of work. Piles of work. Mountains...."

HE DREAMED, nightmares of wandering through mountains of bodies, piled sky high, looking for Charles. He'd catch a glimpse of what he thought was him, and climb up the piles, stepping on arms and legs and faces bloody and waxen in death, and hear the moans and cries of the wounded, who all seemed to be buried inside the hills of bodies. But when he'd climb to where he thought he'd seen Charles, it would be a stranger with dead eyes, and he would know Charles was lost, lost forever in the mountains of corpses and soon-to-be corpses. Weeping, he would climb back down and wander more, lost himself among the dead.

When morning finally came he was not much more rested than he was before, but the watery sunlight was a relief from his dreams. He managed to get himself up to his room, the sole spot in the house aside from the maid's room not occupied by wounded soldiers, since even the room Will and Reston shared had a few extra pallets in it, and washed and changed his clothes. At least he felt a little more refreshed after that, and went down the stairs without having to hold onto the railing.

Reston was waiting for him at the foot of the stairs and led him into the kitchen, where toast and eggs and ham were set on the table. He fell on them as if he were starving. In between shoveling eggs into his mouth, he asked, "What's the word from the field?"

"Will's gone to find out," Reston said. "I sent him to the Richmonds'; we thought that their servants would have the most recent reports. Your patients are all stable; we've fed the ones that could eat and given them all water. Their dressings still need to be changed."

"I'll do that while we wait for Will," Tristan said, "then I've got to go out and find Chamberlain. He was still working when I left last night."

"Mr. Chamberlain came 'round about an hour ago. He said for you to stay home, that Mr. Maartens had told him that most of the wounded would be tended on the field, the fighting having stopped about midnight. The local doctors would be dealing with those that came in overnight, and they would call on you if they had need. Mr. Chamberlain also said he was going to go home and 'Get around a beefsteak, then sleep for five hours, battle be damned.'" He coughed delicately. "That was a quote, sir."

"Do we know the results yet?" Ham. Had Tristan ever appreciated the taste of ham before? It was amazing, sweet and salty and tender. "No. That's right, you sent Will to the Richmonds'. God, I'm tired."

"Perhaps you should take Mr. Chamberlain's course of action, sir?"

"Perhaps," Tristan said, folding a piece of toast around a pile of eggs and stuffing the whole thing in his mouth. Reston only smiled and poured him more coffee.

HE WAS just finishing up when the kitchen door burst open and Will flew in. "We've *won!*" he shouted, then he noticed Tristan sitting there and reined himself in. "Good morning, sir!" he chirped. "Boney's beat and the Prussians are chasing him back to Paris!"

"Hurrah!" Tristan said, grinning at the footman. "Tell us more."

"I don't have much more than that, sir, just that the French made one last big push late last night, and thought they had us, but the Duke had kept some troops in reserve and they stood against them just when the French had thought they'd won through. Broke them entirely and crushed them between our forces and the Germans, just about ten o'clock. The Duke sent Blucher after them." The jubilant grin faded from Will's face. "I guess our troops were pretty badly shattered for the Duke to give the Germans th' honor of pursuit. They say there are too many wounded to even take them off the field. Nowhere to put them."

"Piles of wounded," Tristan murmured. "Mountains...."

"Sir?"

"Never mind, Will. Go on."

"Not much else to say, sir, only that the Duchess of Richmond told her majordomo to tell me to tell you that if you'd like to stop by today, she'll be happy to give you what news she has. She said she'll be receiving after lunch."

"Thank you, Will." Tristan pushed away from the table and rose. "Well. Excellent work, Will. Reston, see that the staff gets something in honor of the good news, and some rest. I'm going to take Mr. Chamberlain's advice and sleep a little longer; if he comes by, wake me." He nodded at Reston, Parks the cook-maid, and Will, then went back upstairs. Lying on the bed in his clothes, he stared up at the drapery of the bed curtains. The battle was over, won—at ten o'clock, Will had said. It was five now.

Seven hours. And no word from Charles.

It would have been a busy seven hours, he was sure. The Duke was a demanding master, and Charles's job wouldn't have been done just because the battle was. He was probably riding hither and yon, coordinating follow-up efforts for His Grace. Someone had said last night that a number of the Duke's staff had been killed or wounded; that would have put more responsibilities on Charles's shoulders. It would probably be three or four hours before Charles would have the opportunity to send word to Tristan. Maybe more. He should sleep, and when he woke, Charles would have sent word, or better yet, arrived. He would wake Tristan the best of all possible ways, with gentle hands and kisses, climbing into bed with him and holding him safe. Safe. The two of them, together, safe.

The thought gave him hope, and he drifted off into a more restful sleep this time.

BUT Charles did not come. Early in the afternoon, Tristan had Brat saddled and rode out down the Waterloo road to seek his own answers, rather than getting them thirdhand from the Richmonds. The road was crowded with soldiers heading back to barracks, wounded limping along with the help of their compatriots, baggage wains, carts of wounded, even carriages that had been co-opted or volunteered to carry the injured. Brat picked his way along the muddy verge, shying at every opportunity, too fresh from being kept cooped up for several days. Tristan knew how he felt.

At every juncture, he heard the same information about the battle, and nothing about Charles. The farther he got from the suburbs, the worse the traffic got, so he turned back toward the city. When the way was clear, he gave the gelding his head, and if his vision grew blurry, he blamed it on the wind whipped up by Brat's passing. He needed the exercise every bit as much as Brat; tired as he was, he needed this, the speed, the exhilaration, the freedom. He always found that the faster he went, the less he thought.

He didn't want to think at all right now. If he could have flown, he would have, at a thousand miles an hour, faster and faster until he was nothing but a blur, a streak across the sky, a nothingness. Free, empty, mindless and careless.

THERE was a strange man standing in front of the house when Tristan rode up. The groom came from the side garden at the sound of Brat's hooves, and Tris dismounted, giving the reins to Michaels and turning to the soldier. He wore sergeant's stripes on the shoulders of his muddy red uniform. "May I be of assistance?" he asked politely, then saw the rectangle of pasteboard in the man's fingers. It was soaked with blood, but the embossed black letters were clear against the brownish-red stain. *Tristan Northwood.*

"I'm looking for Mr. Northwood," the soldier said.

"I'm Northwood."

"You'd be a relative of Major Charles Mountjoy?"

There was a roaring sound in Tristan's ears. He clenched his fists against the blackness that threatened to overcome him. "He's my brother-in-law." His voice sounded very far away.

"My name's Keighley. I'm with the 52nd. I found this in the major's pocket so I knew where to come. He's hurt, badly. He's laid up at a farm not far from here, about ten miles out toward Wavre. If you know a doctor, you might want to bring him."

"*Michaels!*" Tristan shouted, "bring my horse!" He demanded, "Where is your mount?"

"Not a cavalryman, sir. I walked...."

Michaels reappeared, Brat dancing alongside him. "Sir?"

"Major Mountjoy is injured and I'm going to him. I need you to fill the carriage with blankets, pillows, whatever you have, and drive it toward Wavre. We'll meet you on the road. You, sir, will come with me." Tristan threw himself into the saddle, and reached down a hand. Keighley stepped on his foot and scrambled behind Tris.

Just as he did, Derek Chamberlain came around the corner on foot. "Hi, Northwood!" he called. "Where are you off to?"

"The sergeant here has brought word of Charles. He's injured, somewhere out on the Wavre road."

"You'll need transport. Can I help?"

"Michaels will follow with the carriage. But we probably will need help. Care to ride along with him? It's only about ten miles; shouldn't take more than an hour, unless the traffic out that way is as bad as it is westward."

"Certainly. But you'll need your medical kit. Particularly if the carriage is delayed."

"Damn it! You're right."

"Hold on a moment," Chamberlain said, and he ran into the house. He came back a moment later and tossed the bag up to Keighley. "Hang on tight to that, man. Tris, I'll see you in an hour or so, hopefully."

"Bless you," Tris said, then, grimly to Keighley, "hang on," and he kicked Brat, who took off like one of what Charles called "Whinyate's rockets."

He didn't let himself think of Charles. He didn't dare imagine what condition he was in, how badly hurt. He focused on keeping Brat moving, never more glad for the gelding's energy and temper. They flew down the road, keeping to the center and out of the ruts as much as possible, although sometimes they had to resort to leaping to the verge to pass some vehicle struggling along in the mud. Thankfully, few; there wasn't the traffic he'd encountered on the way to the battlefield.

Keighley hung on tightly, a steady, silent, balancing weight at Tristan's back, one arm clamped around Tristan's waist and the other around the bag with his kit. He'd apparently had some experience with riding pillion *ventre-a-terre* and neither shifted nor spoke during the whole ride. When he finally spoke, it was to shout, "There! There, sir!"

Tristan pointed at the crossroads. "Which way?"

"Left, sir. It's just over the rise."

Tristan obeyed, and a few minutes later was dragging Brat to a halt in a small farmyard. A woman was dumping a bucket of dirty water on the grass at the side of the house; she turned and raised a hand to her brow to see who had arrived. "*Qui est-ce?*" she called in Flemish-accented French.

"I'm looking for a wounded British soldier," Tristan replied, throwing his leg over Brat's withers and sliding down to the ground

She laughed shortly. "You have your choice, *m'sieur*. We have several." Then she saw Keighley scramble down from the horse. "Sergeant! You are back."

"Aye, Missus Pauwels."

"*Venez*. Come in, then." She set the bucket on the wooden bench by the side of the door and went inside. Tristan took the bag from Keighley and followed her in.

There were four or five soldiers lying on pallets in the small main room of the cottage, but Tristan only had eyes for one. Charles lay against the wall, asleep or unconscious—Tristan prayed it was only one of those—in his shirtsleeves. His shirt bore patches as scarlet as the coats some of the others wore, and his hair was sticky and dark with blood. An effort had been made to wash his face, but there were brownish stains on his neck and around his ears. No wonder Tristan's visiting card had been soaked. Surely that couldn't all be his? No one could live having lost *that* much blood. "Good God," he prayed as he dropped to his knees beside him.

"It ain't all his," Keighley said. "I found him pinned underneath that big ugly piebald of his. Shell'd taken off his forelegs and the major had put him down with a knife. Blood everywhere."

Tristan barely heard him. He pressed his fingers to Charles's red-stained throat and felt the pulse: rapid, erratic, but strong enough. There was a thick bandage in the hollow beneath his right collarbone. Without being asked, Keighley said, "I got him behind the lines to a surgeon but all he could do was stitch up the bullet hole. Went through him, so that was good; no ball to dig out. But he couldn't do nothin' for the leg. Had him and the others on a cart to get them into town, but it busted an axle a half a mile from here. The farmer and his boys carried all of 'em here."

"My husband has gone to Wavre for a wagon," the farm wife said, coming back into the house with a full bucket of water.

"Where's the captain?" Keighley asked her.

"In the henhouse," she said. "Killing chickens for soup. He has promised to pay."

"'Captain'?" Tris echoed as he stripped the thin blanket from Charles. The left leg of Charles's trousers had been sliced open to the knee. "Oh, *Christus*," he said, echoing Derek's favorite curse, and carefully unwrapped the bloody bandage from around the purple, swollen calf. "Oh, God."

"Looks worse than it did before," Keighley observed.

The fracture was compound, the end of the shattered bone visible, poking out against the bloody wrapping. The delay in treatment had meant that the leg had swelled with inflammation. "The surgeon said he couldn't do anything for it but amputate, but the Captain and I wouldn't let him. Wouldn't even try to set it."

"Thickskulled bloody bastard," Tristan swore viciously. "Ham-handed fathead. Bacon-brained puddingheart. Bloody hell. Keighley, I need your help. Can you find that captain of yours? We'll need him too." *This wasn't Charles*, he said to himself, *this is a patient. That's all, just a patient. You can do this. This is a patient.* He repeated it to himself over and over again, until his hands steadied.

And then the door opened and Francis Randall came in. He stopped and stared at Tristan as if at a revenant, then swore, "Bloody hell! *You* here? Keighley, you idiot, I sent you for a *doctor*."

"I *am* a doctor," Tristan snapped. He was. The hell with Crosby and his dismissal; he knew he could do this. A sort of cold peace settled over him, a distance, a disconnection. "And I need your bloody goddamned help, so get your supercilious arse over here and *help me*."

Startled, Randall obeyed. Tristan had him kneel at Charles's head, holding his shoulder steady, then bade Keighley kneel beside Charles's lower leg, and showed him how he needed him to pull: slow, steady, no quick jerks but slowly, gradually increasing the pressure so that Tristan could guide the bone back into place and wrap the leg tightly with the clean bandages from his kit.

To his surprise, when he looked up the farm wife was standing there, holding two pine planks out to him. "Last year, my second-born broke his leg," she said. "You will need these."

"I do," he said, and he took the planks, binding them to Charles's leg to keep the bone in place and immobilize the knee. Then he carefully removed the pad of lint from the wound in his shoulder. The stitches were sloppy and apparently done in great haste, but the great tear in the skin was ragged enough to account for it, and there was no sign of infection yet. He replaced the dressing with a clean one. "That was the exit wound," he said. "Did the surgeon do anything about the entrance? I'd like to avoid shifting him if I could."

"Said the ball was small enough there wasn't a lot of damage. Bandaged it, told us to watch for more bleeding." Randall had sat back on his heels. "Where the hell did a dandy like you learn battlefield surgery?"

"Corinthian," Tristan corrected.

"What?"

"I'm a Corinthian, not a Dandy. I don't wear my shirt points impossibly high, I wear a reasonable number of watch fobs, and I have never needed sawdust to pad either my shoulders or my calves. And in answer to your question, at St. Joseph's Hospital in Spitalfields, thanks to this man here." He reached up and lay a hand on Charles's brow. He was warm, but not quite feverish. Yet. And he was still unconscious. "Now, what about the rest of these fellows? Yours, I presume?"

"Most of them. Three are from my company, the other from the 22nd. They didn't report in after the skirmish, and Keighley and I went looking for them." He glanced down at Charles. "Keighley spotted that ugly piebald of Monty's; said it couldn't be anyone else, that nobody else *had* a horse that ugly. Took both of us to move that bloody bastard; thank God for mud slippery enough to help us out. If it had been dry we'd have needed a block and tackle. But I imagine we did more damage to Monty, shifting the horse."

"Needs must when the devil drives," Tristan said. "Any of them in need of immediate medical care?"

"Pattinson's got a wound won't stop bleeding," Keighley said. "Most of the rest of them are managing."

"Let's take a look at Pattinson, then." Tristan rose from beside Charles and went to the pallet Keighley indicated. The surgeon's sloppy needlework was evident here too. "We need to apprentice that lad to my wife," Tristan said to Pattinson in a cheerful voice. "She'd soon have him taking tidier stitches, I tell you." He took his needle in hand and set to work. A few minutes later, he redressed the wound on Pattinson's leg and turned to the next pallet.

When he'd examined and made repairs to the rest of the wounded, he stood up, stretching. "I need some air," he announced, and went outside.

Sitting on the bench, he quietly went to pieces, drawing his knees up and resting his heels on the bench and burying his face in his arms. He tried to keep his sobs quiet, so the men inside wouldn't hear, but they wracked his body until he ached from it.

Finally, he came back to himself enough to realize that there was someone sitting beside him. He looked up into Derek Chamberlain's worried face. "Tris," he began, but Tristan shook his head.

"He's alive. Has a shattered shinbone that wasn't set. I set it, but I don't know if it will heal properly. He has a bullet wound in his shoulder. He's unconscious, but he's not showing signs of shock; how that is I'll never know. He should be in shock. I know I would be. It's just—damn it, Derek. Damn it!" and he started to weep again. "I was never a, *hic*, watering pot before I met Charles," he sobbed. "It's all his fault."

"You never cared before you met Charles," Derek said quietly. "You never loved before you met Charles."

Tristan jerked his head up and stared at Derek, who gave him a tired smile. "I know, Tris."

After a moment, Tris said, "How did you find this place? I meant to send Keighley back down to the road...."

"The lad waiting at the crossroads said Keighley had sent him. At least, I assume that's who he meant by '*le petit sergent*'."

Tristan snorted a laugh. "I'm sure Keighley wouldn't appreciate being called '*petit*'. I wouldn't repeat that."

"I shan't. He may be on the short side, but he has a fierce look about him. I had a sergeant like him in India. Utterly fearless." Derek trailed off and looked over Tristan's head.

Tris followed his gaze. Captain Randall stood in the doorway, watching them. Chamberlain rose and held out his hand. "Derek Chamberlain," he said. "Solicitor."

"Francis Randall, captain of the 52nd," Randall said, shaking his hand. "Friend of Northwood?"

"Yes. Came to see if I could help."

"Mr. Chamberlain has been working with me assisting the wounded in Brussels," Tristan said distantly, his voice cool.

"Has he." The captain's voice was equally cool.

Chamberlain said, "I have the distinct impression a conversation is imminent, and one that does not involve me. So if you will excuse me...." He sketched a bow to them both and went off toward the carriage, now drawn up blocking the lane.

"Am I needed inside?" Tristan asked coldly.

Randall regarded him expressionlessly. After a moment, he said, "I cannot... *approve* of the feelings you have for Major Mountjoy, but I also cannot deny that they seem real enough. Although I have counted him a friend for many years now, I cannot judge what he feels for you—I only hope for the sake of his honor, his career, and his immortal soul that he does not reciprocate. However, he does seem to care for you." He hesitated, then went on, "That man—Chamberlain—what is he to you?"

"A friend. Nothing more." Tristan's eyes narrowed. "Why?"

"It's only…." Randall frowned. "I am not sure this makes sense. And I am not sure of how I can explain it. I only feel this: if you hurt Charles in any way, I will *kill* you. Do you understand me?"

"Of course I do," Tristan said. He cocked his head. "Do you think that I am betraying Charles by having Derek as a friend?"

"'Derek,' is it?" Randall's voice was dry.

"He is a friend. He is not a rival to Charles."

"I wish he was. That way you would not be tempted to drag Charles down with you," Randall said savagely.

"I will drag Charles nowhere. Neither would I ever betray him." Tristan was suddenly very tired, and put his head down on his knees. "Are you quite finished, captain?"

"I suppose there is nothing more to be said," Randall said. Again, the hesitation. "Under the circumstances, I feel that I should report what I saw in the alley that evening to no one. For now, at any rate. I suppose that is between you and Charles."

"Thank you," Tristan said to the ground. He heard Randall's footsteps and looked up to see him walking toward the carriage where Chamberlain was standing talking to Michaels. Then Tristan got up and went in to sit on the floor beside Charles.

CHAPTER 25

HE WAS moving again, but this time the discomfort was muffled through thick layers of softness. He dreamed he opened his eyes and saw Tristan beside him, his face set in high relief by the glow of carriage lanterns, but that wasn't possible, was it? Tristan was home in Leicestershire, at that whimsically named hunting box, what was it? Lilac Cottage, yes, with Charlotte and the children; not here in this place of smoke and fire and fog. Smoke in his lungs and fire in his body and fog in his brain. But thinking of Tristan, thinking of him here, beside him, comforted Charles, and he drifted back into darkness willingly.

WHEN next he opened his eyes, it was to stillness, and pain. And light. He blinked in the bright sunlight through open windows.

"He wakes," Tristan's voice said. He sounded hoarse and tired. He glanced over to see his lover sitting in a chair by the bed he currently lay in— Tristan's bed. Why wasn't Tristan beside him? And then he moved slightly, and the pain slammed into him, and he realized why. "I was wounded?" His own voice sounded strange too; raspy and dry.

"Just a little. You don't remember?"

"No. Wait. Something about drowning."

Tristan blinked slowly, the long dark lashes sweeping down over the beautiful silver eyes and back again. Charles watched, fascinated. "Drowning?" Tristan echoed in confusion. "You weren't drowning. Your horse fell on you."

"Damn clumsy of him."

"Had something to do with not having any legs left," Tristan said in the same mocking tone as Charles had spoken in.

"Ah. That would do it." He flexed the fingers of his right hand, wondering at the dull ache there. They didn't seem to be injured; he cast a quick glance at his side to see the hand still there, so it wasn't the ghost pain he heard sometimes came with amputated limbs. "My hand hurts," he said curiously.

"That would probably be because of the death grip you had on that little boot knife I gave you," Tristan said. "You wouldn't let go of it until we got back here. Then you opened your eyes, said my name, and dropped the knife."

"I don't remember that."

"You probably will, eventually."

"Yes, probably." He tried to raise his head but it made him dizzy; he laid it back down again. "How long?"

"Four days."

"The battle?"

"Over. We won. The Germans even now are pursuing Napoleon back toward Paris. Reports are that his attempts to stir up resistance are failing; people are trading the cockade for the fleur-de-lis again."

"Mm." It was difficult to care.

"Your Duke has been by twice to see you, and Mr. Keighley and Randall. Are you thirsty?"

Charles considered. "As the devil," he decided.

Tristan lifted him gently, but he still nearly screamed at the pain in his shoulder, panting breathlessly. Tris waited until he'd recovered a bit before pressing the rim of a mug against his lips; Charles opened his mouth obediently and swallowed. "Gah," he said, "what was that?"

Tristan laughed, the sound open and delighted. "Your beloved skullcap tea!" he chortled. "See! It *does* taste dreadful!"

"You prepared it that way on purpose," Charles accused.

Tristan snorted in amusement.

"So what is the damage? My shoulder, I know. But everything hurts right now, and so I can't quite do an inventory."

"Your leg," Tristan said. "Broken when Patch came down on you."

"Patch? Not Paragon?"

"No, Paragon's in my stables, eating his head off. As is Betsy. But poor Patch is dead. And he broke your shinbone in the process."

"Badly?"

"Quite bad enough. Fortunately it seems as though you avoided infection, despite the mud that got ground into it."

"Lucky."

"It is. We cleaned you up, and I think it was a draw between mud and blood for which substance you wore more of." Tristan let Charles drink a bit more of the tea—it was really horrible, Charles thought—then eased him back down on the bed. "Your idea of washing the wound in whiskey seemed to help; neither your leg nor your shoulder took infection."

"Mm," Charles said again, not really caring. His lids were growing heavy and he missed the warmth of Tristan's arm around his shoulders. "Tris?" he essayed.

"Yes, love?"

The word made him smile, and the kiss on his forehead too. "Tired," he murmured.

"Sleep, love." Then, softly, "I'll be here when you wake."

TRISTAN tucked the sheets closer around Charles's shoulder and went to the foot of the bed, adjusting the ropes of the makeshift traction device slung over the canopy. Maartens had recommended the use of Desault's splint in the treatment of Charles's shattered leg, but Tristan remembered that Crosby had thought that full immobilization of the leg in similar cases had led to increased muscular degeneration, and suggested light traction in combination with periodic exercise of the knee to keep those muscles active. Crosby's suggestion made more sense to Tristan, and he knew that if Charles had ever a hope of retaining his ability to ride, he needed to keep the leg mobile as it healed. But he had no idea of the extent of the nerve damage, and had swallowed his pride and written to Crosby asking for his advice. He sighed, and arranged the bedcurtains so that Charles's face was shaded, but still getting fresh air—another Crosby quirk. Fresh air and common sense. Tris could manage the former, and only hoped he possessed the latter.

Then he went downstairs to check on his other patients. Most of them had been sent back to their billets or to their regiments for care, but there were two who still suffered from the fever and it was decided that it was unwise to move them. Three of Randall's lambs had joined them—two of his own and the private from the 22nd—but their injuries were far less serious, and Tris fully expected them to be on their feet again by the end of the week.

There were voices in the drawing room, now back to its original purpose, with the dining room now the only hospital ward. Tristan rubbed his forehead. Was he expecting anyone? Reston didn't seem to be in sight, so he pushed the half-open door all the way and walked in.

There were three people in the room, two of them strangers. The Duke of Wellington he knew well; he'd become a regular visitor in the last few days, checking up on his injured soldiers. But the others, a slightly built, dark-complected man and a dainty, fair-haired woman, were unknown, though there was something vaguely familiar about the woman.

"Ah, Northwood, there you are," the Duke said, and turned to the others. "Madame Contessa, Conte, may I present to you Mr. Tristan Northwood?"

The woman shook her fair ringlets and came toward him, both hands outstretched. "My dear Tristan—I must call you Tristan, for I feel as if I know you! And you must call me Liesl. I am so happy to meet you at last!" Her voice was sweet and light, with just the faintest hint of a Germanic accent.

So this was Lottie's friend Liesl. Tristan took her hands and bowed over them. "Certainly, Madame," he said.

"'Liesl'," she corrected, and she released his hands to reach up and cup his cheeks, drawing him down so that she could kiss them each resoundingly. "Officially I am la contessa di Montolivo, but amongst us we are merely Liesl and Antonio. Goodness! Charlotte said you were tall, but you must be nearly six foot! Almost as tall as *mein Junge*. How is he? I have been so worried."

"He is recovering, slowly." Tristan turned to shake the count's hand. He was a pleasant-looking man with a broad grin on his face. "Sir."

"As my wife says, you must call me Antonio," the count said, "for we are family now."

"From Lottie's letters, I understood you were fixed in Sicily with King Ferdinand."

The count waved a dismissive hand. "The king is in Naples again; Signor Murat is gone away for nearly a month now. Now is the time for the politics and I do not like politics. So when my Liesl says she must go to Belgium to Charles, I say, 'Why not?' and thus we are here."

"I had a *feeling*," Liesl said.

The door opened and Reston entered, followed by Will with a tray of tea things. Liesl took over their disposition, with her husband at her elbow to do the heavy lifting. They were obviously a fond couple.

Wellington took the opportunity to ask in a low voice how Charles did. Tristan grimaced and said, "He woke briefly and took some tea, but at least this time he was aware of being in pain. The last few times he woke he was disoriented. I suppose this is progress, but for his sake I'd wish him in less pain."

"Understandably," Wellington said. "I'd hoped to have a moment to speak to him before I left, but the army is setting off after Napoleon and I must be off as well. I expect to have the former Emperor in hand in a week or so, and then we'll see about doing something for Mountjoy. I imagine you'll be here for a fortnight or so at least."

"At the least," Tristan said. "I've written to my mentor Dr. Crosby for his advice, and am waiting to hear. The wound seems stable, at least, and he's avoided the worst of the fever, so I have hopes that Charles will recover completely. My main concern—aside from his continuing lack of fever—is that the leg will heal enough for him to return to riding. It's a bad break for something like that."

Wellington nodded. "Well, if anyone will manage it, it's Mountjoy. Appropriately named—he's a centaur."

"Come," Liesl said, "have tea. Then Tristan will convey me up to see Charles."

"I need to check on my other patients first," Tristan said.

"Tea first," Liesl said firmly.

TEA drunk, Wellington dispatched, and patients examined, Tristan led his guests up the narrow staircase to his bedroom. Montolivo was fascinated by Tristan's description of the block and tackle machinery used to move Charles and the other wounded from the ground to the first floor through the windows, to avoid having to shift them through the tight turns of the staircase. "Ingenious!" the count said admiringly.

Charles was still asleep when they came in the room, Tristan first to make sure he was decently covered, as he wore only a loose nightshirt. "Poor *Liebchen*," Liesl crooned softly as she sank into the chair Tristan placed beside the bed and took Charles's hand. "But so well attended. You have my gratitude, Tristan."

"He is not only my brother-in-law," Tristan said stiffly, "he is also my very dear friend. Although were he not, I could do no less. He is by far the worst injured of those yet installed here; I must needs pay more attention to him."

She waved one hand dismissively. "Of course you would, but the others matter not to me, and he does."

Charles opened his eyes, stared at the canopy above him a moment, then turned his head, frowning. "Mama?" he asked in puzzlement.

"Oh, he knows me! Yes, my love, my *Liebling*, your mama is here for you."

Mama? Tristan blinked. "You're his *mother*?" he said in confusion. "I thought Lady Chilson was dead!"

"Oh, no. Of course, how should you know? You would have been a little boy at the time." Liesl was serene in her dismissal of his shock. "I shall explain all to you later. It is very bad of Charlotte to not tell you, but that is Charlotte all over. Charles, my love, how are you feeling?"

"Thirsty," Charles said, his voice rasping. Tristan immediately fetched a glass of heavily watered wine and brought it to him, raising him carefully with an arm under his shoulders. Charles drank, then smiled his thanks to Tris. "And confused. What are you doing here, Mama?"

"I have come to nurse you," she said, surprised. "Of course. I had the feeling something was wrong and when I heard of the battle here I knew that was it. So Antonio and I came from Naples *macht schnell*, or maybe *tout de suite*, since we are in Brussels, and here we are." She shrugged. "Naples was boring and noisy and dirty, anyway, so it is no great loss. And my beloved Tristan is busy with other sick men and so I will help him. And Antonio."

"'Other sick men'?" Charles echoed, frowning at Tristan.

He shrugged. "A few injured left in my care. I helped out with the wounded as they were brought into the city."

"Did you set my leg?"

"Yes. Are you in pain?" Tris asked anxiously.

"A bit, but that's to be expected. I think you said Patch fell on me?" He raised a hand and rubbed his eyes tiredly. "And my shoulder hurts. Was I shot?"

"Yes, but the bullet went through…. Oh, my dear lady, I do apologize," Tristan said penitently. "I should not speak of such things in a lady's presence."

The count laughed heartily. Liesl sniffed. "Nonsense," she said, "I know all about bullets, and it is quite good that the bullet went through him, otherwise there would be digging in the flesh with knives, and concern about infections, and things like that. I have done that, and it is not at all pleasant."

Tristan blinked. The count laughed again, then said, "My Liesl was in Naples when the French came, oh, quite twenty years ago now. When she says she will nurse Charles, you may be assured there is no one more capable of it. Now you, my friend, look as if you could use some rest. Leave Charles to us—you go and sleep for a day or so."

Tristan looked at Charles, who regarded him with a long, slow look, then said, "You look like hell, Tris. Go sleep."

He returned the look, then gave Charles quick grin and a nod. "I will if you will," he said.

"Agreed." Charles lay back on the pillows and smiled up at his mother. "Hullo, Mama," he said softly.

"Hello, my *Liebling*," she replied, her voice gentle.

Tristan looked at them, and at the calm, confident expression on the count's face, then bowed politely and went to find a bed.

"IT IS very simple," Liesl said.

They had finished supper; the table had been cleared and port brought, but with it being only the three of them, Liesl had refused to withdraw and accepted a small glass of port herself. "Eustace and I were in Paris in the summer of 1795; he was there with the British embassage during one of their negotiations. Believe it or not, Eustace was quite an effective speaker in his youth. Charles and Charlotte were, I believe, about eight years of age at the time, Daniel about sixteen. I met Antonio there." She reached across the corner of the table to clasp her husband's hand. "And fell madly in love."

"Ah, my darling girl," Antonio said softly. "You make it sound as if it were your fault. She behaved with utmost honor," he told Tristan, "and would have returned to England with her husband, but that he discovered that we had met twice—in all innocence!—and was infuriated. He cast her off, divorced her in the French civil system, and refused to permit her to see her children again." His voice was low and angry. "He cast off the most loving and loyal woman he would ever know and left his children motherless. He let the world think that she had died, and for her protection, her friends who knew the truth allowed him. But he could not keep her from writing to her children; first to a friend who smuggled the letters to them, and later, when they were older, directly to them. By then, he was too deep in the drink to care any longer. Charlotte's letters—and Charles's, when he found time to write—have been Liesl's greatest joy and comfort over the years."

"Not quite," Liesl said, smiling at him. Antonio raised her hand to his lips.

"Still, I am grateful for Chilson's foolishness, because his loss is my gain—and *my* greatest joy and comfort."

"Lottie never told me you were alive." Tristan thought a moment. "Of course, I think I just assumed you were dead and never questioned it. She always referred to you as 'Liesl' and I assumed you were a cousin or some distant connection. It never occurred to me to question it."

"Indeed, and why should you?" Liesl said practically. "Now. We will stay this evening in Charles's room and you will sleep in the other room, if you would be so kind, and I will nurse Charles and you will rest tonight. Tomorrow Antonio will arrange for an hotel for us, and we will set up a schedule of nursing until Charlotte arrives...."

"Charlotte?" Tristan blinked.

"Yes, Charlotte. Ellen is perfectly capable of taking care of the children, with the help of the nursemaid and wet-nurse, and Charlotte is perfectly healthy, so there is no reason why she should not be here with her husband. Brussels is a disaster, but I do not believe the gloomy-guts who insist there will be plague here; the Bruxellois are a tidy people and will have these bodies cleaned up quickly. Antonio will advise them."

Antonio just smiled at his wife.

"I believe you are quite mad," Tristan said to his new-found mother-in-law, "but I quite like you."

"Good," Liesl said. "I am quite prepared to like you as well."

CHAPTER 26

BY THE time Charlotte arrived a week later, Liesl's prediction had come true and Brussels was beginning to return to its normal state. Out near the battleground the situation was still bad, with the dead in great piles; along with the other doctors and surgeons in residence around the city, Tristan had begun riding out on a daily basis to find and treat those still alive among the dead. As the days rolled on, however, there were fewer of the injured to find, as those succumbed to their wounds and to exposure on the killing fields. The shock and horror Tristan had experienced on his first foray to the battleground had subsided to a grim determination to do what he could, as little as it was. Like the moment he saw Charles wounded and knew he had to swallow his personal fears and despair, and focus only on what he needed to do, out on the battlefield, he closed his eyes against the carnage and focused only on what he could do for those yet living, and, later, on helping to lay the dead in the mass graves dug for them.

He had just returned from the latter task and was taking a much-needed bath when he heard voices downstairs. He was bathing in the room once "assigned" to Charles; the count and countess had repaired to a hotel for their residence, but Charles was still installed in Tristan's bed and Tris did not want to disturb him. Rising from the bath, he dried himself off and dressed quickly in fresh clothing before checking quickly on the sleeping Charles, and then heading downstairs.

Liesl was holding court in his drawing room; he noticed Charlotte at once and went across to her, his hands outstretched. "Lottie," he said gratefully, drawing her into a hug. "You look well."

"You," she said, drawing back and regarding him thoughtfully, "look dreadful. Have you actually slept at all these last weeks?"

"Occasionally," he said with a laugh.

"See who I have brought with me," she said, and she pushed his shoulder gently to turn him.

He blinked in disbelief and Dr. Crosby laughed. "Surprised to see me, Northwood?"

"I stopped in London on my way to Dover," Charlotte said, "and asked Dr. Crosby and Dr. MacQuarrie to join us here. You had expressed concern that you were over your head with trying to treat Charles as well as manage all the other things you have on your plate."

"Mixing metaphors, my love," Tristan murmured, then he nodded curtly at Crosby.

"Both of us would have been a bit much," Crosby said, "so we drew straws. I won. It's no hardship to be out of London in June."

"Certainly," Tristan said stiffly. "I suppose you'd like to see him immediately, to confirm that I am just as ham-handed as you expect, and have him removed to some place where he can get more effective care?"

Crosby blinked. "I beg your pardon?"

"Tristan, don't be an ass," Lottie said. "Dr. Crosby had nothing but good things to say about you on the journey."

"I'm sure he was just being polite," Tristan said coolly.

"Which you are not," his wife said. "Come and sit down and have some tea, and *try* to be civil, will you? The children are fine, the wet-nurse you got for Caroline is excellent, and Ellen is delighted to play nanny for a few weeks, not that you've asked. How is Charles?"

"Sleeping," Tristan said. "He will insist on getting up for a short time every morning and trying to exercise his limbs; he says he's seen more men crippled by wasted muscles than by broken bones. It does not seem to hurt him, but he is usually exhausted after an hour and will sleep until suppertime."

"He's right; as long as he is not putting weight on the broken bone but is only exercising the muscles around it, he should do himself no harm," Crosby said. "Some surgeons believe the patient should be kept immobile, but I agree with Mountjoy."

Tristan closed his eyes a moment, then said with hard-won calm, "Yes, Charles is a very sensible man."

"I have always thought so," Liesl said.

"I looked in on him just before I came down," Tristan said, "and he was asleep. If you would give me your direction, Doctor, I will be happy to send 'round for you when he wakes."

"Stop bristling, hedgehog," Crosby said. "I know I am not your favorite person...."

"Nor I yours, I'm sure," Tristan said, "but it is not me you are visiting, so that makes no difference. My only concern is Charles's health. I am grateful you condescended to make the trip."

"I like Brussels, so it's no hardship. And I like Mountjoy." Crosby took his card-case out and withdrew a card and pencil. Writing on the back, he said, "I'm staying with friends in the rue Bologne. It's only a few streets over. I'll drop by this evening if that's acceptable?"

"You aren't leaving already? Tristan!" Liesl was dismayed.

Crosby laughed. "No need to fret, Countess. I hadn't planned to stay more than a moment; my baggage is still in the coach, and I really do need to get settled before I engage in any more medical activity."

"Then you must come for supper," Charlotte said, holding out her hand.

He bowed over it, said his goodbyes to Liesl and the count, and then turned. "Northwood—walk me out?"

Reluctantly, Tristan nodded and followed him into the hall. On the steps, Crosby turned and said, "I know you hate me for dashing your hopes, but I wasn't just considering your future patients' welfare, and if you hadn't gone haring off to the country the next day, I would have called 'round to explain my decision. I know I'm a bit brusque, but you're equally sensitive, and that's part of my concern."

"It's immaterial," Tristan said curtly. "I've no need to rehash the conversation."

"Well, I do, so shut your gob," Crosby said just as curtly. "You've got a damn haughty way about you, Northwood, which I suppose is natural given your ancestry and upbringing, but I've no patience with histrionics."

"Histrio—"

"Shut up and listen to me, damn it. You've the potential to be a damn fine physician *and* one with surgical skills as well, which is rare, and never mind the ballocksed-up rules that say you can't be both, though I have found that most men are one or the other. Mountjoy, for example. He's dedicated to medicine, but accepts his limitations, and he does have them, despite what your hero worship might tell you. You are limited only by your past poor decisions. It grieves me, because you have the soul of a surgeon; there aren't many who can step back from their emotions and treat the injury for what it is. Damn fewer who can look at the patient and treat him as well. I've seen it in the cases you've handled in the hospital, listening to the patient and figuring out not only how he was hurt but how he was likely to be hurt again, and coming up with ways to change that. That bricklayer with the cough and the sprained wrist—not many would have realized the cough was from the brick dust and the sprain from the way he was working, and sent him to MacQuarrie's group to deal with the cough when they were finished with the sprain. That took brains, and heart. You've got them.

"I got a note from the Duke of Wellington a fortnight ago. You had mentioned in passing that you had studied under me in London. He wanted to thank me for taking you on as a student, because it had made an enormous difference in the lives of the wounded here." He paused, swallowed, and went on, his voice a shade raspy. "To hear that a student has made a difference is one of the greatest joys of teaching. I have never regretted taking you on as a student. My only regret is that you hadn't discovered what it is you wanted to do ten years ago, before the drink had ruined your nerves."

Tristan's eyes were stinging; he stared up at the sky until they cleared, and said quietly, "I wish I had, too. Now...." He spread his hands, staring at them. They seemed steady enough, but he knew that Crosby had been right. They shook when tense, and that—*that*—was all his fault.

"Now you take a different tack." Crosby studied him. "You come back to London, finish your studies, get additional training. Medicine's not like surgery; you need education for medicine, instead of just apprenticing as a surgeon, so it's going to take you longer than you might have expected at the outset. You've got your Cambridge degree, though; I'll wager you can do the medical program in a couple of years. It'll take Mountjoy a year or two longer, since he hasn't the degree. It's supposed to be five years, but that's ballocks. You both need to apply at St. Joseph's as students, but that's a formality; MacQuarrie and I are on the board there. Mountjoy said once he'd hoped to go into practice with you as his partner, after you both get your licenses. MacQuarrie and I think that's a splendid idea, based on your skills, your interests, and your characters. You've the imagination; Mountjoy has the steadiness. Between you, you'll do well. Now. Go back in there and apologize to your wife for being a boor, and I'll be by for supper."

"Eight o'clock," Tristan said dazedly.

"I'll come by at seven and see to Mountjoy first. Good day to you, sir!"

"Good day."

Tristan watched him climb back into the coach and give the driver the signal to start. A gloved hand flapped at him once, then the coach rattled around the corner and was gone. He stared after it a moment, then went back in to apologize to Lottie.

CHARLES lay still, gazing up at the canopy overhead. It was robin's egg blue, which should have made it feminine, but the folds of fabric were crisp and the matching bed-curtains tied back in almost military order. He knew them well, down to the individual folds—too well. And he was bloody sick of them. Sick of them, and of the silk-papered walls and the Brussels-scented breeze that came in the window, and the window itself, and the traction machine that held his leg up.

It had been nearly three weeks since his injury, and he was desperate to escape, both the room and the endless pain in his leg—to walk out of this bloody room on his own two feet, to ride again, to feel the sun on his face. The short walks around the room and up and down the upstairs corridor he'd taken with the aid of a pair of crutches that made his gait awkward and ungainly. But his leg still couldn't take his weight. He knew well enough it might never take his weight again, but he was bound and determined to avoid that fate. He was *going* to walk again, and he was *going* to ride again, and by *God*, he was going to make love with Tristan again.

Tristan.

Again, the snort, this time even less amused. Tristan, who worked carefully with him, always pleasant, always patient, always encouraging, always helpful. Always… *careful*. Careful not to hurt him, careful to only touch him in ways that wouldn't distract him from whatever torture he was putting himself through, careful not to let Charles's increasingly bad humor upset him. It did upset him; Charles could see it when he snapped at Tris and Tris's mouth would go flat a moment, only to curve back up again in a patient, understanding smile. He wanted to *slap* that smile off Tristan's face. He wanted to hurt Tris, and that shocked him.

And then when he was done with his self-torture, and Tristan had helped him back into bed and hooked his leg back up into the traction machine, Tris would arrange his pillows so that he was comfortable, give him his tea, and then kiss him gently—*carefully*—on the forehead before leaving him to "rest."

Charles was sure there was laudanum in the tea, because he did rest, despite the pain, falling asleep moments after Tristan left. Even though he was angry, and frustrated, and hurting, in more ways than one. When he woke hours later, groggy and ill-tempered, the frustration and anger seemed even more intense. The gentleness Tristan showed him was completely devoid of anything resembling passion, and Charles's fury was honed by the fear that Tristan no longer felt about him the way he felt about Tristan.

Indeed, why should he? Tristan was a Corinthian, a hale, healthy young man obsessed with the physical. Charles… was not. Not any longer, at any rate. He was determined to walk again, and ride, but he knew he might never have the other physical abilities he once took for granted; might never box, or fence, or hunt again. He couldn't expect Tristan to wait for a recovery that might not happen. He didn't expect Tristan to wait.

But this patient, careful treatment frightened him. Had Tristan already given up on him? Was his kindness merely the care he had for a brother-in-law, and no longer the desire he had for a lover? Charles closed his eyes against the thought, his heart aching as much as his leg. It was possible. It was probable. Hadn't he himself called Tristan a skylark? Hadn't people—hadn't Tristan himself?—warned him about Tristan's inconstancy? He'd come to believe that he had been wrong, that Tris was different, that Tris was loyal. And he was, in his own way, loyal to Charlotte, loyal to his friends, to his children. Even to Charles himself. But Charles didn't want just loyalty. He wanted devotion. He wanted love.

He wanted Tristan.

His throat was raw from the tears he refused to shed, but he swallowed anyway, relishing the burn. He needed to think, but the pain left him weary, and the laudanum left him thick-skulled, and he wished he could just close his eyes and it would all go away. He understood at last the frustration and despair that had once driven Tris to contemplate suicide, and even as that thought went through his mind he castigated himself for feeling so pathetic and helpless. He might be a cripple, but he wasn't helpless. So what if he couldn't ride again—that was what carriages were for. And if he had to walk with a stick, that was all right too. There were plenty of older doctors who used a stick.

And if he lost Tris? Then Tris was never really his to lose.

There were voices in the street outside; the breeze carried the sound through the open window. He recognized Tristan's, but the other voice was harder to place. He thought he might have heard it before but couldn't remember where, and the breeze wasn't strong enough to carry their words, just the sound of the voices. The other voice spoke at length, then there was the sound of a coach on the cobbles, and the front door closing. He wondered who it was that had visited; if it was someone he knew or some friend that Tristan had made in Brussels, who had visited before and Charles had heard his voice in his sleep, or on the stairs. Perhaps on the stairs as they came up to bed—perhaps it was a new lover Tristan had taken. He swallowed again. He was thirsty, but the carafe on the nightstand was a reach, and he really wasn't feeling up to it. It was easier to lie here and feel sorry for himself. He grimaced and reached for the carafe.

A few minutes later there were footsteps on the stairs: Tristan's and a woman's. His mother's? But no; when the bedroom door opened Charlotte came in, her face bright and her step light as she rustled across the floor to his side. "Charlie, you foolish, foolish boy," she scolded.

"*Kleine Schwester*," he said. "What are you doing in Brussels?"

"Visiting you, silly. What else would I be doing? Purchasing chocolates?" She hugged him gently. "How are you feeling?"

Like shite, he wanted to answer, but he glanced past her to see Tristan looking anxious, and he smiled instead. "Oh, far better than before. Between Tristan and Liesl, I have had excellent nursing."

"I fetched Dr. Crosby with me on the way through London, and he'll be dining with us tonight. He'll visit you before supper, Tris says. Shall we have Reston set up a table in here, so you can join us?"

Charles glanced at Tristan again. "It's entirely up to you," Tristan said. "If you feel comfortable enough dining with us. I imagine that the count and countess will also be joining us; it will be quite a party to sit down together." To Charlotte, he said, "I haven't bothered with regular meals up 'til now, but I suppose with you to manage the household, that will change."

"It certainly will," Charlotte said. She beamed at Charles, then turned away. "Now go away, Tristan, and let me have a nice cose with Charlie. You have had him all to yourself for weeks now, and we have much to discuss."

"As you wish, my dear." Again, a quick, anxious look at Charles, followed by a careful smile, and then Tris was gone.

"Now," Charlotte said as she drew up a chair beside the bed, "tell me what is really wrong, Charlie."

He looked at her beloved face and to his horror, his eyes filled and tears spilled down his cheeks. With an effort, he managed a weak, watery smile and shook his head.

"Oh, my love," she said, and climbed up to sit beside him, her arms around him. "Shh," she crooned. "Shh...."

He sobbed into her shoulder, hating this, hating the weakness and the foolishness, but grateful that she'd come, that she was here. Even more than Mama, it was Charlotte who had always been his comfort. Finally, he drew away. She fished a handkerchief out of her bodice and wiped his eyes, then held it against his nose. "Blow."

He took it away from her and blew, thanking his stars that practical Charlotte also preferred practical handkerchiefs. "I'm not *quite* as young as Jamie," he said dryly.

"Men never really do grow up," she said mildly. "Can you talk to me now without turning into a watering pot?"

"It isn't anything, really," he prevaricated, "just general misery and boredom. Remember how cranky Tristan got when he was starting to feel better after his illness? I suppose it's just the same."

"Mm," she said. "But you are feeling better? Tristan was talking about how improved you are; that you're walking with sticks and exercising, and that he expects you to be able to negotiate the stairs in a week or so, and by then the soldiers who are cluttering up the dining room will have gone away and we can put you in there instead. So you won't have to worry about the stairs, and can have visitors, and so on."

"Soldiers? He said there were a few sick men he was housing, but…."

"Didn't he tell you? When you were rescued, there were four other soldiers rescued with you. I think Tristan said they were from your friend Captain Randall's regiment or something. He's been tending them, although he said none of them were as badly injured as you and will be sent back to their families or their billets tomorrow or the next day."

"Tristan's been tending *five* of us?"

"Oh, that's nothing," Lottie said airily. "During and after the battles, he had as many as thirty men here in various states of injury at any one time. Reston said the house was quite full; even the servants were doubling up for space. Wellington has been quite complimentary about Tris, according to Dr. Crosby." She frowned faintly. "I'm quite glad Mama has come, and that I did not heed Tristan's instructions to remain home. He is looking quite drawn. I suppose it is difficult, after working so hard to make men better, to go out day after day to help bury them."

"*Bury* them?"

"Oh, not the ones he treated—well, I suppose some of them did die, at least I think Tristan said so, despite all his hard work. But from the battle. The casualties were *awful*."

"How many?" Charles asked.

"I don't know. Twenty, thirty thousand? That's what the papers were saying at home, although I expect they don't know any better than anyone else. Wellington says every man on his staff was either injured or killed." She kissed his cheek. "I'm so glad you weren't among the latter."

Twenty or thirty *thousand*? The Staff all dead or injured? He wanted to ask—to demand!—of Charlotte an accounting of his friends and fellow officers, but she wouldn't know. He doubted Tris would, either. Then something she'd said struck him. "Have you *spoken* to the Duke?"

"Me? Oh, no. It was just something I'd heard he'd said. He's not in Brussels; he's gone off with the army. I think they're expecting to capture Napoleon soon, if not already. You know how slowly news moves. Now, tell me again how you are feeling, and without the waterworks, if you please."

Despite himself, her matter-of-fact attitude made him smile, and he settled down for a long conversation.

"WELL, you're looking a damn sight better than you've any right to."

Charles smiled up at Crosby. His visit with his sister had gone a long way toward restoring his usual equilibrium, and he felt quite up to dealing with the brusque surgeon. "It was the only way I could get a rest," he said, "with you and Mac driving me like a cart horse."

"Well, you've some way to go if you plan to keep pace with your young surgeon friend here. He's learned more about treating injuries in a fortnight than he would in a year of following me around. Grant's quite pleased with him, and so is the Duke. Let's take a look at what he's accomplished here. Whose idea was the traction?"

"I don't know. I was up in it when I awoke, so I suppose Tristan."

"Hmm," Crosby said. He investigated the apparatus, prodded at Charles's leg, inspected the wound, inspected his shoulder, prodded his ribs, and all the while carried on an interrogation of him regarding Tristan's treatment and Charles's recovery. He was especially interested in some therapeutic activities with sandbags Charles and Tristan had worked out, and the daily walking, and picked Charles's brain until his head spun. Finally he sat back down in the chair and regarded him with narrowed eyes.

"What?" Charles asked.

"You're doing well. I'm quite impressed. And the sand weights for therapeutic muscle-building—that was quite a clever idea. I might have to steal it for use in my own practice."

"I'd noticed that the injured who returned to work earlier—even if the work was at a slower pace, or less demanding—seemed to have a better long-term recovery," Charles explained. "The same in the army. My leg still won't bear my weight, so I must keep it strong in other ways."

"It takes about six weeks to heal bone," Crosby said. "The tibia is a primary weight-bearing bone so I'd advise you stay off it for an additional two weeks. Traction for the better part of the day and at night, to keep you from doing it additional injury. Still a lot of pain?"

"Not really," Charles said evasively.

"Ballocks."

Charles laughed. "All right, then. Yes. A lot of pain. I don't like laudanum, but I'll bet money Tristan's been dosing me with it, and in a way I'm grateful. But it has to stop, and I'm not looking forward to dealing with the pain without it. Skullcap can only go so far, even augmented with willow and butterbur."

"You and your damn herbs," Crosby snorted, then added, "You know, don't you, that you're likely to end up with that leg shorter? Even if you do walk again, you'll have a limp. Never met a survivor of that particular type of injury that didn't. You'll limp, and have to use a cane, in a best-case scenario. But you've made it through the worst of it. No infection. You were lucky."

"I know it."

"He's a good man, Northwood. Not what I expected—he's got bottom. Steady, reliable. Doesn't fit his reputation. Sorry I didn't catch him before he wrecked his nerves with the drink."

"He's no drunkard," Charles said. "He stopped drinking even before he started studying under you. I've known men who are addicted to it, but once Tris had something else to think about, he didn't need the liquor any more. I think he drank out of boredom and frustration more than anything else."

"Stands to reason," Crosby nodded. "Bright lad, forced into shoes that didn't fit—of course he drank, and whored, and gamed."

Charles grinned. "Tris doesn't gamble. Says it's boring."

"Knew he was sensible."

"And I'm relatively sure he's faithful. Now, at least." To whom, Charles didn't specify; he only hoped he was right.

Crosby slapped his thighs. "Good, good. Means he's found focus. Man will make a damn good doctor if he keeps up with it. Now. You. You can keep up working with the crutches, but no weight on that bone for, hmm, five more weeks, at least. Exercise the leg, by all means; it will keep it from shortening more than necessary. I agree with you on the laudanum, and will talk to Northwood about it; keep it for the worst times when you can't bear the pain any longer, but switch to one of your mad herbal concoctions for the rest. I'll be in town here for another five or six days; I'll want to see one of your exercise sessions for myself."

"Come by in the morning, then. I like to start my day with extreme pain and misery. Makes anything that comes after tolerable by comparison."

Crosby laughed and rose from the chair. "Your sister said something about dining here. Are you up for it?"

"Yes—tell her to bring in the troops, if you will. If you don't mind the excessive casualness of dining not only *en famille*, but *en boudoir*."

"Well, I haven't done *that* in a long time, but it's not quite the same thing, is it?"

Despite himself, Charles laughed.

CHAPTER 27

"I'M SURPRISED to find you still at home," Derek Chamberlain said as Reston ushered him into the former butler's pantry, now remade into a bookroom for Tristan.

"Maartens informed me that there was no need for me to come out to the battlefield any longer. The Bruxellois have it well in hand, and aside from a memorial service once the burials are finished, the rest of us Englischers are superfluous." Tristan set the book in his hand aside; he'd finish the chapter on debridement and curettage later. "Plus Dr. Crosby's coming by for one last visit with Charles before he returns to London." He gestured for Derek to sit; his guest obeyed, dropping into the wing chair opposite Tristan.

"Oh, he's off too, then?" Derek said.

Something in the way he said it made Tris cock his head and study his friend. "'Too'?" he echoed softly.

"I leave with the Seymours in the morning." Derek closed his eyes and leaned his head back against the chair back. "I won't say I won't be happy to be back in my rooms at home, but... things are different now. Things have changed. I've changed."

"I know what you mean," Tristan agreed. "To have been part of something this important, to have participated—even if on the sidelines—in an event of this magnitude, has to change one, doesn't it? Even if a hundred years from now no one even remembers the name of Waterloo?"

"Oh, they'll remember, I wager," Derek said. He opened his eyes and looked at Tris. "I borrowed Lord Seymour's bay again; would you have time for one last ride in the park before I return to my deadly dull solicitor's life?"

"I'm assuming you mean your life is dull, not the solicitor," Tristan said with a smile as he rose. "Dr. Crosby's not due for an hour, and even so, it's Charlie he wants to see, not me, so yes, I've time for a quick jaunt. Just let me have Paragon saddled." He rang the bell for Will and gave him the order, then the two of them strolled out to the front of the house.

"That's not the Brat," Derek said when the groom brought Paragon around. Tristan checked the girth, then swung himself up into the saddle.

"No, it's Paragon, Charlie's horse. I've been keeping him exercised. Brat is quite jealous, but he's enamored of Betsy, Charlie's other mount, so he's easily distracted. Paragon is much better mannered than the Brat."

"Lives up to his name, does he?"

"He does. Come on, then."

They rode sedately to the large park several streets over, then let the horses shake out their legs. It was midmorning; the early risers had already been and gone, and the late risers were still drowsing over their breakfasts. The beastly hot weather had broken, and the morning was cool and sunny, without a hint of the humidity that had made the summer so unpleasant.

Paragon was as fast as the Brat, but without the gelding's nervous twitchiness; his gait was smooth and flowing, and riding him at a gallop felt like flying. Tris laughed from the sheer physical joy of it. He set the horse at a low hedge, and they flew over it with barely a bump. Near the center of the park, he drew rein and let Paragon drop to a trot, and then a walk; he leaned over to pat his neck and found him barely even damp. "Ah, I see why Charlie calls you Paragon," he said in a soft voice, and the horse's ears flicked back toward Tris. "Sweet gait, sweet nature, and strong as an ox, aren't you?"

Derek rode up, panting, his horse lathered. "Dash it, Tristan!" he complained good-naturedly, "that horse is secretly a racehorse, don't deny it. You'll be entering him at Epsom Downs, no doubt."

Tris laughed. "Ah, would that I could! But he's Charlie's, and a hunter, and the Derby's for thoroughbreds, isn't it?"

"I'd think you'd know better than I," Derek replied in confusion. "I can't bet on races on a solicitor's salary, but I thought you would have done so a dozen times by now."

Tristan shook his head. "Not interested in racing," he said dismissively. "I prefer hunting. Standing watching perfectly good horses running around a track is deadly dull."

"Well, you're the only person in the British Isles that thinks so," Derek said, snorting.

They rode on in companionable silence for a while, only breaking it to comment on something innocuous. When they came upon a bench in a shady nook, Derek drew up and dismounted, leading his horse over to the bench, where he sat down and looked up at Tristan. "I wanted to talk to you," he said soberly.

Curious, Tristan followed suit, wrapping the reins around the arm of the bench as Derek had. "What about?"

Derek didn't answer right away. Instead, he leaned forward, his arms on his knees, and stared at the fountain splashing merrily a dozen yards away. Finally, he said, "This is more difficult than I expected it to be. I practiced it, you know. Thought I had it all down pat. But now… it's hard."

"Just say it," Tristan said. He felt suddenly chilled. He'd grown to like Derek a great deal, and had hoped to renew the friendship when he returned to London, but from the tone of his friend's voice, there was something wrong. Was it that he had decided he no longer wanted to be friends with someone of Tristan's persuasion? Was he going to warn Tristan to stay away from him, or worse, was he intending to lay charges against him when he returned to London? Tristan knew he and Charles had been discreet there; it was only here, in Brussels, that their carefully constructed house of cards had come tumbling down. He swallowed hard.

"I love you," Derek said.

A bird chirped nearby, and a tree frog sang. Tristan sat frozen in shock. "What?" he managed finally.

Derek gave a soft, unamused laugh. "I said 'I love you'," he repeated. "I know. I'm mad. And I know that you're devoted to the major. But I can't help it. I'm in love with you. I just thought you should know."

"I don't know what to say," Tristan said, "except, for God's sake, *why*?"

"Oh, Christ, Tristan, I don't know where to start! You're brave, and beautiful, and strong, and smart, and intelligent. You're this perfect—perfect *paragon* of a man, and it makes me long to be like you. To be *with* you. I'm torn, I really am; I wish you would leave the major, but if you did, you wouldn't be the man I love, and I don't want that, really. I didn't even realize I loved you until I saw you with him, saw how you cared for him, and I knew I wanted that from you, and can never have it." He put his gloved hand to his eyes. "God, I sound like a female in some Gothic romance. I shouldn't have said anything. But I couldn't go back to London knowing you might be there sometime soon, and if we encountered each other, you all unknowing—I might not be able to hide it so well. So I thought I'd warn you." He put his hand down on his knee and stared straight ahead. "I'm a fool. I'm sorry."

"You are a fool," Tristan said. Derek's head jerked up and he stared at Tristan blankly, his eyes wide. "You are a fool to think that of me. That I'm any of those things. I'm *none* of them. Whatever I am, I am because of Charles." He swallowed hard. "Before I met Charles, I was setting my affairs in order with a view to putting a period to my existence. I was a worthless drunkard, with no redeeming qualities whatsoever. Charles changed that. He showed me a way of thinking that had never occurred to me—introduced me to people like Ian MacQuarrie and Bennett Crosby and their compatriots, who think nothing of spending their time and money and energy helping other people, while expecting almost nothing in return. I'm not that good, Derek."

"But all those soldiers you treated, the hours you worked until you dropped...."

"Which you did, as well." He held up his hand when Derek, shaking his head, started to protest. "You did. So you didn't have the little bit of training I had—that only made it braver, for you to try to help when you weren't sure what to do. I *knew* some of what I could do. You didn't, but you tried anyway. You worked just as hard as I did. Besides, all I could think was that perhaps Charlie was out there, injured, alone, and I could only pray that someone would take care of him as I was taking care of the others. I wasn't being selfless, Derek. I was being as selfish as I possibly could be, because helping those men helped me too." He shook his head. "I'm no hero. God, I'm barely a decent man. I don't know why you've decided that I'm any better than anyone else. Because it's not true."

"You make me love you even more," Chamberlain said. He essayed a brave smile. "But that's all right. I don't believe you."

Tristan chuckled, but he never felt less like laughing. "Derek...."

"It's all right, Tris. It's all right." Derek touched two fingers to the back of Tristan's gloved hand. "I just hope that we can still be friends. That was what I was most afraid of, that you'd not want to see me again."

Did he? Tristan gazed down at the fingers a moment, then Derek lifted them slowly away. Tristan reached out and closed his own around them. "You have been my friend through one of the darkest times of my life," he said quietly. "No matter what, you have earned my regard. I can't be what you need me to be, but I shall ever stand as your friend."

"Thank you," Derek whispered.

Tristan put his other hand over Derek's and held it clasped. "I don't expect to come directly back to London," he said. "I intend to take Charlie back to Leicestershire with us so he can recuperate in the country. But Crosby expects me to return to my medical studies, and I know Charles intends to do the same, so we may be back in town by next Season. I don't know for sure. But I shall send 'round to you when we are. In the meantime, letters sent to

Lilac Cottage, Market Harborough, shall find me. If you need anything, please write me."

"You are entirely too kind," Derek said, his cheeks scarlet.

Tristan patted his hand and let go. "Come on, then. I must return; I'm sure Crosby will have plenty of instructions before he leaves."

"Of course." Derek stood up and busied himself with his horse's reins a moment before swinging into the saddle. He didn't meet Tristan's eyes.

Tristan mounted Paragon and turned his head back toward the rue de Valois. They rode in silence, but it wasn't uncomfortable; just two men wrapped in their own thoughts. Derek dismounted when Tristan did and held out his hand. "Thank you, Tristan."

Tristan took his hand, but didn't release it immediately. "Your friendship has meant a great deal to me, Derek. I should have been quite miserable alone here for these weeks. Please write me when you are settled back at home and let me know you arrived safely."

"I will." Derek hesitated a moment, then glanced around before leaning forward to brush his lips on Tristan's cheek. "Take care of yourself, Tris— and of Charles."

Tristan raised his hand and brushed his fingers across Derek's jaw. "I shall."

Derek gave him a twisted smile, then remounted, snapped a quick salute, and trotted off down the street, his back straight. Tristan watched, his heart aching a little. He'd never broken a heart before—he'd always been careful to choose lovers as jaded as he was. But he'd never expected this— that someone as steady and confident as Derek Chamberlain could possibly have feelings for him.

He felt terrible.

Leaning his head against Paragon's shoulder, he stood in the street waiting for the groom instead of leading the horse back to the mews. The horse was warm and steady under his forehead; he felt the flex of heavy muscle and then the soft tickle as Paragon nibbled at his hair, nudging his hat out of the way. He laughed. "Oh, don't tell me you're besotted with me too, stupid animal."

Paragon snorted and Tristan laughed again, then bestirred himself to bring the horse back to his stable.

RESTON scratched on Charles's door just as Reid was finishing up shaving Charles. In the last couple of days, he'd been able to move to a chair with his leg on a footstool for his morning shave; he'd taken for granted before just how good it felt to have a clean face. Reid had done his best with him in the bed, but it had been a catch-as-catch-can proposition. Now his batman wiped away the last traces of soap before calling, "Come in, Mr. Reston."

"Dr. Crosby has arrived," Reston told Charles. "I just wanted to make sure you were ready for visitors."

"Send 'em up, whoever gets here," Charles said. "I'm ready for anything." He rubbed a grateful hand over his smooth chin. "Mr. Northwood done with breakfast yet?"

"Mr. Northwood went riding about an hour ago," Reston said, "with Mr. Chamberlain."

"Chamberlain? Do I know a Chamberlain?"

"Lord Seymour's solicitor," Reston supplied. "He made Mr. Northwood's acquaintance when they were both tending to the wounded. I understand that he's returning to London with the Seymours tomorrow. Shall I send Dr. Crosby up, then, sir?"

"Please do," Charles said. When Reston had gone, he turned to Reid. "Do you know this Chamberlain, Reid?"

"I've met him, aye," Reid said. "He and Mr. Northwood go ridin' together a couple times a week. Pleasant enough gentleman."

A pleasant enough gentleman. Whom Tris had met while tending the wounded. With whom Tris went riding a couple of times a week. And whom Tris had not thought worth mentioning to Charles.

Or was it that he didn't choose to mention him?

The pleasure over his shave vanished, and it was with a grim expression that Charles greeted Crosby. "How much damn longer will I be laid up here?"

"You tell me," the doctor retorted. "You know as well as I what recovery time for broken bones is."

"Six weeks," Charles snapped. "But one doesn't have to spend the entire six weeks in bed."

"No," Crosby agreed. "So get your arse up on those crutches and we'll see how you're doing. How's the pain?"

"Alive and well," Charles said. "And reminding me of its presence." He grimaced. "I suppose no one can tell how long *that* will be going on."

"Pain is less measurable than bone. Best we can say is the sooner you heal—*don't*, pray, put your weight on it! Damn it, Mountjoy, you know better than that! You, man, hold your master's other arm. Mountjoy, if you ever intend to walk again, you can't bloody rush it!"

Charles sucked hard on the inside of his cheek, cursing the impulsive move that had shot pain up his leg. He did know better, but never had his enforced idleness chafed more that at this moment. *Where was Tris? Surely an hour was plenty of time for a ride—more than enough time. What was he doing with the mysterious Mr. Chamberlain?* With an effort, he turned his attention to walking, using the crutches to support him while he exercised the knee joint in a mockery of his normal gait. "Good," Crosby said, "you're maintaining flexibility in the knee and quadriceps. That's what I like to see. Those weights you're using to exercise the ankle should be very helpful in minimizing muscular deterioration. You will walk with a limp, of course, but I'm inclined to believe you will walk. *If* you don't rush it. We won't know for sure, of course, until you're well enough to put weight on it. But I'm optimistic, and you know I'm rarely optimistic."

When he was finished with his exercise, he swung back into the bedroom, Reid at his heels. He turned carefully on the crutches, balanced, and held out a hand to Crosby. "Thank you for your attention, and for making the trip here. I appreciate it. My sister wants me to join them at the Northwoods' country cottage for my convalescence, but I hope to see you in town soon."

"I expect to see you in town for the Little Season," Crosby said, "though I won't expect you to return to your studies at St. Joseph's until spring, to be fair. MacQuarrie will probably be in touch with you before that; he'll have plenty for you to do whilst you're abed."

Charles laughed. "No doubt," he said lightly, shaking Crosby's hand again. "Good travels to you, sir."

"And you, sir." Crosby nodded and vanished down the stairs.

"Back to bed, sir?" Reid asked, "or would you prefer sitting in the chair for a while?"

"Bed, I think. I've still not recovered my stamina." He pivoted on the crutches and swung over toward the bed.

He was just about to shift onto the mattress when he glanced out the window and saw a pair of horsemen riding up. One was a stranger, but even if he hadn't recognized the second, the horse he was riding was Charles's own Paragon. Tristan. And the mysterious Mr. Chamberlain, he supposed. Charles went to the window and looked down as they dismounted. They spoke too softly for him to hear them, but he could see clearly enough. Could see

Tristan holding the man's hand a shade too long; could see the man lean forward to kiss Tristan's cheek; could see Tristan reach over and touch the man's face. And when the man was riding off, could see Tristan resting his forehead against Paragon's shoulder, as if in grief at the parting.

He hadn't been able to see his rival's face, but in his imagination painted it as handsome and aristocratic as Tristan's own. A solicitor, so probably not of particularly good family, but then Tristan had never been a snob. He would be a gentleman, at any rate, and of good manners; those *would* be important to Tris. Charles could see himself that he was dignified and sat his mount well. Athletic then, like Tris.

Charles watched Tris as he raised his head and caught up Paragon's reins to lead him to the mews and out of Charles's sight. For a long moment, Charles just stared down at the empty street, but when Reid said, his voice tight with concern, "Major?" he shook his head and let his batman ease him into bed.

"I'm tired, Reid," he said, hating the fretful sound of his voice. "I'm going to sleep; I don't wish to be disturbed."

"Mr. Northwood...."

"By anyone, Reid," he said sharply.

"Yes, sir." Reid clicked his heels smartly and took himself off.

Charles lay in the bed, brooding and unable to sleep.

"HOW strange," Liesl said. "No one at all, Mr. Reid?"

"No, Contessa. He seemed quite tired—not at all himself. I did manage to touch his hand when I was tucking him in, and he did not seem feverish. But short-tempered."

"I suppose his visit with Dr. Crosby wore him out," Lottie said placidly. "He has been shorter of temper since his injury but I suppose that's natural. I remember how *vile* Tristan's temper was when he was recovering from his illness."

"Thank you, my dear," Tristan said, bowing politely.

She curtseyed back at him with a smirk.

"Children, children," Liesl said with a sigh. "Well, we shall let *mein Junge* rest. Perhaps after luncheon he will feel more like visitors."

BUT after lunch, Reid brought down the message that Major Mountjoy was quite uninterested in having visitors, and continued to maintain that he did not wish to be disturbed. After dinner, Tristan sought Reid out in the servants' dining room and took him aside, demanding to know what had happened, if Crosby had said anything to disturb Charles.

"Well, sir, I don't rightly know what it was," Reid admitted. "He was his usual self before Dr. Crosby came, but by the time the doctor arrived he was already in the sulks. The only thing I can think of was that Mr. Reston had mentioned you'd gone riding with Mr. Chamberlain; he asked me about the gentleman, but didn't say anything on the subject. It was after that, though, that his temper got worse. I been thinking about it, Mr. Northwood, and that's the only reason I can figure for it."

"What could have disturbed him about my going out with Mr. Chamberlain?" Tristan asked, more to himself, but Reid answered.

"I think it was because he'd never heard of the man, sir. He seemed quite put out about that."

"Never…. Of course he's heard of him. I've mentioned him, surely?" Tristan thought a moment. "I must have mentioned him."

"Not in my hearing, sir, but then I'm not always there when you're visiting the major."

"Well, still, what the devil would he find objectionable in my taking a ride with the man?" Tristan demanded.

"I'm sure I couldn't say, sir," Reid replied with a sigh.

"Well, at this point I'm not interested in what he does and doesn't want. He's sulking for some reason, just as I did when I was unwell, and just as he did then, I shall shake him out of the sulks."

"Very good, sir," Reid said with a smile.

Tristan nodded abruptly, then turned and stomped back into the main part of the house and up the stairs to the bedrooms. Charles's door was closed, but not locked; Tristan opened it and stuck his head in to see Charles awake and staring blindly out the window. "Sulking?" he said.

Charles turned toward him and said bleakly, "I've no need of anything, Tris. You don't need…."

"Ballocks on what I do or don't need, and the same for you," Tristan said ruthlessly, coming into the room and shutting the door. "Now what are you so fussed about?"

"Nothing," Charles said curtly.

"Ballocks," Tristan said again. "What's this about you being jealous of poor Chamberlain?"

"Jealous?" Charles echoed. "What in God's name do you mean jealous?"

"I took a bloody ride with him, to the park and back, and nothing more. What in that is so upsetting that you've got Reid at his wit's end with you?"

"Reid," his lover said austerely, "is not at his wit's end. And if I decided I want a little time away from your poking and prying and my sister's poking and prying and my *mother's* poking and prying, what matter to you, sir?"

Tristan guffawed. "Oh, that's it, is it?" he said, and sat on the edge of Charles's bed. "Put the blame on everyone else. Fine work, Major." He folded his arms and regarded Charles. "For your information, poor Chamberlain is leaving tomorrow to return to London. He shall not be around to take my attention away from you. Satisfied?"

"I don't want your attention," Charles said sullenly.

Tristan reached over and felt his forehead. Charles jerked away with a muttered oath. "I'm not feverish," he growled.

"I thought you might be delirious," Tristan said.

"Go to the devil."

"Charlie."

Charles looked up at him, his expression unwilling.

"There's something going on, more than your resenting Chamberlain's infringement on my time. What is it?"

"Nothing. I'm just… tired, is all." He looked up, then. "I resent anything that takes you away from me," he said wearily. "I'm being selfish. I know you've other demands on your time; Lottie's told me that you're tending to other wounded, and then there are the social demands of my mother and her husband. I've no right to expect you to spend all your time with me, but damn it, Tris…."

"It's all right," Tristan said, and he bent to kiss his forehead.

Charles jerked away. "Stop it," he said savagely. "If you're going to kiss me, then bloody well *kiss* me. If not, then stop throwing me sops."

"I beg your pardon?" Tristan blinked in surprise.

"I'm tired of all this… *gentleness*. I'm not a bloody child, Tristan, nor a woman. I've broken my leg, not been gelded."

"Forgive me for thinking that you might not be up for bed sports," Tristan said sarcastically.

"I'm not asking for sport," Charles shot back. "I'm asking you to treat me as a man."

"I've never treated you as less."

"Ballocks!" Charles roared. "You treat me as a bloody invalid!"

"You *are* a bloody invalid! For God's sake, Charlie, what do you want from me? You're not exactly in a position to bugger me, though I imagine that's what you want. Shall I put my mouth on you? Will that satisfy your need to believe that I still think of you as a man?" Furious, Tristan grabbed the bedclothes and started to yank them down.

Charles caught hold of them and held them. "Damn you, Tris," he panted. "God damn you to hell!"

Tristan shot to his feet and glared down at Charles. "Fine," he said tautly. "I wash my hands of you. Go to hell in your own way, Charles, and leave me to go to hell in mine." He slammed out of the room and went to Charles's old bedroom, where he'd taken to sleeping, and flung himself on the bed. A part of his mind was telling him it was just the enforced idleness and the weeks of pain and inactivity that had soured Charles's temper, but the pain of their argument on top of his own fear was more than Tris could bear. He had been worried about Charles forever, it seemed, and Charles's words had cut deep.

Lottie came in and sat on the edge of the bed. "We could hear you and Charlie shouting," she said. "Is he very angry?"

"He's a fool," Tristan said, his voice muffled by the pillow.

"All men are fools," Lottie said. "I imagine he's worse because he's frustrated. He's used to being up and about. You were much the same when you were ill; although, of course, you weren't cooped up quite so long. Charlie will be better when he's home, and can sit outside in the sun."

"Do you know," Tristan said, "I don't believe I give a damn."

"Of course you do," she said, and patted his shoulder.

"No, I don't think I do. Which is quite all right. He's not in need of my nursing any longer; Reid can manage him, and he has you and your mama to pat his hand and tell him nursery tales." He rolled over and gave Lottie a savage smile. "He really doesn't need me at all."

KindRED HEARTS | 315

"No," Lottie said, "and he's not the only one with a temper and the ability to sulk." She pursed her lips, thinking. "Perhaps it would be better if you didn't dance attendance on him for a while. Too bad Mr. Chamberlain has gone; he would have been good company for you until Charlie is over his fit of temper."

"Chamberlain! That's half the problem. Charles has it in his head that I'm besotted by him or something."

"Hmm," Lottie mused, "that's interesting. I assume by your tone of voice that you are not."

"No, of course not." Tristan put an arm over his eyes. "He told me this morning that he was in love with me, but that he knew I was devoted to Charles. Hah!"

"Well, isn't it true?"

Tristan didn't answer right away, caught up in his own misery. Finally he said, "Yes, damn it, it's true. I may not have been faithful to you, Lottie, but I cannot find it in me to betray Charles."

"Well," Lottie said practically, "that's because you never loved me."

Tristan's eyes burned and there was a vise around his throat, but he managed a brief nod.

"He'll come 'round," his wife said, and patted his thigh. "It's just a fit of the sulks. Give him time." She was quiet a moment, then added, "I think you'd be wise to avoid him for a day or two. Give him the chance to miss you. He's taken you for granted a bit, I think. Leave him to Liesl and me."

He raised his arm and looked at his wife. She was smiling wickedly. "He'll learn to appreciate your kindness."

Despite himself, he laughed.

CHAPTER 28

THREE days later Charles was ready to kill something. Or someone. He drained his teacup and hurled it at Reid, who caught it deftly. "No!" he shouted, "I *don't* wish to see my sister. Or my mother. Or any benighted woman. They tell me I need to stay quiet because my fever has returned—which it hasn't, as I never had a damned fever in the first place—and then talk my ear off! I've no wish to see anyone in skirts, damn it!"

"I'll convey your message to Lady Montolivo," Reid said calmly, and left the room. Charles had the suspicion he was chuckling.

It was a conspiracy, he was sure. Tristan seemed to have mysteriously vanished, and caring for Charles in his place were the two most important, most loved, most *aggravating* females of his acquaintance. After two days of their solicitous, annoying, *fussing* care, he'd broken down and asked his sister where her husband had disappeared to. Her response was an evasive, "Oh, he's around… somewhere." His mother was more straightforward: "He's not interested in seeing you at this moment, *mein Junge*. You hurt him quite badly. Tch! Poor Tristan."

"But where is he?"

"Gone off to some dinner with some friends; the Richmonds and some of their ilk. Lottie was invited, of course, but she has no interest, and we are Not Received." She chuckled. "Poor duchess. She and I are quite good friends, but even in Brussels standards must be met. Did I tell you what she said about Wellington?"

"Yes, four hundred times," Charles said irritably.

She cocked her head and studied him thoughtfully. "Did you wish me to give a message to Tristan?"

"No," Charles said curtly.

That was yesterday. He was regretting his response now. In fact, he was miserable and furious as well as regretful. Three days of lying here, staring at the canopy, or fumbling his way through his exercises with only Reid and the footman—what was his name? Oh, yes, Will—for support. Three days of listening to the women's endless chatter. Three days....

Three days of being without Tris.

He'd gone longer—months longer—before Tris had joined him in Brussels. Why had these past three days been interminable? Was it because before, he'd known how Tris felt for him, had had no doubt as to his love and his loyalty? Had he been wrong then? No, he'd been sure that Tris had been faithful then. Why should he not still be faithful? Was it because he saw Charles as something lesser, something he needed to tend, rather than someone his equal? No, that couldn't be true. He thought sometimes perhaps Tris did still love him, and it was just his own restlessness and frustration that set these demons at play in his mind.

He was lying, brooding up at the canopy—again—when Reid came back into the room. "Captain Randall is here to see you, Major. Shall I show him up?"

"Certainly!" Charles said in relief. "Here, help me up first, into the chair." He waited for Reid to slide his leg from the traction machine, then leaned on his batman to get to the chair. Reid lifted his leg onto the footstool and arranged his dressing gown neatly around him before going back downstairs to fetch the captain.

When Randall came in, he reached out his hand eagerly. "Randy! Good to see you. Are you back in Brussels with your company, or...."

"No, just as a courier to Richmond," Randall said, shaking his hand. "Left my troops in Keighley's tender care. How are you?"

"Crippled with ennui, but recovering. I understand I have you to thank for my timely rescue?"

"Keighley, rather. It was he who noticed that piebald of yours. I was focused on finding the missing members of my troop."

"Well, thank Keighley, then. I was glad to hear that you both came through the fighting relatively unscathed."

"Better than you, at any rate. How are you healing?"

"Slowly, but steadily. I'm managing to get around after a fashion." Charles waved his hand at the crutches beside his chair. "Sit. Reid, bring tea, please."

"Aye, sir," Reid said.

"Now," Charles said, "tell me. How bad was it? I keep getting different reports, none of them good, but one worse than the next."

"Horrible," Randall said. "Worst I'd ever seen, worse than Badajoz and Talavera combined. God. I don't even know how many dead—estimates range from about twenty thousand Allies, and at least that many French, to over a hundred thousand for the full campaign. It was brutal, Monty."

"Is it true the Duke lost his entire staff?"

"Not all of them dead, but none unscathed. Uxbridge lost his leg while sitting his horse right next to the Duke; the ball sailed right over His Grace and struck Uxbridge."

Charles snorted. "So I'd heard. I'll wager His Grace had something clever to say about that."

"Perhaps. I haven't heard."

"You were the one who told the surgeon not to take off my leg," Charles said. "It's the one bit from that time that I remember, and I'm grateful for that."

"I'm not a surgeon, but I've seen worse breaks heal." Randall shrugged. "Too many sawbones are too eager to earn the name. I'm just glad my choice proved correct." He shook his head. "I just knew what I would want in the same position, and made my choice based on that. And it was lucky your friend Northwood was so quick to come when Keighley told him we were laid up in that farmhouse. He not only patched you up, but tended my handful of wounded as well." He paused, then went on, "I was grateful to him for that."

"He's not a bad fellow," Charles said. "A decent surgeon."

"That's the professional soldier talking," Randall said. "I appreciate your discretion, Charles, but you know that I'm perfectly aware of your relationship. I don't approve, and legally I am obliged to report it, but you have been my friend for far too long, and from my observation Northwood is"—he shook his head—"a decent man. If you had asked me a month ago if I could describe a sodomite as anything but indecent, my response would have been quite different."

"People don't fit into easy categories, Randy," Charles sighed. "Take Uxbridge—adultery is far more specifically forbidden in the Ten Commandments, and yet he is not only accepted, but respected, despite having eloped with Wellington's sister-in-law. There's nothing in the

Commandments about 'Thou shalt not covet thy sister's husband.'" He chuckled humorlessly. "Though that is, in fact, the case."

The captain was shaking his head again. "I don't understand," he said. "How can you choose...."

"I didn't *choose*, Randy," Charles said quietly. "This is the way I am. I know, the preachers say that this is a sin, that it's choosing evil. I don't see any evil in it. Yes, of course, I know all the arguments about the devil making sin attractive, but don't you think I would *choose* to be like everyone else? Don't you think I would *prefer* it?" His breath caught in his throat. "Being like this isn't *attractive*. It's what I *am*. How can that be evil? God made me like this, and I thank Him every day that he brought Tristan into my life." He looked up at his friend, and asked painfully, "I'm asking you to betray your obligations, Randy, and leave us alone. I'm *begging* you."

Randall didn't answer right away, and Charles felt his composure slipping even more. He didn't care about himself so much; he'd always known his predilections were illegal, and had accepted the risks, but he was terrified for Tristan, who'd never been forced to consider it until now.

Reid scratched on the door and slipped in with the tray for tea. He set it on the side table and poured out for both of the gentlemen, then slipped quietly away again.

Charles busied himself with buttering bread. Randall refused a slice wordlessly, and sipped his tea. Finally, he said, "I've given it a great deal of thought, Monty. I have to admit, in a sense I've been grateful for the insanity of the last few weeks because I've been prevented from actually having to make a decision. It hasn't been easy."

He looked up and met Charles's eyes. "If I am asked," he said deliberately, "I will not lie. But neither will I volunteer any information. I consider you my friend, and will continue to do so, and Northwood's behavior has led me to respect him, much to my surprise. He seems to be honestly devoted to you."

Something in Charles's expression made him hesitate. "Am I wrong, Monty?" he asked quietly.

"I...." Charles shook his head. "We had an argument," he said. "Probably foolishly. But there's a friend of his, a Mr. Chamberlain...."

"Derek Chamberlain? Yes, I've met him. He came out to the Pauwels' farm to help Tristan cart you back here." He cocked his head and regarded Charles. "I asked him point blank if he was betraying you with Chamberlain. He was furious; as was Chamberlain when I taxed him with it later. Not in the outraged manner that disguises a lie, but honestly, bluntly furious, both of them. It was amusing, really. I think Chamberlain was more indignant on your brother-in-law's behalf than on his own—it was quite as if I'd impugned Wellington to one of his infantrymen. No betrayal—but a bit of hero worship, I've no doubt." He gave Charles a wry smile. "Much as I must admit it, I believe that Northwood is faithful to you—as you believe, I'm sure."

"I do believe it," Charles sighed. "It's just… bloody frustrating being cooped up here and not being able to see things for myself. And to have to lie here for hours with nothing to do but brood. I've tried reading, but it only gives me a headache."

"Reading what? Novels?" Randall picked up the book on the table and glanced at the title. "Good Lord—a *gothic* novel? No wonder you're having headaches. Get Northwood to bring you some of those damn medical books you used to haul around the continent. In fact, I'll mention it to him when I leave. At least you'll find that interesting."

"He's here?"

"Downstairs, visiting with his wife and a strange couple, the Count and Countess of someplace in Italy. She's a German, though."

Charles chuckled. "That would be my mama and her current husband, I imagine. Did I never tell you the story?"

"Good God, no. I understood that she was deceased."

"Oh, no. That novel is her contribution. Here, have more tea and I'll tell you the romantic tale."

TRISTAN and the count were playing piquet for penny points while Charlotte and Lady Montolivo embroidered. Tristan had just discarded when he caught movement out of the corner of his eye, and looked up to see Captain Randall in the doorway. "Ah, Captain. Come in. Care to take a turn at being fleeced by Lord Montolivo?"

"No, thank you," Randall said, and he managed a polite smile. "I have a message from your invalid, however: he would like someone to remove the horrible novel from his bedside and replace it with something more to his taste, regarding obscure Hottentot ritual healing or something of that nature, if you have it."

"I'm not sure I can manage the Hottentot ritual healing," Tristan said, "but I'm sure I can find something more entertaining and equally obscure. How is Himself feeling?"

"Cranky," Randall said. "Well, my message to you has been delivered, and I'm off to see if His Grace of Richmond has an answer to the message I delivered to him earlier. I expect by the time I return to Brussels you'll be back in England?"

"We expect to leave as soon as Charles is well enough to travel," Tristan replied. "Dr. Crosby said another week, and then only if the carriage is well sprung."

"Then, definitely," Randall said. "With Bonaparte fled from Paris and the Royal Navy blockading the French ports, we'll have him in our hands by the end of this month—possibly even by the end of the week."

"We'll be glad for the peace," Lottie said. "I don't know what it will be like—after all these years of war."

"A lot of unemployed soldiers," Tristan said dryly. "What are your plans, Captain?"

"To stay in the army as long as I can," Randall said promptly. "And then cast myself on my family's good nature until I decide on a peacetime career. Not medicine, thank you!"

Tristan laughed. "Well, good luck to you. I hope we will see you again in London, soon."

Randall gave him a queer look, but said only, "That would be pleasant. I look forward to Mountjoy's recovery. Good day, ladies, gentlemen," and with a bow, he was gone.

"Well," Liesl said, "are you going to find something for Charlie to read, Tristan? Or do you wish Lottie or me to go up and drive him mad again?" She gave him a irrepressible grin.

He laughed again, and said, "No, I think I have something in my bookroom that Maartens gave me the other day. It should help him pass the time. Too bad we read the Scott's I bought him for his birthday—that might have entertained him. At any rate, since the good captain has softened him up, I shall beard the lion in his den." He glanced at his partner. "You've won this hand already, Montolivo; I concede with bad grace and retire from the field."

Montolivo chuckled and scooped up the cards. "Liesl, my love?"

She sighed and set down her embroidery. "The things we do for our loved ones," she said dramatically as she took Tristan's chair.

Tris winked at Lottie, and went to find the book.

Maartens had brought over several books from his own extensive library, ones that he had duplicates of, for when Tristan or his invalid guest had a moment to read. The physician was short-tempered, opinionated, and irascible, but over the course of the past several weeks Tristan had decided that he liked him quite well enough, and vice versa. He had joined the pantheon of sharp-tempered mentors along with Crosby and MacQuarrie: intelligent men with no patience for foolishness. They didn't always agree on principle: Maartens was a proponent of bleeding and purgatives; while Tristan admitted the value of each, he disagreed with the Belgian doctor on when they should be used, and had staunchly refused to allow Charles to be bled or purged. They'd also disagreed on amputation of Charles's injured leg, although now Maartens admitted that Tristan had been right "in this instance and this instance only, mind! And you were damned lucky at that!" But he agreed with Crosby and Tristan about the importance of cleanliness of instruments, and the use of waxed linen or silk thread or catgut instead of cheaper alternatives when stitching wounds.

The book Tris was looking for was a review of folk practices and a "scientific" analysis of each. Tristan had to doubt the accuracy of the science, but he thought Charles might be amused by it. He took it upstairs and was surprised to find the bedroom door open.

"Is it safe to come in?" he asked, peeking ostentatiously around the doorjamb.

"Oh, hell, Tris," Charles said disgustedly. "Of course. Come in. Where have you been these last three days?"

"Oh, here and abouts," Tristan said lightly. "Busy social calendar and all that."

"Right. Well, I'm sorry for being such a bear. Bored and miserable and brooding doesn't lead to a happy patient. Will you accept my apologies?"

"Willingly," Tristan said, crossing the room to sit on the arm of Charles's chair and lean over to kiss him. Charles's lips were soft and warm and welcoming, and Tristan sighed, weaving a hand into Charles's tumbled curls as he deepened the kiss.

"Mmm," Charles said when Tristan had released him. "That's more like it. What have you brought me?"

"You sound like Jamie," Tristan said, laughing, as he gave him the book. Charles took it eagerly and flipped through the pages.

"Oh, this looks like fun," Charles said. "It'll be a challenge; I haven't read French for a couple of years, aside from the odd dispatch."

"I'll help you," Tris promised. He rubbed Charles's shoulder through the dressing gown. "Did you have a good visit with the captain?"

Charles glanced up. "What did he say?"

"Nothing of any import. Just that you wanted something better to read than…." Tristan picked up the novel. "Good grief. I thought Lottie's taste was better than this."

"Lottie's is. My dear mama's is not."

"We shan't bother you with this any longer," Tristan said, and he carried the book to the dustbin by the door to drop it in. He stood there a moment, then reached out and closed the door, turning the key.

When he turned around, Charles was watching him, an eyebrow raised. Tristan grinned wickedly. "You're looking much better," he murmured.

"Oh, my," Charles said, mock-faintly. "You have mischief in mind."

"I do—and you at my mercy." He came back to the chair and eased Charles's right leg off the hassock, careful not to jostle the broken one, then gently pushed the hassock a little to the side. "Is that all right?" he asked softly.

Charles nodded wordlessly, his face flushed.

Tristan knelt before him, unbuttoning Charles's banyan and parting it, then pushing the hem of his nightshirt up to his waist. Charles was already half hard; when Tristan leaned forward and placed a soft, wet kiss on the inside of his thigh, he groaned and buried his fingers in Tristan's hair. "Tris," he sighed.

"Yes," Tris said, easing Charles's legs wider and shifting closer to take Charles in hand, his thumb and forefinger circling his shaft and his other fingers curling down to cup his ballocks. Then he drew his tongue up Charles's rapidly hardening shaft, licking under the edge of foreskin and pushing it back with his lips so he could tease the tender head with his tongue. "We can't do much more than this now," Tristan murmured, "but soon, Charlie… soon."

Charles leaned his head back against the chair. "Yes, Tris. Oh, God, yes…."

Tristan took him in his mouth, feeling the flesh thickening and firming beneath his tongue. God, he loved the taste of Charles, warm and musky and always with the faint woodsy scent of his favorite oils. He sucked lightly, then harder, then slid away altogether to nuzzle into Charles's groin, smelling him, tasting him, licking the crease of Charles's hip before returning to worship his thick staff. He slid a finger into his own mouth, wetting it; then as he took Charles's cock deep, slipped the finger behind Charles's testicles and into the heat of Charles's arse.

Charles jerked and groaned at the pleasure, his head falling back against the chair, his fingers tightening in Tristan's hair. "Tris," he moaned.

Busy, Tris didn't answer, but sucked Charles harder as his finger explored the hot, tight tunnel until he found his quarry. Charles groaned again, louder and more heartfelt, and Tristan grinned around him as he put both his mouth and hand to work.

It only took a few moments before Charles arched and spent, spilling into Tristan's throat and tightening like a vise around Tristan's finger. Tristan kept sucking until Charles whined faintly, then released him and reached for his own buttons, stroking himself briefly until he, too, spent, then collapsed against Charles's good leg, panting and hot-faced. Charles had held onto Tristan's hair even as he brought himself off, and now released him, stroking the dark locks gently.

Tristan looked up at him and said fiercely, "You are everything to me, Charlie. I cannot live without you. When we went so long without hearing news of you—when I was so afraid—I promised God I would do anything, give anything except Jamie and Caroline...." He turned his face into Charles's thigh and burst into tears.

Bending awkwardly, Charles leaned forward and rested his cheek on Tristan's head, his arms curling around his lover's shoulders. "I'm here, Tris. It's over—there's nothing more can keep us apart. I won't leave you, ever again. I love you."

Tristan nodded at the words, but he couldn't stop weeping. He remembered talking to Derek about it at that little farmhouse where they'd found Charles, saying he'd never been a watering pot before he'd met Charles, and Derek's quiet answer. And it was true. He'd never loved before Charles, not like this. Not ever like this.

He wiped his eyes with his hand, made a face, and got stiffly to his feet, crossing to the washstand and fetching a damp cloth to clean them both up. When he was finished, he said, "Do you want to sit up a while?"

Charles looked at him, and Tristan saw his heart in his eyes. His own heart swelled. "No," Charles said. "I want to go back to bed. And I want you to come with me."

"Your leg...."

"Not for loving," he said. "Just to lie with me. Be with me."

"Is that all you want?" Tristan asked.

Charles smiled up at him and held out a hand. "No," he said, "but I'll take what I can get."

PILOGUE

London, 1820

SIR CHARLES MOUNTJOY, Fellow of the Royal College of Physicians, glanced up from the paper he was writing on the treatment of malarial fever as his partner came into their shared office and dropped into the chair opposite. "Did you successfully diagnose Lady Weyford's malaise?" he asked dryly.

Dr. Tristan Northwood, Member of that same august body, ran an agitated hand through his already-tousled hair. "Indeed I did," he said with a groan. "Terminal boredom, leading to a fatal case of hypochondria. I *told* her, however, that she had an imbalance of the humors, gave her that green tonic, and told her that she needed to take a brisk walk daily until she perspired, to balance the phlegm, and to take up a hobby that required concentration, like reading or needlework, to balance the sanguinary humors."

"The green tonic?" Charles said thoughtfully. "Is that the stuff that's mostly dandelion wine and mint?"

"That's the one. Won't hurt her, but will have precisely the placebo effect she needs. Charles, you didn't tell me being a doctor was such a charlatan's profession!"

"It's not, really. You judged her correctly. I've been seeing her regularly for the past year for exactly that thing. She'll follow your prescription for a while, show a distinct improvement, then slack off and the 'symptoms' will return. So we try something different."

"Don't you feel awkward taking money from her?"

"Why? She's taking time from me, and I can afford that less than she can afford my fees. Plus patients like her support the ones like Mrs. Hill, who *can't* pay."

Tristan chuckled. "Ah, then it's worth it. She is amusing, though, isn't she?"

"As long as she doesn't bring that damn pug in with her any longer," Charles agreed. "That beastly thing stank. I told her it was in danger of infection, dogs being far more susceptible to human illnesses than humans are."

"And her social standing improves our reputations," Tristan pointed out. "Which brings more patients who can pay, so that we can treat more patients who don't. Are you on for rounds at St. Joseph's tomorrow?"

"Yes, for my sins. MacQuarrie will never forgive me if I renege on the agreement we made before we opened this practice. He's making retirement noises again today; was talking at lunch about Sicily, or perhaps Egypt— someplace hot and dry for his aching bones. He has been shifting some of his younger patients this way, you know. Mr. and Mrs. Castleton brought their daughter by earlier—they were worried about consumption, but I'm thinking it's more likely allergies, since her respiratory problems seem to be seasonal. I recommended they take her down to Brighton during the summer and see if that makes for improvement, and I thought both Mr. and Mrs. Castleton would fall upon my neck in gratitude."

His partner laughed. It was typical of MacQuarrie to refer younger patients to them, who would potentially have a longer relationship with their practice; they had only been in partnership together for a little over a year, but were already doing well, thanks to the older doctor's generosity. Charles had finished his education before Tris had, despite Tristan's university degree; his experience in the Peninsula and his own research had given Charles an edge. Too, Tristan's father had had a health scare three years ago, and had become obsessed about making sure Tristan was fully aware of the extent of the Ware responsibilities. He'd recovered completely, but his panic had been real. Tris, too, had been frightened; they had wasted so many years at odds that he was afraid that he would lose his father now that he'd finally found him. So he obliged him by taking time off from his studies to enter a very different training program.

Tristan had finally sat his exams a year ago. Charles had spent the intervening months as an assistant in MacQuarrie's personal practice, but when Tristan had been accepted as a member of the Royal Society, Charles judged the time right to strike out on their own, with MacQuarrie's blessing. They'd bought the house on Harley Street, among the other fashionable physicians, and set up their offices and housekeeping, with Charlotte and the children giving them respectability during the Season. Their profession gave them a perfectly acceptable excuse to remain together in Town the rest of the year. *Not a perfect situation*, Tristan thought with a smile, but a far superior one than he'd ever expected.

"Lady Weyford was the last for today. Ready to close up shop?"

"I am." Charles put the lid on the inkpot and his quill back into the mug on his desk. "Are we dining at home tonight?"

"Yes. Charlotte tells me we've no social obligations, so Jamie and Caroline will be joining us. Caroline's table manners have improved greatly."

"Good." Charles smiled as he shifted his weight onto the cane to rise. Tris watched him carefully, but made no move to assist. "You're learning," Charles said.

"You scolded me roundly the last time," Tris said. "Hurts today, does it?"

"Damp and cold will do it. I'm thinking like MacQuarrie—Sicily, maybe Egypt?"

"Not without me," Tristan said.

Charles leaned on his cane and reached up to wrap an arm around Tristan's neck. "Never without you, my love," he said, and kissed Tris gently. "Never without you."

POSTSCRIPT

HIS defeat at the Battle of Waterloo, one of the four battles of the Waterloo Campaign (June 15-18, 1815), meant the end of Napoleon Bonaparte's career as one of the greatest generals of all time. Of the four battles, the French won two outright (Ligny and Wavre); the first battle, at the crossroads of Quatre Bras, was technically a draw, but was tactically a French victory in that it managed to prevent the British army from sending troops to support their allies the Prussians, who would lose at Ligny later the same day. Only the hard-fought Battle of Waterloo itself, on June 18, 1815, was an outright victory for the Allied armies under Wellington and Blucher.

Theoretically, Napoleon should have won the Waterloo Campaign. Although the British outnumbered the French in terms of bodies, much of the Continental army was inexperienced militia, some of which had as much loyalty to the French as to the Coalition forces. The two armies of the Coalition spoke different languages—in the case of the Continental forces, several. The best of the British troops from the Peninsular War, including Wellington's top officers, were in America. Napoleon's forces were almost entirely veteran troops, who flocked to the returned Emperor's banner. He had three thousand more mounted troops, including fourteen regiments of armored heavy cavalry, which the Coalition armies lacked, and nearly a hundred more guns. His generals were all experienced, with major victories under their belts.

The fact that Wellington and Blucher's forces won the field at the pivotal battle at Waterloo was a testament to the importance of communication between allies and the thorough understanding both Wellington and his Prussian counterpart had of their men and of their strengths and weaknesses. Napoleon was a master strategist, but Waterloo was a masterpiece of tactics, of turning seeming defeat into hard-won victory. The losses were tremendous: around 50,000 dead or wounded, with some 15,000 missing, but at the end Blucher and Wellington held the field, and the Emperor was in flight.

WRITING an historical novel requires enormous amounts of research. Thankfully, I didn't have to face it alone. I had help from many sources, particularly Augie Aleksy, of Centuries and Sleuths Bookstore in Forest Park,

Illinois, and Lynda Fitzgerald of Osprey and Shire Books, for books and maps and in Augie's case, a miniature diorama of the Battle of Waterloo, which totally rocked. Thank you so much for your help. Any mistakes are most definitely mine. Thanks also to Lynda for beta-reading and for editorial suggestions that made this a far better story than it was originally. And thanks, of course, to my beta-readers and cheerleaders Patrice, Donetta, and Shannon, and to all the rest of my friends who have to wait for the book to come out, but kept me sane during the process anyway.

Rowan Speedwell
April 2011

An unrepentant biblioholic, ROWAN SPEEDWELL spends half her time pretending to be a law librarian, half her time pretending to be a database manager, half her time pretending to be a fifteenth-century Aragonese noblewoman, half her time... wait a minute... hmm. Well, one thing she doesn't pretend to be is good at math. She is good at pretending, though.

In her copious spare time (hah) she does needlework, calligraphy and illumination, and makes jewelry. She has a master's degree in history from the University of Chicago, is a member of the Society for Creative Anachronism, and lives in a Chicago suburb with the obligatory Writer's Cat and way too many books.

Also from ROWAN SPEEDWELL

http://www.dreamspinnerpress.com

Also from ROWAN SPEEDWELL

http://www.dreamspinnerpress.com

Historical Romance from DREAMSPINNER PRESS

BLESS US WITH
Content
TINNEAN

The
DESIRE
for
DEARBORNE
V.B. KILDAIRE

Madcap Masquerade

PERSEPHONE ROTH

A Secret Arrangement
Farida
Mestek

http://www.dreamspinnerpress.com

For more of the
best M/M romance,
visit

Dreamspinner Press

www.dreamspinnerpress.com

www.ingramcontent.com/pod-product-compliance
Lightning Source LLC
Chambersburg PA
CBHW050032030726

47506CB00001B/244